Thank you for giving my story a try!

The Others

Kristin Bryant (signature)

Kristin Bryant

Sourced Media Books
San Clemente, CA

Sourced Media Books
29 Via Regalo
San Clemente, CA 92673
www.sourcedmediabooks.com

ISBN–13: 978–1–937458–60–7

Printed in Canada.

This publication is designed to provide entertainment value and is sold with the understanding that the publisher is not engaged in rendering legal, accounting, or other professional advice of any kind. If legal advice or other expert assistance is required, the services of a competent professional person should be sought.

—From a Declaration of Principles jointly adopted by a Committee of the American Bar Association and a Committee of Publishers and Associations

To my parents, for listening to my idea and encouraging me to write a book about it. To Kurt, Jake, and Kaden, for allowing me the time to write said book. And lastly, to my amazing extended family, friends, and K-P Nation, for getting me through.

John 10:16

And other sheep I have, which are not of this fold: them also I must bring, and they shall hear my voice; and there shall be one fold, and one shepherd.

Contents

01

Zhimeya, two years ago

Dazzling sunshine poured through the massive skylights, bathing Tribunal Hall in a glowing radiance. One particularly mischievous sunbeam reflected off a polished stone wall and shot its way straight into my eyes like a surgical laser. *Of course* I had the worst seat in the house. I was already perspiring under the stiff fabric of my formal uniform. My only hope was that the thick black coat would hide the resulting sweat stains. That was the last thing I wanted to make tomorrow's headlines.

Mateo passed me a note while Chase, seated next to him, sniggered.

Leksy is staring at you.
All this attention from beautiful women
must be such a heavy burden to carry.

I looked reflexively Leksy's way as she stood at attention in the line of guards protecting the cauldron of holy fire at the side of the hall. Mateo was right. She was staring unrepentantly at me over the simmering flames. I smiled politely. We had gone out once few weeks ago, but I never called on her after. She should have taken the hint, but instead she lapped up the accidental attention and searched my face for more. I minutely shifted in my chair so I wouldn't have to look her way again.

Every inch of the floor of Tribunal Hall was unceremoniously stuffed with leaders, dignitaries, and whoever else considered themselves important enough to take up space. Pretentious women who balanced neck-snappingly heavy headdresses preened and purred while men in gaudy robes tried to shout just a bit louder than the people next to them. The resulting clamor rose upward, mixing dissonantly with the pungent smoke from the cauldron.

I suddenly appreciated my padded chair up on the stand, even if the sun was ever so slowly roasting me alive in front of the entire world.

A slightly raised center platform separated my team from the chaotic floor of the hall. Usually this stage was reserved for those accused of crimes to stand trial. It was positioned facing the only window in the hall, which afforded a terribly convenient view of Black Castle. I tried not to let my gaze rest too long on the moldering capital of Unnamed Territory, the city of the forgotten.

"Ryen! You okay?" Claire whispered from the seat behind me, no doubt noticing the slight change in the set of my shoulders as I contemplated the unhappy memories that being here dredged up. I tried to decide whether it was comforting or annoying to have someone know me well enough to pick up on such a small thing.

I glanced over my shoulder. "Big day," I murmured.

"The very biggest," she said speculatively, her amethyst eyes catching mine briefly, trying to deduce my mood. "Smile for the cameras." She settled back into her chair with passive distaste.

From the back of the hall where the media was relegated, a flock of tiny orb-like cameras rose like bubbles caught in the wind and made their soundless flight toward the stand where we sat. During my youth, I had been known to catch the little flying invasions of privacy and mangle them in interesting and sundry ways for fun. Though I'd outgrown the practice, deep down I constantly fought the urge to take a bat to the ever-present pests.

I did my best to smile dutifully at the mechanical eyes that zoomed close enough to see any trace of lunch left in my teeth because, like Claire said, this was the very biggest day of my life.

These assemblies were nothing new. In fact, the Masters were often brought before the elected Tribunal to report the status of Earth research, especially when the Tribunal called another round of researchers.

But today, I was being called up. Along with a small handful of others, I was finally going to Earth. This was our big send-off ceremony, since we sometimes didn't come back.

As we waited for the Tribunal to arrive, my eyes unintentionally drifted again toward the lone window. This time, I mindfully ignored the spires of Black Castle that broke the horizon and instead examined the hills just outside. The rolling lawns were littered with bodies watching the monolithic walls of Tribunal Hall, which displayed the proceedings on their massive bleached surfaces. Demonstrators for both sides of the great argument ceased their shouting as the Tribunal began to arrive.

"Elia of the Savaun tribe," a booming voice rang out. A young woman came into view dragging an ornate cloak of shining orange feathers from her small, feminine shoulders, her body and face painted like a flame. She carried a shining bowl under her arm. She gave me a coquettish smile and a wink as she floated by, sending Mateo and Chase both into audible spasms of laughter. Claire elbowed Mateo in the gut for me. Elia dutifully made her way to the cauldron of holy fire, dipped the bowl inside, and captured a small ember that burned brightly. She carried it to her chair and sat the bowl on a pedestal in front of her.

"Adan of the Cailida tribe," the voice rang out again.

One by one, every Tribunal member marched in, proudly displaying the marks of their tribe over every inch of exposed skin. Some were decorated in iridescent patterns and swirling designs; some bore the symbols of sacred animals or plants dyed onto their skin. Others were covered in writing, which told the ancient legends of their tribe. Each captured an ember of flame and placed it next to his or her chair—a symbol of The Light.

During the processional, the Masters entered from a side door in a close, silent knot. Gideon, Dai, Oshun, Ecko, and Emani took their places on the platform in front of the gathering Tribunal. I could feel Emani's accusatory eyes on me, but I didn't dare meet her gaze.

As the last Tribunal member took his seat, Jin rose from hers. The nearly blind holy woman was helped to the cauldron by two of her priests. Her misty gray eyes looked like they could see nothing and everything at the same time. Though she was undoubtedly over eighty years my senior, something about her crystalline features was beautiful, almost magical.

Jin sprinkled the fire with a fine powder that made the flames roar up and burn bright white. After a silent moment, she faced the audience, opened her mouth, and began weaving a hymn in the ancient language of our people about The Light— the story of what brought us here today.

From the beginning, mystics and holy men foretold a time when The Light would be born. He would live a perfect life, take all sin upon him, and ultimately lay down his life to save us all from death. An illumination in the darkness. A mender. A healer. A savior. The Light.

There was just one catch.

He would be born in a different world, far away from Zhimeya, our home. He would perform miracles none of us would ever see. He would be tortured and killed by those who didn't believe what he was. But this legendary being, after unspeakable suffering, would sacrifice himself on that distant realm to redeem us all.

And we were supposed to believe that. Without any proof.

Jin finished the ancient strains of The Light's mythology, then the song's tenor changed. She sang of modern Zhimeya, driven by the quest for pure truth, needing to find the proof behind the legend. This was why I was here.

Five hundred years ago, as ancient tribal alliances dissolved in the face of the great religious debate, the first group of Masters had been charged with the mission to "master" the technology necessary to send explorers into space. Their objective, if fulfilled, would serve to be the stepping stone to uniting the tribes once again. Find His birthplace. Prove the existence of The Light, our savior.

Our holy records, ancient prophecies made for thousands of years about the legendary man, had been mangled or lost through the eons. Much of it was still untranslatable to this day. We were missing so much information. It was getting harder to believe or even fully understand the stories that did survive.

After decades of experimentation, the Masters' breakthroughs made long-distance exploration possible. And after more years of exhaustive searching, they finally found an inhabited planet. Earth.

They studied the planet from afar for decades—and when nothing more could be learned from a distance, they sent teams of researchers to walk among the inhabitants. After thoroughly sifting through Earth's religious myths for legends that matched our own, they concluded the Christian Jesus fit our stories most closely.

Humans' scriptural records state that this figure died and was, to borrow a word, *resurrected*. He then came again to his followers and said, "Other sheep I have, which are not of this fold: them also I must bring, and they shall hear my voice; and there shall be one fold, and one shepherd."

Had this Jesus been talking about other worlds? Could *we* be the others?

Our own confusing records were read by some, believed by a few, and disregarded altogether by a growing number. Many were not even sure if the scriptures retrieved from Earth described the same being we understood from our records. There were similarities, to be sure, but nothing proving beyond any doubt that the two mythic figures were the same.

Lately, Zhimeyan history had become defined by nonstop skirmishes, with the accompanying loss of life. Disagreements over land and resources became more pronounced when our people were already split over religion.

If the Masters could find proof that a savior existed, that our stories were true, my people would have no choice but to believe and to start healing the breaches between tribes.

This was my mission—to find that proof.

The strains of Jin's hymn came to a close just as the heavy, ornate golden doors at the back of the auditorium opened. We all stood as Aurik came into view.

Aurik, Head of the Tribunal, had started looking more worn with each passing year, due not only to his age, but also to the weighty burdens he carried. Even his feathery, silver hair seemed to pull heavily on his scalp. Past Tribunal heads had always worn ornate robes signifying their status. Aurik didn't. He wore a simple brown tunic, tied at the waist with a belt of shining animal hide. Under his arm, he carried a shallow bowl.

His skin bore a mark for each of the one hundred tribes present. The Haven tribe's constellation marks were streaked across his forehead, the Abran tribe's tree symbol ran up the back of his neck, and the ancient creation story of the Kesua tribe was inscribed on the palm of his left hand, to name a few. Aurik belonged to us all, so he wore every mark.

On the inside of his forearm was a complicated knot of lines woven together in an unending circle, each line representing a tribe. In the middle was his thumbprint, his signature on the sacred mark. Only the leader of the Tribunal was allowed to wear it.

Aurik made his way to the cauldron, scooped up an ember, and laid it carefully on top of the pedestal next to his podium. He surveyed the Tribunal, each with a shared part of the fire glowing next to them. He raised his painted arms, and the whole world fell silent together.

"Brothers and sisters of Zhimeya, we gather to take part in the free exchange of ideas that marks our society. The Tribunal has come to hear from the Masters of Technology." He turned toward the group gathered in front of him. "Our questions are mostly the same. What have you found? What have you learned?" He paused and took in a long breath. "But I add one more inquiry. You have called yet another round of researchers. This Tribunal wishes to know when these missions will . . . *end.*"

Immediate pandemonium erupted from outside the stone walls, but he continued. "We will decide today whether the Masters will be allowed to continue Earth research."

Claire's breath caught in her throat. I didn't dare look back at her. The cameras, which had respectfully withdrawn as the proceedings got underway, now rained down on us, recording every movement we made. Mateo, Chase, Claire, and I had to be thinking the same thing. Were we going to Earth at all? Were the past twenty years of our lives, spent in arduous training, all for nothing?

The Masters bowed their heads together for one minute . . . two minutes . . . three minutes. Every second lengthened out uncomfortably. Only Dai kept his head raised, watching the Tribunal members carefully. His one purple iris glowed with a rash energy, while his left . . . well, I tried never to look at it. He had lost his left eye in a lab accident years ago. Instead of having a healer fix it, Dai had replaced it himself with a flat black ocular screen. I was never inclined to ask the imposing man why.

Gideon, Head of the Masters, finally broke from the knot and strode forward. He wore the simple rough fabric tunic uniform the head of the Masters historically wore, but Gideon had added jeweled arm cuffs. From his chest swung an enormous medallion of pure crystal torbillium carved in the crest of the Masters. That much raw torbillium was worth a tremendous fortune. He'd commissioned the piece the day he was named Head of the Masters after his predecessor had suddenly passed away.

Though he personally had chosen me to go to Earth, an honor for which I owed him dearly, I now felt a strange surge of aversion when our eyes briefly met. The antagonism emanating from Gideon toward Aurik was painfully obvious. Usually he was a much better actor.

"Honorable men and women," Gideon began when he reached the platform, "we are indeed stunned and distressed by the Tribunal's hasty decision to try to end such significant and vital research."

Some of the Tribunal whispered hotly to each other at the insult; others kept their faces curiously blank.

Aurik's smile didn't reach his eyes. "Eighty long years sending researchers to Earth is hardly hasty, my son. We can no longer ignore the enormous monetary burden of these voyages when our supply of torbillium dwindles. But, more importantly, we are putting precious lives on the line." Aurik pointed at my team with a tired sort of fatherly worry in his eyes. "Every time we send our young ones away, they risk death. It is our duty to question these missions and your motives."

"Our researchers bring back with them invaluable information. Each time these brave men and women return, they bring enlightenment that enriches our world. To stop research now because of the cost of life—or torbillium—is shortsighted and foolish."

"But the original purpose, the reason the Tribunal has allowed these expeditions to continue, Gideon, is to find evidence of The Light on the planet where he was born and died. You have yet to prove that Earth is even the correct place!"

Gideon's eyes burned viciously, but Aurik continued.

"Your mission was to help heal the breach between the believers and unbelievers. If no actual proof of The Light exists on Earth other than ancient text and second-hand accounts, the likes of which we already have, there is no reason to send these young ones into danger."

Nervous eyes darted around the room as the argument volleyed back and forth between the powerful men. Gideon glanced behind him at the Masters, catching Dai's intense stare. He nodded at Dai, who strode forward quickly. Emani followed closely behind him.

Emani's heavily tattooed arms peeked out from below the red and gold robe she wore loosely belted over a short black dress. Her unreadable ebony eyes glinted under her dyed red hair woven with gold feathers. I wondered how Emani felt just now, standing in front of the same Tribunal that destroyed her family. She threw a quick glance behind her, out the window toward Black Castle.

The three Masters whispered together hotly while trying to keep their faces smooth. I caught just a few lines of the stifled fight.

"*It's time,*" Dai whispered calmly.

"No, it is not ready," Emani insisted. "A rush into action will just—"

"We *are* ready," Dai cut her off with finality. She stared furiously at him, but he didn't seem to notice.

Gideon finally nodded, and the two Masters turned to walk back to the others. As Emani passed, she dropped a note into my lap. I should have thrown the unassuming paper on the floor, stomped on it, set it on fire—I should have done anything except open it. But sheer morbid curiosity made my fingers unfold it. In messy crimson writing, it said,

You can't run forever.

I noticed a few of her fingertips were bound with bandages. She'd written the note in blood. I probably should have been shocked, but knowing her, I wasn't even surprised. This was either a desperate cry for attention, or she was just trying to screw with me.

Or both. Probably both.

Since I'd left her, my only goal in life was to stay no less than a mile away from Emani at all times. What was that English phrase about hell, fury, and a woman scorned?

"Gideon, if you have nothing further, I will put this matter to a vote," Aurik said.

"If you would terminate these missions based on its original purpose, would the Tribunal consider continuing these missions for a different purpose?" Gideon asked.

A different purpose? What other reason could there possibly be for us to go to Earth if not to find evidence of The Light?

Aurik looked the Tribunal over, studying the faces that now nodded in assent to Gideon's request. He sighed and said, "The Tribunal will hear the new purpose, though *you are testing my patience, Gideon.*"

Gideon turned himself to face the cloud of floating cameras that were transmitting his visage to every soul in Zhimeya. "Our original mission hasn't changed. It has evolved. The Light did live on Earth, was killed by the inhabitants, and is even now blasphemed at every turn. This most sacred space needs protection from these violent humans."

Aurik's face took on a grim, chalky pallor as Gideon spoke. The rest of the hall erupted in noise.

"Gideon, are you suggesting an *invasion* of a world that has done absolutely nothing to us?" Aurik's enraged voice rang out above the din of noise inside and outside Tribunal Hall.

"Aurik, would you incite your people into frenzy? I would think you much too diplomatic for that," he said mockingly. "Our people deserve the right to worship there, to have it cleansed of the malignancy that is now being spread by those who desecrate the land. The Holy Land needs to be protected!"

I studied the faces of the Tribunal. Several, more than I would have thought, listened intently to Gideon. It was plain on their faces that they agreed with him.

"The proof that ties The Light to Earth's savior exists, and we will find it. If Jesus is our savior too, do we not have an equal right to worship at his birthplace?"

"This is an outrage, Gideon. I will not entertain the idea a moment longer. I will put to a vote what we were convened here to do in the first place. Tribunal, let your voice be heard. Will you allow the Masters to send one more round of researchers to Earth for *only* the original purpose?"

The members whispered animatedly with one another as they chose their sides. Aurik talked with each member, taking their vote. Claire clutched my shoulder with one hand and held Chase's tight with her other. I put one hand over hers as we waited.

With a defeated sigh, Aurik conceded. "It is against my better judgment to allow your experiments to continue, Gideon. The Tribunal is allowing you one more chance to send researchers to Earth, to fulfill only your original purpose. But *this* will be the last group. This is your last chance."

Earth, present day

I stared down from the Mount of Olives at the crumbling city below.

Jerusalem. I knew every street by heart, searching it as I had. I repeated my reason for being here silently, reminding my feet why they really should keep walking. My feet, however, had unanimously voted against me. I was outnumbered—two of them, one of me—so I stayed put.

Frustrated, I ran my hands through my untidy dark hair, which immediately fell back into my face. Claire said I looked homeless but conceded that my unkempt appearance was helpful in the Middle East. It drew attention away from my ice-blue eyes, a color that garnered too much attention here.

My head ached from staring at the dizzying maze of streets for her—the girl. I wished I knew her name. She had become something of an unintentional obsession of mine. I hadn't seen her today in my wanderings, which put me on edge. And *that* was really stupid, since I had never even spoken to her.

Mortar shells cracked and thudded far in the distance, sending up dust along the farthest horizon. Surrounded by so much volatility, it made me even more nervous for the girl I hadn't seen today.

Above the far-off din, my stomach growled angrily. It missed pizza. This sudden longing for a slice of heaven on earth (I understood this colloquialism as soon as I had tried my first bite) conjured up a litany of memories from the last two years.

As beautiful as it had been, my sojourn in Italy, where the Masters assigned Claire and me, had been . . .well, not a *waste* of time. Can spending two whole years living *la dolce vita* really be a waste of one's time? But we hadn't fulfilled our assignment, unable to find the evidence we were sent to obtain.

Our time on Earth was rapidly coming to an end. I was getting desperate to find something, anything, to bring back to the Masters. So, just a few short weeks ago, in the middle of the night, I'd decided on a drastic change of course. The next morning, I packed my bags and announced to Claire that I was going to Jerusalem, with or without her. I couldn't leave Earth without stepping foot in the Holy Land, the place at the heart of Earth's savior story. Of course she followed; she was just as curious as I was.

Truthfully, the more arrogant part of me believed that if *I* could get to Jerusalem, *I* would find what all the others before me hadn't. But here I was, overinflated ego and all, still no closer to the answer than researchers before me had been.

Another loud thud boomed in the distance, reminding me that I should probably try to find Claire before it got too dark. I hated her wandering alone through these hazardous areas, her exotic face usually a one-way ticket into trouble. But she did have a knack for slipping right back out of whatever mess she got into.

As though she had been summoned by my silent thoughts, she slapped me on the back, breaking my silent meditation, making me jump just a little.

"Such a good day," she said smugly, satisfied both with how she had spent her hours and that she had startled someone so much bigger than she. After greeting her with a disapproving glance, I slipped back into staring at the city.

"I saw her an hour ago at the Kotel. She's fine," Claire said with a toss of her plum-purple hair.

"I don't know what you are talking about," I murmured. Was I really that transparent? I thought I was hiding my fixation well. My body relaxed out of its tense stance at the news, which Claire undoubtedly noticed.

"Any luck today?" I asked. Claire smirked, seeing through my attempt to change the subject.

"Absolutely. They are simply fascinating, aren't they? So many answers to the questions I've always had!"

"Funny, they don't seem to see it that way."

She nodded her head in agreement, looking across the storied city with me.

"They just don't know what they have is all. Can't see the forest for the trees?" she questioned, unsure whether that particular phrase fit this particular situation.

I grinned as she tried on the expression like a pair of new shoes. "That phrase works. Add it to your repertoire."

She smiled, her eyes squinting in the last of the sun's dying light. Humans usually placed her clear, pale skin and almond-shaped violet eyes as Asian. Her looks were too enigmatic to be easily categorized, which was because, of course, she wasn't Asian at all. She sighed loudly.

"I wonder what Mateo and Chase are doing today."

I didn't answer, lost momentarily in my relief that the girl, as of an hour ago, was safe.

"Ryen!" she yelled, grabbing hold of my arm.

"What?"

"Chase and Mateo! Have you heard from them?"

"This morning, actually. They are leaving Tonga to finish their time in Central America. They stumbled onto some information they want to pursue before we go home."

"Then what are we doing here? Let's go! I can have us out of here tomorrow, first thing!"

"What's the rush?" I asked.

"No rush. Just trying to be helpful," she said, looking decidedly away from me.

Maybe it *was* time to leave. I had already been thinking about joining the boys for our last few weeks, anyway.

There was nothing here for me. No reason to stay.

I really tried to believe that.

"So, is your stomach up for one last adventure?" I asked. Her eyebrows furrowed, remembering how her digestive tract was never as willing to accept new surroundings as the rest of her was. "Come on, let's go meet the boys in Mexico. Sounds like a good time," I said, trying to stir some excitement in myself. "It will be less crowded, less dusty."

"Will there be better food?"

I grinned at her pained expression. "I guess we could try to be optimistic. Though last night I was reading online about something called Montezuma's revenge."

She stopped my teasing by throwing her arms around my neck. And, though I was still trying, I couldn't drum up the same level of enthusiasm at the thought of leaving this place.

All who had come before me had failed. Aurik had made it very clear that ours would be the last of the research missions.

If we didn't succeed, I had an uneasy feeling that our quiet observation of Earth may be at an end. I cringed at the thought of life changing at home *or* here because I couldn't find what the Masters were seeking.

I mentally said a painful goodbye to the now-darkened streets of the old city. I wouldn't miss them as much as I would miss—I stopped the futile thought cold.

I didn't even know her name.

03

Since she had been the one to call the airline, Claire had assigned herself the last first-class seat for our twenty-hour flight (not counting the layover in Atlanta, Georgia) to Mexico. She smiled impishly as she slid into her posh leather seat and I was herded toward the back. She would need to be closer to a bathroom, anyway. Middle Eastern food hadn't agreed with her. And I couldn't stay mad for long; at least she had secured me an aisle seat.

I found my chair next to an uneasy Slavic man with a thin sheen of pungent perspiration covering his skin. As he didn't react to my sitting next to him—didn't even glance sideways—I could tell we would get along very well.

I sat in my uncomfortable chair and tried to relax as passengers slowly filed into the plane. My fingers drummed nervously and my foot tapped the ground impatiently. I wanted to jump out of the cramped seat and pace the aisles to dispel some of the jittery energy I felt.

I didn't want to leave Jerusalem. Well, that wasn't exactly true. I was done with Jerusalem; I really just didn't want to leave *her*—the girl I wanted but could not have. Hopefully putting thousands of miles between us would help me shake this silly fascination.

In the midst of congratulating myself for getting on a plane I didn't want to board, an all-too-familiar face framed with an excess of wavy blond hair caught my undivided attention. Since I had been thinking about her at that particular second anyway, it startled me greatly when *the girl* materialized within twenty feet of me. In fact, I wasn't entirely sure she wasn't just a figment of my imagination. Real or not, I could feel myself start to sweat as much as the sticky man next to me.

A Botticelli masterpiece come to life, she had high, regal cheekbones, expressive, thoughtful eyebrows, fathomless green and gold eyes, and pale pink lips that could only be described as delicious . . . all complimenting a body that hinted at muscular, but somehow retained soft curves.

She wore a thin, white T-shirt and khaki knee-length shorts and had a backpack slung across her chest, her arms wrapped around it protectively. She glanced at her ticket often, not really paying enough attention to her seat number to absorb the information each time she looked at it.

The girl had first caught my attention because she was gorgeous. Simple enough. But this planet was teeming with beautiful women, so her beauty, although exceptional, was nothing especially novel. Her pretty face may have been the thing that caught my attention, but her sharp wit kept it.

I made a game out of counting how many men approached her each day. First, they'd ask her name. She was Lila from Texas, or Deanna from Pennsylvania, or Elena from California—depending on her mood, I suppose. They would eventually get around to asking to accompany her to dinner. That's when the fun began.

"I've taken a vow of celibacy."

"I'm engaged to be engaged."

"I'm taken. My girlfriend is around here somewhere."

"Single, but my doctor says I shouldn't touch anyone when the leprosy flares up," she told one particularly forward Frenchman who wouldn't leave her alone. She was quick and funny. A pretty little liar. I liked that.

But she couldn't keep everything about herself hidden from me. I didn't know her name, but I knew a lot. She always had a beigeleh for breakfast and falafel for dinner from the same street vendor. At least once an hour, she used a small tube of strawberry lip balm that kept her pretty lips that pale pink color. I'd often find her sitting just outside of Damascus Gate on the surrounding stone steps sketching or chatting with whomever sat next to her. She loved to talk about history, architecture, or the best places to find inexpensive delicacies around the city. She gave shekels to beggars, smiles to babies, and always joined in pickup soccer games that children played in the cramped alleys of the Muslim quarter.

At first, I quietly watched for her without ever going out of my way, satisfied by just making sure she was alive and then getting on with my assignment. But my days slowly became consumed by following her, the inexplicable hold she had on me gaining strength as the days wore on.

I was drinking her in, as was my habit, wondering wryly how this beautiful girl would feel about long-distance relationships, when she abruptly came to a stop next to me. My stomach threatened to jump out of my throat and land at her feet if I opened my mouth, so I pressed my lips together tightly, just in case.

"This is me," she said, her eyes sliding to the window seat as her hand made the gesture.

I got up more quickly than necessary and backed into the aisle. The sweaty man in the middle seemed annoyed that we were waiting for him to move from where he was determined to stay planted for the rest of the trip. My biting glare dredged up some semblance of chivalry from the man, and he begrudgingly unbuckled his seatbelt and moved into the aisle with me.

She gave me a quick smile as she passed. Did she recognize me, or was she just grateful I had gotten her out of the awkward position of having to straddle a stranger? As soon as she was seated, our thick friend resettled himself, blocking her from view. I heard him mutter something under his breath as he sat.

By force of habit, my eyes kept trying to find the girl around the unfortunate obstacle between us. I imagined spilling soda on the man's lap, dropping a sleeping pill into his drink, or even stabbing him in the neck with a pencil just to get him out of the way for a few minutes. I had twenty hours to sit just two feet away from the most beautiful thing I had ever seen . . . and I couldn't even see her.

I finally gave up on my sideways glances when, first, I wasn't succeeding in catching her eye and second, the Serbian started looking uncomfortable, as if he thought I was trying to catch *his* eye. Defeated, I pulled out my "computer" to distract myself.

My communication device had been made to look like an archaic laptop so I could use it in public without suspicion. I carried it around in a sturdy computer bag, and it never garnered more than a glance.

The screen flashed.

New messages. A lot of them.

The newest was from Claire—a gloating note about the hot towels and plentiful snacks in first class. I typed back a quick response about how she had begged me a few days ago to kill her during her last bout of gastrointestinal discomfort after eating lunch from a questionable street vendor. I reminded her that my offer to off her still stood. I could almost hear her giggling from eighteen rows up behind the cloth partitions as she read my reply.

I scanned through the messages for the day's headlines from Zhimeya. Most centered around the shortage of torbillium, our most important energy resource. The only thriving deposits left were in Unnamed Territory. The Tribunal had quietly started holding summits with the Unnamed a decade ago, trading medical supplies, food, machinery, and other raw materials for it. It was a terrible precedent to set, but the Tribunal had no choice.

I deleted every request for interviews the media sent. Even as I deleted, more of the same communications popped on screen. Earth had been such a needed break from life back home, where my celebrity status had taken over my life.

Celebrity. A useless title, especially because I wasn't well known for anything I thought was worthwhile. I was just the fabricated face and voice of the Masters, attending events to garner donations, giving interview after interview to the press with absolutely no new information to ever report. My personal life—who I was dating, who I had spurned, what I wore to bed—always made the headlines except when a skirmish among tribes broke out. Sometimes I fantasized about never going back home. Living a small, quiet life on Earth, making a name for myself based on my own merits.

I begrudgingly opened the last message. It was from Emani regarding her sisters. Oshun and Ecko, two Masters who had spent the last two years in China, were going to meet us in Mexico, but only on the day we were all to go home. I didn't care much for anyone related to Emani. They tended to be seriously unbalanced—just like her.

At the end of the official communication was an encrypted attachment. The F key on my computer glowed faintly, waiting for me to press it. If I did, the computer would scan my DNA signature and open the hidden note. I really should have just ignored it. But, glutton for punishment that I am, especially when it came to Emani, I pressed the key with my index finger. The words appeared seconds later.

```
Something's wrong with Gideon.
Please, please come to me or at least
answer my messages. I know you are
reading them. You are all that I have
left. I haven't used in months. I'll
be better this time, I promise.
```

I hit delete harder than necessary, and the communication disappeared. She'd tried this routine before. She just wanted a chance to get me on the line, to beg me to come back. And there was *no way* on this planet or my own that I would ever consider that. I still bore the emotional, and even a few physical, scars from attempting a relationship with Emani. I'd learned my lesson.

So why did I have to feel this all-consuming guilt about ignoring her plea?

She and I had been so young, only children, when her father and brother stood before the Tribunal to be tried for their crimes. She had begged me to come with her to Tribunal Hall that dark day.

"Guilty," the Tribunal decreed.

I remembered so clearly how the two stoic men held themselves in silent defiance while being stripped of their tribal markings and marched to the border of Unnamed Territory, where they were banished forever. I had held Emani's tiny hand in mine, though I couldn't bear to look at her. There was too much pain in her onyx eyes.

I continued reading other communications absentmindedly, still feeling guilty, until the bold letters of a new message caught my attention. It knotted my stomach and started my heart beating wildly. The headline read,

Tribunal dissolves over Masters' plan for Earth

It had finally happened. Gideon's controversial plan for Earth—a full-scale invasion of our kind—had fractured the tenuous bonds that held the Tribunal together. The article was full of Gideon's beautiful but incendiary words . . . *We must rid the sacred space of the human cancer . . . meet the challenge of this necessary fight to take back what should have been given to us by God in the first place.* He'd obviously convinced enough Tribunal members of his plan to cause this unprecedented break.

Obviously, Gideon had already decided that we had failed our mission if he was still pushing his plan. Maybe he never had any faith in me at all. The barbed thought stung as I realized there had to be some truth to it. Shutting my computer a little too loudly, I leaned my suddenly heavy head back against the seat and closed my eyes, concentrating only on the constant thrum of the engine. I couldn't comprehend the full weight of what I had just read. It was too much.

I had never been more grateful for my uncanny ability to fall asleep at the drop of a hat. I blocked out the words, and the world, and let sleep overtake me.

With a turbulent jolt, the plane dipped and the seatbelt bell dinged loudly, the combination of which shook me out of my uneasy repose. I felt staring eyes and turned instinctively, expecting to see my swarthy seatmate. His chair was empty.

The eyes that were on me now belonged to the girl. Jade green, flecked with gold. Beautiful. And staring straight at me, smiling slightly with that enchanting mouth.

Oh please, let me not have been snoring. . .

"I was hoping you were all right. Our friend got sick a few minutes ago and almost took your legs with him when he left. I got worried when you didn't wake up," she said. I just stared at the empty seat between us.

"Savannah," she said, extending her hand toward me.

I hadn't prepared for this. Not even a little bit.

Either say something witty or write her a note on your napkin that says you're a deaf-mute! my brain finally commanded.

"Ryen," I answered.

Well, that wasn't witty, but it's a start.

I shook her hand and held it for a moment longer than I should have, memorizing the feel of it. She looked expectantly at me, waiting for me to continue talking.

Decision time.

I could drop her hand and look away, effectively ending communication.

Or we could have one conversation.

One short, meaningless conversation.

It couldn't do any harm. It would probably show just how mundane she was. Nothing special, just a pretty face and a smart tongue.

"So, where are you from, *Savannah?*" I asked nonchalantly, wondering, as always, what her real name actually was.

"I'm from . . . uh . . . Southern Idaho. Twin Falls," she said, pausing strangely, stumbling over the words. Usually she supplied a faux hometown seamlessly.

From my study of the United States, I remembered only one thing about that area. Such a beautiful woman probably wouldn't come from a place made famous for only one very boring thing—they could grow a good potato. Obviously she was lying to me, like every other man she met.

"And what are you doing so far from home?" This, of course, was the question I had asked her in my head most often.

She paused for a second, furrowing her brow like she was thinking hard. "I honestly don't know," she finally said with something between a sigh and self-deprecating laugh.

"Does your family know you are wandering through very dangerous corners of the world?" I'd pondered this often while looking for her through the crowded streets, always relieved when I saw her still in one piece. Had she had noticed? Claire certainly had.

"I'm an orphan . . . of sorts . . ." I sensed hesitation in her words again and watched carefully as a deep, genuine sadness flooded her clear green eyes. I listened more intently, leaning over the empty seat, but she didn't elaborate.

"So why are *you* traveling through such dangerous corners of the world?" the girl asked.

"I'm a . . . tourist . . . of sorts."

She grinned at my hedging. I had told her a half truth, which, conversely, made it half a lie. I knew what her definition of tourist was, and she most certainly didn't count interstellar travelers into that mental construct.

"I am a researcher," I said to put a little more roundabout truth in my words. "My research assistant and I work for a group of private collectors of religious artifacts. They fund our travels as we find pieces they may want to acquire." I delivered our cover story easily. Claire and I had fought endlessly as to who would be the head researcher and who would be the assistant. She had awarded me the title when I had heroically gone out one night at three a.m. to fetch her some thick, viscous pink liquid that supposedly calmed her irritated stomach.

"Is your research assistant the woman that is sometimes with you?" the girl asked as she took a rubber band from off of her wrist. I already knew what she was going to do with it. She absentmindedly swept her hair up into a messy knot and secured it in place as she did in Jerusalem when the afternoons got hot.

"Yes . . . Claire. She is my assistant." The girl's eyes brightened dramatically at my explanation.

"Oh! You two seemed close, I just didn't figure it was a working relationship."

She must have been paying some kind of attention if she had picked up on the deep tie between Claire and me. We loved each other, but like family. The thought of her in any romantic role involving myself made my stomach contort.

"We have known each other for a long time. She is an excellent assistant." Claire hated the word assistant, which is why I used it as often as possible.

"Have you found anything the collectors want to acquire yet?" she asked.

"Not yet, but they are patient." *Or they used to be.* "We are on our way to start on another project." To leave empty-handed. I was almost sure of that.

"Where are you going now?" she asked in such an urgent tone, I leaned back in my seat. "Sorry, I don't mean to pry. I forget we're strangers," she said, her cheeks flushing.

Had the girl not completely stolen away my every thought, had I not been completely caught up wondering whether the words she spoke to me now were truth or yet another fabrication she was so good at weaving, I would have remembered to lie to her. Protocol forbade sharing any type of plans we had with humans. But more than that, my own well-documented weakness for her should have been enough for me to shut up. But of course, in the moment I should have held my tongue, the word came gushing off of it like water from a bursting dam.

"Mexico," I blurted out.

"Mexico . . ." she said as a calculating look crept into her eye. "I hadn't considered Mexico . . ."

"I'm sorry, what?"

"I was going to get off the plane in Atlanta and see what the next flight available was, you know, like they do in the movies. But I've never been to Mexico before!"

"Wait a minute. You are just wandering around with no plan, no escort?" I asked. I looked hard at the girl, more carefully than I ever had. Those eyes looking back at me were fearless and determined, more so than was good for her. "It's your life, but that doesn't seem very safe," I said, shaking off the moment, trying to sound detached.

"You're right. It's not safe," she agreed quickly. "But I really don't know what else to do other than wander right now."

"You could go back home." I offered the safest option I could think of as an alternative to traipsing around the globe with no rhyme or reason.

"No. I can't," she said, biting hard into her bottom lip. The sudden heartbreak in her tone disarmed me. I was about to try to talk some sense into her, but her gaze shifted over my shoulder. I turned slowly, unwilling to let our neighbor have his seat back. I still had too many questions to ask her. Maybe we could continue our conversation by throwing notes over his head.

I was stunned into silence, my mouth dropping open like a dead fish, when the addition to our party turned out to be my very own *research assistant*. There Claire stood nonchalantly in the aisle, holding three very large cookies.

"I thought you could use some company, Ryen," she said lightly as she swung into the middle seat. She folded down the tray table and placed the confiscated goods on top. "The food back here must be awful! I could smell what was passing for dinner all the way up in first class."

"I'm surprised they allow the upper crust to mingle with the commoners back here in steerage," I smiled.

"Oh, *we* are allowed back here. *You* just aren't allowed up there." She then turned her attention toward the girl. "You look *very* familiar," she said, her voice full of innocent surprise. I started to wonder whether Claire could have possibly hacked the airline system and placed her here next to me on purpose. Just then, Claire turned toward me and winked unrepentantly.

I knew it. I'd probably get in trouble if I threw her out of the plane without a parachute. . .

"Yes! I'm Savannah. It is nice to finally meet you."

"That's a big name for such a small thing," Claire said, who was half a foot taller than the girl. "I think I'll call you . . . Savy."

"That's not her name, Claire. Don't be rude," I said, though what I meant was, *don't get attached, like a child who names a stray puppy they can't keep.*

This one conversation was just that—one conversation. It would end. We would part. Life would go on as it always had.

"Nope, I like Savy. I'm going with it," she said, handing the girl a cookie.

"I like it too," Savannah decided after a moment of consideration.

Claire shifted back to me just a bit, though not excluding the girl from the conversation. "Ryen, I come bearing bad news," she said dramatically. "Christine isn't going to be able to make it to Mexico in time to help us with our next research assignment."

"Christine who?" I asked, puzzled. Claire faced me fully, widening her eyes and giving me her patented "you are a total moron" look I knew so well.

"Christine Miller, from the university, remember? She was going to help us with our *research.*" Her eyes got even wider as she tried to communicate something to me I still wasn't getting.

"What are you talking about?"

"And now we are one man, well, one woman down!" she wailed, ignoring my question. "Maybe we should just reschedule this whole thing. We *really* need one more helper . . ." she trailed off, cocking her head to the side.

Then it clicked.

Oh no, this couldn't happen. Involving a human in our search? *This* human? I took a breath to calm myself, to stop from following through on my burning desire to chuck Claire from the airplane's exit.

"Claire," I said with a hint of panic, "we have more than enough people to continue. If you disagree, then go ahead and reschedule the trip."

"No, I don't want to reschedule. There must be some other way." Her face turned calculating. I should have dragged her into the aisle and dropkicked her back to first class right then.

She didn't understand the damage she was doing.

I had physically *ached* to talk to the girl so many times. But I had kept my distance. Instinctively, I knew she wasn't like other women—human or Zhimeyan. She was like nothing I had ever encountered before. She had a magnetic pull that got harder to deny every time she walked past me. The harder her gravity pulled, the farther away I stayed, because honestly, her power over me scared me.

Women had always let me get away with way too much. There was always a never-ending line of them at my door. I was an expert at flirting, wooing, and then walking away. But the way this one held herself, the way she looked straight through me even from one hundred yards away, I knew she wasn't one to be played with.

She was all or nothing.

And since there was no possible way I could give her my all, I had settled for nothing. It was one of the most unselfish things I'd done in my selfish life, but I had done it. I had kept quiet, permitting myself only to listen uninvited on the edge of her beautiful conversations with others.

But it seemed my self-denial was going to be for naught all because Claire felt like meddling. I could have killed her.

"Claire, why don't we discuss this later?" I murmured through clenched teeth.

"Maybe we can recruit someone from the local school . . . though that could take some time. Or we could go into Cancún and see if anyone is up for the task." I put my hand on her elbow and tugged lightly, trying to dislodge her from the seat. She knew she was out of time; she felt the dropkick coming on.

"I don't know exactly what you are looking for. I have zero qualifications, but if you just need an extra someone to help carry bags, take notes, do chores, whatever, I could help . . ." Savannah said the words so quietly, I had to strain to hear them. She watched me tentatively.

This wasn't safe.

This was wrong.

Prolonged familiarity with humans was expressly forbidden. It was only a matter of time before secrets started slipping out.

So why was my heart flying?

But she'll be in much less danger if she stays with me, even if it is for just a few days, my selfishness chimed. *Letting her tag along is a kindness.* It was a good story; I almost believed it myself.

"What an *excellent* idea!" Claire practically shouted. "You would be perfect!" She turned back toward me. "Is this what they call serendipity?" she asked quizzically. I refused to even look at her.

Claire was delighted, but the girl looked me over nervously, watching my expression darken as I fought with myself.

The pair went to talking about specifics as I laid my head back and tried to think my way through the situation. Minutes later, our seatmate returned. Claire bounced out of his chair and smiled victoriously at me before strutting back to first class.

"I understand if you don't want me to come along," the girl said as we walked off the Jetway to meet Claire. She stared at the bland beige-and-blue-striped carpet instead of looking at me as we filed out of the Jetway to the gate. These were the first words she'd had a chance to say since Claire left us. "I assume the final say is yours, not your assistant's."

What could I say? I didn't even know what I wanted. No, that wasn't true. I knew *exactly* what I *wanted*. I was torn into two perfect halves—duty versus desire.

But I had a few weeks left here at best. Why put myself through the torture of spending any time with her when I would leave? Of course, others had chosen to stay on Earth instead of going back to Zhimeya in the past . . .

No! No. What was I thinking? How had things gotten so completely upside down so quickly? And why couldn't I find the resolve to stick to protocol? Protocol had always made my choices for me, and here I was, discarding it like a pair of old socks.

"I don't mind you coming." *Understatement of the century.* "But . . . I cannot guarantee that you will be safe. I would hate to put you in any kind of danger."

"I don't mind the danger," she said, and I could tell she meant it. She wore a brave expression that I knew had been earned.

We caught up to Claire then. The girl excused herself to the restrooms lined up outside the gate. What I really should have discussed with Claire was the communication we had both received about the Tribunal dissolving, but there was something much more urgent on my mind.

"What in the name of Zhimeya's moons were you thinking? You just invited a *human* to help us with our research. Do you know how many rules we have just broken? I'll give you a hint. All of them!" I fumed.

"Now you listen to me, Ryen," she scolded. "I'm not blind, though even a blind man could have seen your infatuation with Savy."

"That's not her name!" I snapped. Claire rolled her eyes dramatically.

"She would have gone to some other remote region of the world if she didn't come with us. She was thinking about trying to sneak into Cuba. North Korea was next on her list."

"How do you know that?" I reined in my temper to hear more information about the mysterious girl.

"I followed her to an Internet café and set up a trace from my computer. I recorded everything she did on the Internet. I figured she would send emails, tell people where she was, maybe blog a bit, but she only did research on a few international cities, like Havana and Pyongyang. She never made a phone call, sent an email, zero. What she needs right now is friends, and what you want right now is her. I was trying to help you both," she said with a self-satisfied smile. "Plus, you only live once."

"And what about protocol regarding humans?"

"Ryen, take a chill pill!" She laughed, probably because she had gotten to use the funny expression I had taught her on the way to the airport. I tried hard not to smile but failed.

"By the way," Claire said, seeing that she was out of trouble, "I tried to sit her right next to you on the plane, but she changed to a window seat when she got to the airport. Sorry about that."

"This is a very bad idea, Claire."

"Those are usually the most fun," she smirked.

The girl joined us again. Her hair had been brushed and her face washed. It made me anxious to clean myself up. I hadn't cared what I looked like in a very long time—since leaving Italy for sure. I wondered if my face showed the weeks of neglect.

We walked slowly to the departure gate for Cancún, taking advantage of the time to stretch our legs. The girl excused herself to the counter to purchase a ticket to Mexico. I tried to tell her that we had allotted money to buy her ticket since "Christine Miller" wasn't coming along. She wouldn't hear of it and walked away before I could say another word.

"I could get into the system again and change her seat next to yours," Claire added helpfully.

"You have truly done enough damage for today. Please, please, just leave this one up to fate."

The girl came back, standing close to Claire, farther away from me. She could feel my hesitation, though she had no idea as to the real reason for it. I glanced at her ticket, both pleased and utterly disappointed that her seat was far, far away from mine.

Maybe there was time for Claire to switch her—*no, don't be an idiot,* I told myself. With the girl around, I'd probably be telling myself that a lot for the foreseeable future.

We landed in Cancún a handful of hours later. I almost ran off the plane to the baggage claim, getting more eager with every step, trying to find the two very familiar faces I couldn't wait to see.

I heard them before I saw them. Mateo and Chase were just a little bit louder than they were large. Both had dark, curly hair, light brown skin that matched their eyes, and huge jovial grins, like overgrown puppy dogs. The brothers were identical, though there was a two-year age difference between them.

"What's up, brotha?" Mateo said, excitement ringing in his voice.

"*Malo e lelei!*" Chase added. I knew enough Tongan to know that was *hello.*

"*Fefe hake?*" I asked in Tongan. They both laughed, probably at my accent.

"We are great! Better now that we have someone to get into trouble with. We always get more girls when you're around!" Mateo said, clapping me on the shoulder.

"He's not going to be much help anymore, Mateo. Man, what happened to you? Hit by a bus?" Chase accused, appraising my disheveled appearance.

"At least I can clean myself up. No amount of cleaning is going to straighten out that mess," I said, pointing at his face. He punched me in the ribs for that.

I leaned in closer, making sure no one was within hearing range.

"So, what did you guys think about the last communication? The Tribunal splitting, refusing to reconvene? What do you make of it?" I whispered urgently.

"Not now. We'll talk later," Mateo said, inclining his head toward Claire and the girl turning the corner.

"Claire!" they both yelled.

Claire ran forward, jumping into their waiting arms.

"You know, I am surprised that you two are in one piece and the Tongan islands are still standing. I figured Tonga would have been damaged beyond repair from your visit."

"Oh, baby girl, Tonga will *never* be the same! But I have to admit, we liked it so much, we tried not to do too much damage. All we left behind were some broken hearts . . ." Mateo trailed off in mock sadness. Claire giggled, taking each by the hand. She led them toward the hallway we had just come through. The girl, who was usually never at a loss for words, just stared, trying to take in the brothers, both almost seven feet tall. I always forgot that to a stranger they probably looked a little intimidating.

"Boys, this is Savannah. She will be taking over for Christine, *who cancelled at the last minute.*" Obviously, Claire had already sent a communication to them explaining the situation because they just grinned stupidly—first at the girl, then at me, then back at her again. I nudged Chase in the shoulder so he would say something intelligible.

"Well, you have won the lottery, tiny one. You are about to go on the adventure of your life. I'm Chase, and this is Mateo."

"'Sup?" Mateo said with a quick head nod. I rolled my eyes.

"Claire's told me a little about you," the girl said.

"If any of it was good, she was lying," Mateo said, winking at her. Was he flirting? I needed to put a stop to that immediately. The words *I saw her first* sprang to mind.

We collected our luggage, one suitcase for me, four for Claire, and one duffel bag for the girl. When it came around on the carousel, she strode forward to catch it by the canvas handles. I was there just in time to clap my hand next to hers and take it off the belt.

"Thanks," she said, pulling the bag toward her.

"I've got it, *Savannah Mason*," I said, reading the luggage tag out loud.

Her name really was Savannah. She'd told me the truth.

She again tried to take her bag back since I was holding it suspended in the air, still completely stunned by the fact that she had told me something real about herself.

"I've been your employee for less than a few hours, and already you have more work to do because of me. I'd feel better if you let me pull my own weight."

"Here, Savannah," I said, handing her my laptop case.

"Yeah, because that's an even trade," she grinned as she put the strap over her neck and across her chest.

"Well done, my friend! She is *hot!* It will be nice to have something to look at that isn't Claire," Mateo said appreciatively as the boys and I went to pick up the Jeep from the car rental kiosk. I knew it wasn't going to be a quiet walk.

"How did *you* get *her*? I don't understand what females see in you," Chase said, stymied.

"First of all, I didn't *get* her. We've spoken for a grand total of half an hour. She isn't mine." I heard the letdown in my voice, and I hoped they were too thick to catch it. "And, by the way, I was under the impression that you two had girls at home waiting for you."

Mateo donned a wily smile. "I think both Chase and I decided we were adopting the 'what happens on Earth, stays on Earth' mantra with regard to our girlfriends."

"Do Neema and Joliet know about this?"

"Last I heard from very reliable sources, Joliet's been out with plenty of men and never communicates. Fair is fair," Chase said, always the diplomat.

"If I go back and Neema is there, then it was meant to be. And if not, plenty of fish in the sea, eh? In the immortal words of the Police, 'If you love someone, set them free,'" Mateo quoted. Both brothers broke out into a rowdy chorus of the song.

Earth music, especially rock and roll, had become extremely popular as researchers brought it back with them to Zhimeya. And right now, glam rock was in vogue back home. I hoped that nauseating fad would end by the time I got back.

"Seriously, Ryen, what's the plan? Mateo and I messed around with plenty of girls, but we've never involved them with our research," Chase said.

"This wasn't my idea. You both know this has Claire written all over it."

"Right, but this is *really* against protocol. You can love 'em, but then you are supposed to leave 'em. We told all kinds of stories to all kinds of girls to get out of situations exactly like this," Mateo said.

How could I try to describe this girl's inexplicable hold on me? How it drove me mad that she sketched for hours each day but I'd never been able to steal a glance at the work her hands created? How inappropriately triumphant I felt every time she told a potential suitor to get lost? How could I attempt to put into words how enchanting it was to listen to her explain to a fellow artist how she captures the color of the sky right before the sun comes up in the morning?

All of these musings would be totally lost on the pair, so I settled for hedging.

"Claire thinks she is safer coming with us than being on her own. I'm sticking to our cover story. I'll talk her into going back to the U.S. and it will be over. No harm done, okay?" I was looking for some reassurance on this point. I wasn't fully convinced of it.

"Whatever. You know we are always up for some rule bending. I would bend quite a few rules for a girl with a body like that . . ." Mateo trailed off, and I knew exactly where his mind was going. Not that it should matter to me. *She wasn't mine.*

05

Zhimeya, tunnels beneath Tribunal Hall

Zen leaned his tired head on the reddish dirt wall, enjoying the comparative coolness of it against the back of his damp neck. He'd been standing guard for hours, and his feet were starting to cramp. The earpiece that connected him with his commander and the other members of the guard was silent.

Boring, he thought.

The sweltering tunnels beneath Tribunal Hall were deserted, as they always were and probably always would be. Zen wasn't sure if they had been used in the past thousand years at all. The ancient labyrinth was full of barred cells that stood empty, since prisoners awaiting trial were now housed in much newer quarters above ground. It was pointless to guard the moldering corridors, especially since the full Tribunal wasn't even meeting tonight. Aurik was only meeting with a few of his supporters.

So, so boring.

He and Larkin used the downtime to gossip about their superior officer's penchant for illegal alcohol and younger women.

"He's getting the booze from the Diem tribe by the Kirsh River. You can never trust a Diem," Larkin babbled. "And I heard he was seen with an underage Fauris tribe girl, not that I blame him. My father says that no tribe sires fairer daughters than the Fauris. I'd do the same thing if . . ."

Shut up, Zen thought. *It's too hot to talk or listen.*

His eyes wandered up to the hovering light disk floating above them. It barely lit the dim space with a sickly yellow hue. He did his best to try to look interested in Larkin's clattering. But as he did, he heard another type of clattering down the deep recesses of the darkened tunnel.

"Larkin!" Zen whispered. Larkin stopped mid-sentence and listened with Zen. "Do you hear that?"

"Footsteps. Two sets," Larkin surmised.

"No one else is supposed to be down here," Zen murmured.

Both guards stood silently, the overhead light casting strange shadows down the black hall. They listened to the footfalls coming closer. Zen's hand came to rest on the weapon at his hip. Larkin did the same.

"Identify!" Zen yelled down the dark corridor.

"Clae of the Keeng," a voice called. Both Zen and Larkin instantly dropped their hands from their weapons and straightened up. It was their superior officer. Zen hoped that he hadn't heard them talking about him only seconds ago.

Clae came into view but stopped on the very edge of the shadows. He looked odd, a faint glow coming off of his skin.

A trick of the light, Zen told himself, though he was inexplicably on edge.

"Sorry, sir, we thought we heard two sets of footsteps," Larkin said, looking into the darkness behind Clae.

"You heard wrong," Clae said coldly. Clae had never taken that tone with them before. Zen was now positive Clae had heard them talking about him.

"I'm calling you both off duty," Clae said in a clipped tone.

"But sir, Aurik is still meeting with—" Zen started.

"Are you questioning my orders?"

"No sir," Zen said, bowing low toward the rust-tinged floor.

"Turn around and go back the way you came immediately. Do you understand?" Clae said, just as Zen heard a voice come through his earpiece.

"Zen, Larkin, are you there?" the voice chirped. It was unmistakably Clae's voice, their superior officer's; the exact same voice coming from the man who stood in front of them now. The voice from the earpiece rang so loudly through Zen's earpiece that everyone could hear.

"Don't say a word," Clae warned in a low, dangerous voice, taking a step toward the guards almost directly into the pool of light. The strange glow coming off of his skin intensified.

That's not Clae . . . Zen's thoughts were cut short by a break in the silence.

"Zen, Larkin, please respond," Clae's voice again came clearly through the earpiece.

Zen slowly raised his foot off the floor, and stealthily kicked a small pebble toward the man standing in front of him. The pebble arched through the air, and sailed straight through Clae's leg, hitting nothing but the ground behind him. Larkin gasped. As Zen reached up to touch his earpiece to call for help, the man in front of them dissolved into millions of twinkling stars that rained down onto the earthen floor.

As the man melted away, two dark figures, robed and hooded, rushed at the guards. Something whirred over Zen's head, breaking the light above, leaving them in complete darkness.

"Halt, in the name of the Trib—" Zen yelled into the black, but he was knocked to the floor by one of the attackers. His hand clawed at the earth, dredging up dirt. He threw it where his attacker's face would be. A shrill, girlish voice screamed out in shock.

Zen felt the sharp stick of a needle plunged deep in his neck. An icy cold sensation rapidly took hold of his entire body, freezing him into place.

A thin blue light pierced the blackness. It pointed right toward his eyes. He tried to dodge it, but he couldn't move. He could barely breathe.

He heard a faint click, click, click on the side of his head, and then everything dissolved into something unimaginable. A fiery torture, a pain beyond anything he imagined could exist, overtook him. The last sound Zen heard was Clae through his earpiece ordering him to answer.

06

It was a short hour drive from Cancún to Akumal, a small coastal town close to many Mayan archaeological sites, where we would set up base. Savannah had yet to even ask where we were going. She truly didn't seem to care.

The jungle blurred past us as we drove, Journey's greatest hits blaring through the stereo. From time to time, small brightly painted Mexican villages or low-lying swampy lakes would appear as we flew down the not-too-often paved road. We reached our destination in the dying sunlight, a gathering of bleach-white bungalows that opened onto a beach lined with fishing boats rolling in the gentle water. Peaceful, quiet. Such a change from the busy streets of Jerusalem.

The girls decided to share a room, as did the brothers, which left me to myself—a welcome development. I'd shared rooms with Claire too many times before and could always count on about three hours less sleep because of her incessant chattiness.

Finally alone, I took full advantage of the chance to get a good shower. It took me a while to shave, since it had been weeks since I had done so.

The thick clouds had trapped the heat and moisture in the air, so I unpacked with the door open, letting in the weak ocean breeze and the sound of crashing waves. I looked up from my suitcase at the sound of a light knock.

Savannah was leaning casually against my open door, a vision in a tank top, khaki shorts, and hiking boots—my kind of girl.

"Hi," was my novel response. It still felt taboo to actually be speaking to her.

"Hi. Hardly recognized you without the beard. I thought I had the wrong room. You clean up *well,*" she said with a laugh. The sound of it thrilled me. But I, as usual, couldn't think of anything witty to say.

"So . . . I just wanted to thank you again for letting me come. I have a little bit of money, so let me know where I can chip in." As she spoke, a small bead of sweat ran down her neck and fell into the soft indentation of her collarbone. It distracted me completely. I wanted to catch it, trace its trail back up her neck, to feel her skin again . . .

Oh yeah, she was waiting for a response.

"Oh, don't worry about that," I managed, a little late. "Our employers have budgeted for a helper. In fact, I am supposed to be paying *you.*" She had no idea how much money we each had stuffed away in various accounts under various names all over the world. Come to think of it, neither did I.

"In fact, would you rather have your own room? Sharing a room with Claire is a bit of an occupational hazard. She has been known to talk people to death." I winked at her slyly like I had seen Mateo do.

"No, it's really nice to have someone around to talk to, actually." She looked at my luggage open on my bed.

"I'm keeping you from getting settled. I just wanted to say thanks. Again," she said awkwardly, backing out of the room. I dropped the clothes I was taking to the dresser and followed her, my feet acting on their own accord. I had to think of a reason why I was walking out my door with her when I was so obviously in the middle of unpacking.

"Are you turning in for the night?" I asked. Maybe I was going for a walk . . . yeah, that's it.

"No, it's a little too hot still. I was thinking about going for a walk," she said.

Damn. I wished I'd said it first so it looked like she was following me and not the other way around.

"Could you use some company?" I asked, masking my nerves under a cool tone.

"That would be nice," she said, her face breaking into a genuine smile. It was completely different from the forced ones she so easily handed out to her would-be suitors.

We slid into the new night, walking along the white sand leading away from our rooms. I caught a glimpse of Claire peeking out of her window, giving me the thumbs-up.

The nearly full moon was just starting to rise, magnified on the horizon. The breeze that came off the water was refreshing and clean. For a long while, there was no sound except for the ebb and flow of the water and the skittering of sand under our feet.

She finally came to a stop, turning toward the water to face the heightening breeze. She kicked off her sandals and sank down, crossing her legs under her. I sat quickly beside her. She seemed to get nervous as she stared out into the ocean, arms circled around her knees.

"I want to tell you something," she said abruptly.

"What?" Curiosity burned away at my insides.

"I wanted to explain why I decided to come with you. You must think I'm either completely careless about my safety or just crazy."

"I had considered both of those options," I said. She smiled faintly, but it didn't dispel her nervous energy.

"I sort of . . . watched for you in Jerusalem . . . well, followed you would be a more honest description. I never dreamed of interrupting your work, but I just felt safer with you nearby. I had planned, if I ever really got into trouble, to find you and ask you for help," she said slowly.

"What? *Why?* Why me?" I blurted in outright shock.

"You had such kind eyes," she said defensively, though she wouldn't look at me. "You would glance my way sometimes, and it made me feel . . . protected."

Well, yes, she was right. My incessant sideways glances were for her protection, but that wasn't the point. She had gotten extremely lucky putting her trust in me. What would have happened if she'd chosen to trust someone that would have hurt her?

"You should be more careful with yourself, Savannah. I could have been a murderer for all you knew," I said grimly.

"*Are* you a murderer, Ryen?" she challenged, raising one eyebrow.

"No," was my lame response. She started talking before I thought of a better one.

"I've been by myself for a while, and it felt nice to imagine you as a friend. That's what made it so easy for me to come. I had no business staying in Israel as long as I did. I just kept staying because it felt . . ." she hesitated. "I don't know how to explain it. But then I finally forced myself to get on an airplane, and there you were again."

I turned over the words in my head, contemplating the friendship she had constructed between us. She bent her head toward her knees, her truth lying bare before me. I wanted to reciprocate, to tell her even a small part of my truth, as well. But before I could, she started talking again, filling the silence that I didn't.

"You must have noticed me following you like a stalker. Then I show up on your plane like I'd followed you there too. Believe me, I understand perfectly why you didn't want me to come with you," she explained.

Well, that was stupid. And completely backwards. But I couldn't fault her for trying to explain my lack of enthusiasm about her joining us.

"It seems that I have a confession to make too . . ." Now it was my turn to be nervous. "I *was* watching out for you. I couldn't imagine what you were doing there alone. And I never, ever thought you were a stalker. I was kind of thinking you had applied that title to me, actually." The words poured out, the dam in my mouth breaking open again and spilling more honesty than I had planned.

We both laughed hesitantly, feeling completely exposed, as only speaking the absolute truth can do.

"I'm actually very surprised you never needed saving. How *did* you stay out of trouble?"

"I had a few close calls, but I know how to take care of myself."

I wanted to tease her about the unending line of men that had followed her around the Holy Land, but I never got the chance. In the darkness, two voices screamed out an ear-piercing war cry. Stupidly, I jumped up, only giving the brothers a bigger target to hit. Mateo and Chase smashed into me with such force that I was thrown backwards ten feet into the roaring surf. I could hear Claire's arriving giggle over the crashing waves. So much for my shower.

Before I stood up amidst the waves, I collected two fistfuls of wet sand, which I expertly chucked at the boys, hitting Chase on the side of the head and Mateo right in the face.

That did it.

"Aw, you're a dead man!" Mateo yelled as he ran into the water after me. Chase followed behind.

The water felt so good, Mateo yelled at the girls to join in. Claire tested the water with her toes before committing, but Savannah dove recklessly straight in under the waves, surfacing at my side.

"So what's on the schedule tomorrow, fearless leader?" Mateo asked, grinning as we floated in the warm water.

"I called the museum curator at Chichen Itza. She lined up an interview for me out there tomorrow. I didn't want to leave so quickly, but it was all I could get. We can stay out there close to the site for a few nights. Leave most of your stuff here—no need to take everything with us. Claire—"

"I'm not leaving my things here. You never know what you'll need out there!"

"One bag," I insisted.

"Three," she countered.

"Two small bags," I negotiated back.

"Two suitcases and my Chanel tote. Final offer."

I rolled my eyes. "Deal."

07

The clock read 1:00 a.m. when the quick knock came at the door. Claire let herself in with the spare key, followed by the boys. I studied their faces as they entered—jet-lagged to be sure, but also serious, in full understanding of the gravity of the situation at home. It was a drastic departure from the evening of lightness and laughter. Their expressions meant they had already seen the newest communication that reached me only an hour ago. Aurik was missing.

"Let's make this quick," Mateo said, his face hung in a tired frown. His hands were balled up into tight fists, belying his flippant attitude.

"Ryen, what is happening?" Claire wailed, slumping onto my bed.

"The guard are doing all they can to find Aurik. The Head of the Tribunal gets threats all the time; it comes with the job. They are checking every tribe for possible involvement, though my money is on the Unnamed."

"The Unnamed have never escaped out of exiled territory. How could any of *them* have done it?" Claire asked.

"I don't know, Claire. I'm just hoping," I said tiredly.

"We're trillions of miles away from home! What can we really *know*?" Chase asked, frustrated.

"Well, we *know* that since we left, the Tribunal hasn't stopped fighting over Gideon's plan for Earth," I said. "He has a lot of supporters now. The Keeng and the Elan tribes, most of the Western, and even some of the Eastern tribes gave their votes to him. Aurik is losing support daily. It's almost an even split. The last time the Tribunal was in session a few days ago, members started walking out, refusing to meet again until either Gideon was given more power or completely stripped of it. They haven't reconvened since."

"So if the split happened a few days ago, why was Aurik in the hall a few hours ago?" Chase asked.

I shrugged. "He was meeting with a few of his supporters, probably to strategize, so there were only a few guards posted at the hall. The kidnappers must know enough about Aurik's personal schedule to strike when he was least guarded."

"Then maybe it was a Tribunal member," Chase speculated.

"That's impossible! The Tribunal is incorruptible. Isn't it, Ryen?" Claire questioned nervously.

"That's why I *hope* the Unnamed are behind this. If the Tribunal can't be trusted, our whole society breaks down."

"Did you see the notice from the Ayala tribe?" Chase asked.

"No, not yet. I hadn't gotten that far into my communications," I said wearily. My computer had been flooded with messages from everyone I knew telling me the exact same news.

"They've already declared outright war on any tribe found responsible for the disappearance of Zen and Larkin. They're the ones who were guarding the hall and went missing when Aurik did."

"I used to play with Zen when I was little. I had a crush on him," Claire said to no one in particular. "He said he would marry me if I let him have all the pets his mom wouldn't let him have . . ." She trailed off.

"I'm sure they and Aurik are fine, Claire," I said.

"Things are getting bad. Why don't we just call it quits and go home now?" Mateo asked.

"No! Things getting worse at home is the best reason for us to stay here," I insisted. "If we can find what we are looking for, the fight will be over. The Tribunal will have to come together, and Gideon will have no reason to keep pushing his plan for invading Earth to look for evidence. Everyone will be forced onto the same side. Don't you see how much *more* important our job is now that Aurik is missing and the Tribunal is in shambles?"

No one said anything. No one even looked at me. Mateo studied the oatmeal-colored carpet. Chase watched Claire bite nervously at her fingernails.

"There is nothing the four of us can do," I said. "We are staying. Now, we need to focus on our meeting with Gideon tomorrow night."

Everyone still held their silence, but their gazes at least shifted toward my general direction.

"Gideon doesn't have a majority to push his plan through the Tribunal, but a couple of swing votes is all he needs." Mateo's and Chase's gazes sharpened. They were now listening intently. "I need to know where each of you stands. Please be honest. No matter where your loyalties lie, we are all friends here.

"For myself," I continued, "I stand with Aurik. I think it is dangerous and pointless to start a war with a people so wholly unconnected with ourselves, who have caused us no harm, especially over evidence that may or may not even exist."

"Agreed," Claire said, straightening up.

"We are with you, Ryen. We are not willing to fight for the Masters' plan," Mateo said. Chase nodded his head fervently.

"Have any of you had contact with Oshun or Ecko?"

"No, but it's obvious who they would side with if it came to a fight," Mateo said. Claire blanched at the last word. "They are Emani's sisters, and they will side with Emani. And Emani will side with Gideon."

I nodded absentmindedly. Emani always followed the person with the most power. But I couldn't help recalling the last clandestine communication she sent me. She'd sounded almost afraid of Gideon.

"Wait! I think it is a little premature to be manning the battle stations. It doesn't matter which side any of us is on because, like Ryen said, if we do our job, there's only going to be *one side*," Chase insisted.

"You're right, Chase. I just think it is best to be as prepared as possible. We'll be back in Zhimeya soon. We are not in harm's way," I said, looking squarely at Claire. The silence in the room lengthened as we became lost in our own thoughts about possibly being on the front lines of a war we didn't sign up for.

Mateo broke the silence first. "So, on to more interesting topics . . . how was Italy?"

"Claire?" I asked, falling into an uncomfortable wooden chair, sure she wouldn't mind telling our tale. She surprised me by shaking her head.

"No, you talk. I'll add in what you forget." She smiled a bit at the end, but it wasn't wholehearted.

"Well . . . we didn't really find . . . anything," I admitted.

"Gideon has been saving that region *specifically* for *you*! There's supposed to be all sorts of relics from Jesus' time there. You found *nothing*?" Chase questioned.

Gideon was going to have a similar reaction, but much more virulent. There hadn't been another researcher assigned to Italy in sixty years. Gideon had pinned his hopes on Italy, waiting until he found a suitable protégé to send there, which turned out to be me.

"We found nothing that proves beyond any doubt that the Jesus they worship and The Light are the same being, or even that Jesus is the savior they think he is," I said gloomily. "We spent a lot of time in Rome—"

"*A lot* of time in Rome!" Claire said, becoming more animated.

"Thanks, Claire—*a lot* of time in Rome. No religion, scholar, or scientist agrees with another." I stared up at the spackled ceiling, searching for the right words to make them understand.

"There's a cathedral in Rome, *Santa Croce in Gerusalemme*, which claims to have the pieces of actual cross on which Jesus was killed. Of course no one can confirm that the relic is what it claims to be. In fact, countless churches across the world all claim to have pieces of the 'true cross.' Way too many churches in way too many cities claim to have it for all of them to be correct. Rome, Vienna, Jerusalem, Paris, Brussels, Venice . . ."

I thought back to the ornate chapel, the soaring ceilings, the gold and azure apse faithfully depicting scenes of the crucifixion. For days, I watched devout pilgrims scribble desperate pleading words on scraps of paper, shoving them under the protective glass to get their prayer closer to the wood, closer to their God. I wondered if my people would do the same if I brought the relic back with me.

"So there was no way to actually link the wood with Jesus?" Chase looked as frustrated as I felt.

"All they have is an account from the woman who found the cross in the Holy Land three hundred years after Jesus died.

She said a miracle happened when the cross was touched. No testing, no science, just . . . a miracle."

"So what about the Shroud of Turin? You sounded hopeful about it a few months ago."

"I *was* hopeful. But the most recent scientific studies have deemed it a medieval forgery. The Catholic Church will not allow it to be put through the battery of necessary tests to figure out what it is exactly."

"*We* could test it," Mateo said, his face animated. I could tell he had breaking and entering on his mind.

"We could, if we could get to it. It isn't even on public display right now. It's heavily guarded, and security is very tight. We would be in extreme danger trying to steal it. To get anywhere near the Shroud would take an—" I stopped myself from saying the word out loud.

"It would take an army," Chase whispered.

I knew that fact would have to be in the report I gave Gideon. Like so many other of Earth's treasures, someone who wanted it would have to take it by force. Gideon would use it as an example of how the humans were holding important information hostage. It would serve as fodder for his perilous plans.

"It's a fake. There is no need to go after it. There is no army coming. Everything is fine," I stated. Mateo and Chase nodded, but Claire looked like she was about to burst into tears.

"We have plenty of time to talk later, guys," I said tiredly. I could barely keep my eyes open. "I still have to figure out what I am going say to Gideon tomorrow. Mateo, are you presenting with me?"

"Yeah. Don't want to, but I'll be there. 'Night," he grumbled as he got to his feet and stepped out the door.

Chase lingered for a few seconds in the doorway, looking back at Claire and me momentarily. When neither Claire nor I moved, he left too. I settled next to Claire on the bed and pulled her into my side. She laid her head down on my chest.

"I know you are worried, Claire, but we are going home soon enough. And I think things will be much clearer once we speak to Gideon tomorrow. Please don't think about it tonight, okay?" I said with as much compassion as I could muster with so little sleep. I felt her nod.

"So, how did things go with Savy on the beach?" she asked, brightening.

"Before or after I was thrown into the ocean?"

"I tried to make them wait a little longer so you two could talk, but that's like asking the wind not to blow."

"I'm well aware."

"Well, it looked like it was going well. Great body language, she was smiling, all good signs," Claire encouraged.

To show just how unaffected I was by the night's events, it would have been smart not to question Claire further, to pretend I didn't care at all. But since my better judgment had gone to sleep hours ago, I engaged.

"Did she . . . say anything, you know, after?" I heard myself stammer.

"Yes, but I don't know if she said it in confidence or not," Claire taunted.

"Claire, as your superior officer, and as I am about to drop over from exhaustion, I demand you talk."

"Oh, this is fun! Ryen of the Haven, famous researcher, next in line to head the Masters, all in pieces over a girl. I forget sometimes that you're *only* a man."

"*Only* a man? Does that excuse all my foolish behavior in your book?"

"Yes," she said thoughtfully. "Yes, it does." But she didn't continue.

"Claire!" I moaned.

"When we were getting ready for bed, I mentioned that it looked like you two were having a nice time. She agreed. She also said you were gorgeous, but we all know *that*," she teased. "But then she said the strangest thing. She said, 'That boy is *way* too good to be true, so I'm waiting for the other shoe to drop.'" Claire seemed confused about the saying.

Well, now I had my mission. To never let that other shoe drop.

"All right, time for bed," I said, wanting to be alone with my thoughts.

"But I'm not tired, anymore! And why is she worried about falling shoes?"

"If you don't get any sleep, you'll regret it in the morning."

"Yeah, I know. Sometimes I think if morning me ever met night me, she would slap her right in the face." And with that, Claire hopped off the bed and turned my light out, leaving me staring after her in the darkness.

I woke with a start to the sound of laughter coming from behind the wall my wicker headboard rested against—the wall I shared with the girls' room. I knew in an instant it was Savannah's laugh, though I had never heard it so uninhibited. The sound was delicious.

My head longed to go spinning off into romantic fantasies all revolving around the girl on the other side of the wall. So to hold onto reality, I tried to remember what had kept me away from Savannah in the first place—the actual cost of a real relationship with a human. It would mean a complete, permanent severing of all communication with home to stay on Earth, breaking ties with every one of my family members and friends forever. Indeed a high price to pay for the girl I barely knew.

The best option for everyone involved, of course, was to get Savannah to go back to her home, wherever that was. Then I would go home myself when the time came.

And then what? Get married, settle down, have kids—with some other woman? That didn't seem quite fair to my future wife, to have my thoughts light years away.

No, I'd get over this crush. I *would* go back to Zhimeya, fulfill my obligations to the Masters and the Tribunal, and be with my family again. The decision was made.

After pushing the upsetting tangle of thoughts away with some effort, I got on my knees and put my ear to the wall. It hadn't even occurred to me to wonder why she was laughing in the first place. As I listened closer, I heard Claire talking in a low, exaggerated masculine voice. It only took a few more seconds of listening to realize she was doing a very poor imitation of me.

What the . . .

I thought, of all people, Claire would try to make me look good in front of Savannah. I guessed I was on my own in that department.

I banged loudly on the shared wall and heard Savannah gasp. There was a silent pause, and then both of them dissolved into laughter at getting caught.

"Oh, come on, I don't sound like that!" I shouted through the wall.

"You *know* you do! I was telling about when you almost got thrown in jail for yelling at the Swiss Guard outside of St. Peter's." The laughter started again as Claire jumped up and down on her bed, mimicking the flood of insults I'd unleashed at the guard in front of St. Peter's Basilica, one of the holiest sites in Christendom, when they wouldn't let me in because I had the wrong stamp on my documentation. It was a pretty funny story now that I was in no danger of being jailed for threatening the Holy See.

An hour later, I found everyone in the hotel's tiny restaurant. Claire's feet were resting lightly on Chase's lap, her head lolled back, relaxing. The brothers were bowed over an intricate map of roads, and Savannah was sitting next to the only empty chair at the table. Claire had probably orchestrated this seating arrangement as an apology for this morning.

"So," Savannah said as I took the seat next to her, "you swear like a sailor in front of churches? Now, is it *just* churches or elementary schools too? How about nursing homes?"

"Hey, had you been there, you would have understood." I smiled back at her teasing. She lightly kicked my calf with the edge of her boot.

The inn was almost crowded this morning. A soccer team had come in from a neighboring village to play the local team, and much of Akumal had been flooded with newcomers for the games. I gratefully loaded our bags into the Jeep, happy to get out of the crowd.

The three-hour ride to Chichen Itza passed quickly enough. The boys blared their favorite music, and the girls chatted. I was free to add in my comments and relax.

The desert seemed to fight with the jungle for dominance over the landscape for miles until the jungle finally won out as we encroached further into the heart of the Yucatán. Spindly arms of tall cacti mingled with palm trees, mangroves, and ferns, creating an impenetrable wall of fresh yellow-green on either side of us. I enjoyed the rough feel of the unpaved road under the heavily treaded wheels. It was wilder than the silent drive of urbane asphalt highways.

When Claire's favorite song came on, she screamed, stood up on the seat, and stuck her torso out the sunroof, singing at the top of her lungs:

"First I was afraid . . ."

Savannah laughed and followed her.

"I was petrified . . ." she chimed in.

"Kept thinking I could never live without you by my side!" they sang in unison.

I suddenly realized how upsetting it might be for Claire when she would have to say goodbye to Savannah, the first friend she'd had outside of me in two very long years. But, on the other hand, this whole arrangement was Claire's idea in the first place. She *should* share in the negative effects of it. Served her right.

"What's wrong?" Claire asked, seeing my unexpected downturned expression as the song ended. I just shook my head and she left me alone.

The Jeep pulled off the road when a large hand-painted sign directed us to the villas I had booked. The hotel was quiet and clean with a small pool in the courtyard. It looked like the jungle was having a tense standoff with the hotel's groundskeeper— barely being kept on its turf and seemingly ready to swallow the buildings whole at the first sign of weakness. Vines crept up the sides of the stucco walls where it would be hard for a human to reach. Trees leaned heavy and unrepentant on the outer walls.

Geckos and lizards ran over the stone floors, much to Claire's chagrin. I wondered how often I would be called into the girls' room to shoo out a wayward spider. I hoped it would be often.

Even though they were well over a thousand years old, even after the great fall of its people, the mysterious temples of Chichen Itza rose majestically out of the surrounding jungle. The intricate statues and columns were highly weathered, their delicate features having melted away with the elements, and only in a few places were hints still visible of the colored paint that used to adorn the stones. Even still, the grandeur of the ancient city was indisputable.

My favorite building was easily El Caracol, the crumbling observatory dedicated to studying the stars, a subject that I loved dearly. I felt an immediate kinship with these ancients, realizing the time and energy they had expended decoding the cosmos.

El Castillo, the largest and most impressive temple, overshadowed all of the other buildings that surrounded it. Of course, the Mayans had a different name for this important temple: the temple of Kukulkan. The legend of this temple's namesake was the reason we were here.

The most striking features of Kukulkan's majestic four-sided stepped pyramid were the enormous carvings of serpents that ran down the length of the stairs on each face, mouths open at the bottom, hissing, daring anyone to climb to the temple's summit. The Mexican government outlawed tourists climbing the temple when a woman fell to her death while making the treacherous ascent. Savannah was visibly disappointed when she learned she wasn't allowed to climb it. I wondered how much it would cost to have the caretakers look the other way.

We explored the grounds, listening to the native guides taking tourists around the sites. Researchers before us had found that was the most effective way of learning about Earth.

Savannah ghosted behind us, never asking questions or complaining, seeming completely content just to have someone to walk next to. A few times she retrieved the worn sketchbook from her bag, walked a few yards away from us, and drew, like she had in Jerusalem. My curiosity, as always, drove me half-crazy. I wondered if I would ever get a chance to see what she was drawing.

When the tours became less frequent, Claire, Savannah, and I finally sat on the sprawling lawns to rest. We had been silent for hours, listening instead of talking, but right now, it was too quiet. That, of course, meant Chase and Mateo weren't nearby. I became more consciously aware that I actually hadn't seen either of them for a while.

"Claire, where are the boys?" I asked. She just smiled, looking over my shoulder. Sure enough, they were coming out of the trees, covered in mud.

"Where the—" I started.

"We got bored," Mateo said.

"So we struck out into the jungle. Guess what we found," Chase asked with excitement.

"I haven't the slightest," I said dryly.

"A cenote about half a mile away. No tourists, no locals, no 'do not enter' signs!" Chase said gleefully.

"Not that a sign would stop us, anyway," Mateo added. "We're gonna change and go back. Anyone else want to come?"

"I'm in," I said, jumping off the ground. I had been in planes, cars, and cramped hotel rooms too much lately. Doing something kind of stupid sounded absolutely necessary.

"Wait, where are you going?" Savannah asked.

"A cenote, sen-o-tay," Chase pronounced slowly. "It's pretty much just a sinkhole. There's a lot of underground water here, and sometimes the earth above gives way, leaving big exposed pools that people with no sense of self-preservation are going to go diving into!"

"Can't we just go swimming in the hotel pool instead?" Claire asked plaintively. She knew she was outnumbered as she looked at all the excited faces around her, especially Savannah's. "Fine," she sighed, playing the martyr. "I guess it gives me an excuse to wear my new swimsuit. Oh, Savy, you'll love it! I got it in Italy. Ryen says it is scandalous, but it looked so good on me . . ." And she was off, chatting all the way back to the hotel.

The cenote really was just a massive hole in the ground, fifty feet across, thirty feet straight down to the water's surface. What made it mysterious were the dark, dripping vines and thick roots that hung down in heavy curtains all around the opening. The whole atmosphere was intensified by the setting sun's dying rays just leaving the water's surface, making the pool dim and shadowy.

I took the thirty-foot plunge first, tearing through the water's peaceful surface. I swam to the other side before coming up for air, checking for dangerous rocks hiding beneath. I looked up to see both girls peer timidly over the edge. Out of nowhere, Chase scooped Claire up in his arms and held her high over his head.

"Vengeful gods of heaven and earth," he yelled toward the sky in a deep, solemn voice, "accept this virgin sacrifice!" Claire writhed and screamed in his steely grasp, trying to right herself. Her cries fell on deaf ears as Chase ceremoniously threw her off the ledge, still chanting into the sky. He dove in right after.

Savannah started picking her way down the rocks. Mateo followed silently behind her. When she was about fifteen feet from the surface, he rushed forward, grabbing her up in his arms. He winked at me as she pleaded not to be sacrificed like Claire. She clung to him, her arms wrapped tightly around his neck. I had to remember she clung out of fear, hoping she would have done the same to me if I had grabbed her like that.

Mateo finally jumped with Savannah still wound around him. When they emerged, the look on my face made him quickly place her on a rocky outcropping at the water's edge and swim away. I wasn't as bulky as Mateo was, but he knew I was just as strong.

We jumped a few more times into the water from different heights. Mateo and Chase both swung like monkeys from the ropelike hanging vines, spinning and flipping before hitting the water. I decided to execute a few signature acrobatic dives, as well. This was no time for modesty.

"Wait for me!" Savannah called, as I pulled myself onto the highest ledge she was just starting to scale.

"Geez, be careful!" I called down.

"I'm fine," she said tartly, muscling her way to the top. I took her hand in mine and helped her up the last few feet. I stood closer to her than I should have, close enough to feel the heat radiating off her bare skin, close enough to feel her shiver when the breeze picked up. She peered over the side to the water below.

"It, uh, looked so much easier from down there," she said.

"It always does."

"This suddenly doesn't seem as fun as you make it look."

"Oh, it's fun, as long as you obey two cardinal rules. Are you paying attention?"

"Sort of," she whispered, still not taking her eyes off the water far below.

"The first rule is, don't think too much. If you can manage, stop thinking altogether," I grinned.

"Stop thinking," she repeated, squeezing her eyes shut for a moment. "Got it. So what's the second rule?" she asked. I grasped her shoulders, bringing my eyes level with hers. Her breath caught in her chest as our eyes connected.

"Listen carefully. This is most important," I said. She nodded, listening intently. "The second rule is . . ."

And that's when I pulled us both off the edge.

We fell through the air together and plunged into the shadowy depths of the pool. Under the water, time slowed for a silent moment. We were alone. Her arms caught around my neck, and she pressed herself tightly to me, her body rising to the surface slowly with mine. The bubbles from her lips tickled my face. She was just so close! I could meet my lips with hers, just softly. A plausible accident, completely unintentional.

Before I could make up my mind to *just do it already*, someone tore through the water, causing shockwaves through the pool that pulled us above the surface.

"Sorry, Ryen! I was just coming to rescue you. I thought you'd both gone to a watery grave!" Mateo said unrepentantly. Chase and Claire laughed in a dark corner together where I couldn't see them.

It was completely dark before any of us realized it. When we were all safely out of the cenote, Claire handed me a flashlight and pulled the boys ahead with her, using her long-legged stride to put distance between us.

It would have been better for me to stay with the group; any measure of time alone with the girl wasn't smart. But leaving her in the dark by herself while I ran to catch up with my group wouldn't be the height of chivalry.

"This is the most fun I've had since, well, ever," she decided.

"Really? You don't mind the childish antics, the showing off, the reenactments of human sacrifice?" I asked, stealing a sideways glance at her perfect profile as we walked on the dirt path back to the hotel.

"Well, I will have to get used to the human sacrifice, but other than that, no, I haven't laughed that hard in a long time. My ribs kind of hurt," she said with a small smile.

"So, has Claire taken a toll on your sleep yet? I told you that you wouldn't get much with her around."

"You weren't kidding. If she keeps it up, I may have to sleep in your room—" She stopped short, embarrassed by her word choice. I could almost *feel* her blushing. She hadn't meant it as it sounded, I knew that, but I was probably a little red too.

"Uh, but the sleep deprivation is worth it, because she is so easy to pump for *information*," she said conspiratorially.

My heart stopped, as did my feet.

Had Claire let something slip? Had Savannah noticed something about us that was too different, too alien?

I started sifting through the protocols to follow if a human ever found out what we were.

Assess what the human knows. Lie. Escape.

"What do you mean, 'information'?" My icy whisper froze her mid-step. The others were far ahead now, leaving us together in the darkness.

"Uh . . . information . . . about you," she said, looking nervously after Claire's flashlight in the distance.

"*What about me?*" I pressed.

"What you are like, what you do when you are not working. You never volunteer anything about yourself, so you're kind of a mystery," she said, trying to backpedal. "I wasn't trying to upset you."

Relief washed over me. Claire wouldn't be the one to give us away. It would be my ability to jump to ridiculous conclusions and act like a lunatic that would make Savannah wonder about my origins.

My brain blissfully buried protocol three away. Someday I would have to leave Savannah. I was just grateful it wasn't tonight.

"I'm just a . . . very private person . . . I would rather answer your questions myself," I stumbled. "I hate to think what Claire is telling you. She and I have something of a love-hate relationship." I started walking again, as though the last minute never happened.

"There's a lot more love than hate between you two. In fact, I have a hard time believing you are as good as she makes you out to be."

"Either way, let's agree to leave Claire out of this equation. So, do you have any burning questions you want to ask me yourself?"

"Hmm," she said thoughtfully.

I hated the possibility of having to use my already memorized lies if she asked about my past, anything other than where I had been the last two years. She glanced up at me, apparently having decided.

"What's your favorite dessert?" she asked importantly. I laughed out loud, realizing that I had again prepared for the worst.

"Seriously?" I asked, still laughing.

"Are you going to answer or just laugh?"

"Laugh," I replied.

"Well, since we don't know each other very well, we have to start somewhere, right?"

I stifled my laugh and tried to put some thought into it.

In Italy, I had discovered *the* most indulgent dessert on the planet. Gelato. The Italian people had endeared themselves to me quickly when I noticed locals eating it as early as ten in the morning. Gelato wasn't ice cream exactly—it was much more. The flavors ran the gamut from simple strawberry to panna cotta, from chocolate with blood orange to almond coconut to frutti di bosco, and on and on.

"First of all, I only consider Italian gelato worth eating. If I had to have only one flavor for the rest of my life, it would be cioccolato fondente," I said with deep reverence, "the darkest chocolate in the world. Sinful." She smiled widely, as did I. "Of all the questions to ask . . ."

"I usually don't get along with people who don't like dessert," she said simply.

"Ah, then you and I should get along just fine," I said.

She shivered slightly as a stiff breeze swept through the trees. I took my towel from around my shoulders and held it out to her.

"I'm fine," she said, watching my face turn speculative.

"It's a little damp, so it probably won't help much." I wrapped it around her shoulders. "But you're keeping it." My arm was already around her from putting the extra towel on, so I just left it there. I waited for her to shrug out from underneath me, but she didn't. Instead she moved closer into my side. We stayed like that for the remainder of the short walk. I wished with every step that I had offered her my arm much, much earlier.

09

I hadn't slept more than an hour before Mateo was knocking at the door. The recent sleepless nights pressed hard on me, fuzzing my thoughts around the edges. When was the last time I had slept through a whole night in peace?

Mateo looked like he felt the same way I did—dark-circled eyes, his face uncharacteristically set in an exhausted frown.

He spent a long hour rehearsing his findings for me, and when I couldn't listen anymore, he rehearsed them into my bathroom mirror. The fact that his hand shook slightly as he shuffled his papers put me even more on edge. Mateo, who could find humor in anything, was nervous too.

Even though there was no possible way Gideon would see Savannah, it was tough to resist the impulse to get her as far away from the hotel as I could. I hated to bring her into any kind of danger caused by her proximity to me. I lost myself momentarily, remembering the way she felt pressed into my side. It took the edge off my incessant worry about the impending meeting. Like a sedative right before a panic attack—the perfect remedy.

Gideon's communications with us had become increasingly short, ill-tempered, almost disjointed. Sometimes they made no sense at all. It worried me, but I was in no position to question him about it.

Next to Aurik, Gideon was the most powerful man in Zhimeya. As leader of the Masters, his charisma and magnetism were legendary. His influence could raise or demolish an army with a single word. Everyone dreamed of studying at the Masters Institute, though only a select few ever saw the inside of those hallowed walls.

His personal attention had altered the course of my life when he had picked me for the Institute for Earth Research. I studied under him for years, becoming one of his favorite pupils. He made me the face of the Institute. He made me famous.

And though we had worked closely together, though I gave him my all, he always held me at arm's length. I was always just outside his inner circle. At times I saw the indecision in his eyes, like he was debating whether to tell me something important or to keep his secrets hidden. He always chose to keep me in the dark.

But there was *something*. Not knowing had made me all the more willing to prove my loyalty. After years of failing to please him, I accepted that he would never trust me, and I became distant. That distance grew as I had been on Earth.

All he was really looking for tonight was our word. All he needed to hear was that we felt the humans were hiding evidence we needed to prove the existence of The Light, our savior, on Earth. That was all it would take him to act. My biggest fear was the repercussions of not giving him what he wanted. He could cut us off from our world so easily, making it impossible for us to ever go home.

He would be asking us where our allegiance stood tonight, whether we sided with the Masters or with Aurik. The young boy in me still yearned to please him, to try to win his love and trust. But I knew what was right.

"It's time." Mateo glanced at the clock that read midnight. Gideon was already online, so I started the upload.

The small camera mounted in my computer monitor whirred to life, projecting Gideon's three-dimensional image into the room perfectly, even down to his computer-generated shadow.

As he materialized, I was immediately shocked at what I saw. Even under the nondescript dark clothing he wore, I could tell that Gideon had lost weight—a lot of it. His sallow skin sagged over his once-striking features, like melted candle wax over bone. Gideon's proud shoulders were bowed slightly; his whole being was gaunt and hollow. He glowed slightly, as all holograms do, the effect making him look ghoulish.

He had a small earpiece tucked inside his ear and wore dark glasses, both of which assisted him in hearing and seeing everything in our room. I didn't like that I couldn't see his eyes; it was that much harder to tell whether or not he was telling the truth.

We had been trained to let a superior speak first, so we held our tongues as Gideon surveyed his surroundings.

"I don't have a great deal of time, but I didn't want to put off our meeting any longer." His pacing hologram passed right through the bed and nightstand, like a ghost. Even though I was used to interacting with these holographic images, it was always a little eerie to see them walk right through the furniture.

"Mateo, please report." Gideon sat down in a chair in the room he was in, which we couldn't see. To us, it looked like he was sitting on thin air. If the atmosphere hadn't been so tense, I would have laughed out loud at the sight. His foot tapped repetitively, and his eyes darted about the room. I wasn't completely sure that he was paying any attention to us at all.

"Though Chase and I were assigned to all the South Pacific islands, we concentrated our time in Tonga. Historically, the Tongan people have been most successful at staving off European imperialist powers. Their culture was the most untouched by outsiders." Mateo breathed out his rehearsed lines quickly, trying to catch Gideon's wandering eyes.

"These islands, like most in the South Pacific, are overwhelmingly Christian due to missionary efforts of the Americas and Western Europe. The cultures we studied did not have written records before European contact, so there were no ancient texts to be found or decoded.

"They passed their histories down orally, and their religious stories are unrelated to ancient or modern Christianity. Their views of Jesus are no different from most Western European Christian denominations. The island people mostly accepted the religion of whatever imperialist power visited them first."

"A culture at least a thousand years old with no written records? That doesn't seem plausible," Gideon said, drumming his fingers impatiently.

"These people do not claim to have any relics of the Christian Jesus. We found absolutely nothing that would stand as proof that Earth's savior is what they claim him to be, nor did they have anything that would prove their savior stories refer to the same being as ours. I am sure of it."

"Many of these countries still have royalty. Were you able to question royal families? Bribe them? Anything of value would most certainly be in their hands. How much did you offer?" Gideon said, becoming visibly agitated.

"These are simple people, good people, with nothing to hide. That also goes for any royal lines that are left. These people have not changed or modified the Christianity that was taught to them only a few decades ago."

Gideon huffed, standing up out of the chair we couldn't see. "Mateo, you are boring me. You found nothing. A complete and utter waste of two entire years of your life. Such a pity. You were so promising . . ."

Mateo's eyes sparked and his fists clenched, but he kept quiet.

"You have given me no choice but to deem your mission a complete failure," Gideon snapped, pausing to let the words sink in. "Are you absolutely *sure* you have no other information to give me? Because if you were to find the evidence we seek, it would surely mean great things for you and your family for generations to come."

Mateo stood up out of his own chair, looking down on Gideon's computerized form. "Call the mission a failure," he spat. "There is *nothing there,* Gideon. Those people should be left alone. That is my official recommendation to the Masters and to the Tribunal."

Even though Mateo could cause him no physical harm, Gideon cowered as Mateo towered over him. He retreated a few steps and crossed his arms tightly over his chest. His foot still tapped incessantly.

"And you, Ryen, my protégé, the shining star among the mundane," he crooned, waving his hand dismissively toward my partner, "will you be as big of a disappointment to me as your colleague? I should hope you have something that will make me happy."

"Making you happy was not my assignment," I stated. Protecting Savannah's world was the most important thing I could do now. Gideon glanced back and forth between Mateo and me, reading the distrust on our faces.

"Let me remind both of you that you owe me everything that you are or will ever become. What I have given, I can also take away," he threatened. "What is the meaning of this hostility?"

"We mean to be heard clearly so that we are not used for anyone's ulterior purposes," I said.

Gideon looked like he had been slapped. A strange strangled fury shot across his face like lightning.

"If you had *any* idea what was coming . . . If you only knew," he sputtered angrily, clenching his fists open and shut while he tried to slow his erratic breathing. "I need more," he whispered to himself before breaking into a flurry of movement.

He started rifling through drawers that we couldn't see, pulling them open, clawing through them, and banging them shut. "Where is it? *Where is it?*"

"Where is what?" I asked, baffled at his behavior. He looked up surprised, like he had just remembered we were still there.

"Gideon, are you all right?" I asked. He didn't answer. Instead, he reached up and touched his earpiece. His hologram shattered into a million pixels that rained down on the floor.

"What in the name of Zhimeya's moons is going on?" Mateo asked as I sprinted to my computer.

"The signal is still strong. He's still connected, he just stopped holographic transmission," I said.

"This is strange."

"I don't know that strange is a strong enough word for this situation."

"What do we do now?"

"We wait . . . I guess."

The seconds ticked by. Mateo and I stood straight as soldiers, waiting. Finally Gideon's hologram reappeared. His body twitched erratically, but his face was eerily serene. The wave of manic anger was completely gone.

"Gideon, is everything okay?" I ventured.

"Yes, Ryen. Fine," he said serenely. "Back to the business at hand." He resettled himself in his invisible chair, as if nothing had happened. "I have read your initial report on Italy. I've always held out great hope for that area, especially for the Shroud of Turin. Possible DNA evidence and pictorial proof of the Christ. Very important information! But you disagree with me there. First, you couldn't get anywhere near it, and second, you think it is a fabrication?"

"Uh . . . yes," I stumbled, trying to make sense of Gideon's behavior. "The Shroud itself is behind heavy bullet-proof glass and is kept in a case weighing close to two thousand pounds. It is under very tight surveillance and is rarely on display. The last time the Catholic Church permitted testing was in Earth year 1988. So no, I couldn't get to it," I said. When Gideon said nothing, I continued.

"The material itself has been carbon dated by multiple scientists, all finding that the cloth itself was manufactured between the Earth years 1260 and 1390, more than one thousand years after their Jesus was born, though more conclusive tests on the Shroud should have been done."

"So what is it then? And why do countless worshipers still flock to the relic if it is not real?" he asked.

"The newest theories guess that the image on the Shroud may have been placed on it using very rudimentary photographic instruments. The chemically treated cloth could have been made light sensitive, like antiquated picture film. With curved lenses and the right amount of light, an image could have been chemically burned onto the material, like a camera taking a picture. Anyone could have added the blood to the Shroud afterwards. But, there is no way for scientists to test the theory because the Shroud is not being allowed out—" And there it was. I had said what Gideon had wanted to hear.

"But if we were able to get it, we could test it ourselves! This is exactly what I am talking about. The humans keeping precious information hidden. If we got the Shroud—"

"We would see that it is most likely a fabrication. The face on the Shroud is not of their Jesus, and neither is the blood. It is of no value to us."

"If it is a counterfeit, why do humans still worship there?" he asked calmly, a faint smile playing at the corners of his mouth.

"Believers will believe, Gideon, sometimes in the face of overwhelming evidence. I can't explain that. Maybe they worship not because of what it is, but what it symbolizes. A savior who died to save their souls."

"But there are those who still believe in its authenticity?" he pressed.

"Yes." I couldn't lie. Most who made the pilgrimage did believe that their savior's holy redeeming blood stained the Shroud.

"As long as it is believed by any human to be authentic, it is of value to us. Our scientists would glean so much information from it. We could be the ones to discover what it is!"

"The Shroud is a medieval forgery not worth the lives you would waste in fighting to get it. That is my report. Do with it what you will."

Gideon sat silently, mulling these facts over.

"So we agree to disagree on the subject of the Shroud, my son."

I used to love when he called me *son*. Now it sounded strange and forced.

"It seems that way," I said warily.

"Come now. Let's not squabble over these small differences of opinion." These small differences, as he termed them, meant the difference between an invasion of Earth or not. There was nothing small about it. A loud clamor came over the speakers from his side. His face blanched slightly.

"I am growing short on time. Tell me what you can about Jerusalem, quickly."

"I have nothing new to add to the reports made by researchers before me. The Garden of Gethsemane is now just a plot of land. The River Jordan is just a river."

"Do believers still flock to be, as they call it, 'baptized' there?" Gideon asked with fresh curiosity.

"Yes," I said warily again. Tourist groups came by the busloads to the water's edge to be baptized where the Bible said their Christ was baptized.

"And can you not see how monumental it would be to your people to complete this ordinance where their savior was baptized? Can you *now* see the importance of allowing our kind to come to Earth?"

"No lingering part of Jesus is left behind in that river. The water he was baptized in could be part of the frozen tundra in Antarctica now. And it makes no difference where someone is baptized."

"It seems to make a difference to the people you watched travel great distances to be baptized there."

"Are you suggesting that one place is more legitimate than another to be baptized? If that is true, Gideon, our whole planet is screwed!"

"Screwed?" Gideon cocked his head to one side, unfamiliar with the slang.

"It is not worth the lives that would most certainly be lost to bring our people down to Earth to fight over water."

"That seems to answer my last question then. The most important reason I came before you tonight is to see whether you would stand with the Masters as we convince the Tribunal that our people deserve to come to Earth to share a part of the planet where our Lord lived and died."

"I answer for Chase, Mateo, Claire, and myself. We stand with Aurik." I'd been so nervous to utter the words that would drive an irrevocable wedge between me and my former teacher and mentor. But as I spoke, I felt the rightness of my words.

"You don't know *where* you stand. Aurik is gone! You have no leader!" Gideon whispered furiously. The peaceful air about him vanished immediately. "It would be wise of you to forget whatever feelings you had for the old man and his ancient ways."

Mateo and I sat silently, stunned by the outburst. He breathed deeply and smoothed his face out with some effort. "When you get back to Zhimeya, back where you belong, you will see your mistake. You only side with Aurik because you do not see my vision clearly." He was nodding to himself, staring past us both. "Though, as more members of the Tribunal join me, it matters very little whose side you choose. My plan is the only outcome for Zhimeya now. I have a great deal of work for you to do, Ryen, as soon as you come home."

"Our minds will not be changed. We are well aware of what is happening at home," I said, but he held up his hand and cut me off.

"I will forgive your impertinence at present. You *will* change your mind. Find what you can in the Americas. We have so much work to do before the exodus. We haven't even begun to explore the United States yet. So much to do!" he whispered, completely lost in his own thoughts. He snapped back to attention as yelling started again in the distance. I heard Emani's high keening voice over the speakers. He continued.

"Change is coming whether you are ready for it or not. You have two more weeks and I will send for you." In the background, a furious pounding came on the door to whatever room Gideon was in. He ripped off his dark glasses and muttered angrily, his form dissolving, leaving Mateo and me staring at a blank wall.

10

Nanjing, China

"*Ni hao,*" Oshun answered the phone as she lifted a pair of chopsticks and put a steamed dumpling into her mouth. She had to press the phone hard to her ear to block out the noise from the bustling, dirty streets. Vendors yelled, taxis screeched, and flocks of people tittered loudly to each other along the sidewalk.

"If that's Emani, tell her I found the most perfect dress for her yesterday—the one with the slit up the side, remember? But it's blue, not her favorite color," Ecko whispered, twisting her new neon green and blue hair extensions through her thin fingers. "I could have it made in a different color if she wants."

"*It's Gideon!*" Oshun hissed to Ecko, clamping her hand over the small silver phone, as she tried to swallow her food. She straightened up in her chair, as if Gideon could see her.

"Sorry!" Ecko mouthed back to her sister. She kept completely quiet for the rest of the conversation, correcting her posture, as well. She watched her sister's perfect feline features twist from surprise, to confusion, to a devilish delight through the quick conversation. Ecko didn't understand why Oshun would be smiling. She could hear Gideon screaming at her on the other end, though she could only make out a few of the infuriated words. *Ryen, Mexico,* and *insubordination* were the three that kept cropping up over and over.

If this had anything to do with Ryen, Emani would be involved somehow too. And that scared Ecko, because she was a little afraid of her eldest sister. Her mood swings were fierce enough to break anyone's neck.

"It will be done. We will report to Emani when we find them . . . Of course, Master . . . He won't even know we're there," Oshun said around Gideon's shouts. When the line went dead, Oshun put the phone down and looked at her sister conspiratorially but didn't say a word.

"He sounded angry," Ecko said nervously.

"Oh, he is—*extremely*—but not at us," Oshun answered. Ecko relaxed back into her chair immediately, breathing again. They would catch hell from Emani if they had angered Gideon.

"Well, what's going on? Does he want another report?"

"No, we have a change of assignment. A *drastic* change of assignment." The brash excitement in Oshun's eyes burned like black fire.

"A change of assignment? We're going home in a couple of weeks. Where does he want us to go now? We've been all over China! I can't stand to learn another dialect," Ecko whined.

"No, we're done here. You and I are leaving in one hour. How do you feel about committing a little espionage?" Oshun asked. Ecko, still bewildered, watched her sister dial her phone again.

"Hello, yes, I need to charter a private jet . . . To Mexico . . . as soon as possible . . . Name your price."

11

I willed my heavy eyelids to open so I could check the clock. When they finally obeyed, there was an obstruction before my eyes. I peeled the offending Post-it note off my forehead. Of course it was from Claire. Why had I given her the spare key to my room? The sticky yellow paper said:

We are letting you sleep. Make sure Mateo gets up. The rest of us are off to explore. Don't forget your meeting at 1:00.

It was already eleven in the morning. I unenthusiastically got out of bed and into the shower, thinking about how tough it would be to get the wrinkles out of the suit I planned to wear to my meeting with the head archaeologist at Chichen Itza.

Once I was ready to go, I walked to Mateo's room and pounded on the door. A gruff voice on the other side of the door yelled, "*Oh, for the love*—NO maid service, *por favor! Yo quiero dormir!*"

"I'm your wakeup call, not the maid. Let me in!" I yelled back, hearing Mateo stumble to the door to unlock it. He opened it a crack and then flopped back into bed.

"You gotta get up, man. Everyone else is already gone. I am sure they could use you."

"I know, I know. Hey, I never asked if you needed help with your interview today. Could you use a little muscle?"

"No, I'd rather do it alone. I'll be recording it so you can watch it back later tonight after Savannah and Claire go to sleep."

"No way. I am going to bed early tonight. I'm exhausted."

"That makes two of us." I walked out of his bedroom, turning on the lights and raising the shades before shutting the door. He cussed loudly at me as I made my way down the hall.

I stopped at the hotel's small restaurant to grab something to eat. The female cashier eyed me carefully as I grabbed an apple and some juice from the buffet line. She unbuttoned the top two buttons of her white cotton blouse and smoothed her long black hair back when she thought I couldn't see her.

Huh, I guess I did look pretty good in this suit; her unapologetic stares confirmed it. It had been custom made for me by a master Italian designer and cost a ridiculous amount of money, even by European standards. While in Italy, to warrant any kind of respect, I had to dress the part.

I hurried to the register, eager to get to my appointment.

"Buenos dias," the woman said with a coy smile spreading across her pretty face. "You hurry so fast. Where are you going, *hermoso?"* she asked with a thick accent as I handed her the money.

"Just here on business," I said as she counted out my change too slowly.

"That is a shame!" she exclaimed. "What would you *rather* be here for?"

"Just business," I stated again, knowing from experience where this conversation was headed.

"When you finish this . . . *business,* I live just down the street. You come find Marguerite," she said seductively, still holding my change ransom in her hand.

I wanted to tell her that I was in a hurry, that she was coming on a little too strong, or that she was falling out of her blouse, but my training was too ingrained. Every human was important. Anyone could have information that would help my research. Flirting was actually in my job description because it usually got me what I wanted.

Come to think of it, I had always enjoyed that part of the job—suggestive conversations with beautiful strangers. But today, I just didn't have the patience for it.

"Thank you, Marguerite, but I really am just here on business." I held my hand out for the money, but she instead ran her finger down my upturned palm.

"Can I change your mind?" She leaned her head toward mine, locking her gaze on me. I should have been appreciating her sultry looks, enjoying the tease, maybe more. As Claire had pointed out, I am just a man. But my head refused to find beauty in any woman who wasn't the mysterious girl who had been so cataclysmically thrust into my life. That thought was enough to snap me out of my conversation with the sexy cashier.

"Keep the change," I blurted, turning on my heels and bolting out the door. But I felt badly about my curt behavior. Obviously, Marguerite wasn't the kind of woman accustomed to being turned down, so I sent Mateo a text message about the "hot girl" in the restaurant. She was just his type.

As I walked over to the museum, I couldn't help but compare Savannah to Marguerite, and any other woman I had met like her, including Emani. Savannah was soft, smart, modest, and kind. She was sexy, absolutely. But it was effortless, uncalculated, and real. Maybe that's why she was so attractive to me. The Marguerites of the world were a dime a dozen. Savannah was a rare find, something special, something pure.

The museum was right outside the gates of the Chichen Itza archaeological site. I spent a few minutes looking around at the exhibits to use up some time.

"Ryen!" a familiar voice rang out. I whirled around to see Savannah standing right behind me.

"How are you?" she asked, obviously concerned.

"Fine?" I answered, confused by her tone.

"Claire said you had a bad night, sick with the stomach flu?" she asked sympathetically.

Oh come on, Claire!

Couldn't she have explained my need to sleep in for a few hours with anything less embarrassing? I could have gotten in a bar fight and was nursing a wound, or I was out late saving women and children in a nearby village from a fire, wild animals had dragged me away—anything else! Instead, Savannah had to assume I was up late barfing.

"Uh, yeah, Mateo and I got sick, probably from the jet lag and the food and . . ." I said, trying to sound tired. It wasn't hard.

"Are you feeling better?" She reached up and placed the back of her hand against my cheek. "You're not feverish." My temperature was rising, but it wasn't from any kind of sickness, that's for sure.

"Just needed some sleep is all." She nodded but kept looking me over carefully. Was she waiting for me to vomit on her shoes?

"You look very nice in that suit. Sort of perfect," she said with a small smile, tugging my jacket lapels into place and smoothing them down with her hands. Well, Savannah and Marguerite had one thing in common at least—they liked the suit.

"Thanks," I said quietly. Savannah's eyes were still wandering over me, so I took the opportunity to do the same.

She was wearing one of her usual thin fitted vintage T-shirts over faded jeans that hugged her just right. She had left her hair down in thick waves around her face, and she smelled like citrus. Her eyes were an almost emerald green today, standing out from her tanned, lightly freckled skin. *She* looked perfect.

"Claire said I should wait here for you. I'm sorry I didn't dress up." She looked down at her own clothes, dismayed. I scrambled to figure out why Claire would want Savannah to come with me on this interview. I was getting sick of trying to follow Claire's far-flung logic, always a step behind.

"I think I overdressed for the occasion, actually. You look great," I assured her. "Did you want to come to the interview with me? I can't imagine it will be very interesting."

"Claire said there may be artifacts they would let you see. She said I could photograph them or sketch them for you while you are talking . . . to save you time?" she offered, which was better than anything I had come up with for her to do.

"Sounds great."

"Thanks for letting me tag along. I was definitely the third wheel this morning with you and Mateo gone."

"What do you mean?" I asked.

"You know, *Claire and Chase*," she led off suggestively. "I've been wandering around this museum for an hour now so they could have some alone time together."

"*Claire . . .* and *. . . Chase?*"

"Yes, Claire and Chase! They are *together*, right?"

"Last I heard, Chase had a girlfriend," —*who wasn't Claire*— "and Claire would never tell me anything like that. She knows I would just laugh," which I did as I tried to picture Claire and Chase together as a couple.

"Really? I guess I could be wrong, but it seemed so obvious! *Please* don't tell them I said anything."

"You're probably not wrong. I'm just kind of obtuse when it comes to things like that," I said. Savannah raised an eyebrow at me, like I was missing something.

I was still puzzling over Savannah's revelation about two of my best friends possibly being—ugh—together, when the head archaeologist appeared.

"Dr. Mora." I recognized him from his website photo at once and extended my hand towards him.

Daniel Mora was a short, heavyset man in his late forties, with coffee-colored skin and thick salt-and-pepper hair. His flat brown eyes darted about shrewdly. He shook my hand harder than necessary.

"I'm Ryen, and this is Savannah. Thank you for meeting with us today."

"Ah yes, welcome!" he said in a thick Mexican accent, turning his attention to Savannah, appraising her perfect figure. I shouldn't have minded it when other men leered at her since she wasn't mine, but I did. I minded a lot. Knocking Dr. Mora unconscious would probably have tainted the information we would be able to get out of him, so I pretended, with all of my might, not to notice his eyes slithering like a snake around her body.

"Thank you for taking the time to meet with us today," I said stiffly. "We just wanted to ask you a few questions."

"Of course, come with me to my office. We can sit down together," he said, wedging himself between Savannah and me. He led her forward, hand lightly on the small of her back, making me follow behind.

Come on! He's old enough to be her father!

As I followed, I watched his fingers expertly slide the bottom of her shirt a tiny bit away from the top of her jeans, so he could touch the sliver of bare skin on her back. "So, Savannah, is this your first time in Mexico?" he asked innocently.

I expended every ounce of effort and self-restraint I had learned in my twenty-eight years to not break his arms clean off and then beat him with them. Though I was murderously jealous, I kept my face smooth as glass as I had been trained to do. I could be professional. After all, I reminded myself for the hundredth time, *she wasn't mine.* It helped that Savannah didn't look pleased at all by the man's attention.

Dr. Mora led us through a small door to his tiny office filled to the brim with dusty books, rugged topographical maps, broken pottery, and statues of strange anthropomorphic beings labeled with long, unpronounceable names. He offered us the mismatched chairs on the opposite side of his desk as he settled into his shabby seat that squeaked loudly when he sat.

"I am sorry for the cramped quarters. The Mexican government does not offer us much in the way of funding."

"That's quite all right, Dr. Mora. We appreciate it." *You filthy piece of*— "Would you mind if I recorded our interview?"

"I guess not, though I would have worn something more official had I known I was going to be on tape. I might have a nametag here somewhere . . ." he said, searching under piles of papers on his desk.

"The recording will only be used for my own perusal later; please don't give it a second thought," I said, proud of my professional tone. He relaxed and stopped rifling through piles. I opened my laptop and trained the small camera mounted into the back of the screen on his face.

I *was* recording the interview, but he was unaware of exactly how monitored he was going to be. My camera documented Dr. Mora's words, but it also took continuous biofeedback information from him. His heartbeat, breathing patterns, perspiration, and pupil dilation were all being meticulously recorded for any aberration in the pattern, which would point to the subject telling a lie.

Since Gideon believed all humans to be inherent liars and thieves, he demanded we record our important fact-finding interviews for his later examination, though he hadn't asked for the recordings in over a year.

"What can I do for you today?" Dr. Mora crooned to Savannah. "I usually don't get visitors asking for interviews, *especialmente a una mujer bella como tú.*" Annoyed by his blatantly lustful gaze, Savannah narrowed her eyes and pursed her lips. I knew she must have a torrent of things she wanted to say; I'd seen her expertly shut down men like him before. But she surprised me by just giving him a stiffly polite smile. I spoke up so he would have to peel his eyes off of her.

"The group that funds our research is interested in ancient religious artifacts. They have recently turned their attention to the ancient peoples of the Americas. Their financial support helps to preserve archaeological sites if the area is important enough to receive outside funding." Usually the promise of funding was enough to make any academic show or tell us whatever we wanted.

"Well," he said, his beady eyes glinting with excitement, "I wouldn't mind pleading my case for a little extra funding. There are whole cities, only a few miles into the jungle, completely undiscovered because we lack the money to excavate them. If your financial backers are truly interested in preserving ancient artifacts, this is the place to invest!"

He sounded like a bad commercial.

"I'll pass that along, " I said, clicking the record button on my computer. "So, Dr. Mora, what can you tell us about the legends of Quetzalcoatl and Kukulkan?"

"How much time do you have?" Dr. Mora asked with a wry smile. "I know just about everything there is to know."

"We are just starting our research. Just give us the layman's version."

"The two gods you mentioned are from two different ancient cultures—the Aztecs and the Mayans. Their religions have many similarities, especially when it comes to these two gods.

"Quetzalcoatl was one of the most important Aztec gods, and they brought the legend to the Mayans, who named him Kukulkan. Both names translate into the words 'feathered serpent.' I assume you have visited El Castillo, the largest temple here at Chichen Itza."

"The one I can't climb," Savannah said sadly.

Dr. Mora laughed.

"The very same. The giant feathered snakes on the temple represent Kukulkan. In fact, the whole temple is dedicated to him. If you'd like, I could give you a private tour myself, take you where only we archaeologists are allowed to go," Dr. Mora started.

"What were the gods' characteristics?" I asked quickly, stopping him from asking her out on a date with me sitting right there.

"Quetzalcoatl is the god of creation. He was said to have sacrificed himself to resurrect mankind. Some legends say that he promised to return one day to bring peace and a perfect society. Physically, he was tall, white-skinned, and bearded— very different from the ancients themselves.

"In fact, I have a very good representation of that particular god here somewhere." Dr. Mora hastily disappeared into a side closet. Savannah looked at me, exasperated.

"I don't like that guy," she mouthed soundlessly. I tried not to laugh. I also, to put it very mildly, did not like that guy.

He finally emerged with a long, flat stone. It was covered with intricate carvings of a man in an elaborate feathered headdress and holding serpents in his hands.

"Dr. Mora, may we photograph this for our collection?" I asked. "My financiers would enjoy photos of such a well-preserved rendering."

"Be my guest," he said happily. Mentioning people with money as often as possible was going to go a long way with him. Savannah pulled out Claire's camera from her backpack and then paused.

"With your permission, I'd also like to sketch it," Savannah said.

"Of course, *senorita linda! Puedes tener lo que quieras,*" he said, his voice dripping like Spanish honey. From the sardonic look on her face, Savannah wanted dearly to put Dr. Mora in his place. She was holding her tongue, trying to be professional so I could continue the interview.

"If I may venture a thought, Dr. Mora, this god sounds a little like the same god that is worshiped so universally throughout the Christian world."

"Ah, you are referring to Jesus Christ."

"Well, from your description . . ."

"You are not the first to wonder at the similarities," he conceded.

"And when we consider that the Mayans and Aztecs are not the only ones living on this continent to have such a legend, one has to wonder if there is a connection."

"To what other cultures are you referring?" Dr. Mora asked, cocking his head to the side.

"The Hopi Indians' legend of Pahana, their 'lost white brother' that came from the east, who said he would return, bringing with him a new purified society where the wicked would be destroyed. Then there's the Tlingit Indians of the Yukon, with their legend of Raven, who created the world, another bird symbol like Quetzalcoatl, who also said he would return. The Chippewa speak of Waicomah, the pale god who healed any man he touched and brought them religion. The Papago Indians of the Southwest, who talk of the Healer, E-see-cotl, sent by his father from heaven to teach religion. There are dozens of other Native American legends telling close to the same story over and over again across this continent," I said.

"Those are not legends many people know about, even in the academic world," Dr. Mora said.

"The Internet is an amazing tool, isn't it? I do wonder what your scholarly view is of the possible link," I said excitedly, betraying my calm façade. He saw my burning interest; he would use it to his advantage.

"As a scholar, I shouldn't comment on any culture outside of my area of expertise, but here is what I know," he said, leaning across the table. "We must remember a few things when comparing Quetzalcoatl and Jesus. The stories that we have of Quetzalcoatl come from two different sources—hieroglyphics made by the ancients themselves and histories written by missionaries who came to Mexico during the Spanish conquest of Central America.

"Mayan and Aztec hieroglyphics were made prior to Spanish contact so they are untainted by any Catholic influence. But these sources are up to a great deal of interpretation, since they are mostly pictographic.

"During the period of conquest, Christian missionaries came to the native people and tried to 'civilize the heathens.' They wrote down the natives' oral legends in order to preserve them, but sometimes they would *Christianize* the stories, making them seem more Christian-ish than they actually were."

"They purposefully corrupted the native population's oral histories?" I asked.

"'Corrupt' is not the word they would have used. They were trying to save the natives' souls by converting them. Let me give you an example. Jesus was most likely born in the spring, nowhere near December twenty-fifth. Early Christians, in order to bring their religion to the masses, took pagan holidays and turned them into Christian holidays, to help the masses accept the new religion. In the case of Christmas, they took the date of an important pagan festival, December twenty-fifth, and made it the day to celebrate the Christian god's birth. Making the symbols and dates of the two religions similar helped ease the pagans into Christianity.

"Spanish missionaries did the same thing to the oral histories of the Mayans and Aztecs. Sometimes it is tough determining what was pre-Columbian native belief and what was added by the missionaries. But, in this case, there are a lot of places where the sources match, leading us to believe that many of Quetzalcoatl's inherently Jesus-like qualities are not influenced by Catholicism."

"So where does that leave you on the tie between Quetzalcoatl and Jesus?" I asked, exhilarated. Even though I didn't trust him farther than I could throw him, I had to admit that he was knowledgeable.

"Well, the idea is preposterous if you ask anyone in mainstream academia. Even the legend of Jesus making it to the native people of the Americas would make most academics squirm. It has always been believed that the old and new worlds were completely separated at that point in time. *It's impossible.*

"But," he continued, "I have noticed that every time we say something is impossible, it isn't too long until we find that what was once deemed impossible is absolutely not. Man once knew the Earth to be flat. Man once knew the sun revolved around the Earth. These were indispensible facts at one point— but not true."

"Nothing is impossible," Savannah said as she stopped sketching and closed her book.

"Exactly! I don't think academia gives our predecessors the credit they deserve. I think the Americas were very much known to the rest of the world in ancient times. And though my belief is not a popular one, there is evidence to support it. That is why I believe that the legend of Jesus may have made its way to the Americas, but—*que lástima.* We are out of time!" he said, glancing at his watch. This was about the time when scholars would usually ask for a handout in exchange for more information.

"But I am free tomorrow. Would you be interested in taking a hike with me to the nearest of the ancient cities we haven't been able to excavate? I want to show you what a little financial backing could do for this area."

"That could be arranged." He held my interest hostage. He knew it. I was going to pay whatever it took to get more information out of him.

"I will arrange for a crew of men and supply the gear. I will, of course, need money up front to get the ball rolling," he said expectantly. I opened my jacket pocket and withdrew a number of traveler's checks. I quickly signed them and passed them over to him. His eyes lit up as he added the amount together in his head.

"Will that do?" It was more than enough. Much, much more.

"This will do just fine," he managed to choke out.

"Well, that was interesting," Savannah said after we escaped Dr. Mora's office and made it to the museum cafeteria. She completely ignored the food I had set in front of her. She looked a thousand miles away.

"Yes, it *was* interesting. What are you thinking about?" I asked.

"About how life is just *like* that. Just when you think you are sure about something, just when you think you *know*, life has a way of showing you how little you actually *know*. It's fascinating."

"Nothing's impossible, right?"

"I guess not," she said.

A sudden urge to blurt out my secrets caught me off guard. I violently wanted to tell her everything that I was keeping hidden. But that was completely ridiculous. How exactly would that conversation go?

Oh, by the way Savannah, aliens do exist. In fact, you are talking to one right now. Also, Earth may be in a great deal of danger from said aliens. In addition, I really want to kiss you. I want it so much that it keeps me up at night. I could end that ludicrous conversation with, *And did you know that I'm an idiot?* But she probably already knew that.

"Are Mateo and Chase going to go with you tomorrow on the hike with Dr. Mora?"

"It will be dangerous and uncomfortable, so they will be

the first in line. Would you rather stay back at the pool with Claire, since we are probably spending the night in the jungle?"

"Isn't this the exact reason I am here? I'm supposed to be helping. But even were I not under your employ, I wouldn't miss this!"

"Claire may try to change your mind."

"She can try, but you aren't getting rid of me that easily," she said, slowly sliding her hand toward mine.

In a momentary lapse in my constant calculation and planning, I started sliding my hand to meet hers. I couldn't stop myself. I couldn't even remember why I should be trying to stop myself. Our fingertips connected. I was about to go too far, and I couldn't decide whether I cared or not.

The phone vibrating loudly against the metal hotel key in my pocket broke our trance. It was Claire. I knew it was. Only Claire was capable of such timing. I flipped the phone open.

"Yes?" I murmured.

"Are you *done* yet?" she whined.

"Just now. We're getting lunch," I said in a strained voice, furiously sifting through what had happened in the last few seconds.

"Perfect! We'll be right there!" she said happily.

"Here comes the cavalry," I whispered. Savannah pulled a slightly trembling hand away from mine and sat up in her chair. I did the same.

"Hey, kids!" Claire exclaimed. "Clear the table, will ya?" My computer and Savannah's sketch pad were taking up too much room, so I slid both into my bag absentmindedly.

"How'd it go?" Chase asked lightly, though he exchanged a weighty glance with me.

"We've been invited on an excavation tomorrow with Dr. Mora."

"Sounds like a good time. Are we footing the bill?"

"Of course. Where's Mateo?" I asked.

"He sent me a text an hour ago. He met someone back at the hotel who is showing him around. He said she was a friend of yours. I think her name was Marguerite," Chase said.

I laughed out loud despite myself. The others looked at me with puzzled expressions. "Yes, I can imagine she is showing him around."

Is that what they were calling it these days?

"Claire, what's your plan for the rest of the afternoon?" I glanced at my watch. It was past two already.

"Savannah and I are going into town to explore and shop!" she sang. Having another female to share in her shopping pleasure was the most exciting thing to happen to Claire in months, possibly years. She usually had to settle for me, and I was rarely pleasant on shopping trips.

"There's no shopping around here outside of local handicrafts, which is all junk," Chase said.

"Then we'll buy junky local handicrafts," Claire said tartly.

"Okay, then I don't like the idea of you two going anywhere by yourselves," he admitted. I had been thinking the exact same thing.

"If you don't like it, then come with us," Claire challenged. She knew she had him beat.

"Ugh, fine! Go. Just take your cell phone with you," he said, resigned.

12

I sat down on my bed in a huff, exhausted by spending the last of the daylight hours studying, listening, and compiling information with Chase. He'd called it quits around six and left me to work for a few more hours. I returned to my room and decided to watch the interview again to look for any physiological anomalies in Dr. Mora's interview that would point to him lying. I wasn't going to find anything. He might be sleazy, but he seemed to take his job seriously.

I reached into my laptop bag to grab my computer but my hand found something else—Savannah's sketchbook. I'd forgotten that I'd taken it in the cafeteria. She must have forgotten too.

The thick book's brown cover was soft and worn, the corners tattered and dirty, brimming over with secrets about the girl that I wasn't brave enough to ask.

I'll just look at the sketches of the carving she did today, that's all.
Yeah, right.

That was the stupidest thing I'd ever told myself. The all-consuming need to see what her hands had created overwhelmed my poor conscience, which really wasn't putting up much of a struggle.

The inside cover had what looked like a very long list of cities handwritten in pencil, marker, and multi-colored pens.

The title of the list was scrawled in untidy, juvenile handwriting and read *Property of Savannah Mason, Athens, Ohio.* But then under the first city was a long list of other cities and towns:

Coffee Springs, Alabama

McComb, Mississippi

Cookeville, Tennessee

Cambridge, Ohio

Kewanee, Illinois

Council Bluffs, Iowa

Cottonwood Falls, Kansas

Moorhead, Minnesota

Pierre, South Dakota

Cheyenne, Wyoming

The farther down I read, the more refined the penmanship became. The list spanned almost the entire breadth of the United States. My eyes finally came to rest on the last city on the list: Twin Falls, Idaho

She had told me that she was from Twin Falls when I had first met her. If this were a list of cities she had lived in, why would it be last on her list? Obviously, she hadn't told me the truth. I wasn't put out about it, because if she had asked where I was from, I would have lied to her too.

The first parchment page was covered in charcoal pencil and smudged around the edges from wear. It was a woman's face. And though I had never seen this woman before, the way she smiled warmly back from the page at me was strikingly familiar. On closer inspection, I realized that she looked a little like Savannah, but older. A portrait of her older sister? Her mother, maybe? A relative for sure.

The next pages were scenes from what I guessed were Middle America. Decrepit barns, glassy lakes, cornfields, pastoral expanses . . . I skimmed through these until I came to another portrait of a woman. This face possibly belonged to the same woman as the first, but she looked more aged, thinner. But she still wore the same sweet smile that Savannah must have inherited from her.

I couldn't be sure that the next three portraits I came to were of the same person at all. Each picture was of a woman, each one older, more weary and gaunt than the one that preceded it.

The last portrait I found mixed in with a few more landscapes was done in blue pen and seemed rushed compared to the others. The woman had her eyes closed, a peaceful expression on her tired, drooping face. It was haunting, though I couldn't figure out why. I quickly turned the page, feeling like a sick voyeur looking into Savannah's private life, a place she hadn't invited me.

That really should have stopped me, but it didn't. I was completely disgusted with myself, but not quite enough to stop me from turning pages.

The next sketches were of European countrysides interspersed with famous cathedrals that were familiar to me from my own travels through Europe. Those led into drawings I recognized right away. Israel's Dome of the Rock, the Church of the Holy Sepulchre, the Western Wall, the Dead Sea at midday, the Garden of Gethsemane at sunset. Savannah had drawn them so faithfully, all in beautiful detail. I didn't feel as guilty looking at these—they felt more like postcards of where she had been.

But my hand stopped cold as I turned to the next set of drawings. I looked closer to make sure I was really seeing what I thought I was.

It couldn't be . . . me?

There I was, staring back at myself from the page. She had drawn me, over and over again. In each sketch, I looked frustrated, my eyes far away, searching. Looking at my face set in these expressions reminded me of the way I had been feeling as I wandered through the dusty streets of the Holy City.

The last picture she had drawn of me was completely different. For one, I didn't look homeless anymore. My face was shaved and my hair was washed, which meant that she had drawn this here in Mexico. My whole countenance was different. Happier, more open, without a trace of the frustration I had worn in Jerusalem.

That's when it happened.

The change.

The quick and silent slip from simple crush to something far more powerful. The strange, confusing surge and swell of emotion that followed was a bizarre blend of euphoria and bewilderment. I was falling—too hard, too fast, too much.

And it was extraordinary.

Maybe this was evidence that she could have some sort of deeper feelings for me too.

That thought should have brought me some measure of elation, but it had quite the opposite effect. I could want her from a distance; I wasn't hurting anyone besides myself. But to hurt her when I left? That was unacceptable.

My one hope was that the drawings meant nothing to her. Maybe she just found my face interesting from an artist's standpoint.

As I reached the end of the pages from a book I was never meant to see, the guilt arrived, right on schedule, and I realized what I had done.

I had let the other shoe drop. And I couldn't shake the faces of the women, all seeming to judge my actions.

I had to give her the book back. Now. I shoved it back in my bag and walked quickly out of my room without thinking through what I was going to say to atone for my sins. Would she be upset? Would she be hurt? A fresh gush of shame gutted me.

I reached her and Claire's room, still not sure what I was doing. I half hoped they were already asleep. I leaned my ear to the door and heard Claire's high chirpy voice, babbling away. I knocked quietly. Frantic rustling came from the other side of the door, then Claire yelled, "Come in, Savannah!"

Come in, Savannah?

I walked into the room only to find Claire blushing tomato red as she sat awkwardly on the edge of her bed and Chase leaning on the far wall, looking terribly uncomfortable.

"What's going on? Where's Savannah?" I asked.

"She and I got home from shopping, *if you can call it that*, and Chase came over to say goodnight. She all of a sudden decided that she wanted to go swimming," Claire said nervously.

"And you didn't go with her?"

"She said she wanted to go by herself. She's a big girl, Ryen—" Claire started.

"How long ago did she leave?" I demanded.

"Uh, I don't know. Chase?"

"I came over around eight, so an hour ago. Mateo crashed early. I was just checking in on the girls before I went to bed, to make sure they'd gotten home safely. Savannah left a few minutes after I showed up, so I figured I would just stay for a while," Chase overexplained.

"Are you two . . . *What is this?*" I asked, my eyes narrowing. They glanced at each other awkwardly and then back at me.

Claire gave me a desperate look while Chase didn't seem able to make eye contact with me anymore.

So Savannah *was* right about the two of them! And it looked like it was so early in the "relationship" that maybe they hadn't even defined what they were yet. Since Savannah had asked me not to say anything about it, I begrudgingly let them off the hook.

"Never mind. I'm going to go make sure she's okay." They both relaxed as I walked out of the room.

When I got to the hotel's small pool, it was empty, with no puddles or wet footprints on the cement. No one had been swimming recently. A twinge of alarm skittered up my spine. I called Claire.

"She's not at the pool. Did she say anything else?" I asked nervously.

"No. She took a towel from the bathroom and had her swimming suit on under her clothes. Do you want us to come and help you look?"

"Take the restaurant and the hotel grounds. I'll go farther out. Call if you find her." She hung up as soon as I was done barking instructions.

I should have given Savannah a cell phone or something. I never thought she would go off without at least Claire with her. We were in the middle of the jungle. There was danger everywhere. What was she thinking?

In answer to that, Claire's words echoed through my head.

She's a big girl, Ryen.

She was free to do what she wanted. Maybe I shouldn't go running off after her. She didn't owe me a call or explanation whatsoever. *She wasn't mine.*

But even if she wasn't mine, my job was to keep her safe, which was the whole reason I'd let her come with us in the first place. I couldn't let anything happen to her out here.

I stopped walking in the middle of the hotel's large courtyard and put my fingers to my temples, trying to concentrate. She must have said something to me in the course of the last day or so that would lead me to her.

Then it dawned on me. I knew *exactly* where she was.

I ran toward Chichen Itza, less than a mile down a dirt road from the hotel, ducking through the dense jungle to the side of the entrance gates to bypass security. I slowed up at open fields around the ancient temples, hoping to find her sitting on the grass. No luck. I picked up my pace and ran toward El Castillo, the temple she had been so disappointed that she wasn't allowed to climb.

She wasn't in sight, but if I were her, I would have climbed up the eastern side facing away from the entrance so I'd be less likely to be spotted. I rounded the corner, eyes straining into the darkness.

"Savannah!" I called as loud as I dared.

"Ryen? What are you doing here?" I heard her call in utter astonishment from high up in the darkness.

"I'm looking for you!" I called out in relief.

I flipped my phone open, dialed, and waited for Claire's hello. "Found her," was all that I said before hanging up. I pushed the power button so she couldn't call incessantly for more details.

"What are you doing here?" I called.

"Making bad decisions. This all went so much better in my head!"

"Did Dr. Mora bring you out here?" I asked, trying to make out his shape next to hers.

"Of course not! That guy is a creep," she said. I took a second to laugh.

"Are you okay?"

"Well, I got about halfway up and a stair gave way. I cut my leg in a few places. This is probably why no one's supposed to climb up here, huh?" she said in a nonchalant voice, which made it more comical.

My eyes were adjusting to the darkness more each passing minute. I could see her now against the nearly full moon. She was wearing a tank top with minuscule jean shorts and sandals and had the hotel towel wrapped around her leg. The stairs below her were spattered with a good amount of blood. I scanned the steps to find the safest pathway to the top.

"Stay where you are, I'm coming up," I said.

"I'm not going anywhere," she called back.

When I reached her, she threw her hands around my neck, pressing her forehead to mine. She must have been either more scared or more hurt than she let on. I let my hands rest on her shoulders, but that was all I allowed myself. Even that was almost too much to handle.

"This was a stupid decision," she said.

"If we keep to the right, the stairs are less weathered. Can you make it to the top?" I asked, pulling away from her, trying hard to ignore the nearness of her lips, the scent of her skin.

"You're not mad?"

"You're allowed to make stupid decisions. So, can you make it?"

"Wouldn't it be better if we just went back down?"

"If you're ready to call it quits because of a little blood, you are not the girl I thought you were," I challenged. "Besides, I want to see the view from the top."

"So do I," she admitted.

I led the way slowly toward the safest part of the stairs.

"Did you know," I said, trying to distract her from the precarious climb, "that this pyramid has ninety-one steps on each side?"

"I wasn't exactly counting," she said sarcastically.

"At ninety-one stairs per side, that would make three hundred sixty-four stairs all together. If you count the very top platform step, which the Mayans did, you get three hundred sixty-five stairs. The exact number of days in a year," I said.

"So this isn't just a temple," she guessed.

"It's also a calendar. It traces the vernal and autumnal equinoxes too. For the Mayans, this is where art, math, and religion met. Fascinating, don't you think?" I asked, helping her up the last stair to the temple platform at the top.

"Yes. I can now appreciate it as I am currently not about to fall to my death." I helped her sit carefully on the top step. I sat down next to her and unwrapped the towel to examine her leg. She laid it gingerly on my lap and leaned back to give me room.

"Hmm, all the cuts look superficial," I lied coolly. The blood was still spilling freely out of the worst of the wounds.

"Really? One of the cuts looked pretty deep."

A human doctor would have definitely given her stitches. But we were pretty far from any reputable medical center, and she needed help immediately. Luckily, I always carried a few emergency medical supplies from home with me.

"It just looks bad because of the blood. Some antiseptic, ointment, and a few bandages should do the trick."

I ripped a packet of ordinary antiseptic open with my teeth and started cleaning the worst of the cuts. She cringed as the alcohol hit her skin.

"It would have been a lot safer to wear pants if you were planning to go climbing. Some sturdier shoes would have been smart too," I teased.

"This wasn't planned," she said tartly. "Chase showed up at our hotel room with *the look*," she said, raising one eyebrow.

"The look?"

"Yes, the look. The hungry look, the 'I want Claire now' look. I'd know that look anywhere."

"Would you?" I asked fervently.

Did she see it in my eyes every time I looked at her? Could she see it written plainly across my face at this very moment as she held my gaze? Could she see me burning from the inside out because of her nearness?

I looked away from her searching eyes. I was being stupid. She wasn't mine, and she never would be. Showing her the way I felt would only complicate matters. I busied my hands with cleaning the cuts on her leg. She winced in pain.

"Uh, so I volunteered to go to the pool to get out of their way. That guy has a one-track mind," she said with a nervous laugh.

"All guys have a one-track mind. It is one of the great *universal* truths," I said sardonically.

She was still watching me intently, probably trying to decipher the meaning behind my pointed words. I fished the canister of sealing salve from my bag, a Zhimeyan concoction that instantly sealed most cuts closed.

"Keep watch for security," I said, trying to distract her. She did as she was told and studied the fields below.

I pulled the largest laceration closed and used just a dab of the salve. I could have used more and spared her a scar completely, but that would have raised her suspicion.

"So, you went to the pool . . ." I prodded.

"Oh, right. I went to the pool but then decided what I really wanted to do was come here. It would have been too awkward to knock on the door again to ask for my jeans. I didn't know what they were up to, and I doubt she had a necktie in there to hang on the doorknob to warn me," she said with a tentative laugh, trying to lighten the mood.

I didn't know what she meant, but I laughed with her so as to not give me away. She must be referring to some American custom that I wasn't familiar with. I placed the last of the butterfly bandages and she took her leg back.

"You never told me how you knew where I was," she said quietly.

"You seemed so disappointed when you found out the temple was closed to the public. And Dr. Mora did say he wanted to show you around. I thought maybe you took him up on his offer," I joked.

"Oh yes, a date with him would be *impossible* to turn down," she laughed. "You shouldn't have to worry about me, but in this case, I'm glad you did."

"Glad to be of service," I said, glancing up at the sky.

"I've never seen so many stars," she said in awe, looking upward with me. I wondered how much more beautiful she would find the stars from space, as I had seen them.

"So, did you decide to come up here because you crave danger, or are you trying to get away from something?" I meant it as a glib remark, but her face fell slightly.

"I kind of wanted to just get away from everything for a little while."

"I can understand that. This world can be a little rough. I'd like to escape from it sometimes too."

"A little rough," she whispered mostly to herself. "Sometimes when I get homesick, I feel a little better looking at the stars. They are quiet, peaceful, unchanging."

"I know what you mean." How often had I stared up into the sky, missing my home? I always felt closer to everything I'd left behind by just looking up. As I turned over my thoughts, she took her hair down from the band that held it back. A few tendrils of it were swept up with the light breeze toward me, washing me with her clean scent. I breathed her in.

"Savannah, do you believe in God?" I asked abruptly, startling myself.

She looked at me seriously, maybe to make sure I wasn't kidding.

"Yes. I have to," she answered earnestly.

"You have to?"

"I have to believe that there is a higher purpose, a reason for this existence," she said. "If this is it, if this life is all we get and then we just . . . cease to exist, it would be beyond useless for me to go on." She cut off quickly, unwilling or unable to finish her sentence. After a quiet moment, she looked away from me, returning her gaze back to the sky.

"And what about you? A man who scours the world for priceless religious artifacts, do you believe in God?"

I shrugged my shoulders. "Anthropologically speaking, almost every culture from the beginning of history claims the existence of a higher power. Billions of people can't be wrong, can they?"

Or could they? Could two whole worlds teeming with life all have faith in a power that didn't exist?

"Is that a 'yes'?" she questioned.

"It seems that the universe is too full of amazing things for it all to have happened by chance." I glanced at her face, pale white in moonlight, an example of exactly what I was talking about. "I just wish there was more evidence, you know? Proof enough so that faith wouldn't be necessary."

"Evidence? More than nature, the ordered universe, you and me? Isn't that evidence?" she asked.

"I'm looking for something unassailable. Can you imagine how the world would unite around undeniable proof that God exists?" I asked.

She thought about it for a minute.

"Yes, it would make things easier. But I kind of think God lets us go without concrete proof so that we can choose which path to take. If we all had proof, there would be no choice. God gave us our lives to do what we want with it," she said simply.

Zhimeya was split over this exact difference of opinion Savannah and I were discussing. Many of my people believed that God wouldn't have left undeniable proof for us to find, on this planet or ours. Some even believed that our pursuit to prove the existence of God or The Light or a savior, whatever you wanted to call Him, would evoke his judgment upon us, not unlike what God had done to those who had built the biblical Tower of Babel to reach Heaven.

That Savannah would disagree with my mission objective, were she to ever find out, was frustrating. She, in so many words, didn't think I would find the evidence I was looking for. All the more reason for me to do whatever I could to stop Gideon from disturbing her world, from taking innocent lives over evidence that didn't exist.

We had been quiet for some time, both wrapped up in our own thoughts. She yawned, reminding me of the late hour.

"So, have you had your fill of danger for one night?" I asked.

"Definitely. I think I've sacrificed more than enough blood to appease the Mayan gods for now." She picked herself up slowly, so as not to disturb the bandages. "Huh, you must have done a good job. I can barely feel the cuts anymore." Pain relief was a side effect of the sealing salve, but she didn't need to know that.

On the walk back to the hotel, I regaled her with tales of Claire's more embarrassing exploits since Claire had no qualms about doing the same to me. It was petty to pick on Claire, but making Savannah laugh, even at Claire's expense, was just too much fun to resist.

The walk passed too quickly, and the bag hanging on my shoulder got heavier and heavier as we approached her door. I had to give her back her book.

She stopped at the door, with her hand on the knob, and turned back toward me to say something. She was startled silent by my suddenly nervous expression.

"Savannah . . . I was coming to bring your sketchbook back to you. That's when I realized you were gone." I handed it to her. She took it out of my hands and clutched it to her chest as the smile slowly drained from her face.

"Did you look through it?" she asked pointedly.

"Yes," I said quickly before I could lie to her.

"All of it?" she asked. Her beautiful green eyes burned, belying her blank expression.

"Yes," I said quietly.

"Wow, that's . . . disappointing," she muttered, looking straight through me with her devastating stare. "I was hoping you would be different. You seemed different, better. But you are just the same as all the others. It was my mistake to have trusted you."

"No, I—I just wanted to see what you had created. You have an amazing talent . . ." I sputtered out stupidly.

She laughed a hard laugh once. "So you like what you saw, then?" she said with an acidic edge. "You have a beautiful face. You are *well aware* of how attractive you are. So I sketched you." It wasn't a compliment at all. I should have known the sketches of me meant nothing more to her than that.

"I'm sorry," I mumbled.

"Ryen, I am damaged, probably beyond repair." Her tone was cold, clinical, as if she were discussing a medical diagnosis. "I have a lot of issues, trust being the biggest one. So tell me this. How am I supposed to learn to trust when no one I meet deserves it?" Without another word, she turned away from me and shut the door resoundingly behind her.

13

Zhimeya, at the home of Adan of the Cailida tribe

It had been a long day of battle on the Tribunal floor, and he was tired. With Aurik missing and the Tribunal split into warring factions, all anyone did was yell, scream, and blame.

Gideon was the only constant in Adan's life now. Always there, always pressuring Adan for his vote. Adan had made it very clear that he would rather die than give Gideon his support. He would never vote to allow Gideon any measure of power beyond what he had. He had scheduled an emergency meeting with the elders of the Cailida tribe to tell them about Gideon's intimidation. The Cailida tribe would *not* be bullied.

He thought sadly of the Cailida children. What would this disunity mean for the future of their tribe? Their planet? It wearied the old man to shoulder the weight of his Tribunal appointment at such a disturbing juncture in history.

Adan was relieved to have finally reached his home, until he saw it—a sealed envelope resting at the bottom of his front door, the crest of the Masters plainly stamped on the front.

"An outrage," he said angrily, as he tore the velvet sheath open. A piece of heavy parchment fell out, covered in elegant script. He unfolded it and read it once, twice, a third time.

Adan of the Cailida Tribe,

Last chance.

Come to the Tribunal building immediately if you have decided to change your mind. Consider this my last offer and your last warning.

Gideon

"Despicable!" Adan spat furiously, crumpling the note and throwing it to the ground. For good measure, he stepped on it with his heel.

He positioned himself in front of the door, bringing his mouth close to the small microphone hidden inside. In a low voice, he spoke the door's password, his very favorite scripture from the human Bible. Words their Jesus had spoken eons ago, so far away from here. But time and distance didn't matter. The Light transcended both. The phrase had anchored deep into his soul the first time he had heard it.

"Be not afraid, only believe," he said. The door sprung open for him, letting him into his darkened home.

Adan moved through the house slowly, unwinding from the stress of the day. He took time to water and prune the plants, vines, and trees that grew freely through the sandy soil floors of the home.

He finally reached his bedroom, ready to lay his weary body down for the night. He turned on the light and jumped at the sight before him.

Adan knew the pair. Emani and Dai, both Masters and advisers to Gideon. Dai lounged casually against one of the moss-covered walls while Emani sat nervously on the edge of his bed. Adan was taken aback by how striking they both were, as beautiful as they were dangerous. Even with one missing eye, Dai was still undeniably handsome. Emani, one of his own, a Cailida, was even prettier than her late mother, who was a famous beauty herself. Both wore nondescript black clothing and gloves.

"Adan," Emani said in despair, "you are just gathering your things before you go to Gideon, *right*?"

"Hold your tongue, Emani. We've been waiting for you, Adan," Dai explained, his whole being aglow with rash excitement. He flexed the muscles in his arms, warming them in case Adan tried to run.

"This goes beyond intimidation! To stalk a member of the Tribunal, to break into his home," Adan said, trying to keep his tone even. "How did you even get in?"

"We had the password."

"Only one other person knows that password. What have you done to her to get it?" Adan accused.

"I assume you have rejected Gideon's last offer since you are not currently on your way back to him to receive your mark and pledge your vote."

"You assume correctly. Now get out!"

"Gideon has been patient with you. Your vote could have done a great deal to sway others in the Tribunal into giving their support, but you stubbornly withheld," Dai said mockingly.

"That man is insane. I am meeting with the Cailida Elders tomorrow to place sanctions on the Masters for coercion of Tribunal members. Both of you, along with Gideon, will have your tribal marks removed. You will become Unnamed, exiled from society. Are you willing to pay that price just to serve Gideon?"

"That's very brave talk from someone who is outnumbered," Dai said scornfully, pushing his jet black hair away from his one electric purple iris. He held up a small silver device, thin as his finger, no more than six inches long. When Dai clicked the end of it, a blue ray of light shot from the opposite side. "Do it, Emani," Dai ordered.

Adan didn't notice that Emani had moved until it was too late. She kicked his knees, which threw Adan off balance into the wall. Dai pounced on Adan's slumping figure and pointed the end of the mechanical wand onto Adan's temple, though careful not to bruise the skin.

"What is that?" Adan screamed, panic-stricken.

"Well, it doesn't have a name yet, it's just a prototype. If it doesn't work, you'll die. If it does, you'll still die, just not for a few days."

"You will never get the Cailida tribe's vote. My people will not be bullied or bought."

"We already have the Cailida vote. It was given to us by Cyrenia," Dai sneered.

"Cyrenia doesn't have the power to vote in the Tribunal. That power is mine. She is the second in command."

"She'll be first in command soon enough. She is at the Tribunal building right now meeting with Gideon, receiving the mark. Everyone has their price."

"Cyrenia," Adan uttered in horror. "*She* gave you the password to my home? My oldest friend!" he lamented.

After a few stony seconds, he snapped out of his stupor and started struggling again against the hands that held him. "Emani, you're my blood! A Cailida! How can you do this?" he screamed. "Please do not squander your gifts for these evil purposes!" he begged, staring up into her eyes.

She was transfixed in the gaze of a man she had once regarded as a father. He had been the one to recommend that she and her sisters enter the Institute for Earth Research. He had encouraged her gifts. When Emani's father and brother were banished from society and her mother had committed suicide because of the disgrace, Adan had cared for her and her sisters. He was a good man. He was innocent.

"I tried to convince you of Gideon's plan. I tried to save you," Emani whispered, tears welling up in her eyes. She quickly pulled out a syringe and injected a clear serum into his neck. Adan tried to fight, but paralysis was spreading through his limbs like wildfire.

Dai turned the dial on the end of the wand. Click, click, click.

"Good night, Adan, former Father of the Cailida tribe," Dai said pleasantly.

There was a surge of heat in the middle of Adan's brain, a fiery torment he could not extinguish. He tried again to move, but he couldn't find his body anymore. The heat and pressure mounted to an unfathomable degree. He stared bravely up at Emani, even through the torture.

Emani stared back at him in horror. She thought she had been ready for this, but it was too much for her to take.

With a loud pop, Adan of the Cailida was dead. Blood and smoke sizzled from his nose and ears. His eyes were still boldly held wide. Dai pulled the weapon away from Adan's temple. No mark was left.

"Clean that up," Dai said.

"Me? This mess is your fault! He wasn't supposed to die!" Emani cried, trying to mask her anguish with anger.

"Well, this thing still isn't working right. I used the same setting as I did with Zen and Larkin, and they are only brain dead," he said, tapping the instrument in his hand.

"But he was old! You can't use the same setting on everyone! Brain damage and death are not the outcomes Gideon wants!" she screamed, inconsolable, but not because the weapon wasn't working.

"Okay, next time, just two clicks," Dai said coolly. "We have plenty of people Gideon wants dispatched. There's time for practice. Clean up the blood, and we'll put him in bed. Remember to get the note from outside," he ordered.

Emani tried to hide her shaking hands. She hated taking orders from Dai, but he would tell Gideon about any reluctance she showed. This had been a test of her allegiance, and she had followed through.

Emani looked down at Adan one last time, lightly placing her fingertips on his eye lids to shut them, unable to stand seeing her reflection in his eyes as she destroyed the evidence.

14

"Oh, how the mighty have fallen," Chase called out as I entered the hotel's small restaurant.

"Over a skirt, no less!" Mateo exclaimed.

"You are in *trouble*," Chase sniggered over his plate of greasy chorizo and eggs. "Claire told me what happened."

"Please, *please* let it go." I slumped into an empty chair, letting my head fall on the dingy table. If there weren't so many people around, I would have pounded my forehead a few more times for good measure.

"Like we're going to just let this slide." Chase laughed at my misery again.

"Ryen, I would have looked through her book too, don't get me wrong. But I never, under any circumstances, would have told her that I had! Lie, son!" Mateo exclaimed.

"You *should* have just kept your mouth shut, brother," Chase added.

"Yeah," was all I could say, picking my head up and staring at the ceiling stained with old rainwater leaks. I didn't feel like arguing with them about ethics.

"Aw, don't beat yourself up too badly. Claire thinks there's a very slight chance Savannah might forgive you someday. Claire did everything she could to make you look like a good guy," Chase said as I drowned in my own private pool of self-loathing.

"No, I'm pretty sure I've completely blown it."

"So what, Ryen? If you did, it will make it all the easier to go back home, just like you had planned to do, anyway. I think this is a good thing. We'll get her on a plane outta here, and we can get on with our lives," Mateo said, trying to be helpful.

"That's not the point. She's here because I want to help her, not hurt her." This was what had kept me up all night. It was obvious that Savannah had lived through something traumatic, though I could only guess at the details, and here I was doing more harm than good.

"Did Claire really think she might forgive me?" I asked.

"Well, we're about to find out. Here they come." Mateo inclined his chin toward the door, signaling the girls' entry. I straightened up nervously.

Savannah's eyes were cast downward, but Claire's were trained directly on me, two white-hot lasers of seething disapproval trying to burn me where I sat. Chase pulled out the chair next to him for Claire, but she stopped him.

"Thanks, but we ordered room service," she said, giving his hand a squeeze. "Chase, Mateo, can you come with me? I need some help."

"Help with what?" Mateo complained.

"It doesn't matter!" Claire glared at them with an intensity that should have lit them on fire.

Neither brother moved at first. They both wanted to see their fearless leader decimated by a tiny human. They finally exited, though I could hear them guffawing from the lobby.

Savannah sat down slowly, stiffly, still not having made eye contact. Her scent hit me hard with a sudden shift in the breeze, the scent that always drove me crazy.

I reminded myself that Mateo was right. None of this should matter. It shouldn't matter that I hurt her. It shouldn't matter what her opinion was of me. My goal was to get her on a plane bound for wherever I wasn't.

But the thought of her actually boarding that plane, walking out of my life forever, caused me enough physical pain to take my breath away.

She lifted her eyes, bottle green today, and read the agony that was clear on my face. Her demeanor softened minutely.

"That book is more than just sketches to me. My mother gave it to me when I was ten," she said too calmly. I wished she would yell or at least hit me.

"You made me feel exposed and embarrassed." She paused, letting the words stick into me like poison-tipped darts. "You have no idea know how much—" She broke off, took a long breath, and continued in a different direction. "Claire seems to think that I should forgive you. She said you would beat yourself up more than I ever could."

"She's right." I didn't know if I was allowed to talk, so I kept my words short.

"In fact, I wanted to come earlier, but she said that a little extra self-flagellation was good for you." Her expression hadn't changed yet. I had no idea where the conversation was going.

"I thought about it, and I came to the conclusion that if I weren't so messed up, I probably wouldn't have been as upset by the situation as I was. It *was* a scummy thing to do, but I assume you probably didn't mean to actually hurt me."

"No, of course not! I would never—" I rushed, but she held up her hand to stop me.

"And I appreciate your honesty, but, Ryen! Come on! You should have just lied! Why would you fess up to looking through that book?" A smile spread across her face, as bright as the sun breaking over the horizon after my long, desolate night. "Your conscience is going to get you into lots of trouble." She was siding with Mateo and Chase. I hadn't seen that coming.

"So . . . we're okay?" I asked tentatively, taking courage in her upturned expression.

"Yeah, we're okay," she said. The relief was so severe it hurt, like air rushing back into my lungs after nearly drowning. "I figure a guy who rescues me off the side of a Mayan temple in the middle of the night deserves a *little* credit."

"I'm sorry," I said with all the feeling I could manage, reaching out my hand for hers without thinking. She took it and braided our fingers together.

"I still hope that you are different. There's something about you that's special, so don't prove me wrong."

"You have my word."

Dr. Mora was waiting for us at the agreed-upon spot, impatiently tapping his small foot. He had eight Mayan men with him, all much shorter and darker than he. He watched Savannah and Claire with a greedy twist to his fleshy smile.

The ten-mile hike into the jungle should have been grueling for us, but it was almost like being at home again on Haven tribal land. We'd all grown up in the heart of a rainforest, so we glided easily along with locals through the copious greenery. Only Dr. Mora and Savannah struggled to keep their footing among the thick underbrush. Even the light backpacks they carried slowed them down considerably. I offered to take Savannah's at least ten times, but she wouldn't hear of it.

The machete-wielding Mayans hacked a path through the thick tangle of plant life barely big enough for us to squeeze through. As soon as everyone was through the carved-out tunnel, the trees moved back in to fill the hole, sealing us further into the heart of the jungle. We kept our step in time with the blips of the GPS device Dr. Mora held.

I followed Mateo in line for the first half hour but quickly ended that practice after the fifth time he bent back a thin, springy tree and hit me right in the face when he let go of it. I gladly settled into walking behind Savannah at the back of the line, happy to watch the rhythmic swing of her hips and shoulders as she walked.

"Dr. Mora, how did you find this area in the first place? I can't imagine anyone just stumbles this far into the jungle accidentally," Claire asked, sounded genuinely interested. Only I heard the hint of boredom in her voice. She knew the answer to this question but was trying to make him feel like the expert, as was her job. Men fell quick prey when she turned her charms on them. Idiots.

"We find these hidden cities through what we call *remote sensing*. Finding anything in the jungle is almost impossible on foot, so we look from above. We use satellites and radar, which take pictures of the Earth's surface from the sky. Then we use those pictures to find what we cannot see from the ground."

"So, you find an ancient city buried in the jungle, then . . ." She trailed off to let "the expert" finish the sentence.

"Then we mark it on a map. After that, I pray that someone with money and a penchant for archaeological digs comes my way."

"The gods have been good to you, then, to bless you with our presence," Claire quipped, winking at him over her shoulder.

"Yes! You, beautiful Claire, are a godsend." Dr. Mora grinned. Chase whipped his head around, watching the exchange between the man and his, I guess, girlfriend.

It was good to see that I wasn't the only jealous one in the group.

The technology he was referring to was absolutely archaic. Having to use something as antiquated as radar to map out the Earth's surface was slow and never rendered clear-cut results. The photographic technology on Zhimeya was, like most things, much more advanced. The Masters had done a great deal of "remote sensing" themselves, looking at Earth from a great distance through these advanced technologies before sending the first wave of researchers.

"So what would this area have looked like a few thousand years ago?" Savannah asked.

"Ah, good question," Dr. Mora said, walking slower and letting her catch up to him. "We would see the remains of great cities that once housed thousands of people, *mi querida*. This whole area was a great thriving state that rivaled almost any in Europe, the Middle East, or Africa during the same time period." Savannah looked enthralled by the pictures he was painting for her but kept her distance. "Great houses, wide roads, markets, temples, schools," he babbled on. I had another burning question so I rather rudely cut him off.

"When we ran out of time yesterday, Dr. Mora, you had said something about new facts that may prove that the people of ancient America were more closely linked with the people of the Middle East than previously thought."

"You wanted to know whether I thought that the Quetzalcoatl story could be influenced by the stories of Jesus Christ," he said.

"Exactly," I said.

"In my estimation, it's very possible that the legend of Jesus could have easily traveled to the new world. I would point to the evidence now known as the 'cocaine mummies,'" he said mysteriously, letting his words hang in the air for drama's sake.

"Are you going to elaborate?" Mateo asked rudely.

"During the early 1990s, German scientists were conducting studies on three-thousand-year-old Egyptian mummies. Among other things, they were doing toxicology screenings looking for traces of drugs left in the hair shafts of the bodies. What they found was astonishing." He paused for effect. Mateo glared at him again, so Dr. Mora started talking more quickly this time.

"The mummies had traces of cocaine in their bodies, which is derived from the coca plant, which grows *only* in the Americas. Of course, the whole academic world condemned the scientists for producing such ridiculous results.

"The only 'logical' explanation was that the mummies were fake, the tests were faulty, or some extinct plant the Egyptians used resembled cocaine closely enough that it made the drug test results positive.

"But after further scrutiny, the mummies were proven to be authentic, the tests were rerun with the same result, and no plant has ever been found that looks like cocaine on a tox screen other than cocaine.

"These findings suggest that ancient peoples may have been closely connected with one another, trading goods over the vast oceans that separated them. If cocaine made it to Africa, ideas must have been transmittable too. Even the temples that we find here in Central America look very much like the pyramids in Egypt and have very similar construction."

"So if we accept that ancient peoples were in contact with each other across oceans, then you believe the legends and stories of Jesus could have made it across the ocean, as well?" Chase asked.

"It's possible. Another option is that Jesus actually came to the Americas himself. The last option is that multiple tribes across the continent simultaneously came up with similar stories about a god with similar attributes. Pick whichever option you like. None of them can be proven at present."

This gave me a lot to ponder. If I were to accept, no matter how they got the information, that Quetzalcoatl, along with the god so many other Native American tribes described, were all speaking of Jesus, then that would definitely add credence to the Christian legend. More witnesses make for stronger evidence that such a being existed and was, in fact, what he claimed to be.

Maybe the Masters had been short-sighted never sending researchers to the Americas before. Perhaps, if I could get in touch with the Tribunal, I could talk them into giving Gideon and the Masters more time to send more researchers here. I'd volunteer to stay. Maybe Gideon would be more patient with his plans, as well.

"Okay, this is as far as we can go without going straight up," Dr. Mora said, checking the coordinates on his GPS device. He pointed to a small piece of exposed stone wall amidst the green leaves and vines. It was so thickly covered, I would have walked straight into it had he not pointed it out. The vine-covered walls I started to make out all around us reminded me of home so precisely, I felt the first rush of homesickness I'd experienced while on Earth.

The natives set to work clearing pieces of the giant stone wall in front of us. The freshly exposed rocks were covered with very light grooves that had once been beautifully carved murals, worn away by the millennia.

"Remember this moment—on the other side of this wall are treasures unknown. Remind your financial backers of that!" Dr. Mora exclaimed, sounding like a salesman.

"This city has a large wall around it; this side is the highest. We should send a team around to the adjacent side, to look for an easier way in." Dr. Mora looked at me to start dividing my group.

"Chase, Claire, do you want to go around to the next wall?" I asked, knowing they would be more than happy to go off exploring together.

"No problem!" Claire exclaimed, grabbing Chase's hand and pulling him away. Three short men jogged after the departing figures, trying to keep pace.

"The rest of us have two options. We can keep walking the perimeter of the city to look for a way in, or we can climb the wall," Dr. Mora said.

"We're climbing," Mateo said, rubbing his hands together.

"Someone will have to free climb and sink anchors for the rest of us," Dr. Mora explained.

"I'll do it!" Mateo yelled, shoving past me.

"We'll both go. We will be here all day if we are all using one set of anchors to get everyone up," I said.

"These two men are very good belayers." Dr. Mora pointed to two of the locals. "They don't really speak English or traditional Spanish, but they know enough to understand your commands." Since the two men were already setting the lines up and getting the harnesses out correctly, trusting them seemed to be the best option.

I looked up the straight wall; eyeing a few rocky outcroppings that I could use to make my way up. I started stretching my arms out, warming up for the climb. I caught Savannah watching me with a somewhat distracted look on her face. She flushed light pink and looked away quickly.

Once we were set, Mateo started scaling the rock like a possessed lizard. I turned toward Savannah, realizing that she would be left by herself with the strange men below.

"Are you going to be okay down here by yourself?" I asked. The locals looked safe enough, but I really didn't trust Dr. Mora.

"I can take care of myself," she said.

"You sure?"

"Go!" She laughed and pushed my shoulder. "I'll be *fine!*"

"Ryen, we're losing daylight!" Mateo yelled from far above.

The ascent was exhilarating. Me versus the wall. I had missed the feeling of the chalk on my hands, the stress in my calves, the fatigue in my fingertips. It took all my concentration to map out my next few moves, like a complicated vertical chess game.

"Just like old times," Mateo said from behind a small outcropping that hid him from view. "Though this climb's got nothin' on Ma'agi Mountain."

"Now that was fun," I agreed, remembering the near twenty-thousand-foot climb we'd done as teenagers. The ascent up the sheer cliff had taken us almost four days to complete.

We fell quiet for a few minutes, both lunging for holds farther up and sinking in anchors as we went.

"So what are you going to miss most about Earth?" Mateo asked, climbing back into my view just in time to see my quick glance at the girl below.

"Ugh, besides the obvious. Ryen, you are kind of starting to scare me, you know that? The human's getting a little too close for comfort," he said seriously. I didn't make eye contact with him and kept climbing. "Trust me, brother, you only want her so much because you can't have her. She's forbidden fruit, which makes her all the more tempting. After we leave, she'll be out of your system in no time," he said with more conviction than necessary. "You *literally* have an entire planet of women waiting for you back home."

"Mateo, I told you, as soon as I can get her on a plane back to the United States, I'm done with her," I said forcefully, masking the twinge of discomfort that skittered up my spine at the thought. Would I really be able to walk away from her?

"So this *thing* between you two, it's nothing?"

"Absolutely nothing," I lied.

"All right," he said impishly. He didn't believe me, not one bit. A mischievous smile spread across his face, which meant he was planning something.

"So how about you, Mateo, what are you going to miss most?"

"The women," he answered back quickly.

"Oh, come on, *besides the obvious*," I managed to chuckle.

"The food."

"You have a one-track mind, my friend. No wait, a two-track mind. Sorry."

"That's right."

"You're as deep as a thimble."

"Yep, keeps things simple," he explained as we both took a huge upward lunge, finally coming to rest on the top of the wall.

The view would have been beautiful were the jungle not blocking it completely, pressing down on us like an emerald tsunami of leaves.

"I'm gonna see how far this wall goes. There's got to be an opening somewhere. You staying here?" he asked.

"Yeah, I want to keep an eye on things below."

"Of course you do," he grumbled as he walked off.

I looked down and located Savannah. She was facing into the forest, arms crossed over her chest defensively. She looked like she was trying to ignore Dr. Mora, who was obviously talking to her. Dr. Mora stalked closer, but she decidedly kept her back to him. Then he reached out and grabbed her shoulder greedily. His hand slowly ran down the length of her arm and past her waist, coming to rest on her soft curves below. I nearly jumped off the forty-foot ledge.

But what happened next froze me in place. Savannah's body twisted away from the man like lightning. Her leg swung up, her foot catching him hard on the side of his face. The next thing I knew, she was standing behind him, pulling his bent left arm behind his back, shoving it upward roughly by his elbow. She was speaking in a calm voice as he sunk down to his knees, yelping in pain. He tried to get back up, and she forced his elbow higher, sending him to his knees again.

It took only a few seconds for me to repel down. I had completely forgotten to warn my belayer. Good thing he was quick. He helped me down, one eye on me, the other on the altercation.

"What do you say?" Savannah asked him in a clear voice, behind the man writhing on his knees, nose plainly broken.

"I'm sorry!" Dr. Mora said quietly.

"Excuse me? I can't hear you," she said, yanking up harder on his elbow.

"I'm sorry!" he yelled pathetically.

"Yes, you *are* sorry!" Savannah repeated.

She looked up and saw that I was almost to the ground, so she let go of Dr. Mora's arm. I took off my harness and ran over and shoved him away from her. He toppled over a fallen tree stump and lay in a heap on the ground.

"What happened?" I asked grimly, eyes trained on the cowering man.

"I warned him," she said. "I said I wasn't interested. *He* said it isn't a woman's place to tell a man no. But he has learned his lesson, haven't you?" She started tracking toward him again. I caught her wrist.

"Hey, let me have a turn," I said. She nodded.

"I told you Ryen would be angry if you messed with me!" she taunted as I heaved Dr. Mora into the forest. It was hard not to smile just for a moment.

When we were far enough away from the group, I threw him against a young tree, which buckled and broke under his weight. "You pull a stunt like that again, and I will resurrect some of the bloodier sacrificial rituals the Aztecs made famous," I whispered furiously as I picked him up and threw him against a second tree, which shuddered and snapped as he collided with it. I picked him up by the neck, cutting off his air supply.

"I'll start by ripping your heart out, and then we'll move on to the disemboweling and blood drinking. Do I make myself *absolutely* clear?" He nodded wretchedly as his feet dangled in midair.

"Where I come from, we treat women with respect. Consider your financial backing cancelled. Don't even think about looking Savannah's or Claire's way again or I will *end* you," I vowed, dropping him to the ground. He cowered there until I forced him back up to standing and shoved him back the way we had come. He tripped fearfully ahead, barking orders at the local men in their native tongue. They all gave Savannah a wide berth.

Dr. Mora, still hissing instructions, ran off in the direction Chase and Claire had gone. The men put Savannah into a harness. I indicated that they should help Savannah climb first. Just in case she fell, I would be there for her this time.

"Are you okay?" I asked, grabbing her shoulders, looking her over carefully. She had a little dirt on her cheek, which I rubbed off with my thumb.

"I told you that I can take care of myself," she said, walking away from me toward the wall.

"You were *amazing*!" I said in awe. "What other powers are you hiding from me?"

"No powers," she said. "My mom just made sure that I knew how to defend myself from creeps like him, that's all," she said, finding her first foothold. "For my tenth birthday, I wanted roller skates. I got pepper spray."

"There's a story behind that, isn't there?"

"Yes."

"But you don't want to talk about it?"

"Not right now."

"Later, then?"

She just shrugged her shoulders and kept climbing higher. I wanted to push the issue, but she was right, this wasn't exactly the ideal time for soul baring.

"I told you that Mexico might be dangerous when you decided to come with us," I called up.

"And I told you that I didn't mind the danger," she yelled back.

"Just remind me never to get on your bad side!" Her answering laugh trickled down the rock to my ears, washing over me like rainwater.

The climb was much faster with help from the anchors and the men below. As soon as we were at the top, the hired hands dropped the ropes and made their way toward the side of the wall Claire and Chase were exploring, leaving us alone. I couldn't think of a good way to bring up the previous conversation, so I sat quietly, hoping she would broach the subject. She didn't. Instead, she stood up and carefully started picking her way across the top of the wall. I followed, keeping my arms stretched toward her in case she lost her footing.

"So, you told Dr. Mora I would be angry if he messed with you?" I chuckled hesitantly.

"Sure. I mean, you've rescued me before. You seem to take very good care of your . . . *employees*," she said, glancing quickly over her shoulder, gauging my reaction. I stopped walking.

"My employee . . ." I choked out the word like it was a bug I'd swallowed.

A *business* relationship. That's all this was supposed to be.

"Yeah, that's right. I nearly killed a man because you are my employee," I whispered vehemently to myself.

She turned, her eyes carefully trained on mine. "Do you have something you want to say?" she challenged. "That's what we are, right? That's all I am to you."

No.

Of course not. What a ridiculous question.

In fact, Savannah, you've quickly become the only thing I ever think about. It's a bit maddening, actually. I never felt truly complete until you came accidentally tripping into my life, and now I greatly fear I will never be completely happy without you next to me. My mental well-being has suffered greatly because of you. I've been lying to everyone, especially myself, about this inexplicable hold you have over me that I can't seem to break.

So no, Miss Mason, you are not just an employee.

I'm absolutely in love with you.

There it was. The truth.

I'd finally admitted it, if only to myself.

But I couldn't say the words out loud. Loving Savannah came with a price tag that I wouldn't pay. I wouldn't leave everything behind, everything I'd ever known or loved, to stay with her if she wanted me. Even though I ached to tell her how I felt, even though it was the absolute, undeniable truth, I kept quiet.

And it was absolutely devastating.

"What else are you supposed to be?" I said icily and clenched my jaw shut. If I opened it again, it would be too easy to tell her the truth, to take us past the point of no return.

I burned, I suffered, in silence.

Her eyes searched my face, and I knew what she would find there—rejection. It had to be this way. It was better for both of us.

Her eyes slowly dropped from mine—and even though she hadn't taken a step, I could feel her pulling away from me.

The heartbreaking silence was shattered by a fearsome yell that came out of the jungle.

"Oh, *hell* no!" Mateo cried out, sending a multitude of brightly colored birds flapping into the air. "Ryen! Where are you?"

"Southwest corner. What's wrong, Mateo?" I called, still reeling.

"They're gone!" he yelled again. He broke into view a few seconds later. "They took off!"

"Who took off?" I asked in a loud, but calm, voice.

"Everyone! Mora and his team. They left us here!"

"That's ridiculous," I said flatly, scanning the forest, looking for a rustling in the sea of trees. Nothing. "They just went around to meet Claire and Chase's team on the opposite side since we were already up the wall."

"No, they left us too." Claire yelled from far away. "They helped us up and left. I thought they were on their way to help you!"

I turned toward the jungle and shouted, "Dr. Mora! Daniel Mora!" No human sound came from the trees.

"Why would he leave us?" Claire asked, bursting through the thick overhanging canopy. Chase followed close behind. "Ryen, what did you do?" she accused.

"Me?" I yelled. Claire didn't even flinch. She just kept barreling down on me.

"Fine! It was me! He came on to Savannah." All eyes turned to her while I explained. "She had to break his nose to get him to back off."

"So he left us here because he got beat up by a girl?" Chase asked, unconvinced.

"No, not exactly," I hedged. "I told him that because of his actions, there would be . . . no possibility of further funding."

"Did you say that as you were choking him, perhaps?" Claire scolded.

"I had to make sure I got my point across!" I retorted.

"So you made it perfectly clear that we were absolutely of no use to him, so he decided to stop wasting his time and leave us here!" Claire screamed.

"This is my fault, Claire. I didn't have to break his nose," Savannah said.

"No, *you* had every right to defend yourself, Savannah. *Ryen's* job is to get as much information out of Dr. Mora as he can, promise him *anything*, put up with *anything* to get what we need," Mateo said, decidedly not looking at my furious glare. Now *he* was getting way too close to telling Savannah too much. "But he *completely* blew that one."

"He's right, Savannah. No one blames you." I conceded gladly. "So, now that we have established who the idiot is here," I said, raising my hand, "let's figure out how to get out of this situation."

"There's not enough light to get us safely through the jungle. A storm's coming. Wherever Dr. Mora is, he'll get caught in it too," Chase said, looking up at the gathering storm clouds. Even as experienced as we were at traversing jungle terrain, we'd never make it out safely tonight.

"At least they have camping gear, propane, and sleeping bags. Without shelter, this is going to be a long night for us," Mateo said.

"We'll find something. And we have enough food and water to get through," Claire added, trying to mollify him.

"The safest place for us is going to be inside the walls. We need to start a fire as soon as possible. We're not safe unprotected; this is jaguar country," I said.

"Don't forget the coral snakes, venomous spiders, scorpions, and crocodiles," Claire shivered.

15

Zhimeya, Emani's laboratory

The smell of chemicals bubbling away, mingling together and changing, soothed Emani's fragile nerves. Science itself was blessedly amoral—no emotion, no judgment, no wrong or right—a welcome refuge from her waking nightmare of a life.

She kept as busy as possible, shunning sleep. If she could have managed it, she wouldn't even blink. Every time she did, Adan's face was there. Sometimes the damning blaze of hellfire burned in his dead coal-black eyes; at other times, he was peaceful and patient, his countenance radiating fatherly forgiveness. She didn't know which was worse.

Emani's hands, sheathed in thin metallic gloves, slowly moved and nudged the molecular strands suspended in front of her into different arrangements. As she spoke, the glowing holographic compound grew another arm according to her directions. She stared at the new formation, willing the answer to show itself.

"I'm missing something," she whispered in frustration. The task was taking both a mental and a physical toll. She looked longingly at the small black box in the corner of her lab. Half of her body strained toward the substance she wanted so badly to be coursing through her blood, the drug that would make Adan's face a distant memory. The other half of her tried to stay planted where it was. She almost shook under the intense struggle.

The addict inside begged, pleaded, raged. She ignored it as best as she could. She had purposefully only made enough for Gideon so she wouldn't be as tempted to use again.

I told Ryen I wasn't using.

She didn't want to turn that into a lie.

"There's no time left," she said to her two halves, trying to get them to come together.

The answer was out there. Every poison has an antidote. There had to be a way to undo what she had helped create.

The weapon. Gideon had named it "Obedience" because of the intended effect it had on its victims. The tool that could end a whole world. More death, more destruction, more ghosts haunting her at every turn.

If she could find a way to undo what she'd done . . .

Could she invent penance?

Bottle forgiveness?

She would try. Maybe God would see her attempt and weigh it in her favor. Maybe there was hope . . .

No, I've taken a life. There's no forgiveness for me now.

It had been so easy to make something destructive—Why was it so much harder to undo the damage? The simple truth was this:

I can't make good things. I'm *not good,* she thought in defeat.

Destruction had always come so effortlessly.

Her hands cramped uncomfortably as she manipulated the molecular chain into a new pattern and added a carboxyl group. The chain unraveled, unable to support itself naturally.

"There's no time, no time, no time," she chanted, looking hungrily again at the locked box. Something to calm her nerves and stave off the visions of Adan. Surely a little wouldn't be so bad . . .

"NO!" she screamed, tearing the gloves from her hands, and throwing them onto the floor. The holographic chain that had been floating in space disappeared.

"I need—" Emani couldn't finish the sentence. There were too many things she desperately needed. She needed her mother back. She needed to see whether her father and brother were still alive in Unnamed Territory.

But one need outweighed the rest. She needed to see *him*, to hear his voice.

He'll know what to do.

She turned toward the screen that took up the entire west wall, speaking out loud the long codes she knew by heart. She added a distress code at the end so he would know it was an emergency. She checked the signal. It was strong. The two distant planets were almost completely aligned with nothing but space between them tonight. He had no excuse not to answer.

The signal connected.

"Please, please, please answer. Please be there," she said, smoothing down her hair and wiping the sweat off of her face. She had to talk to him. Ryen would know what to do.

"Ryen," She wrapped her arms around herself and tapped her foot. "Please answer. Please," she whimpered, trying to hold herself together. "I need help. Gideon made me—"

He made me kill, she finished in her head, unable to say it out loud, even though she was alone.

Frightened tears ran down her hot cheeks. She whisked them away as quickly as they fell. "You're in danger too," she muttered, holding herself even tighter. "Please answer me!"

She would have written him a communication, but Gideon had recently started tracking all messages she sent, his distrust growing. He'd even found away to open locked attachments. He would kill her if he knew she was working on an antidote for Obedience *and* looking for help from Ryen, who was on the verge of being considered a traitor to the Masters.

The seconds ticked by.

A minute. Another. And another.

The signal remained unbroken. He was receiving the call on his computer, the one he was supposed to have with him at all times. He was ignoring her call for help, abandoning her all over again.

He doesn't care, Adan's ghostly voice whispered into her ear.

She was alone. Completely and utterly alone.

Adan's mocking laugh rang through her ears. She screamed out loud, flying through the room, looking for the biggest thing to break. Her hands caught with a rack full of thin, crystalline laboratory equipment, all of the finest quality. With all of her might, she pushed the rack off balance. It fell to the ground. The shattering of crystal and glass resounded throughout the small lab and echoed the way she felt inside.

Like shattered glass, she was irreversibly broken.

Any instrument that survived the fall, she picked up and threw against the walls, sending a rainbow of crystal shards sparkling to the ground.

She looked at the computer screen again, still sending out the distress call to a man who didn't care.

"I hope Gideon destroys you too, Ryen!" she screamed. "You don't deserve me or my warnings!" Emani threw herself down on the cold, stone laboratory table in the middle of the room and sobbed uncontrollably. Angry, frightened, frustrated.

Alone.

She didn't know how long she lay on that table in the basement underneath her house. She had half convinced herself that she was going to stay down there forever when she heard a noise. It was coming from the computer. Her heart leapt. She tried to clear the tears from her eyes well enough to see the screen. When she could finally read it, her world came crashing back down again.

It was just her sisters. Oshun and Ecko.

"Answer," she barked at her computer. Her two sisters, wearing dark glasses and earpieces, materialized inside the room with her. Neither of the glowing newcomers moved as they looked warily around the wrecked laboratory.

"Emani, are you all right? What happened?" Ecko asked carefully, a little afraid of her older sister, and with good reason. Emani had proven herself ruthless, cunning, even brutal on several occasions.

"*What do you want?*" Emani demanded, pulling herself to sitting on the table.

"You told us to call you as soon as we found them," Oshun said flatly.

Ryen. They had found Ryen. Maybe he had a good reason for not answering her calls.

"Speak," Emani ordered.

"Okay," Ecko said, wondering why Emani looked like hell. She didn't dare ask. Her sister's hair hung limply around her face, an ordinary light brown—her natural hair color. If Emani wasn't changing her hair color daily, something was definitely wrong. "We found Ryen, Claire, Chase, and Mateo. As far as we can tell, they look like they are following protocol. Ryen has been meeting with a scholar about the ancient people here in Mexico. We tapped Claire's computer. It was full of notes and photos from today. All the standard stuff."

"Except for the female," Oshun added. Ecko's eyes darted nervously at Oshun.

"What female?" Emani asked, her attention spiking.

"Ryen has a female with him," Oshun said vindictively. Emani had always gotten whatever she wanted to Oshun's chagrin—*except for Ryen.*

"Who is she?"

"Vermin, just like the rest of humanity," Oshun said.

"Is she a scientist? A historian? Is he using her for information?" Emani demanded, clinging with bloody fingernails to her sanity.

"We . . . don't know. She is young. She doesn't look like a scholar. But Emani, we just got here. She could be anything," Ecko said quickly.

"What are you hiding? What don't you want to say?" Emani snapped.

"Decide for yourself," Oshun said, as she uploaded the video she had shot yesterday.

Ecko filled the uncomfortable silence by chattering on about their flight and the inconvenience of paying off customs to let them through in a hurry, but Emani wasn't listening. She was watching the images that were now flickering through the air.

The scenes were all different, but exactly the same. Ryen, achingly beautiful as always, walking next to, sitting next to, and laughing with a human female.

She studied the human's face carefully. She was pretty, but so was Emani, so that didn't bother her. What Emani concentrated on was the hollow look in the human's eyes. She noticed it immediately, because it was like looking into a mirror.

The human is broken too, just like me, Emani thought with wonder.

She watched the pair exchange soundless words and smiles. Ryen's attentions warmed the human's face, made her sad eyes come alive. With every word, every touch, he healed her. And she was letting him. What Emani hadn't let Ryen do for her, he was doing for this human.

Emani tore her eyes away from the human and watched Ryen. He wanted the girl. His eyes were full of a painful longing for her. It was unbearable to watch the fierce protectiveness that emanated from every part of him when he looked at her.

He was in love.

Unable to breathe, Emani clutched at her chest, sure that she would find nothing there but a gaping hole. She was genuinely surprised that she was still in one piece. She focused on rhythmically pushing air in and out of her lungs.

I have to remove the human. Even if I have to kill her.

Disgust rolled through her in nauseating waves, but it didn't dampen her resolve.

If that's what it takes to separate Ryen from the girl, I'll kill her myself. She imagined the human's ghost following her forever too, but she didn't care. She had to get him back.

She wondered what it would take to cure him of his love for the girl. Time? Torture? She imagined taking Ryen to the point of death, burning the human out of him, making him promise his love to her.

It's his fault. All his fault. He's forced my hand. He should have stayed with me.

"Really Emani, you have nothing to tell Gideon. They are following protocol," Ecko said, watching her sister's face turn pale white and murderous. "I'm sure the human is nothing more than a passing fancy."

"Keep following them. Watch the human. I want to know everything about her."

"Yes, Emani," they said in unison.

"Leave," she said quietly. When the sisters didn't disappear immediately, Emani picked up a chair and threw it at them. "LEAVE!" she screamed. Oshun and Ecko's forms disintegrated as the chair sailed through their holograms.

It was too much.

Too much to take sober.

No one should have to endure this kind of pain without pharmaceutical help. She hurried to the nondescript box in the corner, feeling Adan's haunting eyes on her. But that only made her work faster. She spoke the password into the lock and heard the latch pop open.

The small box held the most important objects she owned. The first was a crystal tube full of white powder, her very own drug of choice. Second, a prototype of Obedience, the weapon she and Dai had created, which she was now using to find a cure for its destructive properties. Lastly, an unassuming silver vial rolled around at the bottom of the box. For now, it was empty.

Gideon was going to be angry when Emani was short on his "treatment," but she didn't care. She'd take the punishment. He wouldn't kill her over it; she was the only one who knew how to make the drug he needed so badly. A small part of her felt ashamed for breaking her promise to Ryen, but the other, much larger, part of her laughed. What was the point of trying to be good for a man who didn't care?

She slipped the vial into her mouth, let the contents slide onto her tongue and, like so many times before, faded away into the welcome nothingness.

16

The thirty-foot-high city wall may have kept warring tribes out of the city a thousand years ago, but the silent stone sentry could do nothing to keep out the jungle. It had found ingenious ways to climb over, crawl under, and sometimes just break straight through the guarding wall to swallow the ancient city inside. What the humans had carved out, the unrelenting jungle destroyed, claiming back the land. I could almost hear the trees say, *Sure you can cut us down, but we'll be here long after you will. We've got time.*

And when you start thinking the jungle is talking to you, you know it is time for some rest.

After lowering ourselves into the city, we split up to find shelter. I volunteered to go alone. I surveyed the layout of the ruins, though only hints of its former grandeur were visible through the dense blanket of growth. Once-great houses reduced to vine-covered rubble crowded the paved walkways. Thatched roofs that had adorned the tops of homes had long since disintegrated, leaving bare stone walls sticking pointlessly out of the undergrowth. Some of the more fortunate houses still boasted all four walls and intact wooden doorframes.

My heavy footfalls sent unseen creatures scurrying for cover. Hopefully, I was the largest predator they had seen in a while.

Rain started to fall steadily from above. *When it rains, it pours,* I thought wryly, not having shaken off the misery from the last hour of wholesale lying to both Mateo and Savannah. I felt hollow, as though the storm winds and rain were passing straight through me.

The worst part of all this wasn't the pain I was causing myself, though it was torturous. But I expected it and tried to take it in stride. The worst part of it all was the indecision in my decisions. In the past few weeks, I had made the absolute decision not to talk to Savannah, then not to touch her, and especially not to fall in love with her. And somehow, for all of my trying, they had all happened anyway, one right after the other. Like I had absolutely no choice in the matter.

I was getting very tired of the fight, especially because I kept losing every single battle. The only option I had left was to physically separate myself from her. As soon as we were safely out of the jungle, I would put her on a plane and get her as far away from me as possible. Even better, I'd make Claire do it so I wouldn't know where she had gone, just in case my resolve broke and I tried to follow her.

There. Done. Decision made. And this one had to stick.

I took out my frustration on a particularly heavy hedge of vines, slashing them to confetti, and found what used to be a large gathering place, possibly a temple. Tall, sculpted steps led up to an empty stone platform. Only one of the walls was still standing straight. The opposite wall had fallen into it, leaving a triangular opening just large enough for all of us to sleep sheltered for the night. I entered the makeshift room to check for its sturdiness. The fallen wall still had much of its original painted stucco. The bright, beautifully colored pictures that ran the length of the slanted wall conveyed a scene of Mayan harvest.

It was a priceless work of art lost in the depths of the jungle. My eyes were possibly the first to see it in millennia.

I called to the others, who came quickly to get out of the now torrential rain. We spent time unpacking our backpacks and setting up for the night. I made absolutely sure I kept myself as far away from Savannah as possible in the crowded space.

When the rain finally let up, Mateo and I, with a great deal of work, got a fire started just outside our shelter. For dinner, we feasted on granola bars, hotel sandwiches, and bottled water that Claire had fortuitously brought.

"Time for some fun!" Mateo said happily after swallowing a mouthful of granola. "As long as we are stuck here, we may as well make the most of it, right Savannah?"

That caught her off guard. "Sure . . .?" she said hesitantly.

"Excellent," he said, winking at her. "Chase and I have been working on a little something for just such an occasion."

"We have?" Chase asked, puzzled.

"You came prepared just in case we were left out in the jungle to die, huh?" Claire asked dubiously.

"We didn't have this *exact* occasion in mind. But when you are stuck on an island in the middle of the Pacific Ocean for months with spotty access to electricity, you have to learn how to make your own fun. Here's something the Tongans taught us."

He took off his shirt and threw it at Savannah. The envy I felt over such a small thing was ridiculous. Somewhere deep down, I knew that. But it did nothing to dampen the fire.

Mateo, now shirtless, sauntered over to the other side of the fire. He said something in Tongan to Chase, who rolled his eyes but began singing a staccato melody while Mateo danced along to the rhythm. The girls clapped loudly when they finished. I didn't.

Mateo settled himself back down close to Savannah and gave me an evil grin, which I pretended not to see. He was about to start whatever he had been planning on his climb up the wall. I braced myself.

"So, Savannah," Mateo said, trying to sound casual.

"Yes?" she asked.

"Truth or dare?"

"Are you serious?" I asked hotly, beyond annoyed.

"Well, what I just did could definitely count as a dare, so now I get to pick someone. Savannah, truth or dare?"

"Uh, truth, I guess," she said reluctantly, glancing at my cold, vacant expression.

"Well, we all know way too much about each other, but we don't know anything about you. What's up with that?"

"What do you want to know?" she asked bravely.

"Past romantic history. What's your story?" Mateo asked, inching closer to her. I knew what he was doing. He was trying to force some kind of reaction out of me, to see whether I had been lying about my feelings for her. I would have stormed out, had I anywhere to go. But since I was stuck, I pretended to find the mural above my head fascinating.

"There's nothing interesting, I can assure you. I've gone out with guys, had a few short-term boyfriends, but never anything serious."

"That's hard to believe, coming from such a pretty girl," Mateo said flirtatiously, his eyes darting from hers to mine.

"Thanks," she said a little nervously, leaning away from his advances. "My mother was, to put it mildly, overprotective. So when she finally decided I was old enough to be let out of her sight, she disapproved of any guy who came my way. Catch-twenty-two. I was allowed to date, but not any of the guys that asked me out.

"So, being a teenager, I went through a rebellious period where I chose guys based solely on how much my mom disliked them. Of course, she always disliked them for good reasons, so I never really got into any serious relationships."

"No nasty breakups? No intrigues? Nothing?" Mateo pressed, leaning closer to her still.

"I am terminally boring, I promise. Hardly good company for the likes of you four. But if you are satisfied, I think it is my turn to pick someone," she said.

"Now we're getting somewhere!" Mateo exclaimed.

"Ryen," she said stiffly. Everyone's eyes shifted toward me.

"What?" I said, like I hadn't been paying attention. Like I hadn't been hanging on every single word she said.

"Same question. Romantic history. I assume you have a much more interesting story than I do," she said. The boys hooted with laughter.

"Oh darling, this man's got some stories!" Mateo roared and rolled onto his back, forgetting his mission to encroach on Savannah's personal space.

"He could talk all night and not tell you half of it! This one's a heartbreaker," Chase laughed.

"I figured as much," she said. The boys laughed even harder.

"He's the biggest celebrity we have back in Zhim—" Mateo sputtered, then turned white as he stopped his tongue from finishing the word. Savannah heard the pause and watched Mateo more carefully. He pretended to cough and clear his throat. "Gym . . . gym class. High school. He was the biggest celebrity we had back in high school. All the girls loved him."

I had to hand it to him. He covered well, but not perfectly. Everyone had fallen deathly silent. Savannah's eyes searched each of us, trying to find the source of the change.

"Oh, come on, there's nothing much," I said, managing a chuckle through my tight jaw. I could have taken Mateo's head off. "Just a couple of girlfriends."

"That's not what the boys just said," she pressed, still looking around the circle at everyone's forced smiles. "Chase said you were a heartbreaker, so tell me about her, or them," she said sarcastically.

"They're making a big deal out of nothing," I said.

"Are you married?" Savannah asked grimly.

"No! Of course not!" I said fiercely. The group's forced smiles turned genuine at Savannah's accusation.

"Then tell me. Those are the rules of the game, right, guys?" Savannah asked, looking at the rest of them.

"Those are the rules," Mateo said. *Traitor.*

"So heartbreaker, whose heart have you broken?" Savannah pressed.

"I'll tell her if you don't," Mateo warned.

"Okay, fine. I had an ex-girlfriend who took our breakup . . . badly," I said curtly, shifting my eyes up toward the ceiling again. The very last thing on Earth I wanted to talk about was *her.* I didn't even like thinking about her. She still made me nervous, even from billions of miles away.

"Badly doesn't quite cover it. He's trying to be nice. She is totally obsessed with Ryen. Too bad she is certifiably insane," Mateo said.

"Amen," Claire said under her breath.

"She's *not insane*. She had it tough growing up so she turned to drugs. She was already kind of imbalanced to begin with. I ended it when I found out how bad her habit was. It's been over for a long time now. It's nothing."

Savannah watched me, measuring me carefully.

"What's her name?" she asked, her tone warming a little.

"Emani," I said, refusing to volunteer anything else. I was done. Tired, frustrated, and desperate for the girl who sat five feet away from me that I couldn't have.

"So Ryen was popular in high school? I could see that," Savannah said to Claire, drawing everyone's attention away from me. They launched into a conversation about a made-up high school full of made-up people. Claire wove the stories effortlessly as she went.

The talking thankfully died out as they all became more tired.

"One of us is going to have to stay up to keep watch tonight," I said, staring into the fire.

"Not it!" Mateo said quickly.

"We'll all take turns," Chase said, throwing a pebble at his brother.

"I'll take first shift. I'm not tired, yet," I lied. Truthfully, I was completely exhausted. But even if I did lie down right now, I wouldn't be able to sleep. "I'll take from now till one. Mateo, do you want the one-to-four shift?"

"Yeah, sounds good."

"I'll take four till whenever you guys wake up," Chase volunteered.

Our little makeshift camp finally settled down, as evidenced by Mateo's quiet snores a few feet away from me. Claire was nestled comfortably into Chase's chest, wrapped in his arms. Savannah lay close to the fire on the opposite side of me, using her backpack as a pillow. I watched as her breathing changed from quick, rhythmic breaths to slower, deeper ones as she fell asleep.

I stoked the small fire, sending embers popping into the dense jungle air, the smoke marring the priceless paintings above. But I was much more worried about staying alive than preserving artifacts at the moment.

I stared into the hypnotic flames and let my frustrated mind wander. Of course, it ended up where it always did: Savannah. Like being trapped in a bed of seaweed, the more I tried to fight, the more I became tangled up in her.

Again, my mind begged the question, *why fight it?* But I knew very well why I had to fight it.

I watched her breathe. I watched her sleep. I watched her dream. So I dreamed along with her.

I imagined telling her every single one of my secrets here by the fire. And after all that, when she knew everything about me, she wanted me anyway. She had told Dr. Mora that nothing is impossible. Could she extend that logic to include me? I imagined bringing her back to Zhimeya, showing her my home, my life, my family. We could be happy there.

I stared deeper into the blaze, watching the yellow and red flames dance in harmony. My pent-up desire, kept under lock and key, refused to be fettered anymore. I let down my guard and focused on the aching physical hunger I felt for her. I tried never to entertain these maddening thoughts, because it made my unmet need so much harder to bear. But in this moment, I didn't care how much it would hurt later. As the fire twisted and spiraled around itself, I let myself imagine it, our bodies entwined, her mouth pressed to mine, the taste of her on my tongue. Her body burning on mine . . . like fire.

The vision shifted slightly as my head conjured up the perfect image of her angelic face in the smoky light, her gold-green eyes lit by the yellow flames, her hair catching the red glow. It stunned me. I involuntarily leaned forward toward the smoldering mirage, my fiery angel burning brightly.

It was when the image moved abruptly that I realized that this wasn't a vision at all. Savannah actually *was* watching me. She had a puzzled look on her face, probably wondering why I was staring so unrepentantly at her. I shook my head hard to break my concentration.

"Hey, I thought you were asleep," I said, rubbing my eyes, trying to dispel the hypnosis of lust.

"I was," she said, pointing over to Mateo, snoring raucously now. "I couldn't sleep through that," she said. She crawled toward me and came to rest by my side.

"What time is it?" she asked, yawning.

"Almost eleven. It's gonna be a long night."

"Yes, but comfortable at least. I feel very safe, all things considered."

"Hmm," I mumbled stupidly. I wanted to beg her to keep her distance, to spare me the torture of being this close to her without being able to get closer.

"That must be nice," she whispered, pointing toward Claire and Chase cuddled in the corner. She leaned and nudged my shoulder softly with hers.

Oh, why the *hell* was she tormenting me like this?

I employed my only defense mechanism. Silence. If I tried to talk, I would either tell her to get lost or ask her to lie down with me here in front of the fire. And I was pretty darn sure which would win. But any misstep on my part would only push us closer to that invisible line we couldn't come back from. So, at this absolutely critical moment, the moment that could change everything . . .

I didn't say a word.

"So where are you headed after your adventure here in Mexico?" she asked, pulling me from the painful fight with myself.

"You mean, if we live through the night?" I quipped. Ah, sarcasm, another tried and true defense mechanism of mine.

"Yes, if we don't get killed by a jaguar or devoured slowly by mosquitoes, where are you going to go?"

"I haven't gotten my next assignment yet."

"Oh," she said quietly. "Will you get your assignment soon?"

"Very soon," I said stoically.

My decision was made. She was getting on a plane. Maybe talking about the inevitable departure would help keep me firm in my decision.

"How about you? What are your plans when we get out of here?" I asked, though I shouldn't have. I didn't want the temptation of knowing where she was headed in case my resolve broke.

"I don't know. Maybe I'll head south. Learn to tango in Argentina. Tierra Del Fuego is supposed to be beautiful too. I've always wanted to see the Antarctic, so that's another option."

"Be serious, Savannah," I said, angered by her flippant response.

"I *am* being serious. I don't know where I'm going to go."

"You are going back home," I ordered. "Somewhere permanent. Somewhere safe."

"You'll be off to your next assignment soon enough. Why do *you* care where I go next?"

"*Why do I care? I care about you!*"

"Do you?" she whispered plaintively.

"Of course I do," I said softly. My own anger was losing its edge. Her sadness disarmed me. "I just . . . want you to be safe. I thought going home would—"

"I don't *have* a home, Ryen! Haven't you been paying *any* attention? I don't have relatives or friends. I have *no one!*" she whispered furiously.

"That can't be true."

"You can't send me home, Ryen. I don't have one." She leaned away from me, though we weren't even touching.

"Savannah, what happened to you?" I asked, her sadness steadily sapping away my determination to keep my distance. "Won't you tell me? Maybe I can help," I urged.

"Why would I want to talk about a life I am trying so hard to forget?" she asked, finally looking at me with a shockingly pained expression.

"Sorry. I was just trying to help. You don't have to tell me anything," I said, barely above a whisper.

She breathed in deeply and blew out all her air, clenching her eyes tightly. When she opened them, her expression had changed.

"No, you know what? I am going to tell you. I don't want to run from this, anymore," she said.

She absentmindedly reached for my hand and wound her fingers tightly through mine. She then gathered my free hand too. Even though the moment was all wrong—her sadness, my indecision—the heat that flowed from her touch warmed every inch of me, burning away every thought that wasn't about her.

"My mother spent six months falling in love with a man she barely knew—and twenty years running away from him."

I opened my mouth to question her, but she freed one of her hands and held her finger to my lips.

"She was orphaned at seventeen. Her parents died in a car accident. Her two uncles took the little money her parents had left behind. The bank took the house when the money ran out, so she left Louisiana and headed for New York City to become an artist.

"She met my father when she was twenty years old at a club where she was waitressing. She was beautiful, naïve, and completely broke. He was a handsome, successful lawyer. Quite the combination. Maybe he loved her at first, I don't know. She got pregnant with me soon after they met, and they moved in together. He refused to marry her, but he did put a roof over her head.

"He started working late, going on longer business trips, and never answering his phone. He was distant, controlling, and abusive." Savannah's unfocused eyes stared into the darkness beyond the fire.

"He cheated on her all the time. Sometimes women would call the house looking for him. He didn't even care enough to hide the affairs.

"I was just a baby and she had no one to turn to, so she stayed, even as he became more violent. He threatened to hurt me if she left the house or called anyone, though she had no one to call.

"She started to suspect him of criminal activity because of what she heard whispered over phone conversations. He was involved in a cartel that was smuggling drugs into the U.S. from South America. His job was to keep his friends out of jail, and he was good at it. She knew she had to get me away from him and the dangerous people he was involved with. We would have to disappear. To do that, we needed money.

"My father wasn't careful about his phone conversations around her. She heard him talking about a deal that was going to take place at his office, where a lot of money would be exchanging hands. On the night of the deal, she made it inside his office through the back entrance and stole one of the duffel bags filled with money. I was already packed and waiting in a car she stole from him. We drove for three days straight.

"We lived off the money in that bag for as long as we could. Sometimes we would settle down somewhere for a few months if we found a small, quiet town we liked. She'd work as a waitress or in grocery stores, small things like that. But she always felt like we were being watched or followed. When she got that feeling, I knew we'd be leaving. I couldn't talk her out of it. Running away was her obsession.

"Living like that changed me. I never made friends. What was the point when you were leaving?" She stopped talking abruptly. When she did, I noticed the silent tears escaping her eyes. I freed one of my hands and lightly dragged it across her jaw line, wiping them away. She rested her head on my shoulder and continued.

"She started to get sick two years ago. She wanted to keep moving, just like we always had. I never knew how progressed the cancer was until . . ." I felt her jaw clamp shut.

"The pictures, in your sketch book, was that your mother?"

"Yes."

"All of them?"

"She barely looked like herself at the end."

"I'm so sorry."

"She is buried in Twin Falls, Idaho. That was where we finally stayed when she was too sick to keep going. I have lost my mother, my only friend. Now you know why I can't go home. *I don't have one.*"

There was nothing I could say, so I put my arm around her and pulled her close. After a few moments, she picked her head up off my shoulder and looked at me. Her expression was a heartbreaking mix of loss and confusion, a despair and sadness I couldn't fathom.

Then, as our eyes held, her gaze shifted into a vulnerable longing that mirrored my own. I wanted nothing more fervently than to lean down and meet my lips to hers. I had to do it. I needed to.

But I didn't.

I knew myself too well. If I kissed her, I wouldn't be able to leave her. And I *would* leave her. Soon.

Instead, I pulled her onto my lap and cradled her there, wishing for a miracle that would allow us to be together. I held her tight, trying to hold the pieces of her firmly together as she fell apart in my arms.

When she finally fell asleep, I laid her down, resting her head in my lap. I passed the rest of my shift lightly tracing the contours of her face with trembling fingers, memorizing it. While I sat there, I realized two fundamental truths. First, I would never be able to forget this girl. Second, I would never be able to get over her.

Mateo's wristwatch alarm sounded at one. When he found us together, he opened his mouth to start firing questions at me but I shook my head. He rolled his eyes and left the shelter to stretch his legs.

Ignoring my better judgment, which was lying in shreds somewhere by the fire, I lay down next to Savannah, wrapping my arms around her protectively.

A piece of a Hemingway quote came to mind as I lay there with her. I leaned my head close to hers, wishing she could hear me, wishing she could understand.

"'The world is a fine place and worth the fighting for, and I hate very much to leave it,'" I quoted quietly as she slept. It was the best I could do at a goodbye.

17

Zhimeya, Gideon's private office

Stacks of papers littered Gideon's desktop. Requests, orders, love letters from beautiful women. He wasn't interested in any of it. Nothing mattered anymore except the work at hand.

He was tired. But the physical weariness could not diminish the lust that propelled him forward. Power. Control. The only thoughts in his head. The intoxicating feel of the power he was gaining kept him awake at night, away from food, away from the pleasures of the women knocking down his door. He knew better than to distract himself now. All the rest he could enjoy later.

With Aurik missing, it was almost too easy to win support in the shattered Tribunal.

Powerful. Unstoppable. The words revolved through his brain, gaining speed.

His eyes flashed to the door, making sure again that it was locked.

He had painstakingly extracted his most prized possession from its hiding place and held it in his shaking hands. He shoved the meaningless mass of papers from his desk onto the ground to make room for his task. Gideon lovingly spread out the thick roll of parchment on his desktop, smoothing the rolled corners flat.

He glanced at the lock again. And once more. Were the wrong person to wander in now, the parchment would be damning evidence against him and anyone who had pledged their allegiance to him. Its secrecy was vital.

As his eyes surveyed the detailed map of Earth spread out on his desk, a tremor of maniacal excitement rocked through him. Day by day, he made new marks on his map. Day by day, he promised pieces away.

Today, he had promised Zerin of the Ozars most of Africa. *"A wealth of mineral mines and a weak, fractured military presence,"* he had told him as he convinced Zerin to trade his vote for the territory. Gideon drew a large black line around the assigned area, penning Zerin's name in the middle.

Seraphyne of the Teresina tribe had traded her vote for rule over the Hawaiian Islands. *"Warm, crystalline waters and a heavenly fruit called pineapple, sweeter than anything you have ever tasted,"* were the words he had used to win her vote. He darkened in that territory as well.

Ahliya of the Maiko had been harder to buy, but not impossible. She was one of Aurik's closest confidants. When he disappeared, she wavered, and finally fell. But Gideon had had to trade her most of South America for her support. She had wanted Brazil too, but it had already been promised to Tashi of the Dao. Gideon continued to carve up the continents with his pen, cataloguing the day's work.

Every day, he gathered more votes that would legally allow him to use force against the humans, to steal away the land they didn't deserve. Aurik's supporters couldn't stand against the Tribunal's sacred vote, especially without a leader to rally around. He only needed to turn a few more votes his way. It was so close . . .

He then let his covetous eyes slide over the portions of the map where he had inscribed his own name so long ago, when his plans were only in infancy—Washington D.C., London, Tokyo, and Moscow to name a few. The hearts of power. He could give away smaller countries and beautiful islands to barter votes, but he kept the real seats of power for himself.

His greedy, wild eyes settled finally on the city where he would reign. Gideon's holy empire would be ruled from the ancient city that had birthed the most powerful figure in the Universe's history.

Jesus had laid down his life for others, so the scriptures said. But the real power belonged with the man who could inspire others to lay down their lives for him. Gideon had that kind of power. His people already had a savior; now they needed a king. The Light would dim, and Gideon would take its place.

It had been three days since he had eaten or slept. He knew from experience that on the third day of fasting and wakefulness, the angelic voices would begin murmuring, telling him the secrets of the universe, especially with the aid of Emani's special concoctions. She always made such beautiful preparations for him. She had even taught him how to smoke the fine white powder she made. After a few puffs of the dust, God would start speaking to his mind. He lit the end of the rolled paper on fire and breathed in the smoke that made his head whirl. Closer to the heavens with every drag.

The voices were coming, whispering of his future grandeur. He had stopped telling the other Masters about the melodic voices he heard. They gossiped about his visions, called him crazy. But they still followed him. They would follow power.

Well, most of them. Ryen would change his mind eventually. The prodigal son would return. The angels had told him so. Ryen was capable and resourceful. Even as a very young child, he showed great promise. Gideon needed him.

He let his head fall into the high-backed chair, exhaled a cloud of gray, noxious smoke, and stared up at the sparkling domed ceiling above his head. It was covered with millions of polished black tiles that glittered even in the dim light. The inky blackness was only interrupted by small points of light, brilliant silver tiles placed to represent stars. Each star was in its proper order, portraying a sea of constellations overhead. Suspended from the ceiling on thin, wispy wires danced golden orbs, each a replica of a planet in the solar system that housed the most sacred planet, Earth. They spun and moved mechanically on unseen tracks hidden in the ceiling, revolving around a bejeweled, fiery sun. Gideon watched the silent ballet above, though there was a piece missing. The most important orb had been plucked from its place in line with the other planets. Its hook swung empty.

The sudden clacking of high heels and the scrape of heavy boots outside pulled him from his trance. Gideon moved urgently to conceal the map until he heard the familiar, albeit annoying voices from outside the door.

"What do you two want?" Gideon shouted before they had time to question the guard outside the door.

"I have news, Gideon!" she called.

"This had better be important. Enter," Gideon said, resigned. The drug had already started to disconnect him from reality. A conversation would demand all of his concentration.

Emani and Dai entered through the smoky haze. Emani was dressed in the Master's uniform robes, though her skirt was cut short, and the neckline of her polished animal scale corset plunged low. She carried a small parcel in one hand. Dai wore simple black under his scarlet robe. As soon as the door was closed, he unfastened his robe, shrugged out of it, and let it fall to the floor. He absentmindedly pulled the heavy chain around his neck.

"My chemist," he said, motioning toward Emani. "My engineer," motioning to Dai. He tried to keep his tone professional, but his concentration broke when he saw what Emani held in her hands.

"If you have food, you are wasting your time," Gideon said flatly.

"Master, please. We are worried about your health. Eat something. It will keep you strong," Emani said. She had watched as Gideon lost his grasp on reality, even as he became more trusted by the people of Zhimeya. She felt greatly responsible, since she was the one who, in order to gain his favor, introduced him to the drug he loved so much.

"Why did you come? I am busy," he muttered, staring vacantly at the glittering spheres above. He didn't make a move to hide the map now. There were no secrets between the three of them. Emani and Dai did most of the legwork for him, anyway.

"I came to report about what my sisters have found, as you wished," Emani said. She was still coming down from her most recent fix, grateful Gideon hadn't asked her for his allotment of the drug yet, the allotment she had already taken.

"Out with it."

"They've found Ryen, Mateo, Chase, and Claire. They are fulfilling their assignment. But there is an addition to their party, a young human woman to whom Ryen seems partial—" Emani choked on the last words. She couldn't help the surge of blood that turned her alabaster skin scarlet and heated her body to a boil.

He could try to run away, distract himself with other women, but Emani would have him back again. He loved her.

He just had forgotten. He would remember, or she would burn it into him.

"Is the woman a scholar? Is she supplying them with information?"

"My sisters are not sure of her role, yet. But Ryen pays particular attention to her." Another bolt of heat ran up her spine. She shivered feverishly, wishing she still had enough of the drug left in her to calm her nerves.

"Emani, I shouldn't have to tell you that that is part of his job. Every human could have vital information."

"But what if she *isn't* just a human with information? What if he has feelings for her? We may be in danger of losing him, Gideon. He may resign. We've lost men before."

The way Ryen had watched the human, becoming completely lost in her eyes . . . He wasn't coming back on his own accord. She had to make Gideon see that.

"Resign? Ryen? Ha!" Gideon's head rolled heavily toward Emani, his eyes straining to focus through the fog enveloping his mind. "He is loyal to me!" But even as an involuntary laugh escaped his lips, Gideon worried. Could Ryen actually choose to stay on Earth, turning his back on Gideon for good? Ryen had been cold at their last meeting—a possible symptom of impending desertion.

"Has he been communicating with any of Aurik's supporters?"

"My sisters have not intercepted any communications that would suggest that."

"Of course not, of course not. He's loyal to me. He always has been."

"Gideon, please. I am gravely concerned about the girl!"

"Of course you are, you covetous child," he snapped. Dai sniggered out loud. "Keep your sisters near him. Intercept all his communications. If they suspect any type of betrayal on Ryen's part, I'll let you go get him yourself."

"Yes, Master." Emani started to back out of the room, elated about the possibility of both seeing Ryen soon and dispatching the human in person.

"I don't need to remind either of you that Obedience is your only focus right now. How are your tests coming?"

Emani shrank. She didn't want to talk about the weapon, not when she was fighting so hard to find an antidote for what it could do.

"Speak!" he yelled.

"Yes, Master," Dai said, pushing off the wall he had been casually leaning against. He walked closer to the map on Gideon's desk and lightly fingered the edges of it. His single purple eye glinted greedily as he too looked longingly at Jerusalem.

"The last person we tested it on lived for two hours before hemorrhaging."

"Two hours? That's nowhere near good enough. Did they take any direction in the two hours?"

"He stood when told to stand, he sat when told to sit. He remembered his name. When I gave him a new name, he repeated it as his own. Then he died," Dai said simply.

"If I wanted to kill humans, I would turn their own guns against them. They need to tell their secrets before they die."

"We will make adjustments and report as soon as we try again," Dai said calmly, masking the revulsion he felt at taking orders from a drug-addled lunatic.

"Are my new allies coming to the marking ceremony tonight?" Gideon asked. Dai slipped the chain from around his neck and handed it to Gideon. Gideon admired the pendant that was attached—a heavy oval disk with an intricate design of two planets, Earth and Zhimeya, almost touching.

"Zerin, Seraphyne, and Ahliya are here already. Tashi of the Dao is refusing," Dai said.

"Every ally must wear my mark on their skin to prove their loyalty. Let Tashi know that he will either wear my mark or be eliminated."

"Yes, Master. And what about Emani? She doesn't wear your mark," Dai said with a sneer. Gideon gasped.

"You are absolutely right, Dai! Mark her at once!" he said with a rash delight.

"Gideon," Emani pleaded, "you know I am loyal only to you. Wearing that mark wouldn't make me more so." She had seen firsthand what that mark did. Everyone who had been branded with it suffered excruciating pain that never seemed to lessen.

"All must wear my mark to prove their loyalty," Gideon said again, handing the disk back to Dai.

"Dai isn't marked!" Emani cried.

"Is it true, Dai? You haven't even marked yourself, yet?" Gideon asked.

"Of course I wear your mark, Master. I wear it proudly," Dai said as he rolled up his sleeve, baring his forearm. He held his head very still and stared hard at his exposed skin. Gideon's mark stood out plainly. Emani had seen his bare arm an hour ago in their shared laboratory. The mark had not been there. It was completely healed too.

"You are loyal . . . to me . . . only me," Gideon sang, his eyes closing.

"That mark is not real! Gideon, he's using his eye! It's a holo—" Emani was cut off as Dai slapped her. She punched him in the jaw hard enough to stun him, but not long enough to get away. He came at her again, and this time she swung for his missing eye. He caught her fist in his hand and threw it back toward her. The force of it propelled her into the book-lined wall.

Dai pinned her there and yanked down the waist of her skirt, pressing the disk onto her exposed hip. She felt the searing pain, like thousands of needles injecting hot metal into her skin. She bit hard on her lower lip, trying not to scream out loud.

When he was finished, she looked down at her skin, which was broken, bleeding and raw. The mark of the two worlds was hard to even make out. She raised her fist and struck him in the mouth, splitting his lip. He just smiled wickedly and laid his body over hers, pressing her spine into the books.

"If you say a word to Gideon about *my* mark again, I will kill you myself. He'll never know you're dead. You'll walk these halls as a hologram until I don't need you anymore," he whispered quietly into her ear, putting the chain back around his neck.

"There's no way anyone would be fooled," Emani spat furiously.

"Really?" he asked incredulously. Dai stared up at the ceiling and narrowed his eyes in concentration. Angels with glowing wings sprung to life out of the blackness. They soared high above, winding their way along the domed ceiling singing beautiful harmonies that spoke of Gideon's impending greatness. The angelic voices roused Gideon.

"They are coming to me! Do you see? God speaks to me!" Gideon cried. Emani only looked on in horror as the projections streamed from Dai's single black eye.

"If you were wise, you would prove your worth. Because if I decide I don't need you . . ." he trailed off, projecting a new image onto the ground where Gideon wasn't looking. It was a perfect replica of Emani, except that the hologram glowed slightly. She was lying on the floor, gasping for air, a blade stuck deep in her chest. Blood ran thick over the stone floor. Emani stared in shock at the projection of herself dying.

"Now that we understand each other, tell me about our old friend. How is he faring underground?" Dai said, turning his gaze back to the ceiling, projecting pretty angels for Gideon to enjoy.

"He is comatose. The sedatives will not wear off for a few more days," Emani said breathlessly.

"I have much to discuss with him about handing over power of the Tribunal to me."

"Yes," Emani said quietly.

"Don't cross me, Emani. Now that you wear *my* mark, you can't hide. Now leave," Dai commanded. Emani exited as quickly as she could, holding her hand over her branded hip.

Gideon sunk further down into his chair, finally succumbing to the drug's effects. Dai wiped the disk free of Emani's sizzled skin. He walked behind Gideon's chair and pressed the disk into the back of Gideon's neck. As he did, the angels that were sweeping around the room changed. They disintegrated and became new visions—visions of the destruction of cities, countries, continents, a new order rising from the ashes. Dai's new order.

18

The early morning light filtered down softly from the forest canopy, a soggy spring green. I woke up slowly, trying to remember why I was lying on a cold, rocky floor. The memories came back in a sudden deluge.

Savannah.

My arms automatically constricted to find that she was still there, the curves of her body matching against mine perfectly. She felt me move and turned to face me. The planes of her face were full of color and light. I tried to ignore my heartbeat, which pounded at breakneck speed as I looked into her eyes, trying to read whether she regretted sharing her secrets with me last night.

"Thank you," she whispered, her eyes brimming over with all of the gratitude, warmth, and relief she didn't put into words. She ducked her head and pulled herself tighter to my chest.

This was why I couldn't be close to her anymore. Things like This kept happening. It wouldn't take her long to realize the extent of my feelings for her, if she didn't know already.

Maybe all wasn't lost yet. I could still dismiss my actions last night as friendly concern. I hadn't done anything a friend wouldn't have done. She was sad. I was there to comfort her. Any friend would do that. A friend, of course, wouldn't have wanted to hold her tighter, kiss her, confess his love—but I had kept that all hidden. The lie was still salvageable. I still hadn't crossed the shaky line that blurred more and more.

I had spent hours last night wishing for a miracle that would change my circumstances somehow, to allow us to be together and for me to keep my family. But it was impossible. There was no way I could have both. Wishing wouldn't change anything.

So this had to be it, my last few seconds to ever be this close to her.

Savannah gasped quietly, shaking me loose from the silent hell inside my head. I quickly realized what I had done without consciously deciding to do it.

I was holding her so close, I could feel her heartbeat against my chest. My hands were exploring the curves of her back and shoulders. My lips were pressed gently against her forehead. She then turned her head up toward mine and ran the tip of her nose along my neck softly, back and forth. Forget crossing the line; we had long-jumped over it.

I tried to panic, but the emotion didn't come. I felt . . . happy? Peaceful? Boy, I wasn't expecting that. I didn't even start calculating the repercussions of what was going on. I just turned my head off.

And when I did, I fully realized that Savannah was lying *here* with *me*, touching me, holding me. I felt victorious. There would be time for the penance later. For now, I pulled her closer.

The others surfaced out of sleep slowly. Claire looked joyous at finding us together. Chase looked resigned. Mateo wore an "I knew it!" sort of look on his smug face.

Getting out of the jungle was easier than the trek into it. Thankfully, Chase had secretly marked our path with a compass every mile on the way in because he hadn't trusted Dr. Mora. I again kept trying to calculate the damage I had done in the last twelve hours, but my mind wouldn't oblige. I just rode this strange new high and concentrated on nothing else.

Safely back at our hotel at Chichen Itza, while the girls showered and packed, I decided to pay Dr. Mora a visit. Not so much a social kind of visit—more of a breaking-his-face-into-a-few-different-pieces kind of visit. The boys insisted on coming with me. He would suffer; first, for what he had done to Savannah, and second, for leaving us to die in the jungle.

"I get first crack at him," Mateo said, as we walked toward the museum after lamenting the fact that he hadn't brought a baseball bat.

"We're not going to kill him, Mateo. We just want to make sure he understands the consequence of his decisions," Chase countered.

"So wait, will he be walking away from this encounter, or do we get to at least put him in the hospital?" Mateo unbuttoned the cuffs on his shirtsleeves and rolled them up to afford his arms more movement.

"Let's see how apologetic he is, then we can make that call," I offered, taking off my aviators and securing them in my jacket pocket.

Seeing our reflection in the large glass museum front doors as we approached almost made me grin. Three men, all well over six feet tall, wearing dark clothing and even darker expressions. We looked downright terrifying.

"This time, the aliens *do not* come in peace," Mateo said with a frightening smile.

I hoped Daniel Mora could see us. I hoped he was *scared*.

We reached the glass doors just as a small Mexican girl in a museum T-shirt was closing them. Her face fearfully registered our presence. Chase shoved the door open roughly before she could lock it.

"Where's Dr. Mora?" I asked, trying to be polite.

"Museum . . . closed, sir," she managed to say.

"Where is Dr. Mora?" I said more forcefully. "We are friends of his." She looked at us dubiously. We certainly didn't look friendly.

"Please . . . tomorrow sir, museum closed," she tried again in broken English, pointing to the museum hours posted on the door.

"*Donde está* Daniel Mora?" I asked forcefully.

"He's not here," a cool voice answered. I recognized the woman's voice, though I had never seen her. It was Raquel, the museum's curator. She had helped me over the phone to set up my first interview with Dr. Mora. Mateo sized up the attractive woman, grinning appreciatively. I elbowed him in the ribs.

"Where is he?" I asked, trying not to lose my patience.

"He was in an accident in the jungle. He is at the hospital right now. I just got a call from them."

"You really expect us to believe he's in the hospital? Did he tell you to say that?" Chase guessed, looking over her head toward the back of the museum.

"If he's going to be in the hospital, it will be because we put him there," Mateo said darkly.

Raquel stared at him nervously. "I assure you, he is at the hospital. He went on an expedition into the jungle yesterday and was hurt. What do you want from Daniel? Does he owe you money too?"

"He wishes all he owed us was money," Mateo said.

Explaining to Raquel what had happened yesterday was not on our to-do list. Remembering my training, I put on my most charming face and said, "Forgive us, ladies. We apologize for the intrusion. We just needed some information from Dr. Mora, that's all." Both of them melted visibly as I spoke.

"Oh, uh, of course! If there is *anything* else I can do, please let me know. Would you like my phone number in case you think of something?" Raquel offered.

"You are too kind," I said, winking at her. She wrote her number with a shaky hand on the back of a museum information card.

"That's my *personal* number," she whispered as she handed it to me.

"Thank you for your help." I grinned, kissing the hand the she held out with the card. She involuntarily shivered.

"Let me go in. We don't want to draw too much attention, and I know more Spanish than you two do," I said when we reached the hospital. The boys agreed and stayed in the Jeep.

The air inside the small building didn't smell healthy, as though just inhaling could have gotten me sick. When I asked for Daniel Mora, the nurse motioned toward one of the small patient rooms. I followed the sound of beeping instruments and compressing air. A clipboard hung outside the door read *MORA, D., Mordedura de serpiente.*

Snake bite.

I ducked my head through the doorway cautiously. There he was, lying pale and grey in the bleach-white bed, hooked up to multiple tubes. One line was attached to a bag of saline fluid, and another line in his arm led to a bag of antivenin. Different machines attached to every inch of his exposed skin buzzed and clicked away, taking readings of his vital signs. His blood pressure and respiration were extremely low, an effect of the snake venom.

"*Cómo te puedo ayudar?*" A doctor in light blue scrubs came through the door. When he got a better look at me, he asked, "Do you speak English?"

"English is fine. Here." I handed him the clipboard with Dr. Mora's chart. He snatched it away from me. "Can you tell me what happened?"

"Are you a family member?"

"Yes, a cousin," I lied. The doctor didn't believe me but was too tired to inquire further.

"He was out in the jungle on an excavation and was bitten twice by coral snakes, causing respiratory paralysis. He almost suffocated. He also has a broken nose, but none of the men that brought him in would tell me how it happened."

"Will he recover from the bites?"

"Yes, but he will be here for a few more days. He was still miles into the jungle when he was bitten. He's lucky he made it out alive. He won't be awake for a while. Please try back another day."

"Thank you, doctor," I said, trying to pull my face into a concerned frown. I made it out of the room, and out of the hospital before the laugh broke from my lips.

"Well?" Chase asked.

"He's in there, all right. Snake bites," I reported.

"Couldn't have happened to a nicer guy," Chase said.

"Aw, man! It would be no fun to bloody up a coma patient," Mateo complained. "He wouldn't even know we were there! Can I at least go in and unhook a ventilator or pinch his catheter tube?"

"That would just be more work for those poor doctors," Chase reasoned. "It seems that the universe has settled the score for us."

"Boring!" Mateo said loudly.

"If I believed in such things, I would call this karma," I said with a grin.

19

"It feels so good to be back! I can't wait to be with my suitcases again!" Claire cooed as we unloaded the Jeep back in Akumal.

"I'm gonna burn everything I wore into the jungle."

"Do you guys hear that? The music?" Savannah asked, climbing out of the back of the Jeep. I helped her down but dropped her hand the moment she no longer needed it. This morning's high had all but worn off, leaving ample room for the panic I knew would come. "I bet it's the soccer team that came in the day we left," she said.

"Sounds like it's coming from the restaurant. Who's up for making some bad decisions we'll regret in the morning?" Mateo asked.

"Ooh, I *love* dancing. You are all coming!" Claire commanded over her shoulder, looking at me specifically as she towed Savannah back to their room. The boys also departed to their shared room, and I was left alone, standing next to the Jeep.

I'd dressed carefully, choosing to wear Claire's favorite shirt of mine, a short-sleeved cotton button-up that was a sky blue, almost as light as my eyes. My hands twitched nervously, wanting nothing more than to touch Savannah again but, at the same time, knowing how dangerous that was. For the hundredth time, I chastised myself for all of this fresh indecision. My path was set. All I had left to do was to follow it. Get her on a plane, and get her out of my life.

The boys and I were lounging outside Claire and Savannah's room in what seemed like no time. Well, I wasn't so much lounging as standing straight as an arrow, fidgeting nervously.

I shouldn't be here. I could fake a cold or another bout of stomach flu. That would be a lot safer than this ridiculous situation I was walking into.

As I started to turn on my heel to leave, the door opened. Claire sashayed out, wearing a tight, red silk cocktail dress and spiked black heels. She looked like she belonged at a swanky nightclub instead of a makeshift Mexican fiesta. Chase swung her into his arms and kissed her hard. Mateo made gagging sounds while I looked other way, inching back down the hall quietly.

"I believe the expression is, 'get a room,'" Mateo said.

"Fine. We'll try to behave, won't we, Chase?" Claire said, pushing away from him just a bit.

"Only when we are in public," he said, keeping his arms around her waist, "that's all I can promise."

"Listen guys," I started, excuse ready, but then out walked Savannah—and my shaky resolve walked out on me.

She wore a delicate white eyelet sundress with thin straps that clung to her bronzed shoulders. I'd never seen her in anything but old, worn jeans or khaki shorts. The cut of the dress accentuated her quiet femininity. I couldn't keep from imagining touching my lips to the soft skin on her bare shoulder, gently at first and then . . .

My palms started to sweat. I was supposed to be making excuses not to go to this party, but I couldn't remember why anymore. I just walked behind her in silence, watching her every move.

The hotel's restaurant, which was little more than one large room with a few dirty tables and chairs, had been converted to a small club for what looked like the winning soccer team. Paper lanterns lit the small space, making it look more mysterious. The jukebox in the corner banged out a captivating Spanish rhythm.

"*Señoritas, estoy aquí!*" Mateo shouted over the din, stretching his arms out wide. Within seconds he was surrounded by women who pulled him into the crowd. Chase easily took Claire's swaying hips in his hands and pushed her to the dance floor. I glanced at Savannah, who was looking at me tentatively.

"Would you like to dance?" I asked. She nodded and took my hand, leading me to the middle of the floor. The music thumped rhythmically as we moved in time with each other. She wound her arms around my neck, and I set my anxious hands gently on her hips. She ran her fingers under the collar of my shirt, tickling my neck. Did she have any idea what she was doing to my self control? The look in her eyes said she did.

Sultry clouds pressed down under the gunmetal sky, heating the already thick, viscous air. The restaurant opened out to the sand, where a large group of people were already dancing. I was musing over the way the heat made her dress stick to her curves as she pulled me outside onto the sand. We were enveloped by more bodies moving with the music that filled the fog. Without warning, thunder crashed over the ocean, and rain poured from above. I stopped, ready to get her back inside, but she didn't move. Neither did the crowd, which grew more raucous as inhibitions were washed away with the balmy rain.

Savannah looked up to the clouds, raindrops washing away the hair that had stuck around her forehead and neck from the heat. I lifted my hand and gently helped brush it off of her face. I rested my hand on the back of her neck in her tangled tresses. She smiled at my touch. As lost in her as I was, I didn't realize she had again pulled me toward the edge of the crowd.

"Do you want to get out of here?" she whispered in my ear, her breath mixing with the salty air. It sent electricity pulsing straight down my spine.

"Yes," was all I could manage to say.

We broke free of the party, but she didn't stop walking, my hand in hers. I didn't know where we were going, and I truly didn't care. We walked toward the ocean, dimly lit by the moon through small breaks in the cloud bank. As soon as we were out of sight of the party at the water's edge, she stopped and turned toward me. She gazed at me bravely, challenging me with those piercing emerald-green eyes.

I pulled her carefully closer, my hand slowly discovering the beautiful curves of her waist. She ran her hands up my arms and across my shoulders and knotted her fingers on the back of my neck, pulling me toward her. Our lips met, gently at first, hesitantly. But I couldn't hold back my urgency, my absolute need for her. My uncertainty, my indecision, it all fell away with the weight of her kiss. White-hot images flashed and burned through my memory under her touch.

The first time I had seen the beautiful woman lost on the ancient streets of Jerusalem. That same woman absentmindedly holding her airline ticket walking toward me on the plane. Her expression as I asked her whether she believed in God on top of a Mayan temple. That same beautiful face covered in tears as she entrusted me with her deepest secrets. Waking up next to her on the jungle floor.

All of these mixed with her sultry scent, the taste of her lips, the feel of her body pressed hard against mine. I was drowning.

Holding Savannah there, on a small beach in a tiny town no one had ever heard of in Mexico—this was where I decided. Nothing could remove me from her.

I wasn't going back to Zhimeya. There was nothing there as important as she was. I would write my resignation and send it with a smile. I would give up my old life, everything, just to spend my days at her side, wanting nothing more than what I had in my arms right at this moment. The choice seemed so easy. Why had I fought it so hard?

Whether she wanted me the same way I wanted her was irrelevant. I wasn't going to let her get away. I'd follow her around this planet forever.

The wind whipped her hair around me, making me feel like a part of her, inseparable, our lips still pressed fast, moving together.

The finality of my decision rang through my body as she gently pulled away, sighing softly, pressing her cheek against my shoulder.

"Finally," was all that she whispered.

"Finally," I said with conviction, swinging her up in my arms and pressing my lips to hers again. I was holding her so tightly that I felt her shiver as the wind picked up.

"Where do you want to go?" I asked, hating the thought of ever moving again.

"There." She pointed over my shoulder. "The caves on the other side of the beach."

It was more of an indentation in the rocks than an actual cave. I couldn't even stand up straight. But it was warmer and drier inside. I settled myself down into the sand and kept her on my lap. She gently wiped the raindrops from my forehead, ran her fingers through my hair, and touched the tip of her nose to mine. But before she could kiss me again, I pushed her gently away.

"What's wrong?" she asked. I put my finger to her lips to stop her from fretting about my sudden change of mood.

I looked deeply into her eyes, which glowed in the dim moonlight. With complete certainty, I said, "I love you, Savannah."

She froze.

"I—I know it's sudden, but I had to tell you," I stuttered. "And you don't have to say anything if you don't feel the same way."

"It's not sudden. It's right. I love you too."

"I promise I'll never leave your side."

"I wasn't going to let you leave me, even though you really seemed to be trying to." She smiled and then pulled me to her again, kissing my lips and my jaw line, making it hard for me to think straight. I bent my head toward her bare shoulder and kissed the freckles there, making her shiver.

"So, what now?" she asked, as I moved from her shoulder to her neck. "Another adventure?"

"Actually, I've grown very, very tired of my current profession," I said as the tip of her nose trailed down onto my collarbone. "I'd very much like to settle down somewhere. Unless you want to keep traveling."

"No!" She straightened up immediately. "No. I'm done. No more running."

"No more running," I promised. She relaxed into my chest. I wrapped my arms around her shoulders and held her as tightly as I could.

"I want to make friends, make memories," she said quietly.

"Then that's what we'll do. I'll take you to Ravello!" I said, the idea hitting me like lightning. "It's a tiny medieval town in the hills of the Amalfi Coast of Italy. It's so small, cars aren't even allowed inside the city. We can buy a villa with a view overlooking the sea and fix it up together. You can paint, and I can teach at the university," I mused. "Would you like that?"

"I don't speak Italian," she fretted.

"I'll teach you."

"Then that will be perfect." She smiled a little, but there was obviously something worrying her.

"What's wrong?" I asked.

"I was just wondering about Claire, Chase, and Mateo. Will they have to keep traveling?" she asked.

"Yes, I'm afraid they will. We can keep in touch with them through email though," I said, thinking of all of the fake emails and letters I would have to send Savannah over the next few years, signing Claire's name to them. I'd gradually phase them out, pretending they just lost contact with us over time. It was the first break in my night of overwhelming happiness.

"But you and I, we'll be together," I offered. She smiled and then kissed me with renewed fervor, lighting a fire in me that would never go out.

In that quiet space, we talked, laughed, and planned our life together until the storm settled down. The moon finally fully broke out from behind the clouds, casting its silvery glow on the deserted black and white beach that had become my favorite place in the universe.

We were too quickly back at her hotel room door. She said that she wanted to take things slow, to do this just right, everything in the proper order. I tried to talk her out of it. I'd even tried waxing poetic, hoping my literary prowess would win me even just a few more minutes with her.

"*Soul meets soul on lovers' lips*," I spoke against her neck.

"That's beautiful, but I still need to go," she said, running her hands over the planes of my chest.

"*I'll follow you and make a heaven out of hell, and I'll die by your hand which I love so well*," I tried again, breaking out Shakespeare. It had worked plenty of times on lesser women.

"You don't give up easily, do you?" she purred.

"*The only way to get rid of a temptation is to yield to it*," I reasoned.

"You were closer with Shakespeare," she laughed, kissing me one more time, then disappearing behind her door.

But I could wait. Not patiently, but I could. If that's what made her happy.

Claire knocked at my door an hour after I'd gone to my room.

"So, you've finally decided," Claire lamented as she flopped onto my bed.

"Decided what?" I asked, knowing exactly what she was talking about.

"You're staying here with Savannah. I saw you two tonight."

"Yes, I'm staying with Savannah. I tried to walk away from her, I really did. But she needs me—no, that's not true. I need her."

"I knew this was going to happen. You were a changed man the first time you saw her. I've been trying to come to terms with never seeing you again . . ." Her voice broke as she dissolved into tears. "*Now* who is going to keep Chase out of trouble when Mateo throws him a bachelor party?"

"Wait, what are you talking about?"

"Chase and I. We're getting married!"

"What? When did this happen?"

"An hour ago."

"You know that's not what I mean! When did you two become way more than just colleagues? I've been here the entire time!"

"First of all, you are terribly unobservant, but all that doesn't matter right now. What matters is *your* decision. Are you sure about this? This is absolutely, completely undoable."

"I am sure about Savannah. If I could bring her with us, Claire, I would. But she would be tossed into prison or maybe even killed on the spot. Gideon has convinced half of Zhimeya that humans are evil. And what tribe would claim a human? She would be an Unnamed, banished from society. This is the only way. This is the only decision that makes sense for us."

She nodded her head sadly, letting her eyes well up unrestrained again. "You are the big brother I always wanted. I will miss you every day."

"And I will always remember you, especially when things are quiet. I'll wonder what you would be chattering on about to fill the silence."

She threw herself into my arms, blubbering dramatically. I pulled her off of me after a moment and looked into her eyes seriously.

"Claire, you need to do me one last favor, okay?" I asked. She nodded, wiping the deluge of tears away.

"Please tell my family everything. Tell them that nothing except real love could have made me stay. Please, please help my mother understand." It was harder than I expected when I thought of my parents and my sister.

"Of course I will, Ryen. They love you and want you to be happy, though this is going to be tough all around. These rules are ridiculous! I don't see why communication needs to be cut just because you are staying here. You are one of *us*!" Her crying cut off instantly, and her face turned calculating—so very Claire. "Maybe we can find a way around it. Maybe I could talk to Aurik, see if he could change the laws, or at least bend them for you."

"Well, first you have to find Aurik, remember? He's missing at the moment. But if anyone could find *and* talk Aurik into something, it's you. I'll try to get through to my family before they sever the connection completely."

"You can't do that!" Claire looked aghast. "You know what would happen to them if they got caught accepting unapproved communication from Earth—especially from a defector!"

"Then . . . I will be waiting for the phone call."

"I'll never give up trying. And your mother is a force to be reckoned with. Make sure you have a guestroom ready when she commandeers a transport to Earth and drags your family here to come live with you."

"I'd considered that," I said quietly. I'd even selfishly hoped for it, my whole family coming to live here. It would be some sort of happy medium, for me at least. But they wouldn't be happy here, where everything was so foreign. "If you absolutely can't talk them out of coming, tell them to go to Ravello. I'll make sure our house is big enough for everyone." I laughed, but she heard the desperate undertone.

"I love you, Ryen."

"I love you too, Claire." The love I had for my family, my friends, my old life was almost all-consuming. And though it wasn't quite strong enough to pull me from Savannah, it was strong enough to cause me deep pain at the thought of separation.

"This is all your fault, you know. If you hadn't meddled in other people's business . . ."

"You would have never found the love of your life," she finished. I kissed the top of her head.

"So, you are finally settling down, huh?" I teased, wiping the tears away from her cheeks. "I love Chase like a brother, but I can't imagine wanting to wake up to that face every morning. You sure you know what you are doing? This seems really sudden."

"Oh, it's not so sudden. I've always had a big thing for him, and he for me. We've been exchanging communications for the past two years. This is as natural as breathing."

"Well, I couldn't be happier knowing that someone so good will be taking care of you."

My open computer twittered lightly in the corner of the room.

"What's that?" Claire asked.

"Ugh. It's Emani. She wants to talk to me over the camera again."

"Again?"

"She's been trying to contact me for days now," I explained.

"Aren't you going to answer it?"

"Do I look stupid? Last time I answered her call in Italy, she spent an hour on her holographic knees begging me to take her back. I finally had to disconnect the call."

"But the call is coded as urgent."

"With her, everything is urgent, which conversely means that nothing is urgent."

"Wow, ignoring your superior!"

"She won't be my superior much longer."

"Hmm, I guess you're right. Have you written your resignation yet? What are you going to say?"

"I'll start it as soon as Emani gets offline so she doesn't try to call again. I have no idea what I'm going to say. Maybe I'll just write, *I quit. Screw you, Gideon.* That would be fun," I said with a halfhearted chuckle.

"Well, I've got to get back to Chase. We have plans to make and some serious making out to do," she said, giggling excitedly. I gagged. "We still have some time together, a few more days, right?"

"We do. Let's make them happy ones. No more work, all right?"

"Excellent! Goodnight, Ryen!"

I gave her one last hug as she scooted out the door.

I sat in bed and wrote for the next two hours. It wasn't so much writing as it was writing and deleting, repeating the cycle over and over again. In the end, my final draft was only four short sentences.

```
To Gideon, Head of the Masters
Resignation


I, Ryen of the Tribe of Haven, hereby
resign my post as Earth Researcher for the
Masters of Technology. I request to stay
on Earth permanently. I rescind all of my
rights as a citizen of Zhimeya.
```

I attached it in an email and sent it to Claire to get her thoughts. What else could I say, though? The Masters didn't need to know the details of my decision. Claire, with the help of a letter I would write later, would fill in my family as to my exact reasons. All Gideon needed to know was that I wasn't coming home. The Masters had lost five Earth Researchers to resignation, and those five were always vilified for their desertion. My guess was that they too fell in love, maybe not all of them with humans, but with Earth itself.

My light was already off, so I set my laptop down on the side of my large, empty bed. I couldn't help but wonder how much longer I would have to sleep by myself. I left the computer open just a crack, so the screen's glow and the fan's whir would relax me into sleep.

20

"Good morning," Savannah said, stroking my face softly. I opened my eyes and saw her bent over my bed from the glow that was still emanating from my nearly shut computer.

"Mmmm, I could get used to this," I said and pulled her into bed with me. She slid effortlessly into my side.

"You're not even going to ask how I got in your room?"

"I don't care how you got in my room," I whispered, kissing the indentation of her collarbone. A quiet moan escaped her lips.

"Then I'll be sure to practice the fine art of breaking and entering more often." She threw her leg up around my hip and kissed me recklessly. I could feel her quick heartbeat pounding in her wrists as she slid her hands under my shirt, across my chest. My heart sped up too, keeping perfect time. "But thank Claire. She charmed a spare key out of the front desk manager for me."

"I'll thank her later," was all I managed to say before her lips were on mine again. If I could have pulled her closer, I would have. The rightness of the moment hung heavy in the air. This *was* right. This was forever.

"Anna," I whispered under her lips.

"Did you just give me a nickname, or are you thinking about someone else?" She smiled.

"I have to admit, Claire was right. You have a big name for such a small thing. If you don't like it—"

"No, I like it. That's what my mother used to call me," she said with a small smile.

It was terribly sad to come back down to reality to do something as mundane as shower, brush my teeth, and use the bathroom, but I was only . . .

Human.

Now that I was staying on Earth, I had to consider myself as part of this race. No longer an outsider looking in, but a part of Earth itself.

Human. It had a nice ring to it.

I clicked on the lights and TV for Savannah when I finally pulled myself away from her. She laid curled up in her favorite jeans and almost threadbare yellow T-shirt with the words "Michigan State Fair, 1996" scrawled across it.

"I'll be right back. Don't go *anywhere*," I warned, as I shucked off my shirt. She didn't take her eyes off me.

"Hurry back."

I turned on the shower as high and as hot as it would go. I tuned everything out, hearing nothing but the loud buzz of the television on the opposing wall and the water beating hard on my skin. I needed time to think. I was at a loss as to what I was going say to Chase and Mateo. They would be much harder to convince that I was doing the right thing than Claire had been. Hopefully she would explain all the things that I wouldn't be able to.

I toweled off and dressed quickly, impatient to get back to the love of my life, who was still waiting for me in my bed.

When I opened the bathroom door, it was like I had walked into a different dimension.

Everything was wrong. The covers were pulled off the bed. A water glass lay broken by the small nightstand. The front door was ajar. My computer was lying on the floor haphazardly, wide open.

Savannah was gone.

I went to the open door, hoping to find her standing right outside. Instead, I saw Claire running toward me, her face frozen in horror.

"Claire! Have you seen Savannah?" I asked, not understanding the expression on her face.

"Ryen, she knows!" Claire yelled.

"Knows what?"

"*She knows!*" Claire shrieked.

And the world, for a long, steely second, ground to a halt.

"No," I whispered. A wave of nausea hit me hard. I felt my back make contact with the rough stucco wall. I pressed my palms into it to keep upright.

"Ryen, talk to me! How did she find out?" Claire yelled, shaking my shoulders. She sounded so far away.

When I regained balance, I dashed back into my room to look at my computer to see what she had found.

My resignation and research notes were all open. In the corner of the screen was a call log. In Zhimeyan, the message that scrolled across it read, "Communication with: Cailida, Emani. Duration: 11 seconds. Communication Ended."

She knew.

Savannah knew what I was.

"Where did she go?" I yelled frantically. Claire limply pointed toward the beach.

A new thought occurred to me as I sprinted down to the blinding white sand. I hoped to whatever god there was in the universe that Emani hadn't seen Savannah in my room. Without a doubt, she would come to Earth if only to kill her.

Maybe Savannah had thrown my computer to the floor. Maybe the jolt had connected with Emani's incoming call but the two had not seen each other. It was only eleven seconds . . .

I rounded the corner and found Savannah sprinting parallel to the water's edge, with her backpack slung on her back. She was fast, but I was faster. She realized she couldn't outrun me and turned defensively. She held her arms out, holding me at bay. Her face was wild with terror.

"Stop!" she shouted.

"Anna, listen to me. I didn't mean—"

"Don't you DARE call me that!" she hyperventilated. "Who are you? *What* are you? Is Mateo? Chase? *Claire?*" She gasped painfully when she said Claire's name.

"Savannah—"

"Walk away. Now. I'll yell for help!"

" Savannah, *please* just listen. You have to believe me. I am a man. A normal man. I'm just not . . . from here," I said hopelessly.

Her mouth fell open with a popping sound, choking on the impossibilities. I took a step forward, my arms extended to touch her, to hold her there so she would give me a chance to explain. As I did, she bent down and picked up a large jagged rock.

"I *loved* you. DO YOU HEAR ME? You made me love whatever you are. What have you done to me? What have *you* done?" she screamed.

"Savannah, please, I am begging you—" I lunged forward, trying to close the space between us.

She shrieked in fear and heaved the rock in her hand with as much force as she could muster. The sharp, heavy stone connected perfectly with my temple with a loud crack. The last thing I remembered was her horrified expression as I sank into the sand.

I snapped awake, my hands instinctively searching for the injury that I could feel throbbing. Blood and sand were already drying on the side of my face. As soon as I remembered my last minutes prior to the blackout, I scrambled to my feet and sprinted toward the inn.

I ran back to Savannah's door and tore it open. The sketches of me she had drawn were scattered about the room, ripped from her sketchbook. I didn't even notice Claire curled up in a ball on the floor until I was about to leave.

"Ryen!" she cried. "*What happened?*" Tears flowed down Claire's swollen red face. She gasped when she got a better look at me. "Wait! You're bleeding!"

"It doesn't matter!" I yelled, already out the door. She jumped up and ran after me toward town.

"How long ago did she leave?" I demanded.

"Ten minutes."

I called Mateo and Chase, explaining what had happened using as few words as possible, catching Claire up at the same time. They would search the bus station and the southern edge of the jungle.

I hung up, looking at Claire for the first time since I had found her in the room. She was still weeping softly, gasping for air.

"Claire, what did she say to you?" I demanded. I wanted to shake her to get the information faster.

"She called me a liar . . . a monster . . . inhuman. She told me to stay away . . . not to follow her . . ." Her eyes started looking unfocused, and her head lolled to one side. I gave her a few seconds to calm down, softening my hold on her, but only slightly.

"She tore the drawings of you out, threw them at me, took her backpack, and ran. I didn't know what had happened or what she knew so I went to find you." She looked like she was about to crumple to the ground.

"I want you to turn around, go back to your room, and stay there. If she comes back, call me. Don't try and stop her. Just call me," I commanded.

"But—"

"I *need* you there if she comes back. Do you understand?"

"Yes" she breathed. She turned quickly and ran back toward the inn.

She was gone.

Just—gone.

We had searched all day and night, into the jungle, into the nearest towns and airport. There was no trace of her. I shouldn't be surprised; the girl had twenty years of practice running from monsters like me.

It was nearing three in the morning. Claire called and begged me to come back to the inn. She said that it was dangerous for all of us to be out in the jungle without light or protection. I argued that if I was in danger, Savannah was even more at risk. Scared, confused, alone . . .

The life I had dreamed up for us slowly unraveled with each hour that passed. Savannah's whole existence had been defined by distrust, and I had done exactly what she feared the most— lied to her, misled her.

I couldn't shake the image of her face, terrified of *me*. She was so frightened, she felt that she had to defend herself.

To Savannah, I was alien.

I only wanted to make sure she was safe. If she never wanted to see me again, I would grant her that wish. I just needed to know that she was safe.

I went into town to check again. The streets were completely empty; the town's bar was the only establishment open at this late hour. I hadn't the slightest bit of hope she would be in there, but with no other option, I went in.

I sat down, exhausted, and ordered four tequila shots from the bartender, who took in my appearance warily.

"Necesitas un doctor, amigo?" he asked, staring at my forehead. I'd completely forgotten about the wound. I was sweating from the search and the humidity, so the dried blood on my temple had rehydrated and started to run down my face and onto my white shirt, staining it. I was sure I looked ghastly.

"Necesito tequila," I answered wearily, tossing a few bills on the bar. He smiled sympathetically and poured me a fifth shot, on the house.

I knew absolutely nothing about alcohol except that it was expressly forbidden for us to imbibe while we were on Earth. It was outlawed by most tribes in Zhimeya because of the deleterious effects it had on civilized society. I was insanely glad that this was not the case here in Mexico.

When in Rome . . . I thought as I watched him pour. I was well beyond rules. I would do anything that might help numb the excruciating pain of her loss. I lined up the five shot glasses in a perfect row, hoping five would be enough to get me, what was the word? Hammered? Yep, a nice, hard smack to the skull with a blunt object sounded like the perfect remedy to reality.

I held up the small glass, ready to swig, but the caustic smell of the clear liquid set my nose burning uncomfortably. I swallowed a bit, but didn't dare finish it. It was the foulest thing I had ever tasted.

I realized, setting the shot glass down, that I would be even less help to Savannah if I were inebriated. I slid the shots down to my new amigos at the end of the bar, who all hollered an intoxicated thanks. I left, disgusted with myself for too many reasons to count.

I stumbled back to Claire's room, eyes bleary and burning. But before entering, I called the boys to ask them one more time for an update. Nothing. They would start looking again as soon as the sun started rising in a few hours. Neither brother had said one word about this most inexcusable breach of protocol— letting a human find out what we were. Somewhere in the back of my mind, I was grateful.

I leaned against the stucco wall and finally let the tears fall. Savannah. Where was she now? Was she in danger? Who could she trust? Obviously no one, not even the man who was in love with her.

Claire had gathered all of Savannah's sketches of me into a neat pile. I was thankful, not wanting to see the evidence of her frightened exit again.

Claire was on the bed, leaning stiffly against the headboard. The television was on, but she wasn't looking at it.

"She's gone," I whispered.

Claire said nothing.

"Can you ever forgive me?"

"Forgive you?" she asked blankly, still staring indiscriminately at the peeling wallpaper.

I couldn't put into words how many things I regretted, so I decided to apologize for the least painful thing first.

"For breaking protocol. For putting us at risk. Exposing us," I said stupidly.

Claire turned slowly her furious eyes on me.

"How *dare* you," she seethed. "If you really think that is the reason I'm upset, then you don't know me at all. I loved her too,

Ryen, right along with you. This isn't just your loss. We are all sharing in it." Then she went right back to staring at the wall.

There was nothing more I could say. Maybe I should have stayed to try to comfort her, or be comforted by her. Instead, I walked numbly out into the black hall toward my room. I fit the key into the lock blindly and let myself into the desolate darkness.

21

As I pushed open the door, a faint rustling came from the corner of my darkened room. My hand connected with the light switch, and the room filled with weak yellow light. My heart sprinted.

Savannah was standing in the extreme opposite corner of the room, her face wild and fierce on the surface. But I could make out the all-consuming fear underneath.

She thinks she's in danger.

She thinks I'm going to hurt her.

I ventured a step toward her. She shrank back further into the corner, terrified but determined. That's when I noticed the heavy switchblade in her hand. The weak light glinted off its dangerously sharp surface. She held it level with my heart. I stopped my approach and collapsed to my knees in front of her.

"Anna," my heart screamed, though my voice only whispered her name into the silence.

"Look at me," she demanded. Her eyes were red-rimmed, cheeks raw. Her jeans were wet and ripped at the knees, shoes muddied. Shallow scrapes zigzagged over her arms. She shivered hard like she was freezing. She almost looked like a stranger.

"I am here for answers. When I am through, you will let me leave. Don't touch me. Don't follow me. Do you understand?"

"Yes" I whispered, still on my knees.

"Are you from Earth?"

"No." I answered. She made a small sound like she was stifling a scream.

"What are you?" Her terror-stricken whisper cut me through.

"Our genetic makeup is identical to humans. *Identical.*" The alien trying to sound less alien. A hopeless endeavor. "There's not even the slightest difference between our DNA. Nothing separates us except distance in the universe. *God created man in his own image*," I said fervently.

"Where did you come from?" She stared right through me, the tears still rolling down her cheeks, her neck, wetting her already soaked yellow shirt.

"A place not far from here; it only takes a couple of days traveling as we do. My home is called Zhimeya."

"Are you here to cause us harm?"

"Mateo, Chase, Claire, and I are researchers, academics, here to gather information. That's all. But there are others of my kind who would cause the human race harm."

She staggered, almost losing her balance. "It can't be true. Please tell me this is all a joke!" she begged, leaning against the wall for support. I couldn't answer her; as much as I wanted to tell her whatever she wanted to hear, she deserved the truth.

"I love you," I whispered.

"No you don't. Love doesn't lie. *You are a liar!*" she screamed.

"I *am* a liar."

"I thought I found someone to love forever, Ryen. When I met you, it felt like home, even though I barely know what the word means. You were going to be my home. And now, it's gone. I've lost everything again." She wept bitterly, her face losing all color. She braced her hands on her knees, as if she were about to faint.

"Water," she said through dusky blue lips. I didn't move at first. She had told me not to move.

"I need water!" she yelled. I jumped up and ran to the small hotel fridge and pulled out two bottles of water. I opened them, set them carefully in front of her, and moved quickly away. She drained the first completely and half of the second one. Her breathing slowed, though her body still trembled.

Looking a little revived, she stared down at me, her eyes begging for understanding.

"You are from . . . space . . ." she let the statement hang in the air.

"I'm from Zhimeya, a world much like yours. A world that sustains life just like yours. I know how hard this must be for you—"

"Don't tell me that you understand what I am going through, because that's just another lie."

"You're right. I don't know what you are going through. I grew up in a world where aliens have always existed. It was just a fact of life. I always knew there was another planet full of beings like myself in the universe."

Her head picked up slightly. A spark of light cut through the clouds in her eyes.

"I—I hadn't thought of it that way," she whispered. "To you, I'm alien. What a strange thought," she said to herself.

She let herself slide down the wall to the floor and then pulled her knees to her chest. She lost her grip on the knife, and it clattered to the floor between us. She made no attempt to snatch it back. She was gone, far away from me, lost in a swirl of thoughts I dearly wished I could hear.

The mounting silence was more frightening than her rage. I started to worry I'd done some irreparable damage to her psyche.

"Thank you for the water," she finally breathed. Still too quiet. I searched her face for signs of impending collapse.

"Why are you here, Ryen? Scouting for weaknesses?" she asked calmly.

I saw my moment, a lull in her storm, a chance to explain myself.

"I wasn't lying when I told you we were looking for religious artifacts. You have been watching me do my job.

"My people have ancient records that talk of a heavenly being that would sacrifice his life to save us from our sins, who would redeem us. But he would be born and die on a different planet, and we would never share in the miracle. We are here to try to link the savior of our world with the savior of yours. I'm trying to find evidence that they are the same being. You call him "Savior." We call him "The Light."

"Zhimeya is in upheaval. My people are on the brink of war. If I could prove that your Jesus is our savior, too, and bring them evidence that he existed, my people would come together again. I'm trying to restore peace."

"You said you have records?"

"Yes," I said, watching her very carefully, "like scripture, but nowhere near as copious as Earth's. And as you have seen on your own planet, scripture alone is nowhere near enough evidence to inspire all people to the same faith."

"I still don't . . . understand why . . ."

"We wanted to come to the place where we hope he lived to learn more about him. Humans have only accomplished space travel in the last few decades, but we have had that technology for hundreds of years," I explained slowly. "Why do your people send scientists into space?"

She thought about it for a few seconds. "To learn," she finally said.

"Right. Curiosity. That is hardly a strong enough reason to compel a whole world to work together to master space travel. We had a need. We had to find the world where The Light walked, so we could share a part of what he left behind. Every brilliant mind Zhimeya has produced for a thousand years has been assigned to making this exploration possible. It's our religion.

"The great minds of Earth painted, wrote, composed music, built buildings. We invested all our efforts into making technology to bring us here. Different goals, different outcomes," I explained. To my utter amazement, she nodded.

"How did you find us?"

"Our records mention the eastern direction in connection with our savior. So we started searching eastward. This is the first inhabited world we found."

"You aren't sure if this is even the right place."

"No. But our records matched up well with biblical accounts, so we have been here searching out more information."

She was quiet then, which frightened me. As soon as there was nothing more she wished to know, she would walk out the door and away from me forever. I was quickly trying to decide what next to say when she posed her own question.

"Alien abductions? Crop circles?"

"Researchers like myself have only been coming here for the past eighty years, doing no harm, just listening and learning. But if there are two inhabited worlds, there must be more.

"Visitors from other worlds may have come in the past, possibly chasing after the same legends. This world is sacred, chosen by heaven to carry the savior. It stands to reason that there are others out there who have found Earth too."

"It stands to reason," she repeated quietly and said no more. I tried waxing philosophical to fill the silence.

"All around Earth, there are myths about beings visiting ancient man. Maybe they were researchers like myself. The pyramids in Egypt, the statues of Easter Island, five-thousand-year-old Sanskrit legends about flying machines, cave drawings from the U.S. to Australia showing heavenly beings coming down to Earth. Ancient man was always obsessed with the sky. Maybe it was because they actually saw people come down from it. Maybe aliens have always played important roles in human history. So many possibilities."

"Your people have not harmed humans in any way?" she asked tentatively.

"Not to my knowledge."

"But you said something about danger."

"There are those who feel that this sacred planet should be given to my kind so they can have what they feel should have been given to us by God. They are actually the same group who sent me, the Masters. Of course, I don't agree with their plan." I explained to her about my place in the Masters, about the break in the Tribunal, and about Aurik, who was still missing.

She only nodded as I explained, the sharpness in her eyes dulling. The moments of clarity we had just experienced were over. She was shutting down.

"Please Savannah, I am begging you—"

"Stop," she sighed and held up her nearly blue hands. I swallowed back the words I wished I could say. "I have my answers. Now I can go. And you," she paused. "You'll just have to be a beautiful figment of my imagination." She reached her cold hand out and trailed her fingers along my face, leaving a slow burn on my skin. "The happiest of dreams that ended in a nightmare."

"Anna," I pleaded, "I am in love with you. I need you. I was going to give up everything—my home, my friends, my family, everything—for you. Don't give up on this."

She said nothing but pushed herself up to standing. She almost fell back over, but I caught her just in time, righted her, and dropped my hands.

"I need to go," she whispered nervously.

"No! No, you can't. I can't watch you walk out that door right now. It will kill me. I'll leave if you want me to. Just please don't go right now. It's not safe," I begged, still on my knees. "Please, just stay for the night."

She moved toward me. When I looked up, fresh tears were falling from her overburdened eyes.

"I want to love you. I want it so much," she whispered, placing her shaking hands lightly on my shoulders. I buried my face into her stomach, my arms circling her waist, trying to hold her to the spot.

"I'll stay," she finally said.

With that, I let her go. She slipped off her shoes and climbed slowly into my bed, exhaustion dragging at her limbs. She shivered fitfully as she wrapped the blankets around herself. I snapped off the light and slid down the wall farthest away her.

And for the first time in a long time, I prayed.

I didn't even ask God to make Savannah stay with me. I just asked that she would be okay. That was the change that love had made in me. I knew I truly loved her, because I just wanted her to be happy. Even if that meant I couldn't be part of her life, anymore.

As I pleaded with higher powers I hoped were listening, I heard a soft voice.

"I'm cold."

At first I looked up at the ceiling, but then I realized if God were actually talking to me, that's probably not the first thing he would have said.

"Ryen?" Savannah's scared voice split the silence again.

"I'm here!" I rushed to her side, kneeling next to the bed.

"I'm cold." Her body shook again under the covers.

"I'll go get more blankets from the front desk. I'll just be one minute."

"No! Wait. I need you." She found my hand with her freezing ones and pulled me to her side. She turned and curved her body into mine, still shuddering, taking my arms and pulling them over hers.

This is the last time you'll ever get to touch her, my head screamed. So I held her tighter. "Sleep, angel," I murmured. A few minutes later, the shaking subsided, and she finally fell asleep.

When I woke up, the bed was empty. Before alarm could set in, I found her. She was just finishing getting dressed, pulling her shirt into place in the bathroom, steam from her recent shower pouring from the slightly open door. She must have heard me stir, because she spun around and caught me watching.

"How long have you been awake?" she accused.

"Just now, not three seconds!" I promised.

"You'd better be telling the truth, Ryen . . ." She hesitated. "You know, it's very hard to scold you properly when I don't know your last name," she said with an almost imperceptible smile. "That is, if you have a last name," she added.

"I have something like a last name. In Zhimeya, we live in tribes. Each tribe has a name. I come from the Haven tribe. Claire, Mateo, and Chase are all Havens too. You would call me Ryen of the Haven."

"Haven . . . a safe place," she murmured. "What does it mean in your language?"

"It means explorer," I answered.

And then we were silent. She stared tiredly at me from across the room, arms folded tightly over her chest. Even though the curtains were drawn, I could tell it was a sunny morning outside. Now that the danger of the night was gone, nothing held her here. So why didn't she run?

"I have some more questions," she stammered, awkwardly sitting on the very edge of the bed.

"Of course," I said quietly.

"Do you have any . . . powers?" she asked falteringly, unable to meet my eyes.

"No. As aliens go, we are extremely boring. Our only super power is scientific prowess. We would win all of Earth's science fairs hands down. Does that count?" I asked, trying for levity.

"No, not at all," she said, visibly relieved by my ordinariness. "Why can you speak English so well?"

"In Zhimeya, parents have a great deal of say as to what their children become. Tribes are usually known for certain professions. For example, the Guiomar tribe is known for metallurgy and alchemy. They usually become engineers. The Abran tribe is famous for their pursuit of medical knowledge. Abran children usually become healers. We start our training very young."

I paused for a moment, letting her take the information in. When she nodded, I went on.

"The Haven tribe, my tribe, has always been associated with exploration. Anciently, we were the first astronomers. The first group of Masters were all Havens. My parents decided that they wanted me to become a researcher, because I had all of the most necessary attributes."

"Which are?"

"Claire calls them the three B's—brilliance, bravery, and beauty."

"Obviously modesty and humility are not on that list," she smirked.

"Now what would *I* do with modesty or humility?" I ventured a small smile. "I was the youngest child ever accepted into the Masters' Institute for Earth Research. I grew up speaking English and Italian with my teachers, a few of whom had been researchers like myself. That's where Claire, Mateo, Chase, and I became friends."

"So you never got to decide what *you* wanted to do with your life?" she wondered.

"Some professions take a lifetime to train for. Take my friend Nik, for example. His parents wanted him to become a pilot for the Masters, taking researchers to and from Earth, exploring the sky. So he grew up flying, growing accustomed to space, making long, physically difficult flights. He has been conditioned for his taxing occupation since birth. He actually brought me here to Earth. It isn't a pleasant trip if you have to be awake for it."

"And what about money? You seem to have an unending supply."

"When the first researchers came to Earth, they brought gold with them. It is one of the metals our worlds have in common, though we have it in such abundance, it is fairly worthless to my people. The first researchers traded gold for currency—and the bank accounts they started eighty years ago still contain money that we use at our discretion."

"You've mastered space travel, but you haven't figured out a way to print money?"

"We could print any kind of money and have it pass the most rigorous tests. That's not a problem. The first Masters wanted to make a contribution to the world they were studying. We still use the money to fund museums, research projects, and the like in exchange for information. We try to do good where we can."

She nodded but said no more. The silence grew. I finally broke it with a question of my own.

"Why did you come back last night, Anna?" I asked fervently, trying to meet her gaze. She still refused to look at me.

"I came back for two reasons. My father robbed me of a normal life. I never got to tell him what he did to my mother and me. I decided a long time ago that if anyone ever hurt me again, they would hear about it.

"But there was another reason. The morning I came in to wake you, before I knew everything . . ." Her shoulders shivered at the memory. "You were in the shower, and your computer was open on the bed. I was going to look up pictures of Ravello, the city where you were going to take me. But instead, I saw, among everything else, a resignation letter. The words from that letter pulled me back here to face you. I *had* to know whether you really were going to leave your whole entire life behind to be with me. Is it true?" She looked into my eyes tentatively.

"Yes, I was going to leave everything behind for you. I still want to."

"But we *just* met," she whispered. "Your letter made it sound like this decision was a forever kind of decision."

"It *is* a forever kind of decision. I wouldn't leave my life behind for anything less than you," I said fiercely, reaching for her hand. She jerked away from me and started for the door.

"What am I still doing here? This is crazy."

"Anna, stop," I begged, jumping up and putting myself between her and the door. "Please hear me out, because the decision you're making right now is also a forever kind of decision. If you refuse me, I will go home. But I will always love only you, no matter where I am."

"Please let me go."

"If I've broken this beyond repair, if you feel absolutely nothing for me anymore, then you should go. Get as far away from me as you can. But if you still feel anything, anything at all, then I'll follow you around this planet until you forgive me."

"How can I make that kind of decision?" she cried. "How can I make a rational choice that will not only alter the course of our lives, but cost you everything, before the transports come?"

"Transports? Where did you hear that word, Anna?" I demanded.

"The woman from your computer. She said the transports would be here for you today," she answered, watching me carefully.

Eleven seconds. It had only been eleven seconds. But eleven seconds had been enough.

"What did she look like?" I asked nervously, though I already knew.

"Tattoos, pink hair. She appeared out of nowhere and said she was coming for me," she said. "Ryen, what's going on?"

I could feel my face draining of color as I let out a long string of Zhimeyan profanities.

"It looks like your choice was made for you. We need to leave *now*, Anna. That woman *will* hurt you."

"What are you talking about? Am I in danger?"

"I know I've given you no reason to, but you have to trust me. I'll explain everything as soon as I get you to a safe place," I pleaded, putting my hands squarely on her shoulders. "Please believe me."

"You'll be stuck here forever, won't you?" she asked anxiously.

"Grab what you can, and come back as fast as you can."

"But I—" she protested.

"Go!" I yelled. She nodded numbly and ran out the door.

23

I pulled all my traveler's checks out and counted them. There was at least two hundred thousand dollars there—more than enough to start a new life. I grabbed whatever I could and pushed it into bags. I opened up my computer, hoping to have enough time to send my resignation to Gideon, severing any claim he had on me. It was taking too long to connect, so I started packing again. As I gathered up all of my belongings, I noticed the switchblade Savannah had left on the floor from the night before. Maybe she'd want it back; maybe she'd never want to see it again. I picked it up and shoved it into my back pocket so I could offer it to her later. If she still didn't trust me, maybe she'd want it as protection.

I went speedily to the bathroom and was gathering up whatever I had left in there when I heard the doorknob to my room turn. I rushed back into the room.

The face that I saw waiting for me was not Savannah's. It was the absolute antithesis. Standing in the doorway was Emani, flanked by two armed men.

"*There* you are." She waved her hand, and the two men lunged forward, slamming me into the wall with the force of a wrecking ball. The drywall cracked behind my skull.

Emani had fresh tattoos on her bare midriff, chest, and neck, the skin still red from the ink. Her dyed black hair was pulled back severely, accentuating the snake-like sneer on her face. She slinked across the room, taking my face in her hands.

"I told you that you couldn't run forever. There's nowhere you could go that I wouldn't follow." I tried to shake her off. She slapped me.

"What the *hell* is wrong with you? Why are you here?" I fought uselessly against her men.

"I came to claim you," she said innocently. "And since Gideon considers you something of a flight risk, I brought help. I wanted to make sure you didn't escape me again. Do you like my new marks?"

I looked more carefully at her new tattoos and found my name in white ink etched into the skin covering her exposed sternum, just under her collarbones.

"What would possess you to do something like that?"

"You made a very deep mark on me, Ryen. Do you remember those days? The chemical reaction between us?" She stared up at me, her face twisted in maniacal longing.

I did remember those days. Vividly. We were like gasoline and an open flame—combustible, explosive. But, like gasoline and fire, as soon as the initial reaction was over, the fire died, leaving nothing but ash behind.

Beneath her indescribable beauty lay a sad, schizophrenic, lost little girl. And though I had tried, I couldn't save her from her own self-destruction. "You have my undivided attention, Emani." I glared at the guards. "What do you want from me?"

"My sisters have been watching you. They intercepted the resignation you sent to Claire. Gideon insisted that I come immediately before you made such a stupid mistake," she snapped. "You don't belong here, Ryen. We are *better* than this!"

Her breathing spiked as she ran her fingers down my face, my name rising and falling fast on her chest.

I'd forgotten how beautiful you are," she whispered quietly, almost to herself. "Gideon has a favor to ask of you, and I think you will find it hard to say no."

"He knows where my loyalties lie. He has nothing that will tempt me."

"I didn't say he was offering you anything. I've been trying to contact you for weeks, but you ignored me again and again. You deserve this. This is *your* fault," she said angrily. She looked toward the door and shouted, "Come!"

Two more men entered, dragging a body. Savannah's eyes were bruised, her nose and mouth were dripping blood, and she had two distinct burn marks on her neck. Her backpack was slung on her back.

She had been beaten and shocked, but she was breathing. She was still alive. One of the men that dragged her had noticeably broken fingers. The other's face was swelling on one side. Both had bite marks on their arms. She'd put up a fight.

The sight of her broken and in the arms of enemies sent me over the edge. I let out an inhuman growl and lurched against the men, but they threw me back into the wall. This time, pieces of the ceiling rained down from above. I had to calm down. I couldn't help Savannah if the guards killed me.

"Was that necessary, Emani? It looks a little like jealousy got the best of you."

Emani's cheeks heated to crimson. "You know me so well," she breathed. "I thought if I made her a little less pretty, you would be able to think more clearly and do the right thing." She stepped lightly on Savannah's neck with the toe of her knee-high leather boot. Savannah's chest stopped rising and her body jerked from the lack of oxygen.

"No!" I roared. With a fresh surge of adrenaline, I managed to throw one of the men off balance. I lunged toward Savannah, but Emani crouched on her like a tiger over her kill. She pulled a short, dull-looking dagger out of the holster on her hip and clicked a silver button on the blade's hilt. The blade turned from flinty gray to a glowing, pulsating white, a concentrated beam of energy focused at the top of it. She hovered the blade inches over Savannah's chest.

"Stop, Ryen!" she screamed. The glowing dagger pulsed with so much heat that even though it touched no part of her, the skin on Savannah's chest started to split and melt away. I stopped instantly, letting the men pull me away.

Emani looked down at Savannah's body in horror. "Look what you made me do! *This is your fault!*" she screamed, turning off the blade and throwing it to the ground. She tried to sop up the blood gush from Savannah's chest with a bed sheet.

"You've forced my hand!" Frantic tears welled up in her black eyes. Looking at her crying and covered in Savannah's blood, I almost pitied her. She took out a canister of sealing salve in her pocket and worked furiously to seal Savannah's burns shut. Finally finished with the repair, she stared at me, reading my agony as I watched Savannah fight to keep breathing.

"What has happened to you?" she asked wretchedly, standing up again. "How can you care more for this human than you do for me?"

"Because she is nothing like you, you sadistic little—" Emani silenced me with a perfectly placed kick to my stomach. My head bowed low as air tore from my lungs.

"You need to start thinking about your future, love. There is *nothing* here for you, especially if I kill the girl. Come back with me. Gideon will forgive you. Just give him what he wants, and we can be together again! I promise, I'll be better this time. I'll be whatever you want me to be!"

"You can't change! Look around, Emani. Do you see what you are capable of? Do you see the destruction you cause?" I raged.

She slapped me hard again and then gasped, looking at her hand as if it had acted on its own accord. "I'm so sorry! Please, please forgive me, love," she whispered, her countenance swinging wildly from ferocity to fear. She pushed her lips against mine violently, but I clenched my jaw against her kiss. Realizing my rejection, she took my bottom lip between her teeth and bit down hard until the blood started to flow. She pulled away, wiping my blood from her mouth.

"I'd rather kill you myself than watch you love another woman." When she brought herself close to me again, I spit the blood that was filling my mouth at her. She screeched bitterly, and one of the guards punched me hard. My ribs snapped under the force.

"You are lucky Gideon wants you back in one piece. I'll ask you one more time. Will you come back to Zhimeya with us with no further outbursts?"

"Yes," I said in defeat. I had no choice. "Just please leave Savannah alone."

"I wish I could, Ryen. Gideon wants her."

"*Why?*" I pleaded, but she ignored me.

"You will come to your senses soon enough," she muttered as she turned toward a white case one of the men carried. She produced three large, black pills and a syringe full of thick, deep blue liquid with the word "Jhayne" printed on the side. "As they say in English, pick your poison, Ryen." She held out the pills and syringe for me to choose between.

I was going to have to take the drug that she was offering. It would slow my metabolism, heart rate, and brain waves to almost nothing so that I could survive the flight back home.

"How do you want your Jhayne? Are you going to take it of your own free will, or do I have to jam this needle in your neck?"

"I'll take the pills," I said acidly.

She slipped them into my mouth, and I swallowed hard. Immediately, my lungs started to feel heavier.

"That wasn't very chivalrous of you. I only had one course of pills left. Looks like the girl gets the stick." She turned toward Savannah and drove the thick needle deep into her throat.

"God will make you pay for your actions!" I yelled.

Her arrogant mask shattered. Real, raw horror stained her features. She didn't even try to cover it up. Guilt, fear, and indecision were written plainly across her face.

"Don't you think I know that?" she whispered, her raven black eyes drenched with terror.

Savannah was dragged to the first of two darkened limousines parked outside the inn. I had no strength to fight anymore. It was a herculean effort to even make my lungs expand and retract.

Claire, Mateo, and Chase were already in the back of the limo I was shoved into. The car doors shut behind me, and the four of us were left alone. They were all sucking uselessly at the air, Jhayne swimming thick in their blood. Their swollen veins stood out like blue-black spider webs through their skin, colored from the drug that would put them into temporary comas. They had just minutes until the drug took full effect.

"I'm so sorry . . . all of you. I never meant for this . . ." I sucked in another labored breath. "Oshun and Ecko have been following us. They intercepted my resignation. Gideon sent Emani to make sure I came back. She'll kill Savannah if I don't do what he wants. If I hadn't tried to resign . . ."

"Your resignation . . . just sped up the process," Chase panted. "There's something much worse going on . . . than we anticipated . . . Gideon is planning something, and we're in the middle of it."

"Savy . . . okay?" Claire gasped.

"They stunned her, which means she fought pretty hard," I whispered.

"I knew . . . I liked her," Mateo wheezed, managing a weak smile.

"When we get home, do whatever you can to get out of his way and back to your families. Blame me for everything," I pleaded.

"Hell no! You mess with one of us . . . you mess with all of us," Mateo said through shallow breaths.

"No! Promise you won't do anything heroic."

Thick, inky black tears colored with Jhayne fell from Claire's eyes. She gave my hand a gentle squeeze and then laid her head on Chase's chest.

"Please . . ." I pleaded uselessly.

The boys slumped in their seats, succumbing quietly to oblivion.

I can't lose any of you," I whispered, but they were too far gone to hear.

The large fallow pasture full of yellow weeds was just long enough to allow for transport landing and takeoff. The bullet-shaped aircrafts stood in a perfect line, facing west. Their mirrored surfaces gleamed cerulean blue, the exact same color as the noon sky, camouflaging them almost completely. The flight crews were the most conspicuous thing, waiting in formation outside of the transports. As the limos pulled up, the landing gear on each transport retracted in synchronization, the bodies of each vehicle resting in the tall grass.

Two female attendants opened the door to my car. I was the only one able to climb out on my own. The men that had held me captive just an hour ago pushed me out of the way to drag my friends' seemingly lifeless bodies toward their transport.

I squinted in the sun's bright light and waited agonizingly to see whether they would drag Savannah's body from the car in front of mine.

I stared down at my useless hands, black lines crisscrossing over every inch of skin. I had brought Savannah into the crosshairs of certain death. I had done this. Emani was right. This was my fault.

Savannah finally struggled out of the back of her car. Her skin bore the marks of Jhayne just as mine did. The blood from her meeting with Emani's guard had dried in thick crimson rivulets along her face. Dark fluid spilled from the burns in her neck—blood mixed with the lecherous drug. But she bravely refused the attendant's help. I had never seen her look more beautiful.

Her head swiveled around until she found me. She nodded quickly, answering all of my silent questions. She was all right. For now.

Emani, holding Savannah's backpack and her own white case, was loaded onto the first, much larger transport with Chase,

Claire, and Mateo. Savannah was loaded into the second, smaller one. An attendant took my hand and led me forward.

A jolt of recognition registered in my almost sleeping brain as I passed the pilot lined up outside with the rest of the flight crew. Nik. A friend. *My* friend.

"Load the human first," Nik told the attendants, who nodded and leaned me onto the side of the transport. He walked to my side and stood shoulder to shoulder with me.

" Nik" I whispered. "You came . . . help us?"

"I *came* because it's my *job*! What is going on? What happened to you?" he whispered in utter shock.

"I can't—" I choked. The world was blurring into black and white. I couldn't talk anymore.

"I know, the Jhayne. Just answer my questions then."

I nodded.

"I overheard Emani saying that you were going to resign. True?"

I nodded.

"Because of the human?"

I nodded again.

"The human is not safe. Emani has been talking about Gideon's plans for her."

I shook my head furiously.

"Nothing will happen to her while I'm in charge. I'll make sure you all get safely home. That's all I can promise, though."

I nodded a thank you.

"You must have something Gideon really wants to make him go to these lengths to keep you. When we get home, I'll alert as many as I can to what I have seen here."

I nodded weakly. Gideon would know better than to let anyone escape who had seen this. Nik was in grave danger now too, just like the rest of us. The attendants were on their way out of the transport to retrieve me, but before they did, Nik whispered urgently, "You're not alone. Gideon is gaining power, but if he wants to go through with his plans, he's going to have to fight all those who still stand with Aurik first."

And there it was—a flicker of hope. A light in the unrelenting darkness.

The attendant laid me on a cold metal table and strapped me down tightly. The machines above my head sent out criss-crossing beams of white light every few seconds, scanning my vital signs. Satisfied, the attendant pushed the glass cover closed over me like a transparent coffin.

Through the haze in my head, I searched for Savannah across the aisle. She was lying in an identical glass case. Our eyes met, and my dying heartbeats quickened. I heard it register on the monitors. If I could only comfort her for just a minute, to explain what was happening, to tell her how sorry I was, to tell her I loved her one more time.

The powerful thrum of the motors filled the quiet air. Savannah moved suddenly, straining her neck toward the glass. She took a difficult gasp and blew warm air on its surface, fogging it. She then took her pinky finger and traced the outline of a heart in the mist.

Could she really love me? After all this?

A dark blue tear fell from her eye and into her gold hair, staining it. It was the last thing I saw before the Jhayne dragged me into the black.

24

Zhimeya, tunnels beneath Tribunal Hall

"I am *too old* for this," he said aloud.

The rhythmic breathing of what sounded like two people he couldn't locate were the only sounds Aurik heard other than his own voice. He hadn't seen light since the kidnapping.

Had it been a kidnapping? The details were still cloudy.

"I was speaking with the Tribunal members," he said. He had already yelled himself hoarse calling for help. He spoke out loud now just to hear something real. "The light went out. There was a sharp sting in my neck." His hand the found the lump that still protruded from his skin. "And I woke up here, buried alive . . ." He trailed off. "I am *way too old* for this."

His hands swept over the dimensions of the cell again. Metal bars lined one of the walls; the other three were dirt. When he had first been elected Head of the Tribunal, he was shown a small portion of the ancient maze located under Tribunal Hall, engineered eons ago during a much darker age. He remembered the stifling heat and caustic smell of rotting metal. Without a doubt, that's where he was now. But knowing he was in the tunnels helped very little. They stretched unendingly underneath the city.

A deafening bang tore through the silence, followed by a mechanical clicking and grinding of gears. Then there was light, enough to illuminate the room dimly, and a rush of cool air that carried the sound of voices with it. Someone was coming.

"Sometimes I'm not sure Emani is as good a chemist as she believes herself to be. How long has he been unconscious?"

"She probably administered too much. He fought hard for an old man," a second voice answered. That shook a memory loose in Aurik's head. Although he hadn't been able see, he'd put up a great struggle. He remembered a man's voice—and a woman's.

Two figures finally came into view.

"Sorry to have kept you waiting, Uncle. I was away on unavoidable business," Gideon said. He carried a thick parchment scroll in his hand, which he fitted into a carved niche in the wall.

Aurik barely recognized the man in front of him.

"Gideon! What has *happened* to you?" he cried. Gideon looked skeletal, worn away and white as chalk. "You need a healer immediately! Call for Zio, he can help you!" He reached out to touch Gideon's shoulder.

"There is nothing wrong with me," Gideon spat, his mouth twitching involuntarily. Without thinking, he reached back and scratched viciously at his neck, where Dai had marked him.

"I thought you and I had reached an understanding, Gideon. Do you know what you have brought upon yourself?" he asked sadly. "You will lose your tribal marks and become Unnamed. There is nothing that I, either as your uncle or as Head of the Tribunal, can do to save you from exile."

"Your worry is misplaced, Aurik. No one is going to find out about this, because you won't tell them."

"Dear boy, I am bound by a sacred oath to tell the absolute truth. Not even our family tie can negate that."

"You don't understand. Listen carefully—"

"You had such promise. You could have brought great peace to our society. Your parents, your beautiful mother, what would they say?" Aurik asked as he reached out to Gideon again.

"Enough!" Gideon stepped back. The voices in his head echoed Aurik's words back at him, amplified. "Do *not* speak of my parents. You've driven me to these extremes! *You* have turned me, your blood, into an enemy."

"My job is to protect my people and preserve peace. Your plan comes with an unconscionable loss of life. I did what I thought was right."

"That choice is no longer yours. I have enough support to push my initiative through. The Tribunal has given me their vote."

"Have they? At what price?" Aurik asked. "I don't know what you have offered them, but let me tell you something I have learned in my long years. Bought support will *never* weather the storm. If they do not follow you with their hearts, they won't follow you for long."

Gideon glanced at Dai, who smiled back. Maybe Gideon just imagined the flash of mutiny burning behind that smile.

"They will follow me as long as I need them to, and then I will do away with them, as well," Gideon answered.

"God will not look upon your actions without judgment, son. I'll ask you again to repent of your actions."

"You stand there, half naked, starving, inside a cell, and lecture me about God and repentance? You should be down on your knees begging me to spare your life!" Gideon yelled.

"My life means very little in the larger sense. I will only beg you again to reconsider your actions," Aurik said simply. "Mailah wouldn't have wanted this path for you."

Gideon flew at the bars that separated the two men and shook them angrily.

"Do not speak my mother's name! She'll hear you!" he stammered, his eyes boring wildly into dark hallways.

"Son, what are you talking about? Please call Zio for help. You aren't well," Aurik implored, placing his aged hands over Gideon's.

"Don't touch me!" Gideon screamed. He ran from the chamber down the black, twisting halls, getting more lost with each step.

"His parents have been dead for years," Aurik murmured to himself. "Dai, he is not well!"

"He truly isn't," Dai agreed with a satisfied smile.

Dai stood very still, closing his working eye. After a moment of meditation, he felt the shift, his brain making connection with the extensive machinery in his empty eye socket. His mind melded with the mechanisms, bringing them whirring to life.

He concentrated, reaching out into the darkness, through the walls, scanning for the chemical signal the mark on Gideon's skin emitted. He found his target easily.

He concentrated harder and the earthen walls started to form in his mind, filling in the darkness completely. He walked down the black hallways until he reached Gideon, huddled in a corner, mumbling.

"I found you," a female voice called menacingly. Dai projected Mailah's frighteningly disfigured hologram inside the antechamber where Gideon was hiding. Gideon cried out, clawing uselessly at the walls to get away from the ghost.

"Dai! Help!" he shouted. "I need more!" Dai smiled at the crumbling shell of a man as he dug inside his robes for the syringe.

He was never as strong as his ambitions. But I am, thought Dai.

"I thought I took enough. But the ghosts . . . Just give me a little more."

"Of course, Master," he said comfortingly, pushing up the robes on Gideon's arm to expose his gray skin. He smoothly injected the drug into Gideon's protruding vein. He slowly let the hologram of Gideon's mother evaporate as the drug took effect. As it did, the irrational light in Gideon's eyes calmed.

After a few somber breaths in the bleak hallway, he stood and floated serenely behind Dai, who led him back into Aurik's cell. Aurik observed the changed Gideon with apprehension.

"Dai, please get him some help," Aurik urged.

"Don't say any more words now," Gideon said calmly. "Listen to your future, because time is running out." Aurik said nothing, but folded his arms patiently across his chest.

"You'll follow my every direction, you'll say what I want you to say, and then you will die," Gideon said. Aurik opened his mouth to speak, but Gideon cut him off.

"Please do not fight me on this. I need your body in working condition." Dai threw a small satchel filled with food and water into Aurik's cell.

"Soon your mind will belong to me. So, Dai, if you will be so kind, tend to my uncle. Make sure he eats. Give him light, books, whatever he wants," he said. Dai nodded and smiled.

"It's all very exciting. You should feel privileged to be a part of such historic times. I can't wait to hear all of the Head of the Tribunal's secrets."

"I would never share these secrets, even if I were allowed to do so."

"It's really up to you. If you don't want to tell me your secrets while you are alive, you'll talk when you are dead."

"Gideon, I don't understand what you are saying," Aurik said, less patiently this time.

"Why does *everyone* keep saying that to me lately?" he asked, cocking his head to the side, dazed. "Get me out of here, Dai. I'm getting dirty."

I found my lungs first. They expanded and retracted too slowly, like a giant weight was pressing down on me. I expected to open my eyes and see the glass that encased me, but instead I found the night sky, black as pitch except for a dusting of glittering silver stars. They seemed strangely close. The surrounding air was warm and smoky.

My gaze swung wider until it found something to focus on. I watched in confusion as sparkling orbs floated and spun almost silently between me and the night sky. At that moment, my body and mind finally connected, and I quickly rolled off the floor to standing.

I'd been completely wrong about my surroundings. I was in a strange circular room that reminded me of the Roman Pantheon, but with a covered skylight at the pinnacle instead of a gaping hole. No light filtered through the oculus now. What I had thought was the night sky was actually a litany of tiny black and silver mosaic tiles that completely covered the spherical roof, mimicking space. A miniature solar system of metallic spheres dripping with jewels hung suspended from wires in the ceiling above my head. The walls I could see were lined with tall bookcases brimming over with books, the titles of which were in thousands of different languages. The largest piece of furniture in the room was a heavy wooden desk, intricately carved with exotic blossoms running up the legs.

The only source of light came from a grand picture window that overlooked a dense forest of trees. I faced the window and found the source of the silvery glow. Two snowy white moons shined through the blackened sky. Zhimeya's twin moons. I was home.

A soft musical sound reached my ears, a faraway melody lilting on the edges of the shadows. The singing grew louder and then stopped abruptly.

"You're here!"

It wasn't a voice I'd heard before, but somehow I recognized it. A woman stepped out of the darkness wrapped in steely gray shadows that stuck to her like clothing. They were alive, writhing and shifting on her form, trying to pull her back into the darkness she was trying to escape. Her long, blonde hair waved around her face, and her green–gold eyes shimmered. She reminded me instantly of Savannah.

"I know you—" I said the first thing that made it through the fog in my brain. The woman laughed quietly. It was a shockingly familiar sound.

"Not really. You know my daughter," she said sweetly, though still straining against the twisting shadows.

"You're Savannah's mother." I matched her face to the sketches in Savannah's book.

"I am, and I'm very pleased to meet you."

"I'm dead then?"

"No, darlin', but you must be somewhere close to it, since you're here. We have some things we really need to talk about," she said in a warm accent.

I nodded quickly.

"But I need to get my motherin' out of the way before we go any further," she said seriously, glancing over her shoulder as if she expected someone to be there.

"Now, you are well aware of the mistakes that I have made with my daughter, dragging her all over God's green Earth trying to keep her safe. I did more harm than good, I'm afraid. But, she's found you," she said softly, "and I'm glad she has. But I need an ironclad promise, young man, that you will take care of her."

"She is everything to me," I vowed.

"All right then, you have my blessing."

"But wait," I sputtered, "You don't care that I'm not . . . like you?"

She smiled very slightly as she shook her head. "We're *all* God's children," she said, touching my face with her small, cold hand. "You'll do just fine for my girl. I've been watching you. You are something special, just like her. Strong, smart, good to the core." She put her hands on my shoulders and squeezed tight. "But we're running low on time, son. Please remember what I am about to tell you."

"Of course, anything," I promised. A lovely tendril of shadow wound its way softly around my wrist, thin as a single thread. I very suddenly longed to close my eyes.

"I did a few things right by my girl. I made sure that she learned how to defend herself."

"She wanted roller skates, and you gave her pepper spray," I remembered, watching with amusement as another shadowy tentacle twisted its way around my bicep. Two more softly swept around my neck.

"Soon enough, you won't be able to protect my Anna. But she is her greatest resource. Show her that you believe in her strength. She's going to need that, understand?"

"Yes." I tried to memorize her words, but I didn't understand the urgency in her voice anymore. What could be wrong in this beautiful place?

"There is one more thing. You need to find the map."

"You need a map?" I asked slowly. My eyelids were so heavy. My only wish was for the beautiful shadows to sweep quickly over me so I could finally rest.

"No son, *you* need the map. It's here!" she yelled, pointing to the polished stone floor.

The shadows had grown like thick vines up my legs, around my middle, and across my chest. They started to contract, tightening around me, pulling me towards the darkness from where Savannah's mother had come.

"Oh no, Ryen! You can't follow where I'm going," she commanded. "Anna needs you. Your world needs you! You must leave this place!"

A loud crash came from outside the picture window, like a roll of thunder. The lovely shadows tore violently away from my body. The thunder crashed again, straight over us this time. My heart sputtered, stopped cold, then jolted in my chest, like it was trying to crack straight through my ribcage.

"Listen to me—Earth is the key!" she screamed over the earsplitting sound.

Another crash. This time, the pain of it knocked me back to the cold stone floor. I searched for Savannah's mother, but the steely shadows had pulled her to the edge of the darkness where she forbade me to follow. Then she disappeared.

Everything disappeared.

I was drowning, plummeting, falling through the bleak and fiery torture. Blistering, searing pain, like a chain around my middle, pulled me through the void into sharp consciousness. An unfamiliar face hovered inches over mine. Her hands held metal paddles with remnants of my skin still sizzling on the surface.

"Breathe!" she ordered.

I did as I was told. It was excruciating.

"Sorry about that. Your heart kept stopping. But you should be fine now. Please rest as we make our landing," she said with bored courtesy.

I scrambled to sitting, still breathing hard. I located the needles in my arms that supplied the antidote to the Jhayne and ripped them out, spilling blood all over the clean metal bed. The attendant rolled her eyes and handed me bandages.

As she moved toward the front of the transport, I searched across the aisle to find Savannah, whose heartbeat still registered on the monitor above her head. I wanted to cross the space, shatter her glass confine, and wake her up myself, but the attendant was already wiping the paddles clean of my skin and preparing them for her.

She looked so fragile and helpless with bluish-yellow bruises marring her beautiful features. I needed to see the jade green of her eyes, fringed with gold lashes, that I'd first fallen in love with. I wanted to run my fingers through her tangled curls, to trace her small feminine curves with my hands, to hold and protect her in my arms.

The attendant finally lifted the glass and sunk two needles into the top of Savannah's wrist. She then tore open Savannah's tattered shirt in one easy stride and placed the paddles directly over her heart.

"Wake up, wake up, wake up, wake up," I chanted quietly. The woman pressed a button, and Savannah's body contracted upwards for a second and then slammed back down on her bed.

The attendant placed her fingers on Savannah's neck, counted her pulse, and then pressed the button again. Savannah gasped awake this time, terrified. I pushed the attendant to the floor and lunged toward Savannah, grabbing her up.

"I'm so sorry," was all I could manage over and over again. I stroked her hair, her back, her face. She wound her arms and legs around me tightly. The attendant came back over with two canisters of liquid, though she didn't bother wearing her fake smile anymore. I opened one of the canisters and gulped it gone.

"Water, drink," I gasped. She nodded and drank hers obediently. "Are you okay?" I took her face in my hands, assessing the damage.

"No worse for the wear," she lied, putting on a brave face. I loved her for it. I buried myself into her again.

The attendant handed us both black shirts with the Masters' crest just over the heart. We stripped away our tattered clothes and dressed.

Seconds later, the transport touched down. We were on Gideon's terms now.

"Anna, stay next to me and keep quiet. I'll translate anything that is important for you to know." She nodded.

"I will do everything in my power to keep you safe. But I need you to remember something." I desperately tried to recall her mother's words. "You are your greatest resource, okay? You are strong and smart, and you know how to fight. You need to stay alive for me. Do you understand?" She started to protest but something in my eyes made her nod. "And if I don't get a chance to tell you again, I love you," I said, kissing her forehead.

The front hatch swung open, and Emani stepped on before Savannah could say anything. Emani's footing wasn't sure; she was still working off the Jhayne just like we were.

"Come," she commanded. We descended the stairs and were met by the same men that had captured us. The two that had captured Savannah walked the farthest away from her.

The transports had landed on the very edge of a primordial forest. Trees taller than skyscrapers soared into the sky. I immediately wished I had told Savannah more about Zhimeya when I'd had the chance, because at that same moment, she looked up to see two bright moons gleaming in the sky. She let out an audible gasp.

"Zhimeya has two moons," I whispered urgently. "Mars has two moons. Neptune has thirteen. Jupiter has more than sixty. So Zhimeya having two is actually not *that* universally strange," I whispered apologetically.

"It's beautiful." Her voice was full of genuine wonder. I pulled her tighter to my side, pressing my lips to her forehead again. I could still smell the sweet saltwater breeze of the ocean on her skin.

A rustling in the distance made her pull away from me and look backwards into the ancient forest. The moons' intense glow reflected off the backs of three beasts as they wove gracefully between massive tree trunks.

"Are those . . .?" she whispered nervously. She stared as the giant straje moved quietly among the trees, their violet and crimson scales shining.

"You'd probably call them dragons. It's a bizarre coincidence," I said lightly, trying to distract her from our dire circumstances. "So many cultures on Earth have myths about winged serpents that never existed. And here they actually do exist."

She stared off into the distance after them. "They fly, but not great distances," I said. "They are much like dinosaurs, actually. The carnivorous straje were hunted almost to extinction because they were so dangerous. Most wild straje are herbivores. Some people keep the smaller species for transportation."

Emani, whom we had been following through the darkness, turned to face us both.

"I'm sorry," she said, holding my eyes. She sounded like she really meant it.

I was about to ask exactly which part of this nightmare she was most sorry for, but I never got the chance. A guard from behind slipped a metal halo around my head and pushed it down over my eyes. It attached itself with a painful, sucking tightness. A blinder ring. They were only ever put on the most defiant prisoners, and only when the Tribunal expressly ordered their use.

"Emani, you know it's illegal to use blinder rings without Tribunal authority!" I yelled.

"I'm sorry," Emani said again.

Savannah screamed as she was ripped out of my arms.

"Anna!" I shouted, trying to pull the mechanical ring away, but a sharp blow to my spine brought me low. Heavy bodies forced me to the ground. Savannah's screams came from farther and farther away. She was screaming for me. I kept fighting until Emani brought me down again with an electric shock to my spine.

"She's gone. It's over. Stop fighting," Emani whispered, barely audible over Savannah's retreating cries for help.

They dragged me into the back of a vehicle that flew like a wraith through the night, skimming just above the ground. Between the blindness, injuries, and leftover drugs in my blood, I only kept a very tenuous hold on consciousness. No one spoke, though light fingers touched me often—running the length of my arm, caressing my cheek, twisting in my hair softly. Emani. I remembered her touch.

The vehicle finally halted, and I was dragged to standing and made to walk. The air outside the vehicle was sweltering, heavy with a sulfurous haze I could taste on my tongue—the Zhimeyan underground.

"Where are you taking me?" I demanded. I was answered with a kick to the stomach. I could feel the blood blooming under my skin.

They shoved me up a mountain of endless twisting stairs that seemed to be carved straight out of the ground itself. The dirt stairs finally gave way to stone ones, as the air shifted from oppressively hot to mechanically cooled. At least we were above ground now. But my relief evaporated when I heard the chilling voice.

"Ryen of the Haven, you've returned to me," Gideon sang, only a few paces away.

"Give me back my sight," I demanded.

"Of course! I've heard those are very uncomfortable," he said.

The blinder ring was disarmed and taken from my eyes. Everything was excruciatingly bright. Some prisoners reported severe damage to their sight after the ring's use, even permanent blindness. I started to worry that that was the case with me. But my sight finally returned in slow increments. My audience kept silent as I struggled, except for Gideon, who hummed and tapped his foot impatiently.

My surroundings finally came into focus. A mock night sky above, a heavy wooden desk, jeweled planets spinning above my head just out of reach . . .

"Did you have a nice trip?" If the man hadn't spoken in a voice I would know anywhere, I wouldn't have recognized him. For a few seconds, I just stared in disbelief.

Gideon was bone thin, his chalky gray skin peeling away from his face in some places. His once fierce eyes were now red and gaunt. His long hair hung limply, slick with oil. It clung to his face and neck like hungry leeches. He radiated a wild, yet tenuous, excitement.

"You've had me beaten, drugged, blinded, and dragged through the universe. *What do you want from me, Gideon?*" I snarled.

"You! I want you! Oh, it's *good* to see you!" He clutched me in a tight hug, kissing both my cheeks. "I need your angel face. That's it. Would you be so kind as to lend it to me for a few hours?" he asked.

"I *resigned*. You have no claim on me. Let me go!"

"I received no resignation letter. I have no idea what you mean," he said, nearly giggling. His mouth twitched, and he reached up to scratch wildly at the back of his neck. "Lyre, Jory!" He leaned toward two guards. "Did you see a resignation from Ryen?" Both guards shook their heads. One rolled his eyes. "Did anyone here see a resignation?" he shouted, instantaneously enraged. No one dared move. The anger quickly dissipated, melting into maniacal energy once more.

"See? No resignation. You may have sent it to Claire, but you never sent it to *me*. You are still mine, and I have a job for you." He clapped his hands together cheerfully.

"What do you want?" I demanded.

"My plan, the beautiful plan! I have called every important person in Zhimeya together to hear it. I already have the Tribunal on my side, but the rest of them may need some convincing. That's your job. You will testify in front of the world that we must go forward with my plan. Your word will convince young men and women to enlist for service. If I'm taking over Earth, I'll need a little help!"

"And if I don't, you'll kill Savannah?" I guessed. That's what the bad guy did, right? Hold the beautiful girl hostage until the hero gives in.

"Savannah?" He stopped his frenetic pacing, though his body still twitched. "Oh, oh! The human? Your human? Such a strange name. No, I'm afraid she'll die whether you cooperate or not. With her, I thought *theatrics* would be the best way to go." He held his hands above his head, fanning his fingers. "Sometimes the plans in my head are so big, I feel like I'm going to explode!" he yelled at the ceiling, knotting his hands in his hair, pulling it at the roots.

"Sorry," he muttered, letting his hands free of his hair. Some of it fell out and onto the floor. "We were talking about . . ." He paused.

"Savannah," I yelled. *What was wrong with him?*

"Savannah . . . oh, the human. Since she already knew too much, no one would fault me for bringing the human back to keep us all safe. Wouldn't want her ruining the element of surprise!" he said, lost in his own head again. After a few moments, he rejoined us.

"She will stand trial before the Tribunal, a representation of the sins of the human race. She will convince Zhimeya of how necessary the cleansing of Earth is. Then she will meet with Obedience. No one will doubt my plans when they see what it can do!"

"What is Obedience?" I implored.

"Oh, you don't know! The best part. The genius of it! I've kept you in the dark for so long. But now it is time!"

Gideon slipped a silver wand out of his robes and held it to his temple with dusky fingers. "I'm a visionary, but I was never much of a scientist. Every dreamer needs thinkers. Emani and

Dai were the brains behind this brilliance. Explain, dear girl," he cooed like a proud father.

Emani slowly appeared out of the shadowy recesses of room. She stared hard at the polished floor, holding Savannah's backpack to her chest like a shield.

"Speak, Emani," Gideon prodded. When she stayed silent, he crossed the space between them and slapped her. "Speak!" he shrieked. "Tell him all about the weapon. Tell him about Obedience," he said. She shrank away from him but complied.

"The instrument Gideon is holding, Obedience, changes the structure and size of cells in the frontal lobe of the brain. Small tumors start to propagate, impairing judgment. Test subjects become highly suggestible at first—"

"They tell their darkest secrets," Gideon purred. "You wouldn't believe some of the things we have heard from our experimental subjects. Scandals, affairs, debaucheries. But tell him the best part!" He laughed.

"As the tumors grow in size, subjects stop acting of their own will. They become machine-like, repeating anything that is told to them, following any order."

"Dead brains, working bodies—programmable bodies! Just a few choice leaders on Earth, that's all I need. My puppets in motion! Well, at least for a few days, anyway. But Dai is fixing that."

I stared at Emani, begging her with my eyes to explain what was going to happen to Savannah.

"We haven't been able to arrest the tumor growth to keep the subject alive and viable for Gideon's long-term use yet. The tumors grow so quickly, subjects usually die within days," she said while Gideon mumbled behind her, wandering around the room. She took a few steps closer to me and whispered, "But survival outcomes with surgery to remove the tumors and a drug therapy I am working on make me hopeful about reversing the tumor growth—"

"What do you whisper about?" Gideon reprimanded.

"I speak of your greatness, Master," Emani said flatly, stepping away from me. Gideon was immediately mollified.

"So you see, the human—" Gideon started.

"Savannah," I spat.

"*Savannah* will say anything I need her to say. That's also why I don't need your compliance either, Ryen. I'm afraid that if you don't want to help me willingly, I'll have to use Obedience on you as well."

Emani gasped. "You said you wouldn't use it on him! You promised he would be safe!" she cried.

"Out!" Gideon cried. Two guards came from the hallway and took Emani by the arms. She dropped Savannah's backpack as she fought with them. Her curses echoed down the stone hallway outside the door.

"She can be difficult. Brilliant, but difficult," Gideon lamented. "So, here we are. Ryen, I want you to do me this favor so that I can leave your mind intact. I need you to help with the affairs of Earth. I want you at my right hand."

"If you think, for one moment—"

"Just consider it. You will do this, willing or not. Think about your own survival. If you comply, I'll let you go home. Your family and friends are all anxiously awaiting your return. In fact, all of Zhimeya wants you home. Is this really such a big favor to ask?"

I stared at him in disbelief. Something told me his mind was not up to registering facial cues.

"You have a few hours before you need to decide. Until then, good luck in the tunnels!" he sang, buzzing about the room again. Before Jory and Lyre rushed me away, I took one last desperate glance around Gideon's private chambers. I had to get back here. The fate of two worlds depended on it.

Tunnels beneath Tribunal Hall, Savannah's cell

Was that metal ring really necessary? Savannah thought as she rubbed her throbbing eyes. *A nice, conventional bag over the head would have done the trick.*

Her head still ached from the ring, but her sight was returning little by little. Though she was uncomfortably warm, Savannah sat curled up in the corner of a cell dug into the reddish-brown dirt. Three filthy walls and one wall lined with bars held her captive. A strange computerized locking mechanism kept the door shut. All she could see from the twin torches mounted to the wall were a small antechamber outside of her cell and a dark hallway leading away from wherever she was.

A strange animal poked its head out of a freshly dug hole in the dirt wall. The bizarre reptilian creature had a short, scaly black body, a bulbous nose, and no eyes.

No need for eyes down here. It must usually be totally dark.

Since the odd animal skittered quickly back into its hole after sniffing at the air, Savannah decided not to worry about it.

Instead, she looked around at her surroundings that were coming into clearer focus.

They have fire here, she thought wryly as she watched the flames dance toward the clay ceiling, *and dungeons . . . and dragons. All very interesting—in a horrifying sort of way.*

She had tried being scared, since she was completely alone, taken hostage by an alien race. But the fear didn't come—a side effect of the drugs, most likely.

She had also tried to miss Earth, but that feeling hadn't materialized either. But that probably had little to do with the drugs. What had she really left behind? Just her mother's body in a grave. She didn't miss Earth. There was nothing there to miss.

She missed Ryen.

Thinking his name choked the stale air in her lungs. Ryen. The only thing that mattered anymore.

I should have told him that I loved him when I had the chance, she lamented.

When her mother died, Savannah had completely disconnected. Her fondest wish was to be carried away with the wind or dissolved by the rain, to cease to exist. But a funny thing happened when she saw Ryen. She, for the first time in a long time, was there. Present. Attached. Alive.

A hot tear mixed with the sweat that was already falling from her forehead. Her mind called up his features with precision—the ice-blue of his eyes, almost wintry, endless, the depths of which were warmed by the wild, chocolate brown hair that fell into them so often. Artful eyebrows that spoke his every mood better than he could. A strong Romanesque nose. Full lips that were almost too perfect. A squared jaw that suggested fearlessness. Dangerous to the wrong people, protector of the right. Mind of a scientist, face of a destroying angel—a hero sent to save her.

She recalled the moment Ryen had entered into her life at the International airport in Rome.

She'd had enough of Italy, Rome especially. It was too crowded, and her American dollars weren't stretching nearly far enough. She had to leave, though she had no idea where to go. Her feet carried her slowly through the long line leading to the ticket counter, dreading the words the ticket agent would ask . . .

Where are you going?

If only she had an answer for that.

She casually watched people passing by. She envied those who seemed to be in a hurry—people who had a destination, somewhere to be.

She noticed slowly that many heads were turned in the same direction. So she looked too. Then she found the reason for all the staring.

He was truly the most beautiful person she had ever seen. He and an undeniably attractive woman with purple eyes, contact lenses for sure, whisked their way up to the first-class ticket counter, where only three other people waited in front of them. Savannah looked at the man's perfect face carefully, studying the angles and shapes, as if she were about to sketch it. She took the most time watching his eyes, wondering how she would replicate that color blue with paint, if she even could. The longer she stared, the more she realized those beautiful eyes seemed troubled—on edge for sure. As her line moved, she inched closer to the pretty pair, who were arguing quietly.

"For the last time, I didn't come all the way . . . *here* . . . only to miss it. We won't be there long, I promise," the man said.

"Ugh, but it's *so* hot there!" the pretty woman complained. "I was just on weather dot com—"

"Claire, please just do me this favor. Haven't you always been curious about it?" he asked.

"Fine! But listen, Ryen, as soon as the food starts making me sick, we are out of there," she said to . . . Ryen. He had a name. The agent at the first-class ticket counter called the pair forward. She listened as hard as she could to Ryen's voice. It carried easily over the din.

"We'd like the next flight to Tel Aviv," he said. Within seconds, the tickets were printed for them. Ryen and the woman, Claire, still quietly bickering, ambled slowly toward the security checkpoint.

Tel Aviv.

The Middle East.

I can't go to the Middle East.

What the hell was she going to do in the Middle East?

No, that was ridiculous. There was no way she was going to one of the most dangerous areas on Earth to follow a stranger. She didn't care how gorgeous he was or how much she wanted to sketch his perfect features. How stupid was she?

And that's why it had surprised her so much, down to the soles of her old shoes, when the words "Tel Aviv" came out of her mouth without hesitation when the ticket agent asked her where she wanted to go.

She wouldn't take that decision back. Even though it meant she may die here in this cell, she wouldn't change any of it. It was because she had made that decision that even now, trapped in this hole, she could imagine his arms around her. Safety. Happiness. Love. She had finally found someone to love—and he loved her. And *that* was what life was all about.

It was when she thought about everything she had gained in a few short weeks, that she realized how much had been taken away. A tingle of fear started cracking through the drug's haze, sinking its claws deep into her heart.

If Ryen were dead, she would gladly march into the arms of her captors. She had lost too much. No one would expect her to want to stick around after losing everything—twice.

Except that he had told her to fight, to be resourceful. He believed in her strength. *Those were Mom's last words to me*, she thought.

Suddenly, the sweltering heat moved around her, sucked away by some change in air pressure she couldn't see. A cold draft rushed in, cooling the room by twenty degrees at least. It didn't last long. The moldering heat returned, but it brought new sounds with it. Footsteps. A woman's urgent voice, yelling in an unknown tongue. She didn't know the language that was being spoken, but she knew that voice.

Claire!

Claire. Claire. Claire.

Claire finally appeared, pushed by two intimidating guards. One of them unlocked the door's device, opened the bars, and shoved Claire through them so hard, she collided with the back wall. The door clanged shut again resolutely.

"Claire!" Savannah caught her around the middle and squeezed tight. She hadn't seen her since the morning that she had found out what they were. She had called her a monster.

"Oh Savy! You're alive!" Claire hugged Savannah back tightly. "Hold on a minute." She broke Savannah's hold and banged on the bars. "That's no way to treat a lady!" she screamed at the retreating figures in English. "That's right! Run away, cowards!"

Savannah had a million questions to ask, but the first one to pop out of her mouth was, "Why is it so hot down here?"

Claire stared at her. "*That's* your most pressing question? How hard did they hit you?"

"Are you going to answer me?" Savannah pressed. Claire stared at her warily, but she answered anyway.

"This planet is smaller and younger than yours. You don't have to go too far underground to start feeling the heat from the core. Judging by the temperature, we are at least fifty, sixty feet underground—the farthest anyone ever goes. Are you *sure* you are all right?" Claire gathered Savannah's face into her hands, checking for trauma. She was most worried about the black bruises around Savannah's eyes that darkened even as she watched.

"Yes, fine. How long have I been down here?"

"It's been about eight hours since we touched down. Did you talk to anyone? Have you seen anything?"

"No, they took me away from Ryen at the transports and put something over my eyes. It hurt and I couldn't see anything. When they took it off, I was here."

"They used a blinder ring on you?" Claire asked, appalled. That explained the bruises. "That's illegal! Can you see all right now?"

"Yes, it took a while, though."

"I'm sure it did. The ring creates a vacuum that puts enough pressure on your eyes to stop your optic nerve from firing. When we get out of here, you need to see a healer right away to check for nerve damage."

"*When we get out of here*?" Savannah questioned.

"Yes, *when we get out of here*. But I guarantee no one is going to come looking for us in this maze, so we have to find a way out on our own," she said, studying the bars.

"Is Claire your real name?" Savannah interrupted. Claire turned around, watching for signs of delirium.

Claire sighed, still examining the bars. "Yes, my parents wanted me to become a researcher, so they gave me a name that I could use on Earth. Ryen, Mateo, and Chase's parents all did the same thing," she said, feeling the locking mechanism outside the bars with her hands.

"Do you know what happened to Chase and Mateo?"

"No," she said desperately. "I woke up in Dai's quarters. I tried to convince Dai that Gideon needs to be stopped. Boy, was I growling up an incorrect tree," Claire said.

It took Savannah a second to figure out what she was trying to say.

"Oh! You mean, 'barking up the wrong tree.'" Any other time or place, she would have laughed. Not now. "Who's Dai?"

"A Master. Brilliant, power hungry, and dangerous. We grew up together in the same tribe. He asked me out a couple of times, but, like I said, he had some very significant character flaws," she said, dropping her hands from the lock in defeat.

"I'm sure Dai didn't mean for the guards to put me in here with you. They probably got lost in the tunnels and couldn't find another one. So there's some luck!" Claire chirped. Savannah couldn't match her level of enthusiasm. "But they'll be coming to take you to Gideon soon. We need to get out of here."

"There's no way out. I tried digging in the corners. I just ran into rock."

"Then we'll have to find another way," Claire said, rattling the bars.

"I'm sorry I called you a monster, Claire."

"Oh Savy, you had every right to freak out. I would have questioned your sanity if you hadn't," she said.

A cold rush of air cut the heat in the room again. It carried two female voices with it. Claire's eyes lit up.

"Oh! Oshun and Ecko are coming for you. Excellent."

"Who?" Savannah asked exasperated.

"Emani's sisters. This could work, this could actually work," Claire whispered to herself. "Pull your hair back and take out your earrings," she ordered as she pulled out her large chandelier earrings that dripped with amethysts as violet as her eyes. Savannah did as she was told, removing her mother's small opal studs from her own ears.

"What's the plan?" Savannah asked nervously.

"You and I are about to be in . . . I think you'd call it a cat fight . . . and I don't want your earlobes getting ripped off," she whispered.

"I can't do that!" Savannah whispered. "I've just taken self-defense classes. I know how to get away and run for help, that's it!"

"So *defend* yourself until she's unconscious!"

Savannah wanted to roll her eyes, but she kept them trained on the dark hallway, the hair standing up on the back of her neck.

"You take Ecko, the smaller one. When they unlock the door to get you—"

Savannah nodded just as the two women slinked into view on the other side of the bars. Oshun and Ecko pressed themselves against the farthest wall in the antechamber, whispering hotly to each other.

Oshun was tall and lanky, her flame-red hair cropped short and close to her face. Savannah recognized her as Emani's sister because of the flashing onyx eyes. Ecko was short and wiry, with the same enigmatic black eyes.

Savannah thought as she sized up her opponent. She had long, jet black locks, with streaks of neon blue and green throughout—cheap hair extensions from the look of them. Ecko stood rigidly below the torch mounted on the wall, giving Savannah an idea.

"Hello, ladies! What a pleasant surprise!" Claire said pleasantly.

"We are speaking English for the human trash?" Oshun asked.

"I think it's only polite, seeing as she is a guest on our planet."

"You're not supposed to be in here, Claire of the Haven. Who put you in this cell?" Oshun's eyes flashed with frustration at seeing the numbers evened up.

"Two of Gideon's finest, Oshun of the Cailida," Claire said mockingly.

"We have come for the human," Oshun stated, looking only at Claire.

"The human has a name," Savannah snapped.

"The human also has some misplaced courage." Ecko laughed coldly.

"Come and get her then, ladies," Claire's goaded.

Oshun froze in the firelight, vacillating between opening the cell door and running back down the hall for reinforcements. Savannah did the only thing she could think of to keep the sisters there.

"If you don't think you can handle us, by all means, run for help," Savannah said mockingly.

"Gideon sends you to do one small task, but if you feel like bothering him with *every little problem* . . ." Claire added.

The taunting worked. Oshun planted her feet on the ground and reached for the key around her neck.

"We have no specific orders to keep you alive, Claire. I've always disliked you anyway," Oshun said.

"That's only because I'm better than you in every conceivable way," Claire sang. Oshun gritted her teeth, her face turning the same shade of ruby as her hair.

"You'll regret that, Haven," Ecko spat, moving closer to her sister's side. Oshun started to force the key into the lock, but Claire held up her hands.

"Wait. Before we begin, I need to say something." Everyone paused. "I've always thought that you both have terrible taste in men, hair, and, from the looks of it, shoes." Both sisters looked down at their feet, and then back up, infuriated. "There! Feels good to tell the truth!" Claire sighed in relief.

With a wild growl, Oshun shoved the key into the locking device. The door popped open and swung wide on its rusty hinge. No one moved.

The eerie silence was broken when Claire sprang through the air, landing on Oshun and knocking her backwards. Neither Savannah nor Ecko had moved yet, watching the other two wrestle. Oshun caught a fistful of Claire's hair and yanked hard. But Claire, obviously a veteran, expertly reached up and jerked two of Oshun's earrings straight through her right earlobe. Oshun let out piercing howl, soaked in her own blood.

Ecko tried to run to her sister's aid, but Savannah lunged at her, knocking her sideways. She elbowed Ecko in the nose and stepped away to avoid the fountain of blood she knew from experience would result. Ecko swung her fists, trying to connect with Savannah, but missed. Savannah caught one of her flailing hands by the wrist and heaved Ecko into the dirt wall.

Get her over to the fire, Savannah thought, recalling with perfect clarity a day in high school when a stupid, inattentive boy had lit a cigarette too close to a stupid, inattentive girl with bad hair extensions, and the ensuing fiery disaster.

Ecko lunged for Savannah again, this time catching her around the waist and pinning her arms to her sides. Savannah did what was most instinctive, throwing a knee into her attacker's groin. Nothing happened.

Would have worked on a man, she thought with chagrin.

Though Ecko didn't fall to the ground, she loosened her hold. Savannah used the break to push Ecko back onto the wall. She aimed a precise kick into the side of Ecko's left knee. They both heard the sickening pop as her knee gave way. This time, Ecko dropped. Savannah caught her before she hit the ground and shoved her toward the torches on the wall. Ecko fought back, but with her knee broken, her feet couldn't find purchase on the ground.

Savannah shoved with all of her might, connecting the ends of Ecko's fake hair to the fire. The caustic smell of burning hair, real and synthetic, was only overshadowed by Ecko's shrieks. Ecko threw her shirt up around her head, trying to smother the flames. Savannah cocked her arm back and punched Ecko in the jaw. Ecko hit the floor without another sound. Savannah mercifully stomped out the flames that burned closer and closer to Ecko's scalp.

Savannah had no time to revel in her victory, though. A second later, Claire's body sailed through the air. She hit the cell bars with a loud clang and fell to the floor. Both Savannah and Oshun ran to their wounded partners.

Savannah checked Claire's pulse—it was still strong, but she was out cold. She turned to face Oshun, who was missing most of one of her earlobes and large chunks of hair. She had deep fingernail scratches on her face and arms—tell-tale battle wounds of a cat fight, indeed.

Oshun rose to her feet, seething. She towered over Savannah, panting in rage. Savannah was up against the bars, unable to move. She couldn't reach the hallway, and even if she did, she couldn't leave Claire alone. There was no more running.

"It will be my personal pleasure to grind your species into dust," she said.

"I take it you've never been to the Deep South. Where I'm from, you wouldn't last two minutes in a room full of angry rednecks." Savannah smiled devilishly.

Oshun growled and barreled toward Savannah like a freight train. Savannah spiraled out of her way at the very last second, catching Oshun's back and throwing her into the bars. Oshun hit them, face first, and sank to the ground, unconscious.

For a minute, Savannah didn't move. The room was as silent as it had been when she was alone. Only Claire stirring in the corner broke Savannah's trance. She rushed over but Claire waved her off.

"Did you finish up for me?"

"I guess I did," Savannah said incredulously, looking at the two women she had bested.

"Ryen was right. You *are* some kind of superhero," Claire marveled. "Get them into the cell, quick." Claire stood gingerly and helped Savannah drag the sisters into the cell.

"Goodbye, ladies!" Claire called over her shoulder as she and Savannah started down the dark hallway.

27

Right, 100 paces, left, 87 paces, 36 stairs, left, quick right, 84 stairs, left, 300 paces, left, 104 stairs, right, 220 stairs . . .

I rehearsed the directions as I stalked back and forth like a lion in a cage. They had blinded me again on the way to the cell I was now trapped in, but I kept meticulous track of every turn, every stair I descended. I had to get back to Gideon's quarters.

My hands ached from pulling at the bars and beating at the red walls. Though it was no use, I backed up and threw my shoulder into the bars again. It trembled but didn't budge.

Another part of my head was furiously trying to match Gideon's strange behavior to any I had seen before. At first, I came up with nothing except maybe schizophrenia or some sort of mania, though I had only read about those conditions in books. His behavior was somehow strangely familiar, like I had seen it before.

If I could only place it . . .

Tugging at the corners of my mind was a memory. Italy. Nearly translucent young men and women stumbling out of nightclubs in the early hours of the morning. Twitching, dead-eyed, erratic—*high*.

Was Gideon . . . high?

That possibility actually fit. Emani could be supplying him with some concoction of drugs that had rotted away his brain.

Her specialty, I thought angrily.

Whatever was causing the behavior, the most pressing problem was this: how do you bargain with a madman when you have nothing to bargain with?

Bargaining was out. Escape was the only option.

My friends, Savannah, they could be anywhere. For all I knew, they could be . . . I slammed my shoulder into the bars again with renewed force. Still nothing. I yelled out in frustration at the four walls that penned me.

"There's no way out. Please stop hurting yourself," Emani whispered from the darkness.

"What are you doing here? Have you come to torture me further?" I yelled. "Then come! Unlock the door and let's see who walks away," I challenged fiercely.

"I came to talk," she said quietly.

I let out a strangled howl, my hands gripping the bars so tightly, the metal reverberated. She wisely took a few steps back.

"You came to talk?" I shouted. "You want to talk?"

She nodded, bravely stepped closer to the bars, and put her hands over my clenched fists.

"Just listen to me," she said plaintively. I grabbed her by the wrists and yanked her arms through the slats in the bars. I didn't stop until her head thudded hard against the metal. I dropped her wrists and wound my hands around the back of her neck, pushing her windpipe against a rusty bar. She gagged as her air was cut off. I expected her to fight back, but she didn't. She let her arms dangle helplessly at her sides, infuriating me even more.

I needed a fight.

"I should kill you for what you have done!" I roared.

"I wish you would," she croaked.

I dropped my hands as though she had electrocuted me. She collapsed onto the floor in a heap, gasping. The rust had stained her alabaster skin an ugly red. Bruises were already starting to bloom on her neck.

I, too, fell to my knees. My anger was spent. I had absolutely nothing left. "Why did you come, Emani?"

"Gideon means what he says. He'll take your mind from you if you don't cooperate. You need to live. I need you to live."

"Then get me out of here!"

"I can't. Dai told Gideon I couldn't be trusted with the key to your cell because you were too much of a temptation for me. You have to do what they say, Ryen," she begged.

"No, there's got to be another way."

"His plan will go on with or without you . . . intact."

"*There's got to be another way!* You know his plans. Help me! You could save *billions* of lives! You said you wanted to be better!" I implored. She just gave a bitter laugh.

"It's too late for me. I'm damned no matter what I do. I've stolen, I've lied, I've taken life."

"What is that supposed to mean?" I spat, suspecting more mind games.

"I was there when Adan died. I helped Dai kill him," she said gravely, watching my reaction with tortured eyes. "He haunts me. Even now I can feel him watching me."

It was reported that Adan had died of old age in his bedroom. Emani couldn't have been involved—Adan had been like a father to her.

"You're lying and it's sick," I said angrily, hoping to call her bluff. But she continued.

"I'm a fallen angel. That's what you called me when you left. Do you remember?"

"We don't have time for this, Emani! Please! You need to get me out of here!"

"What happened to us, Ryen?" She stared right at me without actually seeing. "Why did you leave me?"

"Why are you doing this to me?" I cried.

"I need the truth."

"None of this matters now! Whole worlds are in danger!" I yelled, shaking her shoulders.

"Please," she begged. "I just need to know."

In her present state, maybe giving her what she wanted was my only shot out of here. I inhaled the dead, acrid air, trying to calm myself.

"I was so attracted to you," I said quietly. "You were wild and beautiful, full of life. Everyone wanted you. I *wanted* you. And I couldn't believe my luck when you finally chose me." I flew with my thoughts back to a time when all I wanted was this girl, now broken and trembling in front of me. "It was amazing at first. Just to be close to *you*. To watch the world move for you."

"But you left," she whispered, a fragile vulnerability spreading thickly across her face. I had only seen that look once before—when I left her. I took her hands into mine. They felt so small.

"I left because—we weren't right together," I hedged.

"Speak the truth, Ryen," she spat, pulling her hands out from mine. "The same thing that pulled you to me was the same thing that drove you away. I'm not *good*."

"That's not true—"

"I'm not like you. There's something . . . fundamentally *wrong* with me. There always has been. I chose you because I thought you could save me."

"I *tried*," I said almost angrily.

"But when you saw that I was beyond saving, you walked away."

Under her wild beauty lay an ocean of extremes I couldn't cure. At times, she was nothing but manic, frenetic energy, but she would always come crashing down from her shaky high, becoming distant, unreachable. She couldn't keep her drug use a secret from me for long, either. The games she played made me jealous and hostile. I hated what I became when I was with her.

"I shouldn't have left without getting you help. I failed you," I said.

"After you left, I went straight to Gideon and offered myself up. He had taken an interest in me before we graduated from the Institute. I knew he wasn't a good man but I didn't care. He made all my decisions and gave me a purpose. He's used my name, my face, and my mind to further his plans. He owns me. There's nothing I can do now."

"You always have a choice."

"Choice?" she laughed coldly. "What *choice* do any of us really have when corruption and temptation can make even the very best of us sell their souls so freely?"

"What do you mean '*the very best of us*?'" It was a title reserved for and applied only to the sacred Tribunal members, the incorruptible—the very best of our kind.

"One by one, almost every Tribunal member has fallen, selling their vote to Gideon," she said.

"The Tribunal is incorruptible," I stated flatly. It was one truth I believed in with my whole heart. The Tribunal could not be bought.

"They have fallen. Nothing is sacred, and no one is incorruptible," she said.

"What could Gideon have bribed them with that would make them deny their sacred duty?"

"When Gideon takes over, each Tribunal member has been promised a piece of Earth. I don't know if Gideon will actually follow through on his promises. He may just kill them. But on the other hand," she said to herself, "he's kept such strict records of every piece of land he traded away—"

"He kept records of the bribes? Proof? I need those records! They would show Zhimeya what Gideon has done. No one would believe the Tribunal members can be corrupted! But if there is proof . . . Where are these records?" I asked frantically.

"None of this matters, Ryen. Gideon will come for you soon. There is nothing that we can do." She sank farther into the floor and leaned her head on the bars.

"Em," I begged, using the nickname I'd given her when we were children. She picked up her head when I said it. "Please listen. Don't give up now. You need to do for me what I didn't do for you. I need you to save me."

She stared at me, profound pain in her eyes.

"Please," I pleaded, "save me."

Our gaze held. Her desperate onyx eyes changed slowly. The hopelessness that had been there started to melt away.

"Do you think . . . there is forgiveness for someone like me?" she whispered tentatively.

"Of course, Em. Of course there is."

"Can *you* forgive me?"

"I already have," I said simply. Her features radiated with a new expression, one that I had never seen her wear before—hope.

"Then I *will* save you, Ryen," she said.

A cold laugh echoed from somewhere down the hewn hallway. "What a ridiculous conversation. I'm surprised you two didn't last longer together, both so stupid and naive." Dai stepped out from the shadows, a pompous smirk swathed across his face. "I was wondering what you were doing down here, Emani."

"How did you find me?" Emani asked warily. "How do you always know where I am?"

"I have a better question, darling. Why would you throw your loyalty away to a man behind bars? Loyalty should always be given to the man with the power; you and I both know that."

Emani pushed herself off the floor and held her arms out defensively.

"I'm done, Dai. I'm done with the destruction and the lies. Let Ryen out."

"I've been patient with you," Dai seethed. "You've been helpful, which is why you are still alive. But your usefulness seems to have come to an end." He pulled out a dull blade with a button on its hilt. I recognized the strange weapon. It was same kind of blade Emani had threatened Savannah with. He clicked the button and the short metal blade turned a pulsating white. I had to shield my eyes from its glow at first. It heated the room to an insane degree.

"Do you have your fire blade?" Dai asked.

"You told Gideon to take it from me, Dai," Emani spat.

"That's right, because he doesn't trust you either. For a fool, sometimes he makes a smart decision."

"Don't move," I whispered in Emani's ear. I reached into my back pocket, remembering the knife Savannah had left on my hotel room floor in Mexico.

"Dai, give me the key. Gideon is deranged. We have to stop him before this goes too far." Emani pulled away from me, out of reach of the weapon I was trying to secretly give her. She was completely unarmed.

"Too far? He'll go just far enough, and I'll eliminate him too. He's only one pill or puff away from death anyway, thanks to you. Now, I'm late for more important things, so let's get on with this." He lunged toward Emani, making a deft arc with the blade. She spun away just in time.

"Dai, let me out, and the two of us can settle this! Leave her alone!" I yelled, trying to distract him. He didn't even acknowledge my presence.

"What do you think is going to happen here, Emani?" He stalked toward her as she scrambled to the opposite wall. "You are unarmed and backed into a corner," he sneered. "Hopeless." He swung the blade again, getting it close enough that the skin on her arm bubbled from the heat. She screeched in pain.

"Dai!" I shouted, desperately trying to grab at him through the bars.

"Helpless." He swung for her again, slicing into her back when she maneuvered away a split second too late. The smell of burning flesh filled the air again.

"Useless," he said coldly.

Emani screamed and bravely flew at him, hitting Dai squarely in the face. He recovered too quickly and, though I couldn't see it, I heard the horrible squish the blade made as it entered her abdomen. Her whole ribcage lit up while the blade was inside her.

Dai clicked the blade off and pulled it roughly out of her. He pushed Emani to the floor, his chest and arms shining wetly, covered in her blood. His face twisted in disgust as he dried his hands on his pants.

"Just look at me, disgusting!" Dai said angrily, not even giving a backwards glance at either of us as he stomped down the black hall.

I stood, frozen, seconds stalling out like separate eternities. Emani's blood ran toward my feet, the smell of it mixing with the sickening scent of seared flesh. Her eyes stared straight up at the ceiling, unblinking. I fell to my knees and reached for her hand. At my touch, she gasped and rolled to her side to face me.

"Emani!" I exclaimed in relief. "You have to get out of here! Get to a healer, go!"

Her ebony eyes were wide, but there was no fear there. She shoved her other hand into mine, pushing a key into my palm.

"Dai always keeps his key around his neck," she said with a small smile. She must have grabbed it when she hit him.

I pushed off the floor and fit the missing piece into the locking mechanism. The door chirped and sprung open easily. I swept down to pick Emani off the floor, but she cried out in agony when I tried to lift her. I eased her down to the floor again and held her tight.

"Em, stay with me. Let me get you out of here." I tried lifting her again.

"Please stop. It hurts," she begged.

I felt along her side until I found the canister of salve she had used to seal Savannah's wounds shut. I pushed the punctured skin on her abdomen together and tried to seal the wound shut with the leftover salve. The skin stayed closed for a few seconds and then disintegrated. Her wounds were too severe, even for a healer.

Since her eyes had never left mine as I worked to save her, she read my horror when I realized she was beyond help.

"Tell me you love me, Ryen," she said calmly.

"Please let me get you out of here. Maybe we still have time," I stammered.

"No, I want to stay here with you. Just tell me what I want to hear, even if it isn't true," she said steadily. I wanted to scream at her, to tell her to fight. But she only had minutes left.

"I love you, Emani," I said solemnly. I was stunned to find that, as the words formed, it wasn't a lie. She was my first love. That kind of tie left a mark deeper than I ever let myself realize. And now she was saving my life by sacrificing her own. I loved her with all of my heart.

She watched me carefully as I realized the truth of what I had said. She smiled radiantly in return.

"Now, let me finish saving you," she said quietly. She pulled the waist of her skirt down to expose her jutting hip bone. There was a strange circular burn mark there—she'd been branded. The mark was of two worlds colliding.

"The traitors on the Tribunal will carry this mark on their bodies. It's Gideon's mark. Gideon's weapon—Obedience. I've been working on an antidote in my lab, but I didn't have the time to—" She gasped in pain and coughed, blood now trickling from her mouth. I caressed her face and held her tight.

"The map, the proof, is in Gideon's quarters. Earth is the key," she whispered. She let go of her stomach and put her arms around my neck.

"I love you, Ryen. Go save the world," she whispered, still smiling.

I started begging, pleading with her to stay. I promised her everything I could think of to entice her wounds to heal, to force the blood back into her body. But she wouldn't listen. She was already gone.

The world should have ended with Emani's last breath.

I wished it would.

But it didn't.

I considered crying, yelling, cursing, even running as fast as I could away from the gruesome scene.

But instead, I stayed.

And even though she was gone, I whispered to her of the faith I had in a merciful God—a God who would see the sacrifice she had just made, who would forgive her and welcome her home.

I closed her eyes softly with careful fingers.

"Goodbye, Emani of the Cailida, my savior."

I kissed her cooling lips and laid her down with care on the warm ground.

28

It was nearly impossible to leave her there all alone, but I had no other choice. If I failed, Emani's sacrifice would mean nothing. Only that truth propelled me off the floor and into the darkness.

I paced carefully down the hall, counting steps in my head. My legs ached to run, but I'd be hopelessly lost in the underground labyrinth if I didn't follow the same path out that I did coming. I tried to be careful, but I may as well have still been wearing a blinder ring. The halls were pitch black.

Earth is the key. Emani's last words. Savannah's mother's last words. I puzzled over the possible meaning as I scrambled through the maze.

I spread out my arms, trailing a hand along each side of the tight hallway, trying to find the correct passages to turn down. Within minutes, I was completely lost, with no idea where to turn next.

I leaned my back on the opposing wall, staring into the black, trying to decide what to do. As my head connected with the wall, faint vibrations came from the other side. I turned my ear to the wall, pressing against it hungrily.

"Okay, fine. If you don't want to play hangman, what *do you* want to play?" asked a gruff voice.

"I'm just saying, playing hangman is a little off-putting because of our present situation, as we may actually very soon *be* hanged men," said another.

Chase and Mateo.

Chase and Mateo were on the other side of this wall. They were alive.

I stumbled down the hallway, listening to the voices growing louder.

"How about we play the 'anywhere but here' game?" Mateo suggested.

"How do you play?" asked an exasperated Nik.

It took me a second to realize that all three voices were speaking in English and not their native tongue. It meant that they were being guarded. None of the three would voluntarily speak English if they didn't have to, especially Nik, who had only spent hours on Earth, picking up or dropping off researchers.

"Just tell us where you would rather be other than here. That's why it's called the 'anywhere but here' game," Mateo answered.

"Does 'anyplace, anywhere, anytime, with anyone else' count?" Nik quipped.

"I'll go first," Chase said. Their voices were definitely getting louder now. I was headed in the right direction.

"Hmm, I would rather be . . ." Chase thought.

"Besides *anywhere* else?" Nik supplied.

"I'd rather be in Ha'apai, Tonga on a deserted beach with . . ." Chase faltered, refusing to say Claire's name. He must not know whether or not she was okay. They were all silent for a moment, probably giving Chase time to recover. This frustrated me, since I needed them to talk so I could follow their voices.

"Mateo, your turn," Nik said quietly.

"I'd rather be . . . Oh! In Chichen Itza with Marguerite. Or in Akumal with Maria, or Dalia or—"

"Point taken," Nik said dryly.

I finally found the pathway that led to their cell. There was a faint glow coming from the end of the hall where torches lit the room. A dark figure reclined against the wall, not paying particular attention to the men, probably because he couldn't understand them. I crept forward and waited in the smallest shaft of light possible. If they were paying attention, the boys would see me before the guard did. I stood silently not moving at first, trying to catch their wandering eyes.

"Don't look now. Pretend our lives depend on it, because they do actually. Someone's come to spring us," Mateo said as nonchalantly as he could manage. I held up Savannah's knife to show that it was all I had as a weapon.

"We have to find our fearless leader a weapon other than that *freaking penknife* he brought with him. Is that the best you could do?" Mateo asked, trying not to modulate his voice. I just shrugged.

"There is a burned-out torch above your head, Mateo. If you reached out of the bars, do you think you could grab it and throw it into the hall?" Chase asked casually. Mateo lazily turned his head in a wide circle. He saw the torch.

"Yep, I can get it," he said with a yawn. "I'll throw it into the hallway, then you come in swinging," Mateo said facing Nik but talking to me.

"Well, here goes nothing," Mateo said. He slowly got off the floor, pretending to stretch. The guard's eyes still hadn't moved from the ceiling. Fast as lightning, Mateo's arm flashed out of the space between the bars. He grabbed the torch from its bracket on the wall and threw it into the passage, where I caught it. The guard snapped to attention and turned to the men. Mateo pointed toward the hall. The guard turned just in time to receive a solid blow to the head. He hit the ground with a resounding thud.

"That was awesome!" Mateo laughed and rattled the bars.

"Good to see a friendly face down here!" Chase said appreciatively but then gasped as I came closer. I looked down at my chest to see what everyone was staring at. I was completely covered in blood.

"It's not my blood. It's Emani's," I explained, trying not to dredge up the memory of her grisly death as I stared at the evidence staining my skin. "Dai killed her. She got me out right before—" I couldn't say any more.

"Well," Nik said, breaking the silence first. "If you don't have a key, you may as well turn around and leave."

"I do have a key. Emani *died* to get me this key." For a second, I felt like leaving Nik locked in the cell.

"I'm just hoping it fits all the locks down here," I said, pulling the metal piece out of my pocket. "Here we go," I said hopefully as I tried to fit the key into the black key box that covered the old rusted lock. We heard the blessed mechanical chirp and pop of the lock as the door swung open. I was caught in a vise-tight hug by the brothers. Nik nodded his head in appreciation.

"Drag him in there and shut the door," I ordered. The brothers took the arms of the heavyset guard and hauled him into the small cell.

"Wait, take his shirt at least. You really look awful," Chase said. He and Mateo stripped the shirt off the guard and tossed it at me.

I reticently removed it and donned the new one. I didn't want to take off my stained shirt, as a symbol of the sacrifice that had saved me. I still had her blood on my jeans, which, strange as it sounds, made me feel better. I could carry a part of her to the end.

"There it is," I said, as I looked at the guard's bare back. "The Master's mark. Emani had the same brand on her. She said all traitors will have it on them somewhere." They all started asking questions at the same time. "I'll tell you everything, but first tell me what's happened to you three."

"Not much to tell. We both woke up on the transport with Oshun and Ecko. Claire and Emani's beds were already empty. We were brought straight down here and locked up," Mateo said. Chase bit back a growl.

"I was forced off the transport and marched unceremoniously down here like a criminal. Since Gideon knows we are friends, he wouldn't let me leave," Nik said.

"I figured as much," I said apologetically.

"Your turn, Ryen. What do you know?" Chase asked. I explained about Gideon, his plan for Savannah and me, and Emani's last moments when she had told me about a map and Gideon's mark.

"The map must be in his private quarters. I've been there, but I now have no idea how to get back," I said.

"That shouldn't be a problem. The three of us put up such a fight that they couldn't take us too far into the tunnels. We are just a few turns from the main passageway I think," Chase said.

"That's a relief," I said, giving my brain permission to forget the memorized steps and turns that had done me no good, anyway.

"We need to split up. I have to get to Gideon's quarters, and I need you to go find people who will stand with us. Tell anyone you trust about the bribery, the map, the mark, all of it. Gideon is taking Savannah before the Tribunal soon. Bring everyone you can to Tribunal Hall. I'll be there with the proof."

"I'm coming with you," Mateo and Chase said at the same time.

"Mateo, I need you to go talk to the Haven elders and convince them of what is going on," I explained. Mateo started to argue. "You can't ask Chase to leave here without Claire. He needs to come with me so we can find her." He gave up and nodded. "Nik—"

"I told you I would alert as many as I could about what I have heard and seen. I'll go with Mateo," he said.

"Then let's get out of here," I said. "And be careful of the cameras. Once we leave this ancient dungeon, they'll be everywhere."

Mateo clapped Chase on the back. They nodded at each other—their goodbye. Mateo grabbed a torch off the wall, and I grabbed the other. We headed down the hopefully deserted passageway.

Claire and Savannah tripped through the darkness that was barely brightened by the light shining from Claire's watch face that Savannah held in front of them. Claire examined her left shoulder with her right hand, feeling for a possible dislocation.

"Setting Ecko's hair on fire—no one saw that coming," Claire said, trying to distract herself from the mounting pain in her shoulder.

"It was easier than fighting with her," Savannah said, trying not to remember the altercation. She still carried the nauseating smell of burning hair and flesh on her.

"And really, she deserved it. Those extensions were criminal. They needed to be put out of their misery." They both laughed weakly, one in too much pain and the other too scared to laugh with any feeling.

"Claire, do you know where you're going?" Savannah didn't want to ask, but they had been jogging along for quite some time, sometimes turning around and going back the way they had come.

"I'm trying to head upwards. It's getting cooler."

"I'll take your word for it," Savannah said. She was just as hot and exhausted as she had been in the cramped cell.

"Claire, tell me about Zhimeya."

"Do you need a distraction?" Claire guessed.

"More than you know," she answered.

"The best way to describe it is that it is much less extreme than what you are used to."

"What do you mean?"

"Well, because it is smaller than Earth, most of Zhimeya has the same type of weather—warm and mild most of the time. Only the highest mountains at the most extreme poles get any kind of snow. Because the weather is so uniform everywhere you go, there aren't as many different species of plants and animals. Earth is all extremes—weather, terrain, flora, fauna, even humans. It's not like that here.

"That's why our people have been able to live so peaceably for thousands of years. We live in close-knit tribes—communities instead of countries. We've always had very similar religions and languages too. Religion is a large part of our world, as well.

"Of course, lately, that has all changed. Everything is in upheaval," Claire explained. Savannah walked along quietly, trying to picture a whole new world existing just above her head.

"Earth has been coveted since its discovery. You come from a place that is not only full of beautiful and mysterious things but most likely carried our savior."

"Ryen told me that Gideon claims he wants to protect Earth and to let your people worship there too."

"Yeah, right," Claire said sarcastically. "Gideon has always been a megalomaniac. I assume he wants the planet for himself."

"How can one person take over a whole planet? Almost every country on Earth has a standing army. It would be impossible!"

"Gideon must have something that would give him the upper hand. A weapon, maybe? I don't know. Before we left for Earth, he was trying to drum up support for an invasion, though he wouldn't call it that. Surprisingly, many Tribunal members agreed with him. And that is really all it would take, a vote from the Tribunal to start preparations for war. Their tribes would abide by their decision."

"They'd just follow blindly? What makes a Tribunal vote so powerful?"

"It's the most sacred of honors to become a Tribunal member. Only the most infallible men or women are elected. They represent the very best of us, or they are supposed to. Gideon has obviously found a way to corrupt the incorruptible. No one would believe it—a corrupt Tribunal! It's never happened before."

"No one will stand up against a Tribunal vote?"

"There has never been a need. But when it comes to something of this magnitude, I would greatly hope that not everyone would go along peacefully."

They were silent again, hurrying along passageways. Before long, Savannah needed to hear Claire's voice again. It was a comforting sound.

"So let's say we do find our way out of our present situation. What will happen to me?" Savannah asked tentatively.

"Let's not talk about it right now, Savy. I don't want to give you anything more to worry about," Claire hedged.

"I want to know, Claire."

Claire sighed.

"As the laws stand now, you wouldn't be allowed into any tribal society. First, you are human. I assume most people would be afraid of you. Second, you are what we call Unnamed. At birth, we are claimed by a tribe and marked. Since you have not been claimed by a tribe, you would be exiled with all the criminals of our world who have had their tribal name revoked and lost their marks."

"You're right. That was one more thing I didn't need to worry about," Savannah agreed.

"Things will work out; I know they will," Claire said resolutely. Savannah had no choice but to believe in Claire's conviction.

"You know, your talents would be in very high demand here. You could teach art in any university. Zhimeya has never made much time for art and music. The ancients painted and composed, but for the last few thousand years, we have focused solely on scientific pursuits. Now that I have been to Earth, I feel like we have wasted a lot of our time. I have seen some beautiful things there."

"Me too," Savannah said, feeling her first pangs of homesickness.

"Would that be something you would like to do? Teach us art and teach us about your world?"

"Yes, I would." Savannah almost laughed at the idea of her standing in front of an alien race as a teacher instead of a prisoner.

"Good. We will survive this, a tribe will claim you, and we will all live happily ever—" Claire paused and then thrust Savannah back into the dirt wall with her good arm. "Quiet!" Claire whispered.

They both stood silently and listened to heavy footsteps coming from behind them. A dim light appeared at the end of the long passage they were pressed against.

"Run!" Claire whispered again and shot into the darkness. Savannah followed as fast as she could. They ran into the black, their footsteps too loud against the earthen floor. Even though Savannah's whole body felt feverishly hot from running, she could tell that the air around her was cooling. They must be near the surface.

A set of metal stairs finally materialized ahead of them, which led them up to a door. Savannah felt a gleeful surge of relief, which vanished when she saw Claire debating on whether to push through the door that was now in front of them. With the footsteps drawing closer, Claire shook her head and pushed it open.

It was almost too cold in the white marble hallway. The lights were too bright and harsh. They were too exposed. For one wild second, Savannah wanted to run back into the dark tunnels and hide among the recesses. But Claire shut the door, and it almost vanished into the wall—there was no handle on this side.

Claire stood frozen looking up and down the deserted hall. "This way, I guess," she decided.

They ran down the curving marble hallways which ended at a hopelessly locked door.

"Come on," Claire said, pulling Savannah back the way they came. They ran the length of the hallway again, but it wasn't empty anymore. Both women stopped dead. A tall, handsome man covered in wet, shining blood blocked the hallway. Savannah stared transfixed at the empty black space where one of his eyes should have been. He pressed a finger to his earpiece.

"Found them," he said. Claire placed herself in front of Savannah and stared down the frightening man.

"Dai," Claire said.

"Claire," he smiled back.

"English please."

"As you wish," he said with a heavy accent Savannah had a hard time understanding. "I was just looking for you. The guards put you in the wrong cell, and I was on my way to put you in the right one. We are all working very hard today. Mistakes are bound to happen."

"Of course," Claire said sarcastically.

"But it turned out for the best. I happened upon a fascinating conversation. Emani and Ryen were together plotting against Gideon."

"Whose blood is that?" Claire whispered urgently. Savannah felt her hand fly to her heart, which was threatening to stop beating.

"All you need to know is that it isn't mine," Dai said simply.

"Whose blood is that?" Claire screamed. Dai's face twisted into a cold sneer.

"You wouldn't *dare* hurt Ryen. He's too valuable to Gideon!" Claire said in disbelief. "Tell me whose blood that is *now*!"

"You are in no position to be giving me orders, Claire," Dai said dismissively. Two of Gideon's guard came running down the opposite end of the great hallway. They were the same two that had brought Claire to Savannah's cell.

"Take them to Gideon's quarters. Do you understand? No more mistakes!" Dai barked. Savannah couldn't understand him anymore. He was speaking in a strange tongue that sounded almost silky, like music but with a hard edge.

If that's Ryen's blood, if he's gone, I have nothing left, Savannah thought numbly as she was pushed along. If Ryen were gone, she wouldn't fear a death sentence. Death would allow her to be with her mother and Ryen soon.

30

The heavy carved doors opened slowly, and the women were pushed into a large, circular room. Light streamed in from the oculus at the top of the black mosaic ceiling and from the picture window. In the middle of the stone floor was a gaping hole with stairs that led down into darkness.

Savannah watched transfixed as Dai stripped the blood-soaked clothing off of his leonine body, exchanging it for long, red robes. There were no wounds on his chest, no marks whatsoever. He had told the truth. It wasn't Dai's blood that stained the clothing.

"Gideon," Claire breathed. Savannah snapped out of her stupor and followed Claire's eyes. A dead, possibly decaying body was laid out on a metal gurney under large brilliant lights that hovered in the air. Two other bodies were laid out on similar metal beds on either side of Gideon. Tubes full of blue blood led from their arms into Gideon's.

"Zen, Larkin!" Claire whispered in silent horror, tears slithering down her cheeks. "My friends!" Savannah gripped Claire's arm tightly to keep her from running to them.

A young man with ocean-blue hair and concentric circles painted on his skin stood at the top of Gideon's bed with a basin of water, washing his limp hair. A young woman with similar markings flitted about massaging his dusky hands and feet. As she rubbed, the color returned to his fingers and toes.

Two more women dressed long steel gray cowl-necked robes monitored Gideon's every move while whispering to each other. Their heads were shaved, and strange plant-like tattoos adorned their scalps. They wore metal gloves, which controlled the movement of the hovering lights that spun and refocused with every movement of their hands.

"Healers, Lais and Tien," Claire whispered. They were the most alien creatures Savannah had seen yet.

Lais turned away momentarily, and Savannah saw that the healer's back was completely bare, except for an intricate lattice of flowered vine tattoos that crawled up her back and neck and onto her head, where the flowers blossomed. The other healer, Tien, had what looked like a trunk of an oak tree running the span of her naked back with a few thin branches tattooed across the nape of her neck.

Gideon looked like he was being resurrected from the dead. Color slowly returned to his pale white face just as the color left the faces of the blood donors. Zen and Larkin's bodies started to shiver, their breathing becoming more labored. Moments later, Zen wheezed violently and breathed no more. Larkin followed soon after. Healer Lais looked like she was going to be sick, but healer Tien unapologetically covered each man's face completely with a white sheet. She rolled their beds into a small closet and shut the door.

Gideon took a deep breath and sat up gingerly. He rolled his neck, stretched his bony arms, and pushed off a thin blanket that clung to his body. The pair who had washed him scurried over with robes and dressed him. His eyes finally fell on Savannah and Claire, huddled together.

"Who are these pretty strangers who stand before me?" he wondered.

"Seriously?" Claire stammered. One of the guards slapped her across the face.

"Answer the Master," the guard said.

"Gideon, it's me—Claire," she said, baffled.

"Of the Haven tribe?"

"Yes," Claire said nervously.

"Is it time for our lessons?"

"I graduated from the Institute five years ago," Claire's said, her confusion and alarm growing.

"You have been away? Have you been looking after my kingdom?" he asked serenely, sitting back down on his bed.

"Kingdom? I have been on Earth with Ryen, where you sent me," Claire said cautiously. A light fluttered behind Gideon's dead eyes.

"Oh *yes*. Forgive me," he said softly. "Time slips away so quickly. And who are you?" He pointed to Savannah with some effort. Savannah stood silently, not understanding the strange, musical language he spoke. "Why doesn't she answer?" he questioned.

"She is human, Gideon," Claire explained.

"Oh, Ryen's human! The sacrifice. I ask for your forgiveness, little one, for what will happen tonight. It's for a greater good."

"She doesn't understand you!" Claire yelled. The guard hit her injured shoulder. She sagged under the blow.

Gideon's tranquil air vanished as his head wheeled around wildly.

"Healer Lais, I need it!"

Lais cringed and then ran to Gideon's side and handed him a vial of white powder. His body convulsed as he emptied the contents under his tongue.

"More!" he yelled, smashing the glass vial on the stone floor. "More!"

"Master," Lais appealed, "your body cannot handle more. You took too much just an hour ago. We had to replace all of your poisoned blood. We were barely able to save you, and there is no more clean blood for us to use."

"Your blood is clean. I'll use yours," Gideon yelled.

"Please, you could die," she stated.

Gideon howled, pulled one of the hovering lights out of the air, and smashed it on the floor. He upturned his bed and threw it at one of the book-lined walls. The gilt globes suspended from the roof shook on their wire hangings. Healer Tien ran to Gideon's side with another vial of white powder. Lais shook her head furiously, but Tien handed it to Gideon anyway. He emptied the contents under his tongue again. Gideon's wild and furious energy dissolved immediately into an eerie calm once again. He threw his head back and exhaled loudly.

"Healer Tien, you will be rewarded," he exclaimed, this time in English. Savannah didn't dare make eye contact with the crazy man, but instead kept her eyes on the healers' intricately tattooed backs. Gideon followed her gaze.

"Your head must be full of questions. Do you know anything about this new world you are so very temporarily living in?" Gideon asked condescendingly. Savannah didn't say a word.

"We are a spiritual people, a ceremonial people. We observe ancient rituals and rites. At birth we are all marked and accepted into our respective tribes. Some tribes mark with paint, but others make more permanent marks. Lais, Tien, come." They fluttered to his side. He turned them both, their marked backs toward Savannah.

"These two healers are of the Abran tribe. You see, when children of the Abran decide to become healers, they choose their favorite medicinal plant and use it as their mark." Gideon pulled the waist of Tien's robe down a few inches, exposing a mass of twisted roots inked on the lowest part of her back. "The first permanent mark each healer gets is the root system of their chosen plant. It represents the base of knowledge the healer receives in youth. As he or she graduates from various levels of training, the root system is added to, and the plant 'grows,'" he said, running his finger up Tien's spine. "Only the most accomplished healers are allowed to have their heads marked to show that they have reached the pinnacle of their practice. They are not allowed to cover their backs at any time, so that everyone knows what level healer they are should someone need help. It's beautiful, these ancient practices," Gideon mused. With the new stolen blood coursing through his veins, he looked like a completely different person than he did ten minutes ago, when Savannah could have sworn he was a corpse.

Claire was staring fixedly over his shoulder to the closet where the dead bodies had been wheeled. Gideon followed her gaze.

"Ah, Zen and Larkin. Failed experiments. Don't worry, they have been brain dead for a while, so they felt nothing. I've been keeping them alive down there in case I needed them," Gideon said, motioning to the hole in the floor. "And their sacrifice brought us so much closer to perfecting Obedience," Gideon said proudly. "Did you know them, Claire?"

"Yes," she muttered angrily. But Gideon wasn't listening. He was searching the room frenetically again.

"Emani should be here by now. Dai, where is she?"

"I don't know," Dai lied. "I am sure she is lost in the tunnels. There will be time to find her later."

"I want her *now!*" Gideon whined.

Dai sighed and touched his earpiece. "Emani, you are wanted in Gideon's quarters." He waited a few seconds. "She is just down the hall. I'll bring her in."

Dai exited briefly and came back in with Emani walking in front of him. Savannah bristled at the sight of the dangerous woman who seemed to float by her. As she walked through a shadowy corner, Savannah could have sworn Emani's skin glowed.

"Emani," Gideon said, "I am sorry I was so rude before. The closer Ryen gets, the more I worry about your loyalty. But let's not let his presence interrupt everything we have worked so hard for."

"Yes, Master," Emani said.

"Please go to Tribunal Hall and oversee the arrival of our guests. Give Dai updates as he needs them."

"Yes, Master," Emani repeated.

She turned and started walking while Dai stared after her with unbroken concentration. Savannah watched Emani's every movement carefully. Something wasn't right. She slid her foot deftly into Emani's path. Emani passed right through her. She wasn't real. It was the same way Savannah had seen her when Emani had materialized out of Ryen's computer. Savannah raised her head and was met by Dai's cold smile. He held one finger up to his mouth as he passed by her, walking Emani out. He came back alone and stood by Gideon's side.

"Ah Dai, what would I do without you?" Gideon cooed. Dai gave him a patronizing smile but said nothing.

"Now tell me of Ryen. Is he still safe?"

Dai gritted his teeth. He wanted to keep Claire and Savannah operating under the assumption that Ryen was dead.

It seemed to have broken them. But Gideon would be furious if anything were to come of Ryen.

"Yes, Ryen is safe," he said reluctantly.

The air started flowing back into Savannah's numb chest. Her blood raced, and so did her mind. If Ryen were alive, that changed everything. She would fight now. She had to stay alive, just like he asked.

"Has he changed his mind? I should very much like to keep him in one piece."

"No, Master. He will need Obedience."

"Well, it's his head," Gideon said, disappointed. "But there is still time. I won't give up on him, yet."

"Gideon, we should just use the human as leverage. He would do anything to keep her safe. We would get more use out of him that way."

"And ruin what I have planned? I brought the human here expressly for the show, and I am *not* going to change my mind just to force Ryen's hand. The human is the most integral part of the performance, Dai!"

"*If* she plays along," Dai whispered to himself. "She's already seen too much." But Gideon wasn't listening.

"So now, dear friends, it is time to depart. Claire, I don't remember calling you here. Dai, take her back to the tunnels," he said.

"There are too many people in the halls now, Gideon. Her face is too well-known. We risk being caught if someone recognizes her."

"Well, why did you bring her here?"

"She *escaped*," he said.

"Really?" Gideon asked enthusiastically. "Claire, you must tell me your secret!"

"It wasn't hard. You have surrounded yourself with idiots that are easily outsmarted," Claire said, steeled for another blow from the guard. Gideon just laughed.

"I cannot be upset at your assessment, Claire. You speak the truth. What is that saying? 'Good help is hard to find?'" he said merrily, waving his hand dismissively at the members of his entourage.

"What would you have me do with Claire, Gideon? Would you like her dispatched?" Dai asked with a pleasant smile, though insurrection burned in his single gleaming eye.

Gideon mulled it over thoughtfully for a few minutes. "No," he finally decided. "We may still need her. She's famous too. If Ryen doesn't survive Obedience, we can try it on her. Put her down in the hole with Aurik."

"*Aurik?*" Claire and Savannah whispered together. Savannah knew that name—the missing Head of the Tribunal, the most important man in this world.

The guards swept Claire up and descended the stairs into the hole while she struggled and screamed. Savannah could do nothing more than watch helplessly. But this was the last time she'd be quiet.

"Savannah," Gideon said, smoothing his robes, "Dai is going to take you to the Tribunal now. You will be standing trial for the sins of your world. Your only job is to take direction and to die. Any questions?" he asked politely.

"Just one. Who would you rather have kill you tonight—Ryen or me?" Savannah demanded. The fear in her heart had been replaced with ferocity. Gideon glided close to her, wound his hand into her hair and yanked viciously, bringing her face up to his.

"Human filth," he whispered, his foul breath washing over her face. "Ryen loves me. He is loyal to me. I am his master!" Savannah stared back at the man fiercely. She heard the doubt in his voice.

"If that is truly the case, then it will have to be me," she vowed. Gideon threw Savannah to the floor and kicked her in the stomach, knocking the breath out of her.

"Gather up the garbage and get her to the hall. The faster she dies, the better," he said as he walked out. She tried to scream at him, but no sound came out.

Dai picked her up off the ground and gingerly set her on her feet.

"I *will* kill that man," she said furiously. Dai chuckled but measured her resolve. She meant what she said.

"Maybe you will get the chance. It all really depends on how long you live after Obedience. If you make it long enough, maybe you can be of some use to me," he mused. "And in that case, I'll need to know where you are. Jory? Lyre?" he called.

Two men strode forward. They took Savannah's arms and pinned her against the wall. She tried to fight but still couldn't manage a full breath. Dai slipped his arms around her waist and pulled her into him. He bent his head and slowly breathed in the scent of her. "If it were up to me, I'd keep you for myself. You look like you would be quite a conquest," he whispered, his hands moving along her hips. "But Gideon is so dead set on tonight's spectacle; we'll just see how things play out."

He freed one hand and slipped a chain off from around his neck. His thumb stroked the raised pattern on the medallion's surface. "Two worlds, one ruler." He pulled Savannah's shirt up just enough to expose her stomach and pressed the brand into her skin. The searing pain of the burn almost dragged her into unconsciousness, but she fought hard against it.

When he finally let her go, she looked down to see the charred burn left on her skin. She swung at Dai, who moved out of her way just in time. "Don't be angry with me, darling. If that is the worst thing that happens to you tonight, consider yourself very lucky."

31

I listened carefully at the door that led out of the horrific maze of underground tunnels as feet scuttled past. When the hall was silent, I pushed it open. The white marble hallway was empty.

"Good luck," I said to Mateo and Nik, who both pushed past me and disappeared around the corner at a sprint.

"Any idea where we go from here? I was blind the last time I came through these halls," I said.

"I think I can make it back to Gideon's quarters," Chase said. He ran down the hall at top speed with me on his heels. We dashed through the dizzying halls, twisting and turning and finally coming to a stop in front of large, ornately carved double doors. I tried the handle, but it was locked fast.

I cursed in frustration, pounding my fists on the door. Light footsteps sounded on the other side. We both tensed as the door opened.

"Ryen!" she said in utter shock. She pulled us both inside and shut the door.

"Lais? What are you doing here?" I asked, just as shocked as she was. She had attended the Masters Institute with me for a few years before deciding to become a healer instead of a researcher. She was probably the best young healer in Zhimeya.

"Gideon threatened to kill my family if I didn't help him. I've seen what he is capable of," she said, dissolving into tears.

"I've seen what he can do to those who don't obey!" She threw her arms around my neck. I hugged her tightly as she cried inconsolably into my shoulder. "So much death and destruction! I wish he would just kill me already! He's going to kill us all anyway, except Tien. She gives him anything he wants!"

"Tien is here?" I knew the woman but not well. She was also one of the brightest young healers Zhimeya had.

"Yes, but she is allowed to leave when she wants while I am stuck in this room for the rest of my short life!" she cried. "And look what Dai's done to me!" She yanked aside the fabric covering her shoulder. It was Gideon's mark—two worlds colliding.

"It hurts," she said, scratching at the raw, blistered skin. "Nothing makes it stop hurting." I traced the shape with my finger.

"Lais, I'm looking for a map . . . I think. Have you seen Gideon carrying one?"

"No, but it might be down there with Aurik."

"Aurik is . . . *here*?" Chase gaped.

"Yes, he's here, but not for long. It's only because of me that he's still alive at all. I've been lying to Gideon, telling him Aurik is too sick for Obedience, that he would die instantly if Gideon tried it on him—" she murmured, unable to finish her sentence. "I am a more advanced healer than Tien, so he believed me. But I don't think he will listen much longer, which means Aurik is going to die soon too!"

"Lais, please. *Where is Aurik*?" I pleaded.

"Here!" she said, stamping her foot on the mosaic floor. "The floor opens up, but I don't know how. He's down there, and so is Claire of the Haven. Her shoulder is broken but no one would let me fix it," she said miserably.

"Claire is here? She is alive?" Chase yelled.

"Yes, for now," she whimpered.

"Shut up!" he snapped. We all stood silently. There was a faint sound coming from the floor. Two voices, yelling for help.

"Claire!" he yelled. He flew into action, tearing the room apart, searching for something that would open the floor.

"Lais, have you seen anyone else? A . . . human?" I asked, readying myself for the worst.

"Yes, I've seen the human. She had a strange name— Savannah. They've taken her to the Tribunal to be put to death," she said.

"No, no. That's *not* going to happen," I said frantically. I followed Chase, pulling books down, looking through the opulent desk for some sort of way to open up the floor.

The seconds flew by. Almost every book that had lined the endless shelves was now heaped onto the floor. I had ripped the tapestry curtains down. The desk was now empty. I had gone to open a small closet, but Lais warned me not to. She had already searched it during her long hours locked in Gideon's quarters.

There was nothing left to look through.

"I don't have time for this!" I yelled in frustration, turning the desk completely on its side. "Savannah doesn't have any time left!"

"You can't go without that map Ryen. It would be your word against his, and he has the Tribunal on his side. You'll die," Chase reasoned.

"I don't have a choice," I said. I ran to the door and grabbed the handle.

But something kept pulling me back to the middle of the room.

The answer was here, waiting for me.

I let go of the handle, walked to the middle of the room, and fell to my knees.

"Please, help me!" I cried toward heaven, raising my eyes to the glittering ceiling above me, appealing to the two women who had brought me here. Chase and Lais looked on nervously.

And as I gazed upwards, it all came flooding back.

A mosaic night sky, glittering silver stars, and jeweled planets floated through the air on wires above me. All the planets spun gracefully in their orbits, except for one. One orb swung softly from side to side, as if it had been recently nudged off balance. I jumped off the floor to look closer at the one gilt planet that didn't move like the rest.

It was Earth.

"Earth is the key . . . The key is in there!" I dragged Gideon's heavy chair under the orb spinning off balance and lifted it off of its hook. The globe easily split in half in my hands. Inside the empty halves was a small computerized chip, the kind found inside voice-activated locking devices.

"It wants a password," I said, finally looking at the faces who were staring at me in wonder.

"It could be anything!" Chase stormed.

"I *know* the password," I said. "Just stand back."

Lais took Chase's hand and pulled him away from the center of the room. When they were safely out of the way, I closed my eyes and brought the device close to my mouth.

"Earth is the key," I whispered.

The silence of the room was shattered by whirring and grinding gears. The small tiles on the floor rearranged and stacked on top of each other, gathering away from the middle of the floor. As the resulting hole got larger, books and papers that had littered the floor fell in and disappeared. A set of stairs materialized. Even before the floor was done melting away, Chase bolted down the stairs, with Lais not far behind.

"Claire!" I heard him yell.

"Chase! You kept me waiting long enough!" she called back.

I made it down the stairs just in time to see them embrace through the cell bars.

"Aurik," I said reverently, falling to one knee in front of him.

"Ryen of the Haven." He reached his wrinkled hand out of the bars to call us forward. "My rescuer has no reason to kneel. In fact, I always found that practice rather patronizing. Stand that I may see you. It's been so long!" He grasped me by the shoulders and looked at me steadily. "You have grown!"

"Aurik, there is a human here—" I began.

"Peace, Ryen. Claire has told me about . . . well . . ."

"Everything," Claire supplied.

"She's been good company for this lonely old man." He laughed. Claire laughed easily with him.

"See? He *likes* my chattiness, unlike some people," she said in answer to my nervous glare. "He said he wants to meet Savannah!"

"A courageous woman indeed. I should like to meet her very much," he said.

"Aurik, I am looking for something. A map, evidence of Gideon's bribery of the Tribunal. Zhimeya will not believe a Tribunal could be corrupted without evidence," I said.

"Could that be what you are looking for, Son?" He pointed over my shoulder toward the back wall. A heavy roll of parchment rested inside a hewn niche in the earthen wall. I strode over to and unrolled it.

"Yes, this is it!" I said, my eyes roving over a picture of Earth with familiar Tribunal member names penned inside each country. "I have to go. Chase, can you get them out?"

"This is just an old rusty lock. I can break it. It may take a while though."

"Aurik, I am going to Tribunal Hall with the evidence. Come as soon as you are free to testify with me. I can't wait any longer," I said.

"Wait! Take my mark! With it, *you* will be Head of the Tribunal," he said. "Hold out your right arm." He scratched at the red earth wall and came away with a handful of dirt. "Water!" he cried. Lais poured water into his hands from a bucket in the corner. He mixed the two together into a thin paste and started painting. "I trust that when this is over, you will give the office back over to me," he said.

"You have my word, Aurik. Just please hurry," I said, trying to mask my impatience. Watching his finger trace the complicated lines was like magic. Every line represented a tribe. He spoke each tribal name as he wove all the lines together into a circle.

When he was finished, he pressed his thumb print in the middle.

"Go. My blessing goes with you!" he called. I was already running up the stairs.

I made it to the door and cracked it open. There were guards and cameras everywhere. I'd never make it through the corridors. There had to be some other way.

The window.

I ran to the beautiful picture window and looked out over the thick forest outside. It would be a much longer run, but I stood less of a chance of running into an enemy outside. I measured the fall, pushed the window open, and jumped.

I never hit the ground. My fall was broken by a transport nestled into the trees, its mirrored surface blending in perfectly with its surroundings. I slid off its roof and tried the handle, but it was locked tight. As I tried the other handles, I saw through the small window that the transport was packed full of tools, raw materials, and food, and sitting on the pilot's seat was Savannah's backpack. I wanted so badly to break the window open to get her possessions back, but it would take too much time. I gave up on that idea and ran at top speed toward Tribunal Hall, praying I was not already too late.

32

Tribunal Hall

The power. It was better than all of Emani's chemical creations. It was better than . . . anything. There he stood, at the crossroads of history, ready to change the fate of two worlds. The sheer excitement of it made his already thrumming heart beat a little faster.

After years of splitting this peaceful planet apart into factions, it was time to stitch them back together again. He would bring Zhimeya together, force them to move as one entity again. They would unite against a common enemy. He'd worked hard to instill fear and hatred of humans into the hearts of his people. Hatred would unite them.

He had the human. He had the audience. He had the Tribunal in his hands. The stage was set. The greatest performance of his life was about to begin.

He faced the small wooden door that would allow him to stand before the world. He pushed it open and stepped into the blinding white light of Tribunal Hall.

The Tribunal was already gathered in their tiered seats, looking down at the podium where he would stand. He glided forward, bowing graciously to his co-conspirators. The few who had held strong to the old ways watched him warily. Their days would come to an end quickly.

Gideon turned away from his bought Tribunal to look at the masses seated on the floor of the hall. Every important dignitary, every holy man and woman, every lawmaker—they were all accounted for. Every voice that mattered in Zhimeya was here. More people were gathered outside, watching the historic proceedings.

At the podium, he waited for the ripple of voices to quiet. He gripped the edges of it so that he wouldn't be able to scratch the skin on the back of his neck where he had been branded. No mistakes.

"Brothers and sisters," he called out.

The silence was immediate.

"A new age is dawning. The time of division is at an end. We, as one united voice, will do better than our predecessors. We will rise together, daring to dream courageously and to follow those dreams with decisive action." The well-rehearsed words tumbled out of his mouth like perfectly timed music. "We have a mission to fulfill. God himself compels us forward!"

It's going well, he thought, looking out at the faces that had been lulled into his trance.

"The Tribunal has asked me here to share our plan for the future. My vision of tomorrow is a glorious one. After years of waiting, watching, and silent study, the proud, noble race of Zhimeya is ready," Gideon exclaimed, his words gaining momentum.

"This is *our* time. The time when our noble race takes what is rightfully ours. Earth." He nodded at Dai, who stood silently by the door Gideon had entered. Dai spoke the codes into the device he held in his palm. At his direction, the massive skylights in the grand ceiling closed, plunging the massive hall into darkness, except for the holy fire that still burned brightly. The guards surrounding the cauldron produced a thick fabric and stretched it over the cauldron's mouth. Many in the audience balked but were too stunned to stop the guards from extinguishing the fire that had burned continuously for hundreds of years.

Dai started the projection sequence by speaking a few more codes. A holographic depiction of Earth appeared over the heads of the crowd. It spun silently in its orbit. All faces reverently turned toward the ceiling to watch the sacred planet move.

"This is the place. The birthplace of The Light, our savior. A planet rich with beauty and wonder, the likes of which we can't imagine." As Gideon spoke, the pixels that made up the silent planet burst in the air like fireworks. They rained down on the audience and slithered toward each other, coalescing into different shapes all around them. Beautiful holographic streams filled with jumping trout ran through the aisles of the hall. Butterflies flitted, and eagles soared overhead. Some even reached out their hands trying to touch the strange animals.

On the north end of the hall, a bank of mountains rose up, capped with a blanket of pristine snow. The south wall melted into a rainforest where parrots squawked, monkeys swung from the trees, and jaguars slinked through the undergrowth. The hologram projected onto the back wall became an elegant city skyline with a billion lights twinkling from the windows. The audience sat transfixed by the mesmerizing sights and sounds.

"I haven't shown you a thousandth of the wonders Earth holds. But this most wondrous and sacred planet is controlled by a wild and bloodthirsty species. They steal, lie, kill. They have perpetrated atrocities on their own kind that we cannot imagine." The tranquil landscapes shattered into millions of shimmering pixels again. Each one that hit the ground morphed into something horrifying. Soldiers with guns in hand ran through the crowd like grotesque ghosts. Human women and children knelt in the walkways begging for their lives. Bodies of the dead who hadn't been spared littered the floor. The once peaceful landscapes changed into bombed out buildings, mass graves, and war-torn wastelands. The audience shrieked and cried, forgetting momentarily the images were not real.

"They have had two, what they call, *world* wars and are constantly on the brink of a third. Hatred and fear are the definition of the human existence. This wicked species cannot be retrained or saved. They are past feeling. The time of man is over."

The scenes of famine, death, and pestilence melted slowly back into scenes of Earth's natural beauty once more. The bodies were replaced by running deer in green forests, the wasteland replaced by ocean tide pools teeming with life. The chaos in the room subsided.

"Our duty is clear," he said, as the skylights retracted, letting in the brilliant light once again. "We must protect Earth from this evil race before they destroy what is left of it. It is time for our people to take it, to save it, to heal it. It is our divine responsibility," Gideon said solemnly. For a long time, no one dared break the silence.

Each mind was choosing a side.

"This . . . is . . . suicide!" yelled a man covered in swirling red and gold paint strokes that made him look like he was on fire; the distinct markings of the Zel tribe.

"Blayz of the Zel. *So good to see you*," Gideon said acerbically, gripping the podium tighter. He longed to strangle the man where he stood.

"You have just shown us the extent of the horrors humans levy upon their own people. How much more violent will they be when faced with an alien species?" Blayz yelled. A chorus of agreement swelled around him.

"You speak nothing but the truth, Blayz. I would *never* lead my people into such danger," Gideon said, his voice full of concern. "But what if I could guarantee a *bloodless* revolution? What would you say then?" he asked. Blayz, intrigued, sat down.

"The Masters' sole purpose has always been the pursuit of technological advancement that would bring us closer to The Light. In that same vein, I have a tool that will ensure very little life will be lost during our transition into power. Dai, bring the human!"

Savannah was dragged through the door to the platform where Gideon stood. Her clothes were ripped and stained with blood and the red dirt of the underground tunnels. She screamed and fought as the guards brought her to Gideon's side.

The crowd broke into a pulsating roar. Many left their seats to get a closer look at her. All were asking the same question.

"Yes, brothers and sisters. A human. A real, live human. It wears no tribal marks. It is not one of us. It is the product of a corrupt society, a wild animal. Keep your distance, for your own safety," he cautioned.

The crowd settled back into their seats in the hall. Every eye was trained on Savannah's smallest movements.

They look like children watching a caged lion, she thought in disbelief, staring into a sea of painted faces and costumed bodies. *Are they afraid of me?* To confirm her suspicions, she kicked out at a corner of the crowd, all of whom either scattered or shielded themselves defensively.

"I would like to demonstrate the technology of which I spoke. It is truly revolutionary." Gideon stepped away from the podium toward Savannah.

"Keep quiet, keep still. It won't hurt for long," Gideon whispered to her in her own tongue as he glided closer.

"You think I'm going to keep quiet?" Savannah seethed as she kicked the shins of the guard holding her right arm. He howled in pain. Gideon just smirked.

"Dai, go to the podium. Tell them she is threatening to kill us all," Gideon whispered. Dai rolled his one eye but did as he was told.

"You are here to stand trial for the atrocities of humankind. You are here to show the corrupt nature of your race, and you are doing a very good job of it. You prove why my people deserve Earth, where our savior lived and died by your hand."

"An event that took place over two thousand years ago. I am no guiltier of that than you are," she yelled.

"Don't translate that," Gideon said to Dai.

"Gideon, she knows too much. Just use Obedience," Dai said quietly in English. Savannah knew her time was almost gone. She had to do something to warn the people about this man.

"Gideon killed Zen and Larkin!" she shouted as loudly as her parched throat would let her.

Gideon's face turned a pale gray. He struck Savannah so hard, her knees buckled and blood poured from her mouth. The murmuring in the crowd grew as Dai failed to translate the fight between the human and the Master.

"Dai, what is the human is saying?" Blayz demanded from the floor.

"The human is screaming obscenities and making false accusations," Dai announced calmly.

"She said Zen and Larkin's names!" A woman from the Ayala tribe called out. "What does she know about them?"

Savannah heard the woman speak Zen and Larkin's names. "Yes! Zen! Larkin! Gideon killed them!" she said, still struggling against the guards' hands. "Aurik! He has Aurik!"

The moment Aurik's name left her lips, the gathered crowd became incensed. Gideon struck her again. She sagged to the floor but got back up on her feet as fast as she could. Chaos was starting to break out on the floor of the hall.

"Does anyone understand me?" she cried.

Savannah searched the room and saw her—a young woman, not much younger than herself. She had chocolate brown hair that curled closely around her delicate face. Her piercing eyes were icy blue, almost as light as . . . *Ryen's*. Those strikingly familiar eyes were full of understanding and great alarm. The young woman whispered urgently to an older couple decorated with brilliant blue markings sitting next to her. The older man in turn whispered into a wrist-mounted device.

"He has Ryen, Claire, Mateo, and Chase of the Haven too!"

The young woman nodded, but Savannah didn't risk looking straight at her for too long, not wanting to give her away to Gideon.

Gideon clamped his hands down on Savannah's throat, making speech impossible. He didn't let up until her lungs burned with the lack of oxygen.

"Brothers and sisters," Gideon yelled, "this is the human race. They are violent, uncivilized liars. This monster has found out just enough about our people to cause a panic among us. Do not be swayed by its tricks! I have with me the remedy!" Gideon produced the instrument from inside his robes. The small device glinted in the bright light of the hall.

"*This* is how we cure the sacred planet," Gideon said, unable to mask his own excitement. Dai left the podium and stood behind Savannah, holding her head in place.

"This is my creation. I call it Obedience. I will show you why." Gideon touched Obedience lightly to Savannah's temple.

Click. Click.

The scene before her swam. A concentrated point of light flooded through her consciousness. It burned bright, growing in heat and intensity. She was burning from the inside out—a funerary pyre inside her own head. The mounting agony completely overtook her.

She saw death on the horizon; a quiet, peaceful place. But she was soundly stuck, wavering between this place and the next. If only she could push her way over the dividing line. She commanded her body to let go, to find the relief death would surely bring. Ryen would forgive her for leaving this life to end the unimaginable torture.

And then, the torture did end. There was no pain. There was nothing. Blissful nothingness. She waited patiently for a voice in the void. When she finally heard it, she knew she must obey.

"Savannah, tell me the *truth*." The man's velvet voice was pure pleasure to her razed mind. Of course she would tell him the truth. She would give him anything he wanted.

"My mother is dead," she heard herself answer, distantly aware of the shimmery sound of a Zhimeyan tongue translating her words.

"Good. Tell me *more* of your truth."

"Aliens exist," she stated. She heard the man's laughter. She smiled at the sound.

"What else can you tell me?"

"I think I will die soon."

"Yes, that is also true. Keep talking. Show my people what Obedience can do. There is no secret you can keep. Won't you tell me what else you know?"

"Gideon killed Zen and Larkin. I think he will kill Ryen." The translating stopped abruptly and hands were clamped over her mouth. She registered anger in the face of the man in front of her and felt shame for upsetting him.

"Dai, keep her quiet." The man to whom she was confiding her secrets walked away to the podium. She wanted to follow him, to make him happy again.

"Brothers and sisters, you can no doubt see the great change that has come upon the human. It is docile, happy to help. No secret can be kept by a mind that has been touched by Obedience." He held the device into the air. "Not only will the human tell you anything, but they will take direction." Gideon turned back toward Savannah.

"Tell everyone your name."

"Savannah."

"That is not your name. Your name is Human. You are nothing."

"I am nothing," she repeated.

"You see?" he asked the congregation eagerly. "A living, breathing, programmable being, completely incapable of violence. Imagine with me the possibilities! Presidents and kings giving their power to us without a fight!" Gideon crowed.

The Tribunal nodded in approval, as did many in the audience.

"Your bloodless revolution!" he shouted, holding Obedience high over his head to the shouts of many on the floor. "The Tribunal has asked me here today, not only to tell you of my grand vision for our future but to fulfill a heavy role. Zhimeya needs a new leader, one who will lead our glorious race in taking back Earth from the villain." He paused dramatically. "The Tribunal has informed me that I am Tribunal's choice—" As he spoke, a dull roar from outside the thick walls reached his ears.

Chanting.

They are chanting my name! Gideon mused.

But he listened a second longer. The crowds outside *were* chanting, but it didn't sound like his name at all. It sounded like—

No. It couldn't be. He's down in the tunnels! Gideon thought. He spoke faster to say the words that would cement him as leader before—

"Brothers and sisters!" he screamed. Everyone was staring at the grand golden door at the back of Tribunal Hall, from where the shouting was coming.

"I humbly accept this position!" he screeched. No one heard.

The heavy golden doors at the back of Tribunal Hall were being forced open, letting in a sea of screaming sound.

33

A group of Fauris women recognized me first as I emerged from the forest. They gasped and yelled out my name, alerting everyone in the vicinity. Chaos broke out before my eyes, and people rushed toward me like a tidal wave. I would never make it to the entrance in time.

With no other option, I threw my arm into the air to show Aurik's mark. The crush of bodies stopped in their tracks and fell to their knees. The mob slowly split in two, allowing me to pass. I wore the mark. For however short a period of time, I was leader of the Tribunal.

A swarm of tiny floating cameras descended from the sky, surrounding me. For the first time ever, I was grateful for them. The towering walls of Tribunal Hall no longer broadcast what was going on inside. I was now splashed across the massive screens. I watched myself running through the crowd chased by the cameras, my arm still held high, showing the mark.

I ran forward as quickly as the crowd would allow, carving a path through the masses gathered on the immaculate lawns up to the imposing gilded doors. That's when the chanting started. It was quiet at first, just one voice calling my tribal name—Haven. Another voice joined, and another. The sound assaulted the white marble walls of Tribunal Hall.

Twenty-five guards stood at the golden doors of Tribunal Hall. More armed men were stationed above my head in levitating watchtowers. The captain of the guard, Ruel, ran toward me. He had been a guard at the Institute for years.

"Ruel!" I said, clapping him on the shoulder.

"You wear the mark of the Leader?" he asked warily, holding his hand out for my arm. I let Ruel examine the mark. He produced a tiny scanner and set it over Aurik's thumbprint in the middle. It chirped twice, confirming the mark's authenticity. "Aurik lives?" he asked hopefully, measuring my reaction.

"He lives and will be here shortly. He lent me his mark to stop what is happening inside. As leader of the Tribunal, I must ask you to let me by. Let Chase and Mateo of the Haven through, as well as anyone they bring," I commanded.

"As you wish," Ruel said. He barked orders at the guards to open the doors. The guards standing at attention didn't budge.

"I said, open the door," he yelled again. The steely line of men made no move.

"So, you stand with Gideon?" Ruel guessed. "You too, Osahar?" he asked one guard in particular.

"We are on strict orders from *our* leader not to let anyone in," Osahar said.

"*He's* your leader!" Ruel yelled, pointing at the mark on my arm.

Osahar didn't move.

"Traitor!" I screeched, the anger, fear, and ferocity inside reaching a breaking point. I ran toward Osahar and buried my fist into his jaw. He hit the ground with a resounding thud. Ruel grabbed me by the shoulder.

"Talk to your people, Ryen. Use your power," he encouraged, turning me toward the masses.

"Aurik is alive!" I yelled at the swarm of cameras. "He has given me his mark so I can stop Gideon from seizing power unjustly. Who will help me tear down these doors and stop the insurrection inside?"

Within seconds, an army materialized out of the masses. Warriors from the Takeo tribe, each towering well over seven feet tall and dressed in shining body armor, came forward. Soldiers from the Tal tribe rode forward on the backs of Uja, oily black serpents with thousands of spindly legs trained to track and kill on command. As my numbers grew, the guards defending the door faltered, broke rank, and ran into the crowd.

"Cowards!" Ruel yelled after them.

The Tal tribesmen sent their Uja after those who ran. They slithered quickly and silently away. The traitors' screams echoed off the walls as the Uja caught up with them.

Ruel ran to the doors' locking device and spoke the password. The doors didn't move.

"The password has been changed. It will take me a while to reset," Ruel said apologetically.

"I'm out of time," I said, motioning my army forward.

"These doors were made to be impenetrable, Ryen."

"We just need to force them open enough for me to get inside. You can work on disabling the password for everyone else after I'm in."

My little army took their place at the doors and started pushing with all their might. The two gilded doors shuttered and creaked in protest but finally started giving up by inches. When the opening was just wide enough, I dove inside. The doors slammed closed angrily, sealing me inside Tribunal Hall.

The hall was deathly silent. I knew almost every face staring at me. Every powerful person in Zhimeya was present.

"Liar! Traitor! Murderer! I yelled, running down the middle aisle. Gideon stood clutching the podium with both hands—shocked, irate, and twitching. He waved his guards forward. They surrounded me, making it impossible to get any closer to the platform where he stood. Each of the guards looked nervously at the mark on my arm.

"Ryen of the Haven! You are home! We rejoice at your safety," he said with false excitement. Still no one in the audience dared to move or speak.

"Gideon, call off your guard. I am Head of the Tribunal." I held my arm in the air. The audience gasped. Those closest to me fell to their knees, causing a ripple effect through the assembly, everyone bowing before the mark.

"Oh dear boy, what have you done? How *dare* you perpetrate such a forgery on our brothers and sisters," he chided. "That counterfeit mark gives you no power. The Tribunal has named me their leader."

"The whole world is watching, Gideon. Your lies can't stand much longer," I challenged. "Aurik is alive. Gideon had him kidnapped and held hostage." I now addressed the crowd. "When I found him, he drew his mark on me, lending me his power until comes. Gideon has had any Tribunal member that has dared to oppose him killed."

"Escort this man out immediately," Gideon said coolly.

"Don't touch me!" I yelled, but Gideon's guards advanced and drew their weapons. Through their closing ranks, I found Savannah on the podium, leaning unsteadily in Dai's arms.

"Savannah!" I yelled out. She gave no response, as though she hadn't even heard me. She stared straight at Gideon, smiling slightly. The light in her eyes was gone. "Gideon, what did you do to her?"

"Brothers and sisters, get off your knees in front of this imposter." The men and women on the edges of the hall stood, but those closest to me, who could see the mark clearly, stayed bowed.

"This man speaks to you of religion, of a peaceful and glorious revolution. He lies! I have proof of his corruption!" I unfolded the map I had been holding in my left hand and held it up for the world to see. "This is a map of Earth. The names written on it are Tribunal members who have betrayed us. They have given Gideon their vote in return for control over a portion of that planet. This Tribunal has been corrupted!" There was uproar from both inside and outside the walls.

"Gideon means to rule you, to subject both humans and Zhimeyans to his will. Follow Gideon and you will be made his slave."

"You have been very busy *boy*, Ryen. Faking sacred marks and concocting stories," he yelled over the din. "You are the only traitor here. Only days ago, he drafted a resignation letter, giving up his birthright as a citizen of Zhimeya to stay on Earth. He has sided with the enemy. He came back only to bring down our society from the inside. Guards, bring him to me!" he screeched.

The men pounced and dragged me onto the podium. Through the mounting chaos and confusion on the hall floor, I hadn't taken my eyes off Savannah. Something was terribly wrong with her.

"Dai!" Gideon demanded.

Dai handed Savannah over to more guards that were surrounding the podium and approached Gideon. Gideon whispered at him hotly.

"Have her open the door. He needs to look perfect. No mistakes!"

Dai nodded and strode over to the small side door that led onto the podium. When he opened it, the shock of what I saw almost killed me.

Emani, alive and well, stood at the edge of the open side door. She helped a small hooded figure walk through the entry. Then the door slammed shut. The only explanation I could fathom was that I was dangerously close to a mental breakdown, to see the dead walking.

Dai followed close behind the small, hobbling figure, staring with fixed concentration. When they had made it to the center of the platform, the figure took off his hood and faced the audience. It was Aurik. Everyone stopped their shouting and dropped to their knees.

"Our beloved leader!" Gideon shouted happily. He bowed shallowly.

"Aurik," I called out, "please help me!" Aurik only gave me a cold, dismissive glance.

"My beloved Zhimeya," Aurik called out, "I was kidnapped by the Unnamed and held captive. In exchange for my freedom, they demanded I step down as Head of the Tribunal, and I have agreed to their terms. Gideon, you have my blessing as the new leader." Aurik bent low on one knee before Gideon.

"I've watched these proceedings on my way here and am deeply saddened," he said, turning to face me. "Ryen of the Haven, you seek to bring down this peaceable government and to install yourself as leader? These are sins that cannot be forgiven. As my last act as Head of the Tribunal, I wish to see this man pay for his blasphemy."

"Aurik, what's happened to you?" I screamed. Aurik's mocking eyes only grazed over me dismissively.

"Members of the Tribunal, I call you together for one last vote under my rule. This voice of treason must be silenced. I sentence you, Ryen of the Haven, to death. Who on the Tribunal will stand with me?"

More chaos had broken out again on the floor. Guards came flooding in from every side entrance trying to subdue the audience. The walls shook from the noise both inside and out. Guards fought with those who were trying to climb onto the podium to rescue me. Others called gleefully for my death. Gideon and Aurik, with Dai standing behind them, stood facing the Tribunal, staring them down. One by one, almost every Tribunal member stood, casting their vote for my death.

"It is decided!" Gideon cried out.

"Wash him clean of the forgery he wears," Aurik commanded. I fought as hard as I could, but there were too many of them. One of the guards pulled out my forearm, spit on Aurik's mark, and wiped it clean. Nothing protected me now.

"Gideon, please show our people what happens to men who steal sacred marks to deceive their brethren," Aurik sneered.

Before I could make sense of what was happening, Gideon drew a fire blade out of his robes. I was forced to my knees by heavy hands.

"This wasn't what I wanted for you," Gideon whispered sadly to me. "If you had just followed me, you could have stood at my right hand. But you've made your choice. Goodbye, my son."

He clicked the fire blade on, the unimaginable heat of it burning me through as my killer strode forward to bury it in my chest.

34

I waited for the full impact of the knife, but it never came. Instead, the burning eased. The pulsating roar of the crowd had silenced, as well. For one long moment, I was sure that I had passed quickly and quietly into the next life.

With great apprehension, I opened my eyes. But instead of Heaven, I saw Gideon standing dumbstruck, staring out into the audience. He lowered his blade, clicked it off, and shoved it into his robes. Aurik stood facing the audience, as well, with Dai directly behind him. Aurik's face betrayed no emotion, while Dai still looked like he was concentrating tremendously hard.

I followed Gideon's incensed stare to the back of the hall where the golden doors stood wide open. Everyone, both inside and outside the hall, was silent, on their knees again.

I wrestled out of the guards' hands so I could see what had caused the mighty change, but what I saw made no sense. Hobbling down the aisle was Aurik, feeble, dirty, and clothed in rags. But that was impossible, for Aurik, who had just condemned me to die, still stood a stone's throw away. Mateo, Chase, and Claire, along with a multitude of Havens, followed quietly behind him.

"Come now. I don't look that bad, do I?" Aurik called out as he ascended the steps, answering everyone's mystified gaze. "Gideon, I've never seen you speechless before. I quite like it." Gideon pulsated with scarlet fury but remained silent.

Aurik approached the smothered cauldron. "Are any of you old enough to remember the fights our tribes had over deciding upon this symbol? A giant statue was proposed, a massive fountain, a clock set to Jerusalem's time—the ideas were endless," he remembered. "But in the end, The Light was represented by light itself. Firelight—the ancient glow that keeps the darkness at bay." He pulled the heavy fabric off of the holy fire. The embers had dimmed considerably, but revived a little as the oxygen flowed in. Aurik fanned the flames with a corner of the fabric and whispered the words inscribed around the cauldron like a prayer. "To dispel the darkness, to conquer death, to deliver us home."

Aurik moved away from the now glowing cauldron and approached the podium to face his identical twin, who was dressed in robes and painted with ceremonial marks.

"Don't let this imposter touch me!" the regally dressed Aurik cried to his guards, taking a step back. They inched forward but did not stop the disheveled old man from coming closer to him.

"Simply amazing," the dirty man said, watching his twin with great interest. "He even has the scar on the right cheek I got as a young boy. Wrestling with my brothers was always a bit dangerous. I've worn the proof of it right here since I was a child," he said, trailing a thin finger down the side of his own cheek, where a matching scar rested on his grimy face.

"Dai, I assume this is your technology. Truly *astonishing*. It's almost impossible to tell it's not real. Where is the projection coming from?" Aurik said, turning his focus toward Dai. He waved his hand between Dai and his twin. The image faltered, and the audience gasped. "Your eye? Incredible. That's why you turned down a transplant so fiercely after the accident," he guessed. The image of the imposter shattered into a thousand pixels, which rained down to the floor and vanished.

"Brothers and sisters, I have been held captive, but not by the Unnamed. The Masters, with Gideon at the head, have kept me hidden away. Ryen of the Haven, along with his brave friends, rescued me from certain death. I gave him my mark and sent him here to stop this mutiny. Instead, he was sentenced to death by the enemy who has infiltrated us. This same enemy has sunk its claws into the highest levels of government. The Tribunal, as Ryen rightly accused, has been *corrupted*."

The whole of Zhimeya clambered together. The unthinkable had happened. Nothing was sacred anymore. No one could be trusted.

"I don't quite know how we will sort out the good from the bad, but—"

"The mark!" I interrupted. Members of the Tribunal started stirring uncomfortably in their chairs. "The traitors wear Gideon's mark on their bodies."

"Guards, please detain the Tribunal while we sort this out." Only a fraction of the guards present followed the order.

"You turned the guard too, Gideon?" Aurik guessed. "A well-laid plan indeed. Are they marked, as well?" he asked, walking over to one of the guards who hadn't moved. He lifted the guard's sleeve and saw the patch of broken and blistered skin on his forearm where Gideon's mark rested.

"Gideon, if you admit your sins now, the people of Zhimeya may spare you. Ask forgiveness from your brothers and sisters, that they may let you live."

Gideon, burning with rage, his body almost convulsing, crossed slowly toward Aurik. "I bow to *no one*. I beg for *nothing*," he whispered fiercely through his clenched jaw. In a lightning-fast move, Gideon seized Aurik and pushed him off the podium into the audience.

"The revolution begins!" Gideon screamed.

The traitorous Tribunal members scattered out of the hall through side doors aided by the marked guards. Skirmishes broke out everywhere, but I paid them no attention. Gideon and Dai, who had grabbed Savannah, were running toward a deserted side hallway. As Dai opened the door, a small army flooded in with weapons drawn, blocking my path.

I reached into my back pocket and found Savannah's switchblade. I flipped it open and threw it as hard as I could at the wall of guards. It sailed straight through them. Over the din, Gideon screamed. The army of holograms shattered and vanished, leaving Gideon, the switchblade sticking deep in his back, exposed. He pulled Dai through the side door, screaming directions. Dai swung Savannah over his shoulder and slammed the door behind him.

I called Mateo and Chase over, along with anyone within earshot. Two guards ran over with equipment that melted the hinges right off the locked door. On the other side was an unending stretch of white stone hallways. I couldn't even hear retreating footsteps.

It would have been completely impossible to trace their path if it weren't for the trail of blood Gideon's wound left on the bleached white floor. We ran like lightning after them, following the macabre stains that grew larger as we followed.

35

Gideon's quarters

Healer Tien had watched the proceedings in Tribunal Hall, and things hadn't gone exactly as planned. She wasn't sure what her love's plan was now, but he would have one. He always did.

After she was done with the assignment he had given her, she went back to Gideon's quarters to wait for her new life to begin. She and Dai would be together. And together, they would rule the two worlds.

She paced back and forth nervously but finally heard the heavy footsteps of two men running toward the door. One of them was panting hard.

Dai strode in, carrying the human over his shoulder. Gideon was hunched over, wheezing. Tien knew that sound immediately. Punctured lung.

Dai threw the human down on the floor. She slowly pulled herself up to standing and drifted toward Gideon, a vacant smile on her face.

"Healer Tien!" Gideon exclaimed. "Help, I can't breathe." He pushed the human away from him. He reached around, held the knife handle tightly, and tugged. The knife came loose, and he threw it to the floor.

"I think you are right," Tien said, crossing over to him. Her training was already taking over. She listened hard to the sound of his breath, guessing the size of the wound, the tools she would need to fix it . . .

"Don't touch him, Tien. Come back to me," Dai said coldly. She stopped in her tracks and obeyed. "Where is Lais?"

"She's unconscious in the transport. She was on Haven tribal land, hiding exactly where you said she would be," Tien reported. Dai nodded in approval. "We don't need her, Dai. I'm just as good a healer as she is."

"No, you're not," Dai said dismissively, ignoring Tien's injured stare.

"Dai, what's going on?" Gideon asked.

"The time has come to part ways, Gideon. But before that, I wanted to thank you."

"What are you talking about?" he demanded, swatting the human away from him again like a fly. This time Savannah stood still, a few feet away from her master.

"I want to thank you for the work that you've done. The way you can move a crowd, the way they follow you blindly. It has brought me so much closer to my destiny. So, again, thank you. You've started a revolution, and I'm sorry you won't be able to see it end."

"Dai, are you . . . turning on me?" Gideon asked with a condescending chuckle followed by a wet rasping cough. "You would be *nothing* without me. Without me, you would still be back on Haven tribal land, eking out an existence tending to your family's farm. You owe me everything."

"I *said* thank you. Would you like me to say it again?"

"And what exactly is your plan? We are surrounded. My Tribunal will lose their marks. They'll be banished and become

Unnamed. And you're a fool to think that your fate will be any different unless we can come up with a plan together!"

"I have a plan. And please don't worry about *my* Tribunal. They will never be able to lose the only mark that matters," Dai said, gesturing Tien to his side. She obeyed quickly. He slipped his fingers underneath the cowl neck of her robe and pulled it down to bare her shoulder. The mark of two worlds stood out on her damaged skin. He kissed the mark softly. "My mark."

"That is *my* mark. Just because you made the branding device—"

"This isn't a brand! Burns heal. My mark never will."

"*What did you do to me?*" Gideon demanded, tearing at the skin on the back of his neck. "*What is it?*"

"I call it 'Reveal.' Millions of tiny needles, each injecting a traceable chemical into the skin. You can't hide from me once you are marked. I'll find the Tribunal, wherever they go. We'll come together again, and I'll finish the revolution you have started," Dai said proudly.

"We can do this together, Dai! You'll be my partner," Gideon promised, trying to rip the flesh off of his neck.

"You are not an asset anymore, Gideon. Look at yourself! Your addictions have almost killed you. It's been months, maybe years, since you've been anything more than a figurehead. I've been covering up your sloppy tracks for too long."

"I don't want to kill you, Dai," Gideon said, reaching into his robes and pulling out his last vial of white powder. "But I will." He emptied it under his tongue and felt the power flood back into his body.

"In the name of the Tribunal, open this door!" a muffled voice called out on the other side of the heavy doors. Gideon and Dai stood, staring at each other, waiting for the other to move. They heard the squeal of tools being used to melt the hinges and the locks off the door. Gideon reached into his robes just as Dai did. Both pulled out their fire blades.

"It doesn't have to be this way, Dai," Gideon said, turning on his blade. As he stalked toward Dai, the human followed behind him, like a shadow. Dai shielded his eyes from the blade's light and then clicked his on, as well.

Gideon made the first move, jutting his blade straight toward Dai's chest. Dai spiraled out of the way and leapt on top of Gideon's overturned desk. He dove off, driving the short blade toward Gideon's abdomen. Gideon let out a howl of pain as it grazed near enough to melt his robes onto his skin. He sunk to the floor just in time to miss the full impact of it.

Gideon regained himself and arched his blade toward Dai's wrist. Dai tried to retract his hand, but he was too late. Four of his fingers, wrapped around the hilt of the blade, fell in a neat pile on the ground. Dai's blade fell toward the floor, but he caught it deftly in his left hand. Gideon stared down at the fingers and then at Dai, who seemed to have barely noticed.

"Fingers are easy to fix," he said with a wild, twisting smile. Gideon shook off his astonishment and lunged at Dai again. The battle between the two men raged on, but Dai was much slower without the use of his good hand. Gideon quickly gained the advantage.

"You're no good with your left hand," Gideon said, with a cough that brought blood up his throat.

"I'm not, but I have two working lungs," he said with another swing of his blade, which Gideon spun easily away from.

"Lungs are easy to fix," Gideon answered, backing Dai further into a corner where Tien was cowering. "Now, I'm going to give you a second chance to be reasonable. Come back to my fold. Your only other choice is death," Gideon said.

Dai lowered his weapon slightly.

"Have you come to your senses?" Gideon asked patronizingly. "Are you giving up?"

"Savannah," Dai called over Gideon's shoulder. Gideon kept his blade trained straight at Dai's heart, not daring to divide his attention.

"Savannah," Dai said again, though Savannah made no show of recognition. "Human!" he finally called out.

She picked up her head, waiting for instruction.

"Do you remember what we talked about right before I led you to the big white hall? Do you remember what you said you were going to do tonight?" Dai asked in his kindest voice.

"Yes," Savannah said, quietly.

He threw his fire blade over Gideon's head. Savannah caught it too close to the tip, burning her hands badly. "There's Gideon," Dai said, pointing at him.

She strode forward and buried the fire blade deep into Gideon's back. Gideon let out an ear-piercing screech as his hands flailed uselessly trying to dislodge it, dropping his own blade on the floor.

"I *will* kill that man," Savannah said, repeating the words she had told Dai just a few hours ago. Dai shoved Gideon backward and he fell to the floor, driving the blade deeper. Light and blood issued from his mouth, ears, and eyes. Gideon, burning to ash from the inside out, screamed in horrendous agony. His body melted away from the blade leaving only ash behind. His wild screams finally subsided and then cut off in a gurgle just as the door was lifted off its hinges and thrown down. Ryen of the Haven, followed by ten men, ran through the doorway just in time to witness the grisly end of Gideon the Master.

36

I sprinted inside toward Savannah, but Dai was faster. He pulled her into him, wrapping his right arm around her neck. Only his thumb was still attached to his right hand.

"Had a little accident," he said nonchalantly, watching my horrified stare. He used his left hand to hold the fire blade against Savannah's stomach, though he didn't turn it on.

"Dai, let her go," I yelled.

"Calm down, Ryen," Dai said coolly. Savannah looked straight at me with no spark of recognition. She didn't even blink.

"What have you done to her?" I yelled.

"Please give me a moment. I need to confer with the healer," he said, pulling Savannah toward Tien, who was still crouching in the corner.

"How long does she have?" he whispered to Tien. The healer assessed her quickly.

"A few hours at best. She's a walking corpse," Tien said.

"You lie!" I yelled furiously. Mateo and Chase caught my arms and held me back.

"All right, Haven," Dai said. "It looks like you have a choice to make. I'll give you back your human, and you let us leave with a bit of a head start. Or you can kill me with the stipulation that I gut the human before you can reach me," he said, lightly pushing the dull blade into Savannah's stomach. Blood pooled around the point of it. "Do we really need to waste time wondering what you'll choose? You seem like the type who really loves a lost cause."

"I'll find you wherever you go. I'll hunt you down," I said viciously.

"Consider me warned," he said flippantly. "Do we have an agreement? The human for a head start?"

I nodded, keeping my eyes trained on the blade Dai was threatening to push into Savannah's stomach.

"All right, Tien, please make your way to the transport." Tien dropped lithely from the window. A few seconds later, the transport below whirred to life. It rose into the air to the level of the window.

"Until we meet again," Dai said, with a nod of his head. He pushed Savannah toward me. I caught her in my arms just before she hit the floor. Dai jumped onto the nose of the transport, swung into its open window, and disappeared.

"Find him!" I yelled. Guards dispersed in different directions, either barking or listening to orders from their earpieces.

I swung Savannah up into my arms and ran back to Tribunal Hall, with Mateo and Chase clearing the way before us.

The hall was still chaotic, but a hush came over the crowd when I entered and yelled for help. Healers ran toward the podium, where I stood with Savannah still in my arms.

Zio, head of the healers, made it to the front first. A tattoo of a majestic tree ran up the length of his spine, the top of which adorned his scalp. Thick branches shot across the back of his ribs and shoulders. A flock of birds leaving their nest at the top of the tree covered his forehead and ran down his face and neck and across his chest. Four other similarly marked healers followed carrying heavy cases.

One of the healers produced a fiber net with which she covered Savannah's head. A three-dimensional hologram of Savannah's brain appeared in the air a few inches above. Zio studied it carefully.

If Savannah were really hurt, she would bleed, she would scream. She wouldn't be lying so peacefully, I hoped.

"She's fine, she's fine," I said quietly in my own tongue and then switched to English. "Savannah, you are going to be fine."

"Savannah, you are going to be fine," she parroted back in the exact same tone. Her eyes stood wide open, unblinking.

"Brain tumor. Small, easily extractable," Zio said, satisfied.

"Brain tumor. Small…" Savannah started. Zio plunged a syringe full of light pink liquid into her arm. Seconds later, she went limp.

"She's sedated. Let's get out of . . ." He trailed off. "Stop. Something's changed." He used his hands to manipulate the hologram floating above Savannah's head. "There's three tumors now. They weren't there a few second ago. Is there something wrong with this machine?"

"No, Zio. It's brand new," another healer said.

"They weren't there," he said.

And then it hit me. Emani had told me how Obedience worked.

"The tumors will spread, multiply, and get larger," I said frantically.

"All the more reason to get her to Healing Tower immediately." He slipped a brace over her head, securing it in place. "Healers, lift on my count."

"Stop! You can't help this human," an angry voice yelled from the audience. "It belongs to no tribe. It is Unnamed. Our laws forbid healers to help any Unnamed." Though I didn't take my eyes off Savannah, I heard many voices call out in agreement.

"It's one less human we have to worry about!" another shouted. This time, I looked up.

"It?" I spat at the angry crowd. "*It* is the same as you or me! We are *all* God's children!"

"Stop, everyone!" Aurik cried out from behind me. The room quieted. "We will not let this young one die. That is not who we are." He turned to me and put his light hand on my shoulder. "But she does need to be marked and claimed by a tribe, Ryen. It's the law."

"Four tumors!" Zio said impatiently. The woman on his right took notes as he whispered to her about the impending surgery.

"Will any tribe claim the girl?" Aurik shouted above the whispers.

"I'll claim her," I yelled.

"You don't have that authority," he said quietly, still looking onto the floor of the hall.

"Aurik, we don't have time to—"

"We will claim her!" a familiar voice answered. My father, along with the other holy men and women of the Haven tribe, fought their way toward us. He held a container of ceremonial stain in his hands.

"Father!" I cried out. I didn't have the authority to claim her, but he did. "Hurry!" I looked frantically from him back to Savannah, who was in the process of dying quietly. Blood vessels burst in her eyes like shooting stars. She couldn't hold out like this much longer.

"Five tumors!" Zio called out, still taking measurements.

"Savannah, they are going to bless you, to claim you a Haven so that the healers can help you. Can you hear me?" I asked. No response. I felt delicate hands on my shoulders; my mother and sister had arrived.

"I'm ready," he told me. "Translate for her."

With the glowing, silvery paint, he drew the symbol of the Haven tribe on her forehead with his finger. The eastward constellation of stars that first led us toward Earth.

"Savannah." He said her name with reverence. "We know not what came before this life." He made the mark of the first two stars. "We know not what comes after." He dipped his finger into the small jar again and drew the third and fourth. "But for these precious moments in eternity, you are ours, a Haven, until our God calls you home." He kissed the last mark, sealing the blessing, and nodded at Zio.

"Now!" Zio commanded. I was pushed to the side so that the healers could lift her all at the same time. The flurry of activity around her moved swiftly away from me and out of the hall before I even had time to stand.

37

The days that followed were a strange patchwork of pictures, more like scenes from an old unfocused movie reel than reality.

My mother's arms around me, pulling me off the Tribunal floor. My sister's steady eyes full of the grief that mirrored my own. Holy men, my father chief among them, hovering over Savannah's unmoving body, staining her skin with the healing marks of our ancestors. Claire and I kneeling next to her low stone altar in Healing Tower, holding her hands through each unending night. Savannah's naked scalp, covered in more deep cuts every day. The smell of charred herbs sending smoke into the air as Haven holy women chanted and lit ceremonial fires around her. A sea of faces parading past my eyes, asking me questions I didn't hear and didn't answer.

Mateo, Chase, and Claire worked day and night trying to give the media all the information they wanted so that they would leave me alone. My mother and sister rarely left Savannah's side. They sang to her, spoke to her, told her our stories and legends. They did it more for my benefit than hers. And even though I didn't show it, I was grateful to all of them.

The only person that could shake me out of my stupor was Zio.

Right after the first surgery, his head shaking in disbelief, he came to us. My parents' arms tightened around me, helping me stand to receive the news.

"It went well at first. I scanned her brain one more time before closing her up, just for good measure. And there they were. Three more tumors. They came out of nowhere. I—I couldn't cut anymore. She's not stable enough for me to even try to remove them right now. We are going to try medications to slow the growth, and then we will operate again tomorrow, okay?"

I gave him no response.

"Ryen, do you understand?"

No.

I made my head nod yes. I didn't want to hear any more.

"Are you all right?" he asked seriously.

No.

I made my head nod again so he would go away.

It went on and on like that. Day after day. Another surgery, clearing out the growths. Seconds later, new tumors.

"I'm cutting her to pieces, Ryen. We can't keep doing this," Zio insisted.

"Yes, we can. We will keep doing this until we win."

"You aren't listening. I'm doing more damage than good."

"Then start another course of treatment, a different medication. There has to be something—"

"Medications are slowing the growth of the tumors, giving Savannah a chance to heal a little, but nothing is stopping them. If we stop treatment, the tumors will overrun her in minutes. In a few days, we won't even be able to keep her alive artificially anymore. You need to start preparing yourself," he said sympathetically, putting his hand on my shoulder.

"Are you giving up, Zio?" I snapped, pulling away from his pity.

"We need a miracle, Ryen. Pray for a miracle."

I turned and walked away, leaving the healer standing alone in the dark passageway.

I stopped at the entrance to her room. The carved stone walls made it look more like a sepulchre than a healing room. I watched Savannah's chest slowly rise and fall on her low altar. She was so beautiful, so exquisite, even as light and life left her in slow and steady increments.

The sight of her there knocked a piece of poetry loose from my memory, famous lines from a love letter written by a human so many years ago, so far away from here. I'd read it at the Institute when I was younger.

I have been astonished that Men could die Martyrs for religion—I have shuddered at it—I shudder no more—I could be martyred for my Religion—Love is my religion—I could die for that—I could die for you.

The lines seemed silly at the time. What was more important than one's own life? But the last lines had stuck with me. Deep in my soul, I yearned to feel what this poet had—a love strong enough to lay down your life for.

I understood him now. I understood with painful perfection.

I knelt on the floor next to her altar made of shimmering healing stones, cut from sacred ground, blessed by holy men. Soon she would be as cold as the stones she rested on, because of me. Her accidental executioner.

Her life would end because she had met me.

If I had *just* walked away . . .

If I had known the danger she was in . . .

If I could just change the past . . .

She would die. Nothing I could give, nothing I could bargain with, would change that. And maybe that was my punishment for my unending selfishness that brought her to this point. I would have to watch helplessly as she died.

If she could just take me with her . . .

No. That would be too easy.

I would live on. And that would be my punishment.

My life sentence.

Living each unending day with what I had done to her.

I kissed her lips and ran the tips of my fingers over her face, memorizing the feel of it, preparing for the final separation that was looming.

"Love is my religion. I could die for that. I could die for you," I whispered.

A miracle. Zio said I needed a miracle.

So that night, for hours, I prayed for a miracle.

I fell into broken, fitful dreams, full of blinding color and frenetic energy, the disorienting kind that catch you somewhere between asleep and awake. Pictures, words, thoughts, and motion all tumbled through my mind at breakneck speed.

But the pace of the pictures started to slow. They crawled and then they stalled, dropping me into a place I recognized. Fuzzy at first, but more defined as I concentrated, a scene unfolded.

I was relaxing in a fallowing field, staring at the indigo sky with Emani by my side. We were younger. Her skin was yet unmarked and luminous; she hadn't started collecting tattoos yet. This moment in front of me was a memory, not a dream.

We lay under the stars together, our fingers just barely touching. My whole body was charged with electricity from her nearness. Her face was bathed in the light of the twin moons rising. She literally glowed.

"I did not cheat on that test! Just because someone does better than you does not mean that they cheated, Haven," she laughed, pulling herself up onto her side, leaning on her elbow.

"Sorry Em, you've just bruised my ego a little. I had to ask." I laughed too, pulling up on my elbow to face her.

"You're just not great with chemistry. You can't always be the best at everything."

"I don't have much patience for science. It's just so boring. Literature and history are so much more fun. Learning about people, places . . ." I trailed off, momentarily more interested in the curve of her lips than the conversation.

"Ugh, I can't stand our history courses! At least with science, every problem has a solution. Every question has an answer. It can all be figured out. That's not the way people work, though," she said wistfully.

The breeze picked up and blew a few wayward strands of hair into her face. I hesitantly raised my nervous hand to brush them away.

The scene changed abruptly. I was pulled into Gideon's chambers, hands bound, head aching from the blinder ring that had just been removed. Gideon was talking, but I was watching the shadows carefully. He was about to call Emani forward.

Then she appeared. Still alive. Still whole. No blood stained her clothing yet. I wanted to scream at her to run away, to save herself. But I was only watching. I couldn't change the past.

She started to speak.

"I haven't been able to arrest the tumor growth to keep the subject alive and viable for Gideon's long-term use. The tumors grow so quickly, untreated subjects usually die within hours, sometimes days. But theoretically, survival outcomes with surgery to remove the tumors and a new drug therapy I am working on make me hopeful about reversing the tumor growth."

"What do you whisper about?" Gideon reprimanded.

The vision changed one more time. The uncomfortable heat was already gathering around me. I was thrust deep into the tunnels under Tribunal Hall, back into my locked cell. My heart broke out in a panicked sprint; I didn't have enough strength left to watch her bleed out on the floor again.

Emani was there, but she didn't bleed. She sat outside of my cell, face calm, almost enigmatic. Her hair was the light, warm brown I remembered from our childhood. Her tattoos were gone, too, leaving no trace on her brilliant alabaster skin. I tried to talk, but the words wouldn't come.

She put her closed fist through the bars that kept me captive. I held my hands up to hers, and she dropped a tiny silver vial into my upturned palm.

"Forgive me," was all she said.

38

I bolted upright on the floor next to Savannah's bed. My miracle had come.

I took both of Savannah's icy hands in mine, ignoring that she looked much worse than she had just an hour ago. In fact, she looked exactly like the last sketch she had drawn of her mother.

"Anna, I have to go. Please hold on a little longer until I can get what you need. I *will* save you." I kissed her and flew out the door as fast as I could.

There were too many reporters and protestors waiting for me at the bottom of the elevation pods that served as the main transportation up and down Healing Tower. My only chance to leave undetected was to make the journey down the mountain on foot.

Healing Tower was carved straight into the side of the sheer striated cliffs of Angel's Communion, a mountain that soared several thousand feet into the air. It was said that the ancients came to this place to converse with angels. Healers naturally brought people here to be healed, where they would be closest to their Maker. The hospital had been built over the ages around the holy site.

An ancient switchback trail was still passable, though it was now only used by the priestesses who kept ceremonial fires burning to protect the sick inside the tower.

I stole out through a desolate passageway that led to the switchback path. A priestess covered in patterned ornamental scars was stationed right outside the door. The sharp earthy scent of the herbs burning over her fire mixed with the sterile smell that clung to me from Savannah's clean room. It was a perfect representation of how the body was healed in Zhimeya with a mix of magic and medicine.

One hundred feet down the switchbacks, a second priestess was crouched low in a small cave cut into the side of the cliff. She chanted quietly and sprinkled herbs into her fire, making the flames pop magenta. Her body was decorated with scars so light and delicate, they looked like fish scales. I passed without her even looking up from her task. Each priestess I came upon, chanting and keeping watch over her fire, was too wrapped up in her supplications to mind me at all.

The path ended deep inside the protected forest at the base of Angel's Communion, a place supposedly full of the souls of those who died at Healing Tower but weren't fit to ascend to Heaven. Of course, the real danger wasn't the possibility of happening upon ghosts.

Since the priestesses insisted no life be forcibly taken by man so close to the sick and dying in Healing Tower, hunting was forbidden in the forest. The last of the carnivorous straje packs had taken refuge on this protected land. No one who had any choice would pass through that forest in the middle of the night. I had no choice.

My quick footfalls thudded too loudly against the soggy ground. The longer I ran, the more the forest awoke around me. Soon, the sound of my footsteps was joined by the rushing of unknown creatures following too quickly behind.

A beast materialized, its scales glittering green and blue in the moons' pale glow. I jolted to a stop, glancing around for an escape, but only found more glittering, moving forms. I had run right into a straje nest.

The largest of the beasts twisted through the primordial trees, its body weaving and bending around them like a serpent. It snuffed the air far above my head and let out a bellow that shook dusky leaves loose from their branches. The other two beasts lifted their heads and bellowed back.

The sound they made was very familiar. It was just like the herbivorous straje I had grown up with, as harmless as horses and just as easy to ride. On closer inspection, these animals were all missing the rows of razor-sharp teeth, jutting tusks, and armored spikes that set the carnivorous straje apart from these beasts.

I approached the most curious of the three. When he didn't shy away, I easily mounted his back, taking hold of the two rough, curved horns on his head. As I started steering him in the direction of Haven territory, the crack of falling trees rang through the forest. The three beasts snuffed the air again warily.

A menacing screech split the silence. I could see the glittering of another straje in the distance. It was red and orange—and much larger than the three herbivores. It knocked trees out of its way with gigantic knife-sharp tusks. This was a hunter.

The herbivores lowered their long bodies to the ground and glided silently in the underbrush, almost flying between the trees. The forest blurred around me as they made their escape, but the terrible screech of the hunter followed.

The two larger straje, sensing the nearness of danger, heaved their plated shoulders against trees, knocking them down, trying to obscure the path of the hunter. My straje threw its shoulder into a massive tree trunk, hitting it with the force of a bullet train.

The crush of the impact threw me off of its back. I crumpled around a tree stump and fell shockingly hard to the forest floor.

The air tore out of my lungs and refused to reenter for a moment. I lay there dazed, listening gratefully to the sound of four gigantic beasts moving quickly away from me.

I was completely wet, covered in what I guessed was mud. I tried to wipe it out of my eyes so I could see better. It was slick, thin, and smelled like copper. Not mud—blood. My blood. It was too dark, and I hurt too badly to tell where it was coming from, but if I could smell it, it was only a matter of minutes before another hunter found me.

Miraculously, the straje's speedy flight had brought me to the edge of the protected forest. As the trees thinned, I could make out the borderline between the Haven and Cailida tribes marked by watchtowers topped with burning cauldrons of green fire. The sight was enough to get my beaten body running toward my destination. Haven territory. My home.

Even though the hour was very late, the compound I ran toward was still lit. I gave three quiet wraps on the door.

"We are not giving any more interviews until the morning, leeches!" Mateo yelled. I knocked more furiously. "Didn't you hear me? You and everyone else like you can go to—" He pulled the door open. "Ryen! Is she . . . ?" he stopped short of saying the word.

"No, she's alive. Barely." I stumbled dizzily into the house.

"Whoa, what in the name of Zhimeya's moons happened to you?" he almost yelled as I sloughed off what was left of my jacket and shirt, looking for injuries. "Did you know you are missing half the skin on your back?"

"Do you have a surgical kit?"

"Just the small one they sent me to Earth with, but you need a healer to close that thing up right. I can see your rib bones," he said, staring at the hemorrhaging laceration that ran the length of my back.

"Start sewing," I ordered.

Mateo got his supplies and sterilized his hands and my skin with a freezing cold blast of cleanser. He brought out a syringe and started preparing the solution to numb the area.

"No time, Mateo. Start sewing." He shook his head and jammed a hook-shaped needle deep into my skin, again and again, pulling the wound closed with the finesse of a bull moose.

"Pyneloas leaves in the front pocket. It'll help," he offered, seeing my white-knuckled hands gripping the stone table I sat beside. I fished the packet of leaves out of the bag, rolled four together and bit down on them hard. The pain relief from the herb was almost instantaneous. Warmth started spreading through my cold limbs.

"Everyone wants a piece of you. Literally," he said tugging the needle through my skin. "Some are calling for the removal of your marks because you've brought a human here. We tried to explain that it wasn't you who brought her . . ."

Chase entered the room. He shook his head at the sight of Mateo sewing me back together and didn't ask any questions. He grabbed a canister of sealing salve and got to work on my other wounds.

"I don't care. If Savannah dies, they can have my marks," I said furiously.

"You don't mean that, Ryen. You wouldn't do that to us," Chase said, hurt by my brusque words.

"Where's Claire?" I asked, changing the subject.

"She's sleeping upstairs. Do you want me to get her?" Chase asked, pulling leaves out of my cuts and sealing them shut.

"No, I don't want her anywhere near the trouble I am about to ask you both to get into. I came here for help."

"Then you've come to the right place," Mateo said, pulling the surgical thread taut and tying it off.

"You may not be saying that in a few minutes. Zio says Savannah needs a miracle, and I think I know where to find one. But it requires some serious breaking and entering . . . "

Both brothers exited the room before I could finish explaining. They returned wearing dark clothing, armed with what they called "useful tools for opening things that don't want to open." Chase handed me a set of similar clothes, which I pulled on gratefully.

I'd forgotten how beautiful the valley that held Haven tribal land was, even shrouded in darkness. Familiar family compounds rose up organically in between soaring trees. Every wall and roof hung so heavily with curtains of vines, it was hard to tell where the earth stopped and manmade structures began. Suspended aerial walkways that connected the compounds would be deserted at this late hour—but even still, we kept to the forest floor. The dense growth and heavy mist that came off Lake Talava would guard us further from discovery.

Two lights burned in the windows of my childhood home; one in my sister's room and one in my parents'. They probably weren't getting much more sleep than I was tonight. It was the first time I'd seen my home since I'd left for Earth two years ago. What an odd homecoming it was.

The border between Cailida and Haven land usually wasn't guarded. But recent events being what they were, the watchtowers were burning bright. Even the light fields were on. I could only think of a small handful of times when our two tribes felt the need to guard our shared border. The last time I could recall was when Emani's father and brother were on the run from the Tribunal, before they were caught.

Makeshift militiamen had joined regular guards in patrolling the border. Each Haven stood facing a Cailida, a shimmering web of buzzing green light serving as the dividing line. Were anyone to cross through the light field, the other side would be alerted immediately.

The light fields were interrupted at strict intervals by watchtowers, each topped with a fire cauldron. Most nights, the fires burned brightly with a comforting golden glow. I used to play with my friends long after the sun went down aided by the light from the tower fires. But just like the light fields, the flames were burning a ghostly green tonight, a warning of the uneasiness between the tribes.

The border ran all the way up to the protected forest around Angel's Communion, though it was never guarded since no sane person would enter the forest. As the three of us approached the border, I marched up toward the bank of trees, fully expecting the brothers to turn back. Neither deviated.

We skirted along the tree line stealthily, so as not to draw attention from the guards on one side or the predators on the other. Within minutes, we had crossed onto Cailida tribal land and started making our way toward Emani's compound.

The front of Emani's massive compound faced the Cailida's tribute to The Light. Almost every tribe had some sort of tribute to the legend on their land, but the Cailida's was one of the most famous.

A hulking stone carving of a man sunk ankle deep in a natural spring of hot water rose up from the mist. A perfectly smooth spherical stone floated before the man at his feet, buoyed up by the fountain of steaming water bubbling beneath it. The man's outstretched arms were held low and outward. Each upturned palm had the symbol for The Light inscribed on it. His face was as smooth and featureless as the sphere in front of him. When proof of what The Light looked like was found, his face would be carved to match. The sphere would be carved to match the features of his birthplace, as well.

Emani had told me I would be the one to bring the proof back, to complete the tribute. I looked away from the statue's blank face, another reminder of how I had failed her.

I approached her compound with growing trepidation. Her presence hung heavy here, as though her ghost could walk out of the shadows any moment to lead me forward.

Light fields guarded the perimeter of her land. Her once meticulous gardens had been razed to ash. Skeletons of the animals she kept stuck out haphazardly from the scorched earth. The symbol for "Unnamed" was scrawled across the front doors in glowing paint, condemning the building and anyone who would dare enter.

"I'd understand if you both just went home. You know the cost of being caught here," I said. Chase and Mateo just walked ahead of me.

"Because it would mean becoming Unnamed too. You'd be banished; they would take your marks away."

The brothers started discussing the best way to get over the light fields.

"There are a few trees still standing right up against the perimeter. If we can get you into the branches, you can climb down behind the light field. I'll stand guard while you both go inside," Chase said.

They vaulted me into the branches of a tree that hung over the light field. A few of Mateo's haphazard surgical stitches on my back popped as I climbed. I chewed harder on the Pyneloas leaves still in my mouth.

Mateo followed soon after me. We crept to the back servants' entrance. Mateo got out what looked like a crowbar, ready to break the computerized lock.

"Wait, let me see if I can get the door to cooperate," I whispered. Though I hoped she would have changed the password to her doors long ago, for her sake, I tried the old password she used when we were together.

"Ryen of the Haven," I said as loudly as I dared. The door, to my relief and chagrin, chirped and swung open. She'd never changed her password. Mateo looked at me with uncomfortable pity.

I led him through the ruined hallways I knew by heart. The great house had been reduced to nothing, a skeleton. Everything left inside was blanketed in thick ash and debris. Her collections of priceless artifacts had been ground to dust. Everything she loved was destroyed.

The worst devastation wasn't the fires they set or the things they smashed. It was the symbol they left on the door. Unnamed. The Tribunal would be posthumously revoking her marks soon. Banishing her even in death. Her people would never be allowed to even speak her name. She didn't deserve that.

The only reason that I lived was because she died. I had already made up my mind to tell her story, to do everything in my power to have her tribe reclaim her. If they wouldn't, maybe the Haven tribe would. She had always wanted to be Emani of the Haven. That would have been her name had I married her.

The mob had been thorough, but luckily they overlooked a small lever hidden in the floor. I found it and pulled hard. Gears groaned beneath our feet, and the small tiles on the mosaic floor started rearranging and stacking on top of each other, pulling away from the wall. The resulting hole revealed a staircase into Emani's laboratory.

The lights flickered on as we entered. There was no trace of destruction down here. Even the white stone table in the middle of the room was perfectly clean. I ran my hand over its familiar cold surface.

"So, what are we looking for here?" Mateo asked.

"A silver vial . . . I think . . ."

"Like these?" Mateo said, surveying row after row of silver vials sitting on shelves that lined the walls.

"Yes. Like those," I said hopelessly, trying not to wonder how much Savannah had deteriorated while I had been away. "Look for one that isn't empty."

We both went to work, overturning each of the thousands of silver vials in the room as quickly as we could.

"Maybe what you are looking for isn't down here," Mateo offered.

"Everything she deemed important would be down here. Just give me a minute to think." I paced along each wall, looking through the stacks of notes and instruments, waiting for inspiration. A small black lacquered box in the corner caught my eye. It was the only thing I hadn't opened yet. I pulled the lid, but it was stuck tight.

"Do you think you can get this box open?" I asked.

Mateo tried for a few minutes to pry the lid open with all of his instruments, but it was no use. The small, unassuming box was completely indestructible.

"It wants a password," I said desperately.

"You once knew her really well. Try a few out," Mateo encouraged.

I tried every word or phrase I could think of. I even tried my name again. Nothing worked.

"This is impossible!" I yelled in frustration.

"I'm sure she locked it with words that were important to her. You already tried your name, but what about her name and your name together?"

"What do you mean?"

"Isn't that what she wanted most in the world? To be with you? Maybe that's what she would have locked the box with," he said.

Hadn't I just been thinking how much she wanted to take my tribe's name as her own? I took a deep breath.

"Emani of the Haven." The words burned like acid on my tongue, a reminder of her pain.

The tiny black box chirped, and the lid sprang open in my hands. There was only one object in the velvet-lined interior. I picked up the single silver vial and turned it over in my hands. One word was scratched clumsily into the metal.

Forgiveness.

This was it. Her penance. My miracle.

"*You* want *me* to just . . . give this to her?" Zio asked in disbelief.

"Do we have *time* to run tests on it?" I bit back. Chase and Mateo stood in stony silence in the corner of Savannah's room, behind me. I could feel their mounting disapproval, even though they weren't saying anything.

"Of course we don't have time to run tests. Look at her!"

I begrudgingly glanced at Savannah and shuddered. She looked dead. *But she wasn't!*

"Where did you get this, Ryen?" Zio weighed the mysterious vial in his palm.

"You really, really don't want to know," Mateo said menacingly.

"For your own safety, please do not ask again," Chase added.

"Fine. So how much should I give her then?" Zio asked all three of us. He held up the vial, the light catching the words etched onto the surface. "How many doses are in here? Is it supposed to be injected? Taken orally? Should I put it into a saline suspension before I administer it? Or maybe it needs to be injected into the tumors themselves. Can you tell me that?"

"I don't know Zio, I don't know! I just know that this is her only chance!" I whispered furiously.

"Whatever healer gave this to you should have their marks removed. Giving you this degree of false hope is disgusting."

"We didn't get it from a healer. You don't want to know where we got it," Mateo said.

"I don't know if I want any part of this. You three show up in the middle of the night, bring me here with talk of a miracle, and expect me to experiment on a dying girl? I should just walk away. In fact, this could cost me *my* marks," he said, rubbing the birds tattooed on his forehead.

"Then walk away, but at least find me a syringe first so I can give it to her myself," I challenged, holding my hand out for the vial.

"Ryen." Zio's voice turned soft, almost fatherly. "You are *not* well. And you are certainly not up to making rational decisions right now. Let me give you something to help you sleep for a few days. I'll wake you in time for the funeral. I can even keep you medicated through the grieving if you want. Sometimes the best thing is to just let go—"

"No!" I yelled. "This is her only chance!" I felt Mateo's heavy hand on my shoulder.

"But look at her. Really, really look." Zio pointed at Savannah. The color had fled her face. The warmth was gone.

"We'll get through this together, no matter what happens," Mateo said quietly.

I jerked out from under his hand.

"I will NOT give up hope when Zio could be holding the cure in his hands! Do you want me to beg again?" I asked angrily. "Because I will. I'm begging you, Zio!"

Zio huffed loudly, still staring at the vial, rolling it back and forth in his palm. He lifted his eyes slowly, watching me, trying to measure my resolve.

"*All right.* If she weren't minutes away from death, I'd never try this. I'll start her on a slow drip of the vial's contents. I'll watch the tumors. That's all I can do."

"Thank you," I said, dropping my head into my hands.

He opened his mouth to talk me out of it again but, instead, he shrugged his tired shoulders and connected the vial to a tube that already led into Savannah's arm.

"Now if you don't mind, I'm going to go check on other patients so that I have an alibi. Good luck, Savannah of the Haven," Zio said. He kissed her forehead, as all healers do when they part with a dying patient.

The amber liquid started to slowly drip from the vial.

"We'll be right outside just . . . just in case . . ." Chase whispered. He walked over and kissed Savannah's forehead and left. Mateo clapped me hard on the shoulder again, kissed Savannah, and followed his brother.

I knelt back down on the floor next to her.

I gathered her hands into mine.

And, as the never-ending seconds crawled by, I waited.

I waited for a miracle.

39

I never planned to step foot inside Tribunal Hall again. I could have used a hologram, or Claire would have gone for me—there were a hundred other options. But Aurik said my presence today might help to stem the tide of violent demonstrations happening around the world over Savannah.

And I would do *anything* for Savannah.

Aurik sent his fastest transport for me. What a beautiful sight it should have been plummeting from the heights of Angel's Communion down toward Tribunal Hall, the expanse of my homeland sprawled out below. But the beauty of the scenery was irreparably marred by the angry crowds coalescing around the great building.

Not that the mobs mattered to me. The whole planet could be imploding, and I wouldn't care in the least. I only concentrated on what Zio had said an hour ago.

Cautiously optimistic. He was cautiously optimistic that the tumors had been eradicated.

We'd watched together as the small silver vial drained into Savannah over the course of the most frightening day of my life. And as the vial emptied, the tumors shrank and started to disappear.

A miracle, Zio had said.

The most terrifying moment came when the little vial finally ran dry. Would the tumors return? If they did, there was nothing left for us to do.

The last drop fell.

Nothing happened.

Nothing grew.

As a result, Zio was cautiously optimistic the vial's contents had done its job. Of course, that didn't stop him from warning me that even though the tumors were gone, it didn't mean Savannah would survive. After so much trauma, he didn't know how her body could continue to function. But the small glimmer of hope in his eye was enough to keep me breathing from one second to the next.

The hall was almost completely empty inside. Only the remnants of the Tribunal and select media were allowed inside today. I tried to quiet my footsteps, but the sound of my boots on the white marble reverberated off the vaulted ceilings. Even the protestors outside weren't loud enough to make my entrance any quieter.

Everyone inside, including the small knot of reporters on the floor, turned in unison to watch me make the never-ending walk up to the podium. A flock of flying cameras descended on me like a swarm of locusts and followed closely as I walked. I hadn't missed this at all while I had been on Earth.

Most of the Tribunal seats stood ominously empty. Only ten men and women still sat in their usual places with an ember of Holy Fire lit by their side—the only members whom Gideon hadn't marked. The rest of the Tribunal, the usual occupants of the empty chairs, were cloistered in the wings, waiting for the trial to begin.

Aurik called me forward with a wave. The rest of the Tribunal did not look as welcoming. They'd obviously been arguing about me long before I arrived at the hall.

"Ryen of the Haven, welcome! Thank you for coming. I know this isn't the easiest time to pull you away from your . . . responsibilities," he said sympathetically.

"I can't stay long. I don't want to be away if—" I started. He nodded sympathetically.

"Of course. We'll be quick. But before we begin the proceedings, I want to publicly thank you *and* Savannah of the Haven for saving my life. While the whole of Zhimeya may not agree," he said, staring into each of the small cameras that buzzed around him, "we *all* owe you both a great debt of gratitude for bringing so many traitors to justice."

"If you please." Saylo of the Harlis tribe stood up from his Tribunal seat, with a little trouble. The giant was big enough to occupy two seats.

"Be careful, Saylo," Aurik warned quietly.

"Excuse me, Aurik, but everyone knows Ryen was close to the Masters. Gideon was his personal mentor for years! I refuse to give over my trust to him as readily as you are."

"There was a time when Gideon and I were close," I said before Aurik could censure him. "But he never trusted me like he did those he named to be Masters. I never knew his more clandestine plans. And I've been checked *several times* for Gideon's mark."

"So you don't have the mark. That doesn't prove anything."

"What about the fact that he almost killed me, right over there?" I asked, pointing to the spot where Gideon tried to run me through just a stone's throw away. "You remember. You were sitting right there when it happened."

"Maybe Gideon didn't trust you, fine. But maybe Dai did. You two are probably still in contact. I'd wager you know exactly where he is hiding since you are the one who let him escape—"

"I let him escape in exchange for Savannah's life!" I growled.

"Oh yes, that's right. You let a murderer escape to save a *human*. Another reason you don't deserve my tribe's trust," he yelled.

"I'm *not* here asking for your tribe's trust! *I'm* not on trial!" I yelled.

"Enough, Saylo!" Aurik barked. "Ryen is not here to defend himself. I made that very clear before he arrived. Ryen, the Tribunal apologizes."

Saylo sat, his chair groaning dangerously beneath him. Sweat poured down his bloated face, ruining the tribal symbols painted on his forehead.

"Preposterous," Saylo whispered loudly to the member seated next to him. "He still defends saving the savage over bringing a guilty man to justice!"

"Savage? Why don't you come to Healing Tower to see what our *superior* society has done to an innocent girl! Don't you dare speak of your prejudices about humans in front of me! You know nothing of them!" I shouted.

"See? See? He defends the vermin that pollute the holy planet!" Saylo sputtered. "You tried to stay there to become one of *them*! Maybe you should be on trial!"

"Enough!" Aurik cried, staring the corpulent giant down. Saylo hissed but didn't speak again. I was seething, holding onto the podium with both hands to keep from crossing the small space and smashing in Saylo's swollen, purple face.

"Again, the Tribunal apologizes Ryen. I'll take over the questioning," Aurik said, his eyes still trained on Saylo. "As you know, when Earth researchers return, they traditionally have an audience with the Tribunal. We'd like to keep some semblance of normalcy, though these times are anything but normal. May I ask you a few questions about your time there?"

"Yes," I said as patiently as I could manage.

"You spent two years researching, watching, and listening. Did you find the evidence you were seeking?"

"No. I don't think what we are looking for exists," I admitted tiredly.

Aurik studied me carefully for a few moments. "As disappointing as that is, I think I am starting to believe that you are right," he said sadly.

"This is ridiculous," Kosma, leader of the Falizia tribe, piped up. It was hard to look at her straight on because of the glare coming off of the hundreds of delicate chains woven through her skin like metallic thread. The red-plumed bird that sat on her shoulder pulled softly at the strands when the light made them flash.

Kosma, like so many others, believed the evidence we were seeking was waiting to be discovered. She had always condemned researchers for not using more subversive tactics to get information out of humans. I'd been very surprised to find that she hadn't sold her vote to Gideon.

"You've lost your faith in Earth research, Aurik, but I haven't. You think over time our people will find other ways to come together again. They won't. Not with the torbillium shortages and all the problems it is causing."

"Kosma, please. Let Ryen speak," Aurik said tiredly, pinching the bridge of his nose with his thumb and forefinger and letting his fatigued eyes shut momentarily.

"*Like I said*, I don't think the evidence we are looking for exists." I remembered back to the starry night, sitting with Savannah on top of the Mayan temple, and repeated the words she had said to me exactly. "I think God lets us go without concrete proof so that we can choose which path to take. If we all had proof, there would be no choice. God gave us our lives to do what we will with it." I had pondered over those words so often, they were easy to repeat from memory, especially since I believed them. "Zhimeya needs to find a way to unite again, but maybe not under the banner of religion. Our people should be free to believe as they choose. If I had found the evidence I was seeking, the Tribunal would have forced everyone into the same belief. Governments shouldn't take away our right to choose."

"Is this what you decided when you were on Earth, Ryen? Before or after you tried to defect?"

"Kosma!" Aurik reprimanded.

"You would want to see our proud people devolve into warring factions with thousands of different languages, borders, and religions. I'm sorry, but I have no interest in my people becoming anything like the human race," Kosma retorted.

"Would you take away our freedom to choose? Would this world be better if we all were forced into believing the same thing?"

"If it would do away with outliers like yourself, maybe it wouldn't be so terrible," she answered. The bird perched on her shoulder screeched loudly at me, sensing his owner's infuriation.

"You can't be serious, Kosma," I sputtered.

"Aurik," she continued, "I didn't come here to argue with a child. We all know you are thinking about shutting down the Master's Institute," she said. "Which would, of course, bring an end to Earth research."

"Is that true?" I asked, turning my attention to Aurik.

"Well, Ryen, the Tribunal wanted your opinion on that, as well," Aurik said. "The Tribunal is exploring our options as it pertains to the Institute. It is full of bright, young students studying Earth and religion, just as you remember it. But, in light of these recent events, I honestly don't know what to do with it. What would you recommend?"

Savannah's body, broken possibly beyond repair, came to the forefront of my mind. If we had never touched down on Earth, she would never have been harmed. She would be safe, whole, and perfectly unaware of my existence. I wanted to tell him to burn the Institute to the ground. I'd do it myself if he would give me permission, fuel, and a match.

But I couldn't blame Savannah's present state on anyone but myself. Her life teetering on the brink between this world and the next was my fault—not the Institute's, not even Gideon's.

"Let me be clear. I don't care what the Tribunal chooses to do with the Institute—"

"I don't believe that, Ryen," Aurik interjected patiently.

"Please, let me finish. A lot of good has come from the Institute. But we cannot ignore what Gideon did there. He plotted an overthrow of the government, he poured funding into making deadly weapons, and he corrupted some of our brightest minds into doing his bidding. I don't know how the Institute will ever be respected after what has happened. It would take so much work!"

"It *would* take a great deal of work. But I think you are up to it," he grinned.

"Me?" I asked, confused.

"You can't be serious, Aurik!" Kosma cried out.

"I am very serious. The Institute needs a new leader, Ryen. I think you would be perfect for the job."

"Please don't ask that of me," I begged. Aurik didn't know what I planned to do with myself if Savannah didn't survive.

"Ryen," he censured, "I must remind you that your people have dedicated a great deal of resources toward your training and mission. You are heavily in their debt. You and your team have a responsibility to teach the rising generation about what you have seen and learned. Tell me you will at least think about it."

"And if the human, Sa-van-nah," Leal of the Alix stumbled through her name, "survives, she would be invaluable at the Institute, as well."

"What? The human cannot stay here!" Saylo shouted. Leal, her skin already dyed a delicate shade of petal pink, flushed an angry magenta under Saylo's glare.

"And why is that?" Leal asked. "Our people brought her here. She's been claimed to a tribe. She should be allowed to stay if she wishes."

"Aurik, the human must be sent back to Earth immediately!" Saylo shouted.

"I wouldn't worry, Saylo," Kosma whispered. "The human will be dead before the moons rise."

The scene around me swam. A red haze of rage clouded my vision. I couldn't even find my tongue to spit out the curses fast enough.

"One more word, Kosma, and I will revoke your seat in the Tribunal," Aurik promised, his amber eyes flashing hard in warning. She narrowed her gray eyes to slits but held her tongue. I stood perfectly still, my hands gripping the podium with all my might. If I let go now, it would be Kosma who would be dead before the moons rose.

"If I were Savannah, I would want to leave immediately after all that has happened to her by our hand. But I do think the only fair thing would be to give her the option of staying," Aurik said more calmly.

"We would have to put it to a vote, Aurik. You can't make that decision on your own," Ordin of the Shae called over the nine other Tribunal members arguing with each other.

I'd had enough.

"Aurik, can I go, *please*?" I pleaded.

"Just one more thing, I promise." Aurik motioned to his guards, and the side doors opened. In marched hundreds of people flanked by Uja, their spindly legs clacking and echoing against the polished floor. It was a staggering sight, especially since most of the prisoners were former Tribunal members. Each prisoner wore a sackcloth tunic, their wrists bound together with magnetized cuffs. Many glanced nervously behind them, out the back window of the hall at the peaks of Black Castle, which somehow looked closer today than usual.

I tried not to make eye contact with the traitors, especially Oshun and Ecko, who looked too much like Emani for me to bear.

The most shocking sight was the glass case wheeled in and set in front of the traitors. Gideon's decaying remains were on trial with the rest of them. Aurik watched over his nephew's body sadly.

Thankfully, they hadn't been able to find Emani's body down in the twisting underground tunnels. If my mind hadn't been so overwrought, I might have wondered about that. I might have thought back to the moment not so long ago when Dai had brought the holographic Aurik into Tribunal Hall and that split-second I thought I had seen Emani standing at the doorway. I may have wondered if it were possible that she had somehow survived, though I had watched her die in my arms. But at the moment, my mind was too full for such considerations.

When the traitors had been lined up across the Tribunal floor, Aurik turned his somber eyes away from Gideon to face them.

"This is indeed a dark day, the single largest trial in our history. We do not take our duty lightly. This trial will take some time. Ryen of the Haven, as the man who brought Gideon's plans to light, what say you to the traitors who wear Gideon's mark?"

"I have nothing to say to those who sold their souls to Gideon. Justice has found them. But I do have something to say to the Tribunal. Gideon's mark on the traitors' skin means nothing. Gideon's map is your most important piece of evidence. Healer Lais, whom Dai kidnapped, and even Savannah of the Haven were both marked against their will."

Zio had found Savannah's mark during the long hours we sat next to her unconscious body. "It's possible that some of our brothers and sisters were marked against their will, as well."

"But what do you think about—" Aurik started.

Ruel, captain of the guard, ran into the hall from a side door and whispered something in Aurik's ear. Aurik spoke urgently now. "Ryen, you are wanted at Healing Tower. Go!"

Without another word, without another thought, I turned and ran from the hall, but not before hearing Kosma's ecstatic cackle.

"The human is dead!"

40

The red bluffs of Angel's Communion appeared in the distance, both moons just cresting over the tallest peak. Soon the ancient switchback path would be lit with dozens of holy fires along the route. Inside a cave carved into that indomitable mountain, her body lay. Dead or alive, I didn't know.

I could have asked the stone-faced guard for the news, but the very last person I wanted confirming Savannah's death was a stranger. So I just sat limply, numbly, like a guilty man on his way to the executioner.

Maybe Kosma had guessed correctly. Maybe Savannah was dead.

If she had passed on to whatever came after this life, I knew my path. I would give up my marks and wander alone as an Unnamed. My life sentence would begin.

As I flew, thousands of Zhimeyans, riding both animals and machines, migrated toward Angel's Communion. Her fate had no doubt already been broadcast across the planet. The sight below me seemed to confirm my fears. These sick voyeurs had come to celebrate her death. I almost couldn't wait to cast off my marks of this corrupt society.

I walked slowly through the familiar passageways in a strange anesthetic fog, my feet trying to delay the inevitable for a few final moments. I thought fleetingly about finding Zio first, so he could administer some sort of drug that would keep the darkness at bay that was threatening to swallow me alive.

Chase and Mateo met me just outside her room. I wondered which one of them was going to tell me.

"Ryen—" Chase said quietly, blocking my way.

"Just let me see her one last time, and I'll go," I said quietly, trying to push past him.

"Wait a minute. Stop!" Mateo said, pushing me back. The shove jolted me from my stupor.

"We don't want you to scare her. She isn't speaking yet . . ."

"She's . . . alive?" I uttered, disbelieving at first. But with manic energy, I threw myself at them again, trying to break through to get to her.

"Stop! We don't know what she remembers, so just settle down!" Chase commanded. I stood motionless for a few seconds, showing them I was in control. They finally let me by.

Zio, closest to Savannah, was talking in a calm voice, checking her over methodically. Claire knelt close to her head, translating. My mother and sister were right behind Claire, watching vigilantly.

I walked slowly into Savannah's view, afraid there wouldn't be any of the girl I loved left inside. My painful heartbeats hammered out anxiously as I waited for her eyes to pass over me.

Savannah looked away from Zio and studied my face carefully.

"Ryen," she whispered.

And my life began again.

I darted toward her, grabbing her up off the altar before anyone could stop me. Zio's voice was somewhere in the background, demanding I let her go, but I couldn't listen. I held her, feeling her breath, her heartbeat, everything that meant she was alive.

"Anna . . . Anna," was all I could manage.

"You are going to hurt her, Ryen!" Zio yelled. This time I obeyed. I brought her carefully into my lap, keeping my arms around her. She wound her fists into my shirt, unwilling to let go of me either.

"You're alive," I whispered, studying her face carefully. The dark circles under her eyes seemed to dissipate as I watched. The hollows in her gaunt cheeks warmed under my cautious touch. I closed my eyes and said a quiet thank you to Emani for giving me Savannah's life back.

Her eyes moved slowly around the room, staring at the faces she didn't recognize. Her eyes stopped at my mother first.

"Savannah," I said in English, "my mother, Hinna."

"Beautiful girl, we are so happy you have come to us!" she exclaimed as I translated.

"My father, Tanion," I said.

"Thank you for your bravery," he said. "You helped save my son's life. We owe you a great debt."

"And this is my little sister, Aleyna." As Aleyna walked forward, there was an unmistakable spark of recognition in Savannah's searching eyes. Aleyna gasped.

"You remember me," she said in heavily accented English. Savannah managed something of a weak smile.

"How . . . ?" I asked.

"Her trial at Tribunal Hall. We were there that awful day. When Dai brought Savannah in, she started yelling in her native tongue about you, Aurik, and Claire all being in danger, so I translated for Father. He sent a message out to the Haven Elders.

Mateo and Nik were already in front of the Elders trying to convince them to come to the hall to stop Gideon. Savannah's story convinced them to come. I thought she saw me that day; I hoped she would remember me."

"I didn't know you spoke English!" Claire said.

"Ryen needed someone to help him practice the languages he was learning, so he taught me everything he learned at the Institute. I'm better at Italian," Aleyna said.

"Yes, yes, that's all great, but please let me check her again," Zio interrupted. Everyone moved away but me. He was about to say something, but the desperate way we held each other made him stop short of ordering me away. I watched his face carefully, waiting for him to give any sign that something wasn't right. But his face remained clinical, even relaxed.

"Such a miracle," he said quietly. "I just wish I knew what to do about that," he sighed, lifting up Savannah's covering just enough so I could see Gideon's mark etched into her stomach. The skin was raw and red but covered in a white salve, the latest concoction Zio was trying. "Nothing is working. I can't heal it. It doesn't act like a heat brand. It acts more like a chemical burn." She cringed when Zio touched anywhere near the mark.

"Well, after I find Dai, and before I kill him, I'll ask him what it is for you," I said seriously.

The passageway outside the room filled with the scraping of heavy boots as a number of Aurik's guard filed in. I held Savannah tight, fearing the worst. Was the Tribunal coming for her already?

Everyone except the two of us knelt on the floor at Aurik's arrival.

"I've told you all a thousand times. No one should have to bow to a government employee," Aurik exclaimed. "I came as quickly as I could to see the Savannah girl!" he said. Savannah stirred in my arms, hearing her name mixed in with the unfamiliar language.

"You're safe," I said hesitantly, unsure of whether she really was or not.

"Aurik, this is Savannah," I said.

"How is she?" he asked Zio.

"Brittle," Zio replied.

"Ah," he said, lowering his voice and moving more slowly, though curiosity burned his eyes. "Then we shall all be very quiet and cautious." He took her hand carefully in his, as if it were made of blown glass.

"She doesn't look very brittle to me," Aurik smiled.

"Of course not. What do I know? I'm only the best healer in the world," Zio grumbled as he walked out.

"A human here in Zhimeya. Never in my wildest dreams did I think I would ever get to meet one," Aurik said, staring at her hand in his. "I always wanted to be a researcher and go to Earth myself, but my parents chose a different path for me. I was never really happy about their choice, but I tried to make the best of it. Sorry, I am rambling. Rambling seems to follow age, and I am very, very old."

Claire laughed freely with Aurik. We all stared at her, shocked. Chase covered her mouth with his hand.

"Aurik and I are old friends," Claire said, pulling his hand away. "We were stuck in a hole together," she said importantly.

"Yes, that tends to build camaraderie, doesn't it?" Aurik laughed. "How are you, Claire? Your shoulder has healed?"

"Doing fine, thank you!" she chimed.

"Good, good," he said pleasantly, but then turned his attention to me. "Ryen, will you translate for me, please?" I nodded.

"I have come seeking your forgiveness for what has happened to you here, young one. Kidnapped, beaten, and nearly killed," he said apologetically, looking over the deep cuts lining the top of her bare head. "Truly, this is not our way. As a representative for my kind, I ask for your forgiveness."

When I finished the translation, Savannah squeezed Aurik's hand weakly.

"Thank you, my new friend," he said warmly. "You are quite the accidental diplomat."

"So, onto my second reason for coming. Well, third, I guess. The first was to meet you, the second was for forgiveness . . . oh yes! And the third was to see when you would be well enough to go back to your beloved home. It will take a bit of planning to collect enough torbillium to make the trip, but we will work quickly."

As I translated, her eyebrows knit together fearfully. She stared up at me, perplexed.

"Home?" she breathed soundlessly.

"Yes, Anna. Earth is your home. Aurik wants to know when you would like to leave for Earth."

"No!" This time everyone could hear her. Tears gathered in the corners of her eyes.

"What does she say, Ryen?" Aurik asked with deep curiosity, but I didn't answer.

"I think she wants to stay," Claire answered for me. I shot her a withering look.

"Really? After everything that has happened?"

"I . . . want to . . . stay here," she demanded, laboring through the words.

"Absolutely not, Anna. This is not a safe place for you. Can't you hear the mobs outside?" I asked.

"I don't care," she said, her eyes full of resolve.

"What does she say?" Aurik probed again.

"She wants to stay, Aurik, but I'll make her see reason. I won't allow her to stay in a place where so many want to harm her."

"It's not actually your choice, Ryen," Claire interjected hotly.

"Shut up, Claire," I warned. "I'll go back with her to Earth if she'll have me. I'll keep her safe." Out of the corner of my eye I saw my mother blanch at the thought of losing me again.

"Ah, she is a brave one. Both of you are, to risk so much for love. Love is truly the only cause worthy of the fight you two have in front of you," Aurik mused. "I will express her wish to stay to the Tribunal, but you heard them, Ryen. I don't know if I can get them to grant her permission to stay."

"She's *not* staying," I said again, but no one was listening to me.

"But she's been marked, Aurik. She's a Haven! One of us!" my father said sternly.

"I'm sorry Tanion, but this is a matter for the Tribunal to decide. If I can find a way—"

"Find a way," my mother said fiercely.

"She isn't safe here, Mother," I said.

"I will not lose both of you. There has to be a way," she said.

"I'll do my best, Hinna," Aurik promised. "I'll do everything I can to keep her here if you are sure you are all ready to take on this fight. There have been threats against all of your lives already. This decision of yours brings everyone here into danger," he cautioned.

"We stand by whatever our son and Savannah decide. If she wants to stay, we will defend her," my father said.

"As will her friends," Chase said.

Aurik smiled. "All right. Keep her safe. Keep her close. I will lend you a few of my guard, but there is only so much we can do if the world comes together against her."

"We are ready," my mother said, standing with my father.

"She has a little time before any decisions are made. Tribes still without a Tribunal representative would never allow such an important matter to be voted on without them having a say. It will take time to elect new leaders. So much to sort through," he said sadly.

"In any case, Savannah dear, a mark made by the Tribunal Leader is supposed to be good luck. It isn't, of course, since I'm not magical—but all the same, it is the custom. May I?" Aurik asked. After I translated, she nodded. He rummaged around in his robes until he found his ritual paint. He opened the small jar and dabbed his thumb in it. He then pressed his thumb onto the inside of both her wrists, leaving his thumbprint behind.

"I very much hope we will meet again soon." His eyes shifted over to the windows. He gave her hand one more squeeze and walked over to look out at the growing crowd below.

"A heartbreaking sight. Hatred and fear taking the place of brotherhood," he said. "Ryen, come to me soon. We have much to discuss."

"Yes, Aurik," I said, as he passed out the door. Soon the shuffle of boots quieted out in the hallway.

I was suddenly utterly and completely exhausted.

"Could you all please . . ." I started to say, but my parents were already pushing everyone out of the room for me.

I gently laid Savannah back down on the stone so she could rest.

"I can't begin to say how sorry I am for every single thing . . . Every bruise, every cut, every drop of blood you've suffered because of me."

She pressed her finger against my lips.

"Please let me get you out of here. I can't stand for you to be in harm's way. We could go back to Earth, just you and me. We'll go to Ravello, like I promised."

"No," she said simply. I brushed her lips with my thumb carefully, watching the color return before my eyes. "You promised . . . no more . . . running. I want to be here. Our family is here."

"*Our* family?" I smiled.

"When you . . . marry me."

"After all of this, you would still have me?"

"*Especially* after all this," she answered, her voice gaining strength with each word. "You are worth fighting *and* dying for. I know, because I've done both." Her bubbling laughter spilled through the silence, painting her with the same warmth I remembered. She was healing.

"I love you, Savannah of the Haven."

"I love you, Ryen of the Haven."

I kissed her then, softly at first. But she wound her arms around my neck, pulling me toward her with more force than I could have imagined she had. At that moment, I knew, without a doubt, she would be well.

As the sun's final rays left the sky, the light from the mob's bonfires lit up the darkness outside her room with an ominous orange haze. The tumultuous sound of yelling grew, becoming impossible to ignore, marring the perfection of this moment. It was a constant reminder of the danger. But Savannah and I would fight. And we wouldn't be alone. We would find a way to be together, no matter what forces in the universe conspired against us.